UTOPIA'S AVENGER

Volume 1

Created by
Oh Se-Kwon

TOKYOPOP®

HAMBURG // LONDON // LOS ANGELES // TOKYO

Utopia's Avenger Vol. 1
Created by Oh Se-Kwon

Translation - Woo Sok Park
English Adaptation - Jai Nitz
Copy Editor - Stephanie Duchin
Retouch and Lettering - Mike Estacio
Production Artist - Mike Estacio
Cover Design - Fawn Lau & Kyle Plummer

Editor - Bryce P. Coleman
Digital Imaging Manager - Chris Buford
Pre-Production Supervisor - Erika Terriquez
Art Director - Anne Marie Horne
Production Manager - Elisabeth Brizzi
Managing Editor - Vy Nguyen
VP of Production - Ron Klamert
Editor-in-Chief - Rob Tokar
Publisher - Mike Kiley
President and C.O.O. - John Parker
C.E.O. and Chief Creative Officer - Stuart Levy

A  Manga

TOKYOPOP Inc.
5900 Wilshire Blvd. Suite 2000
Los Angeles, CA 90036

E-mail: info@TOKYOPOP.com
Come visit us online at www.TOKYOPOP.com

ISBN: 1-59816-670-0

First TOKYOPOP printing: December 2006

10 9 8 7 6 5 4 3 2 1

Printed in the USA

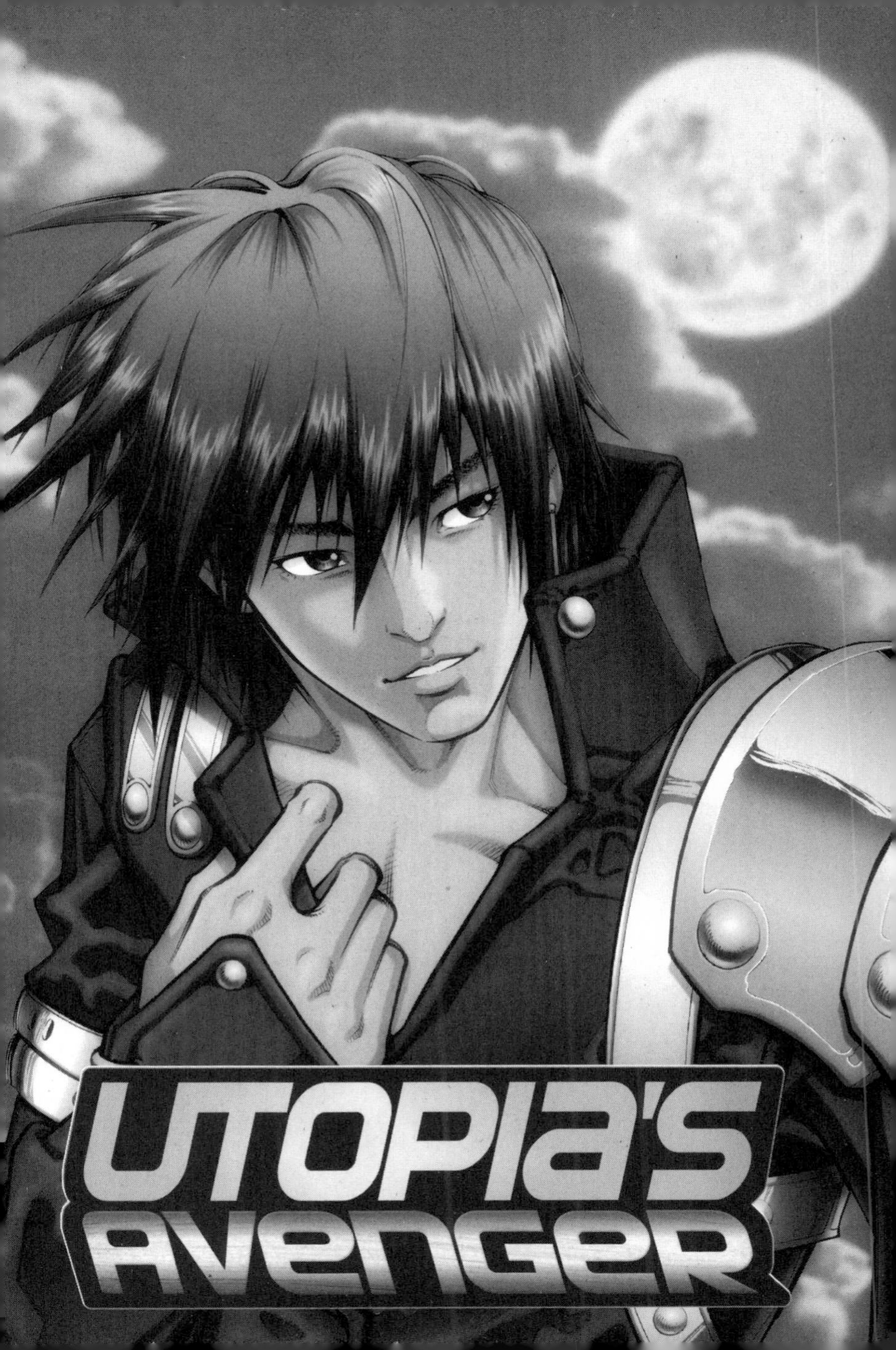
UTOPIA'S
AVENGER

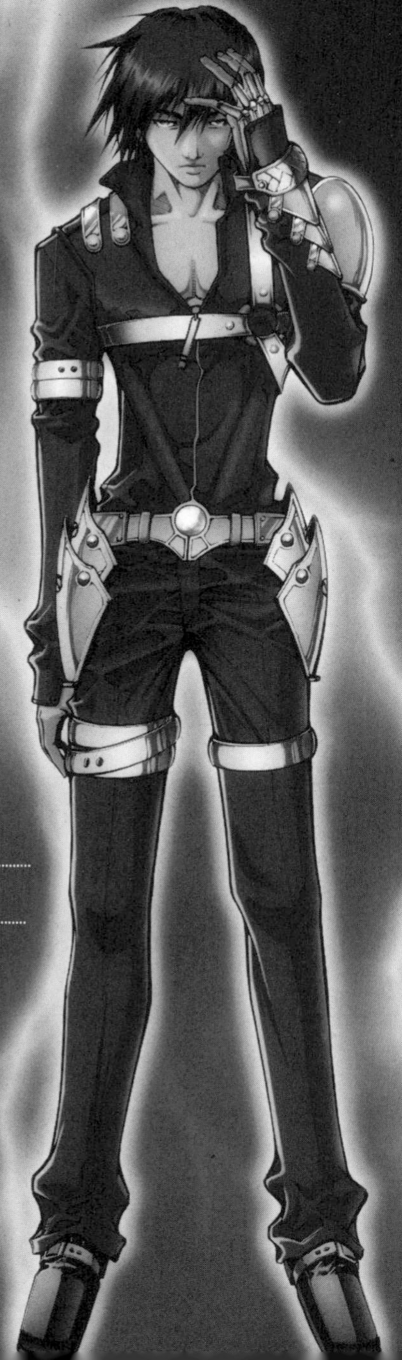

Contents

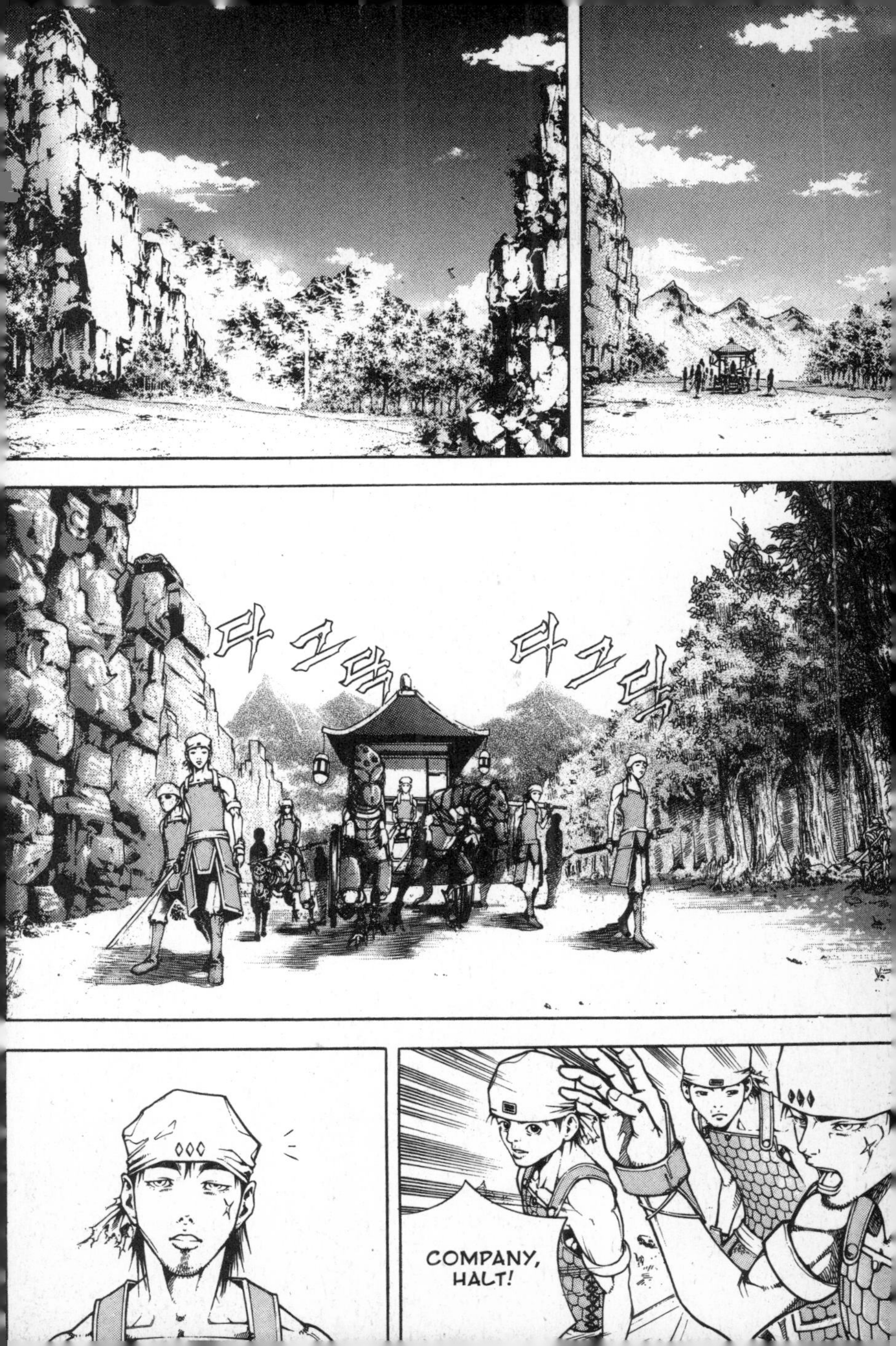
다그닥
다그닥
COMPANY, HALT!

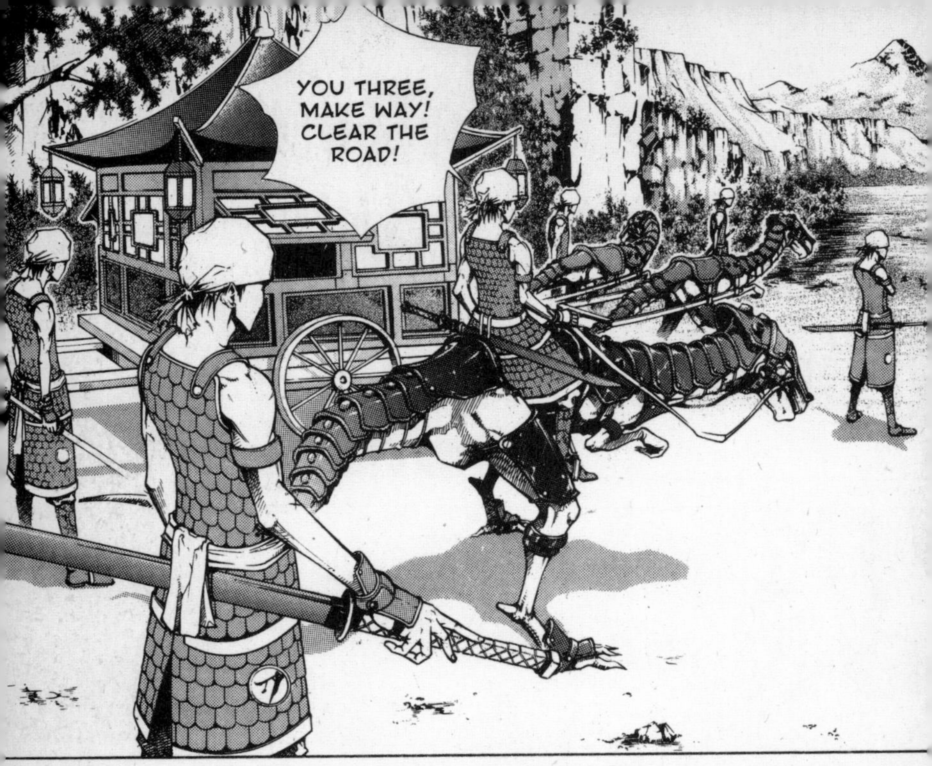
YOU THREE, MAKE WAY! CLEAR THE ROAD!

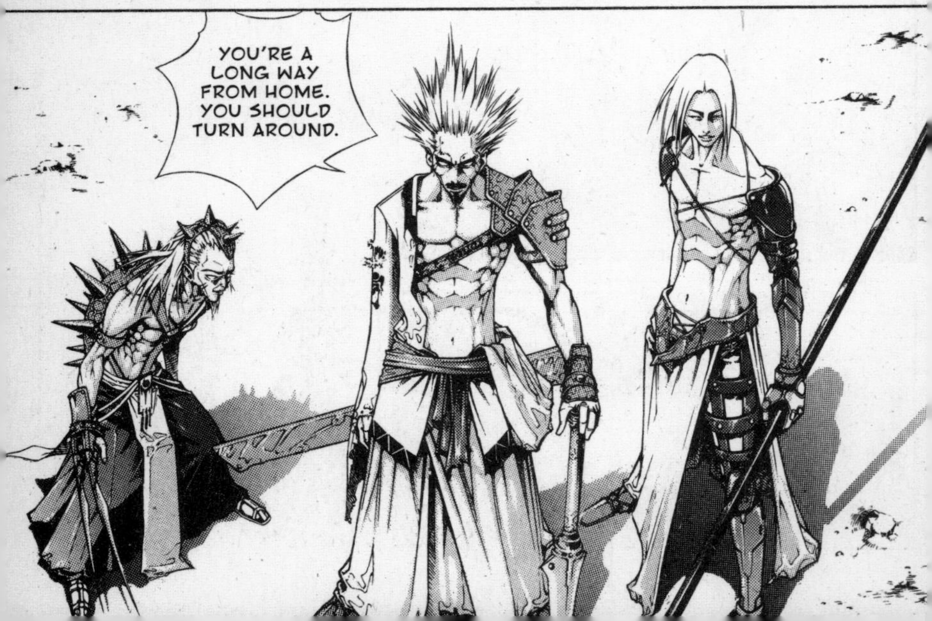
YOU'RE A LONG WAY FROM HOME. YOU SHOULD TURN AROUND.

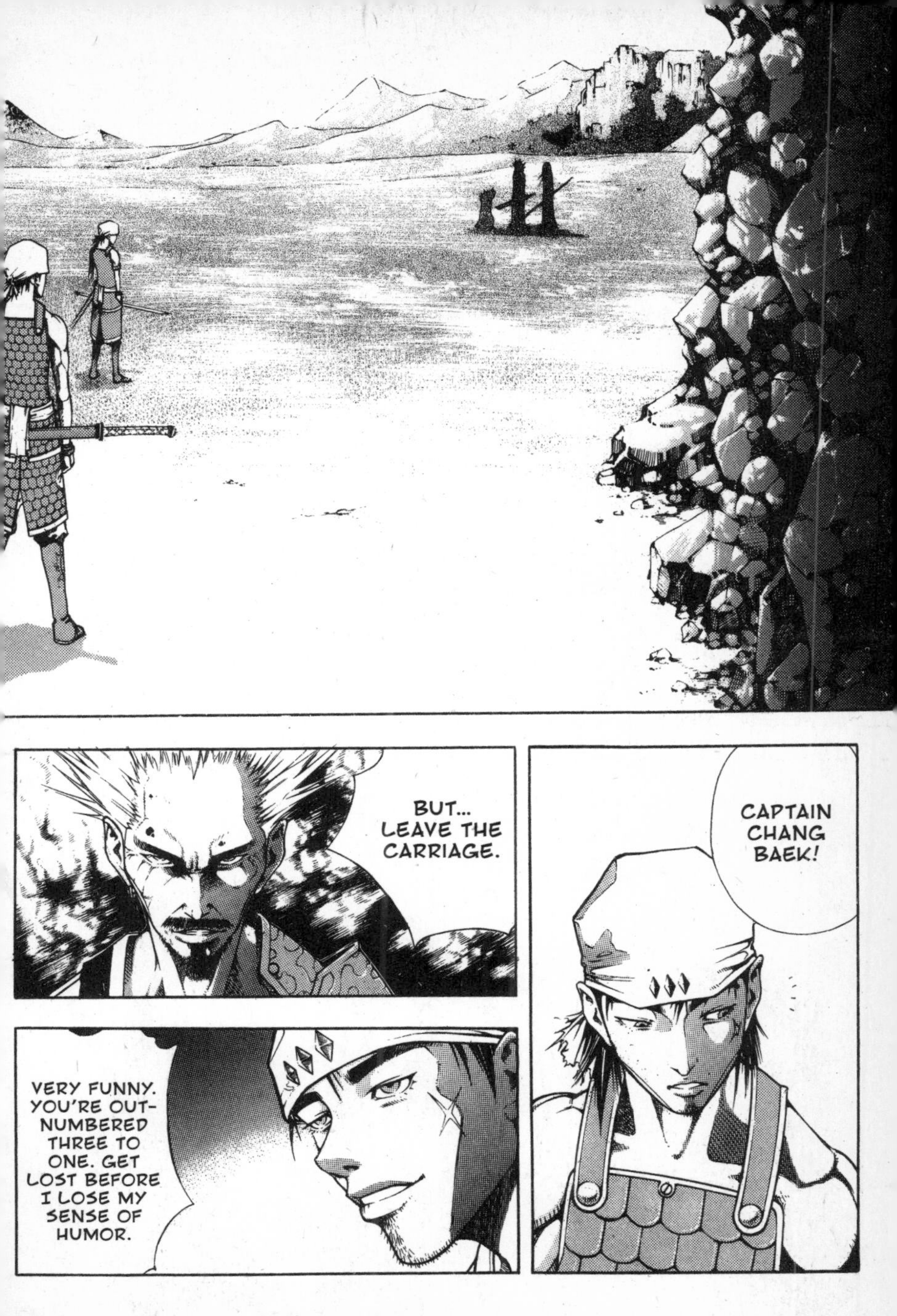
BUT... LEAVE THE CARRIAGE.
CAPTAIN CHANG BAEK!
VERY FUNNY. YOU'RE OUT-NUMBERED THREE TO ONE. GET LOST BEFORE I LOSE MY SENSE OF HUMOR.

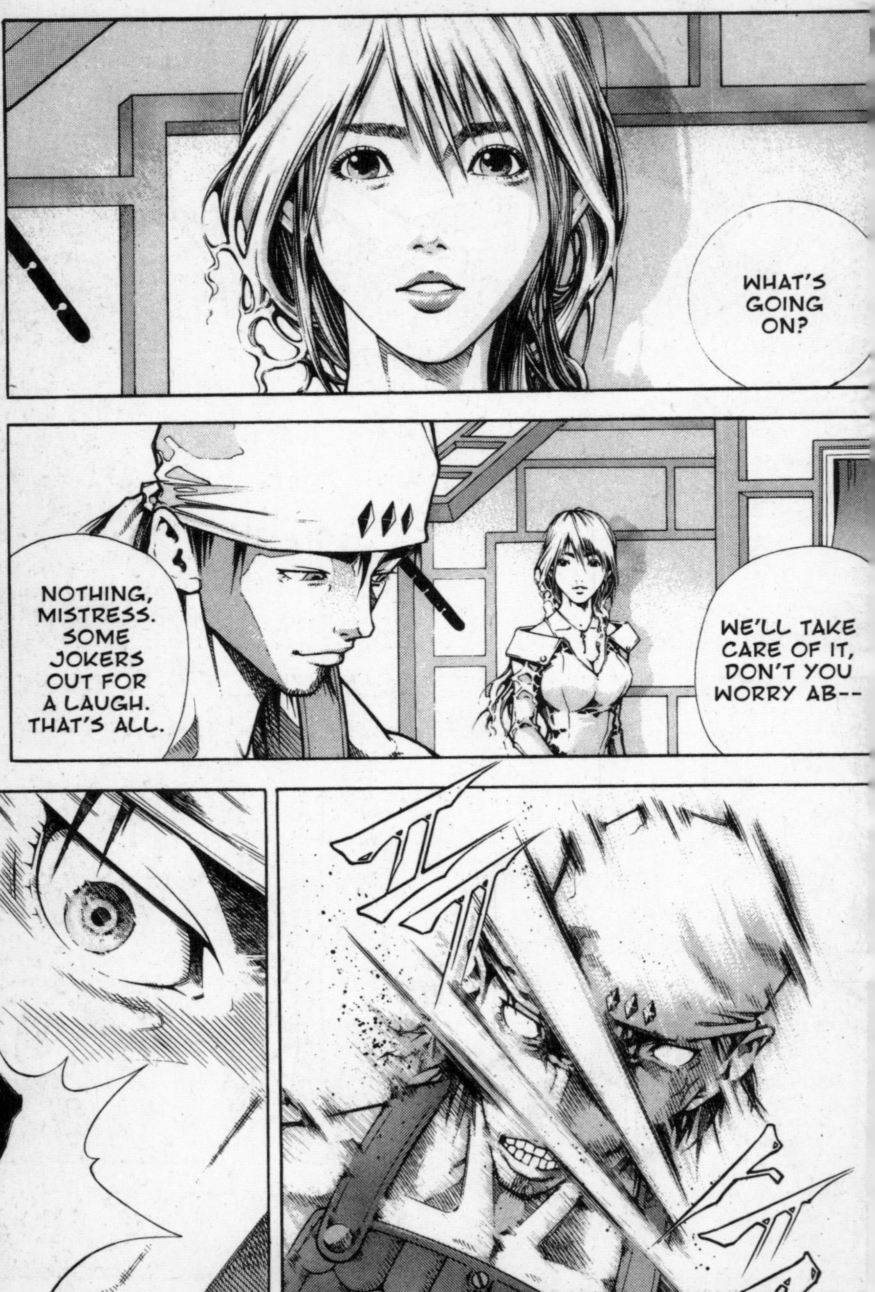

WHAT'S GOING ON?
NOTHING, MISTRESS. SOME JOKERS OUT FOR A LAUGH. THAT'S ALL.
WE'LL TAKE CARE OF IT, DON'T YOU WORRY AB--
!

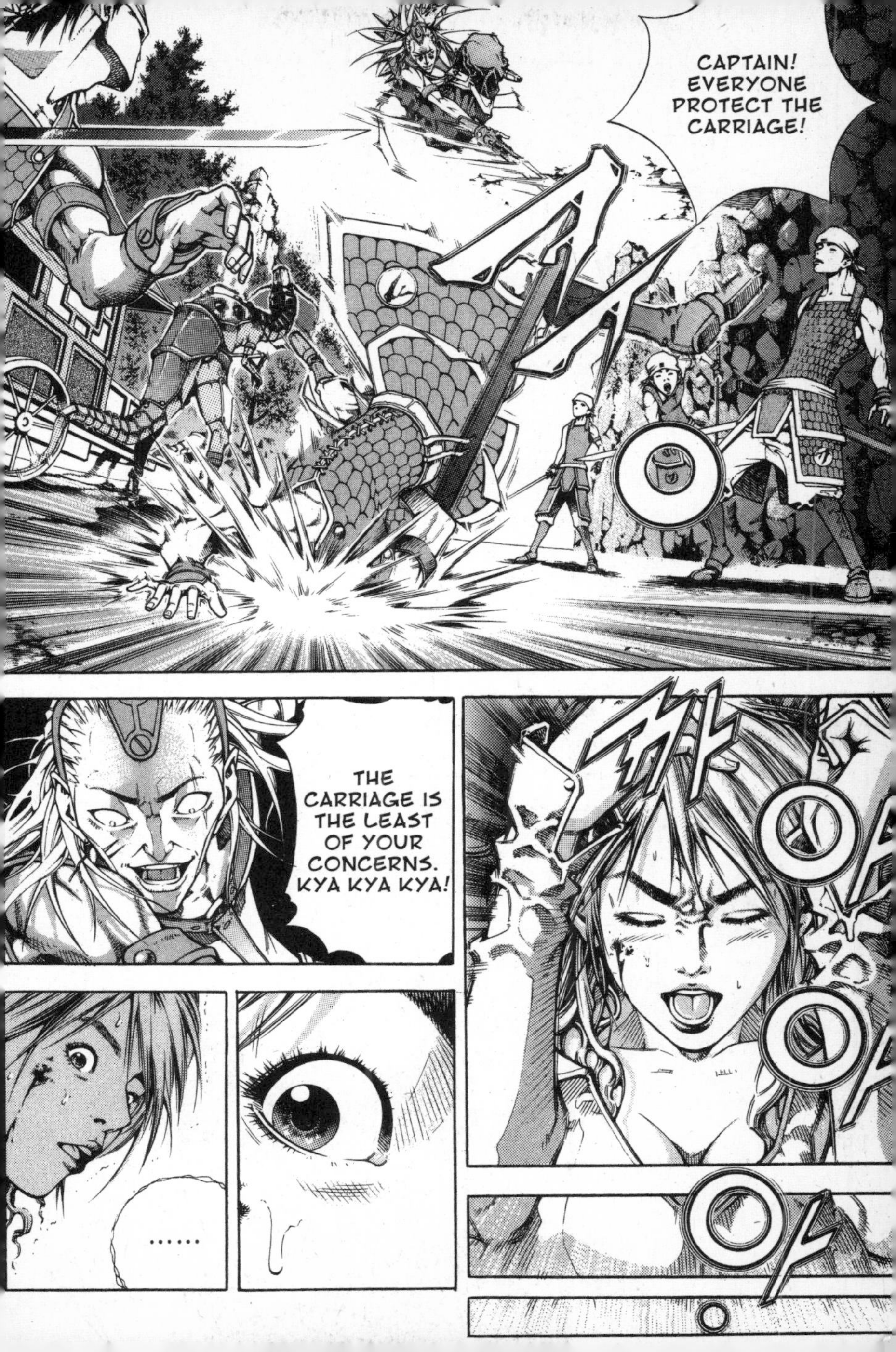
CAPTAIN! EVERYONE PROTECT THE CARRIAGE!
THE CARRIAGE IS THE LEAST OF YOUR CONCERNS. KYA KYA KYA!
....

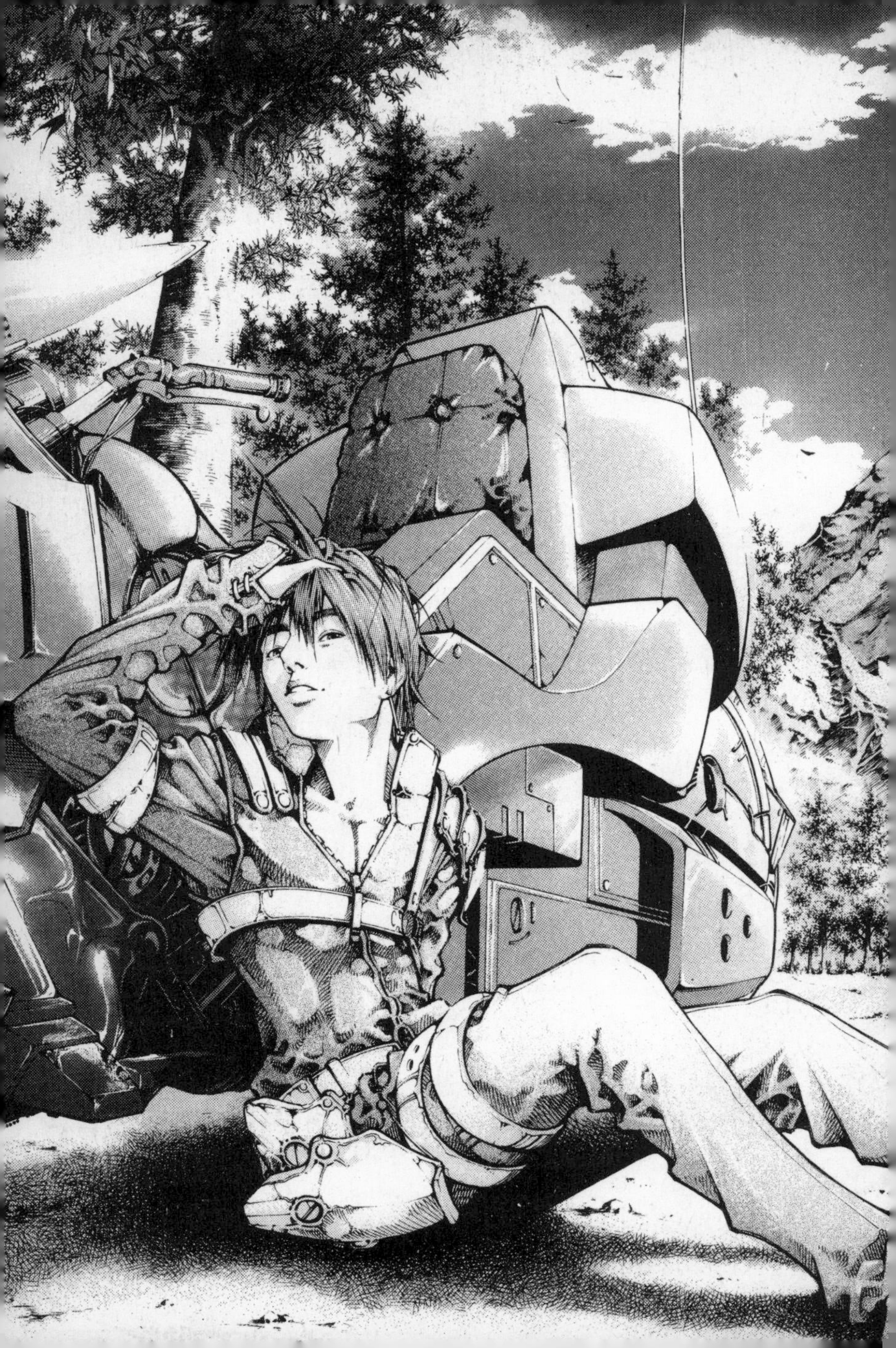

Chapter 1
The Merchant's Daughter

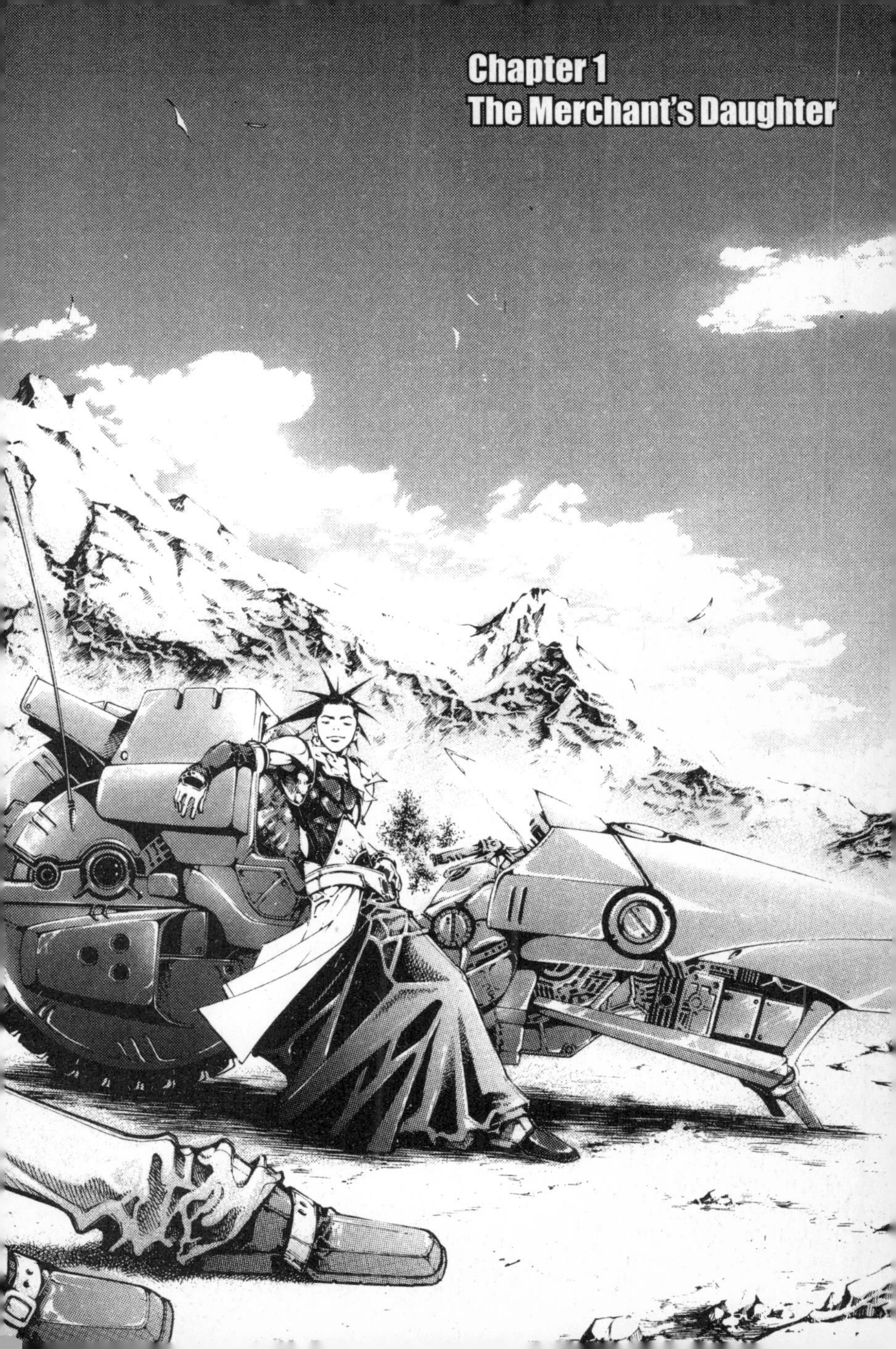

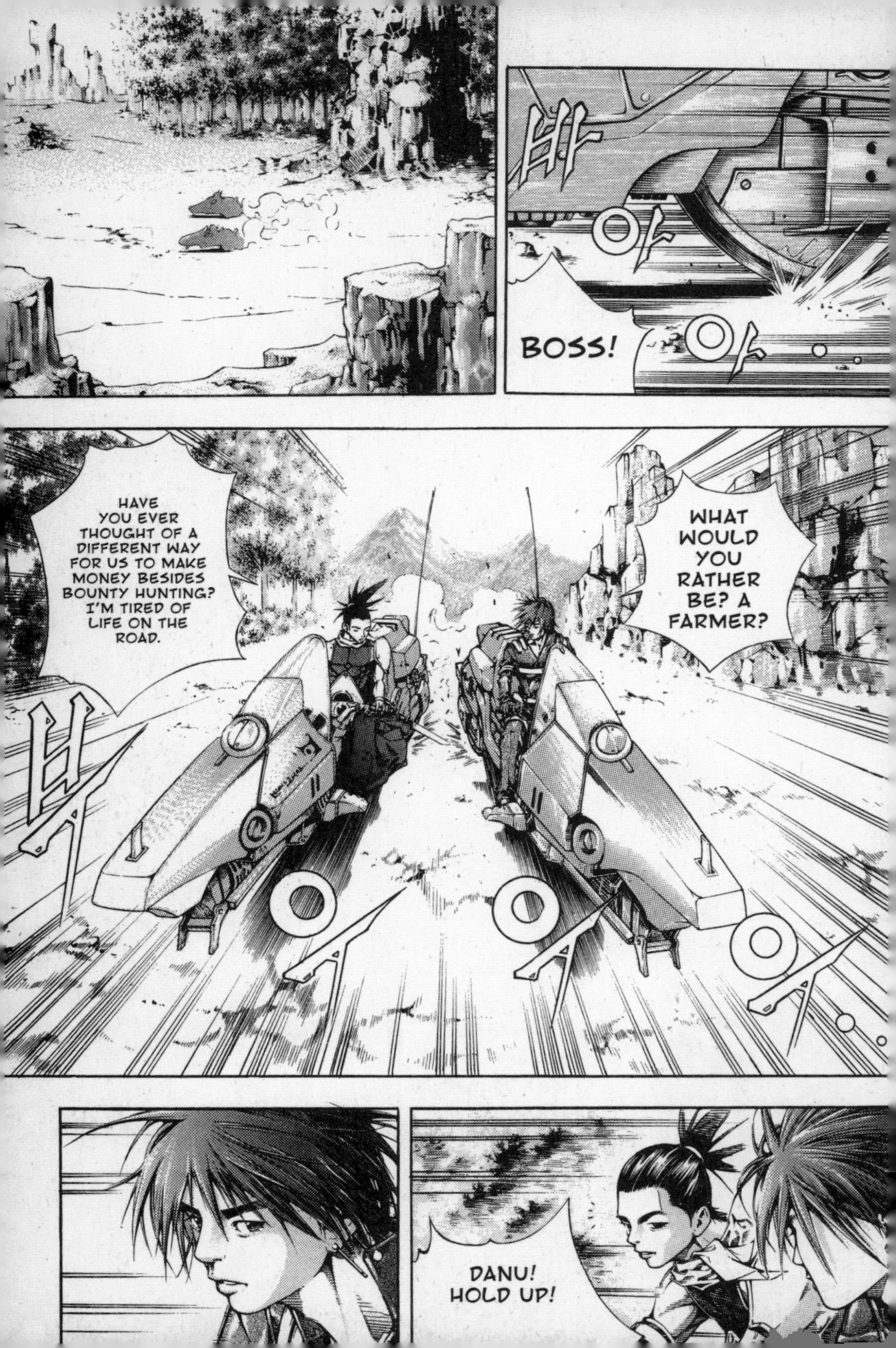

BOSS!
HAVE YOU EVER THOUGHT OF A DIFFERENT WAY FOR US TO MAKE MONEY BESIDES BOUNTY HUNTING? I'M TIRED OF LIFE ON THE ROAD.
WHAT WOULD YOU RATHER BE? A FARMER?
DANU! HOLD UP!

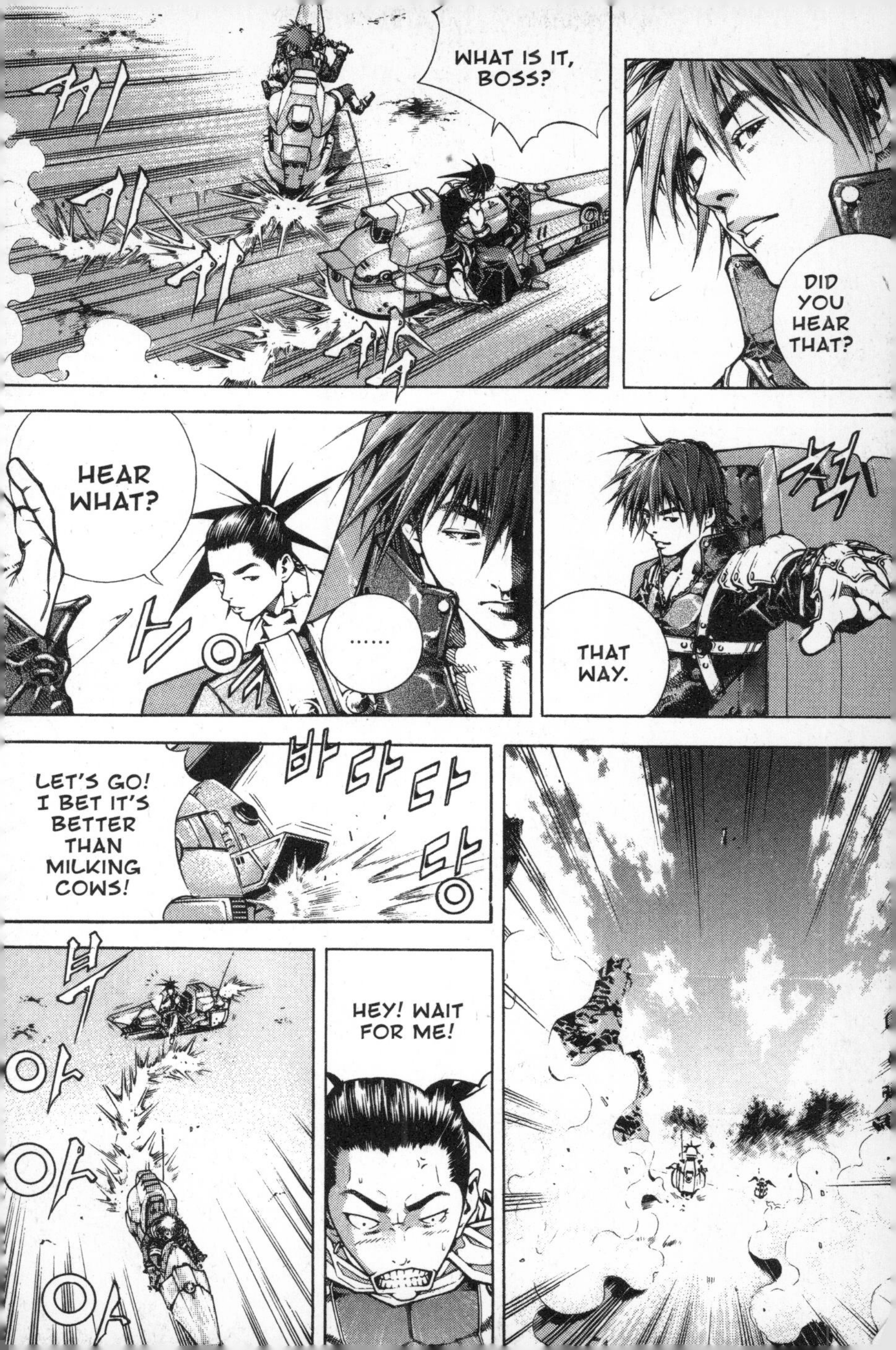
WHAT IS IT, BOSS?
DID YOU HEAR THAT?
HEAR WHAT?
......
THAT WAY.
LET'S GO! I BET IT'S BETTER THAN MILKING COWS!
HEY! WAIT FOR ME!

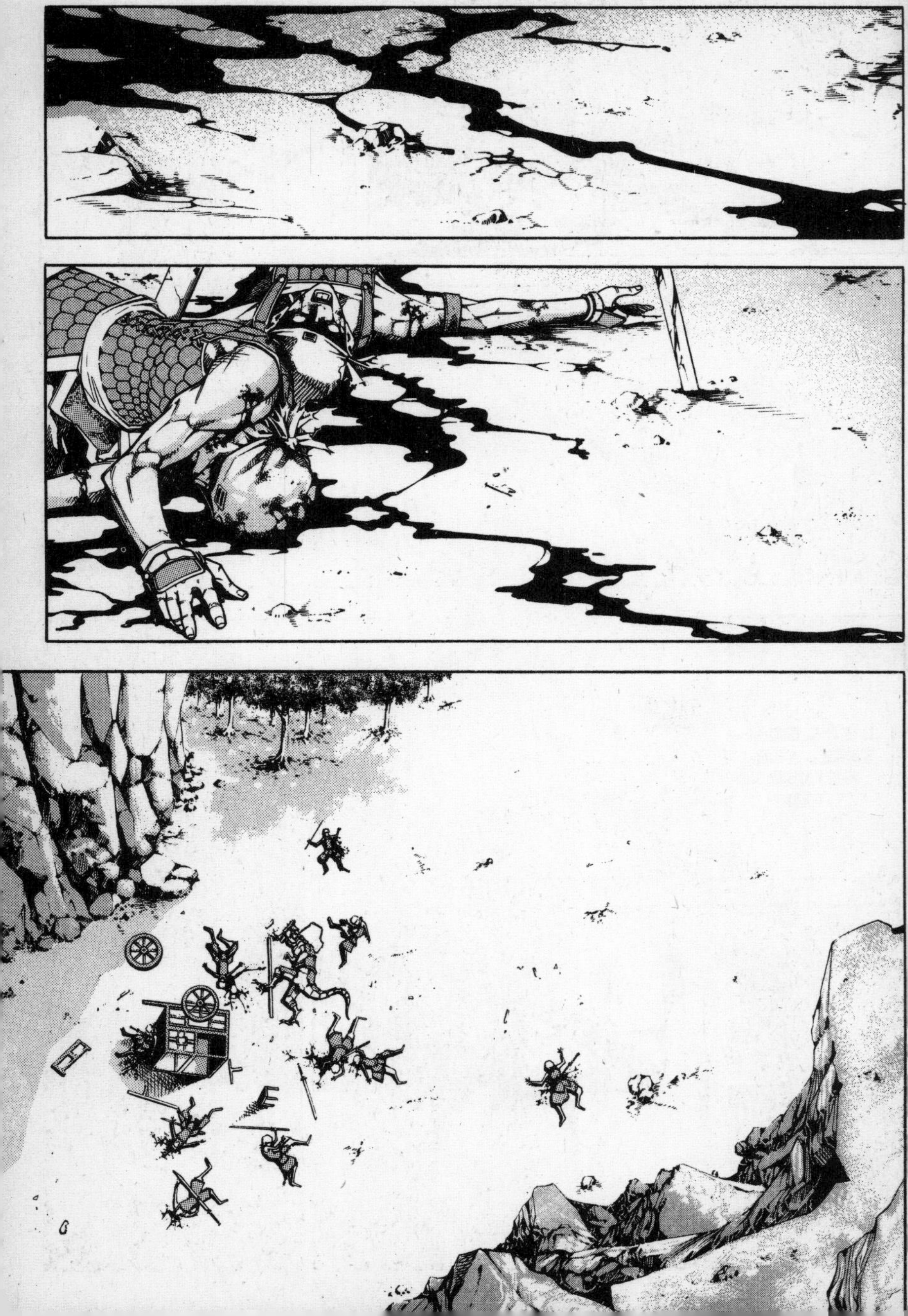

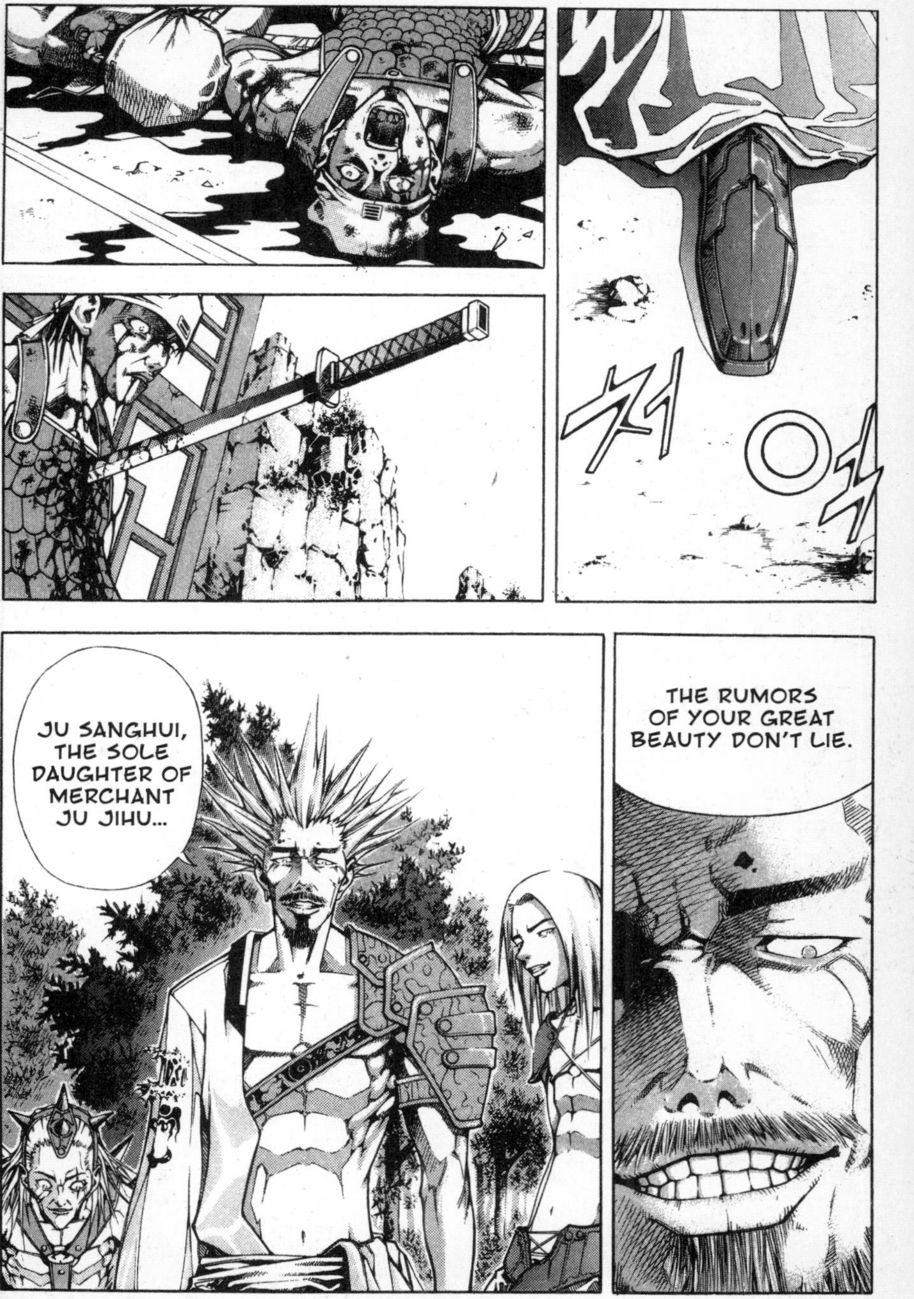
JU SANGHUI, THE SOLE DAUGHTER OF MERCHANT JU JIHU...
THE RUMORS OF YOUR GREAT BEAUTY DON'T LIE.

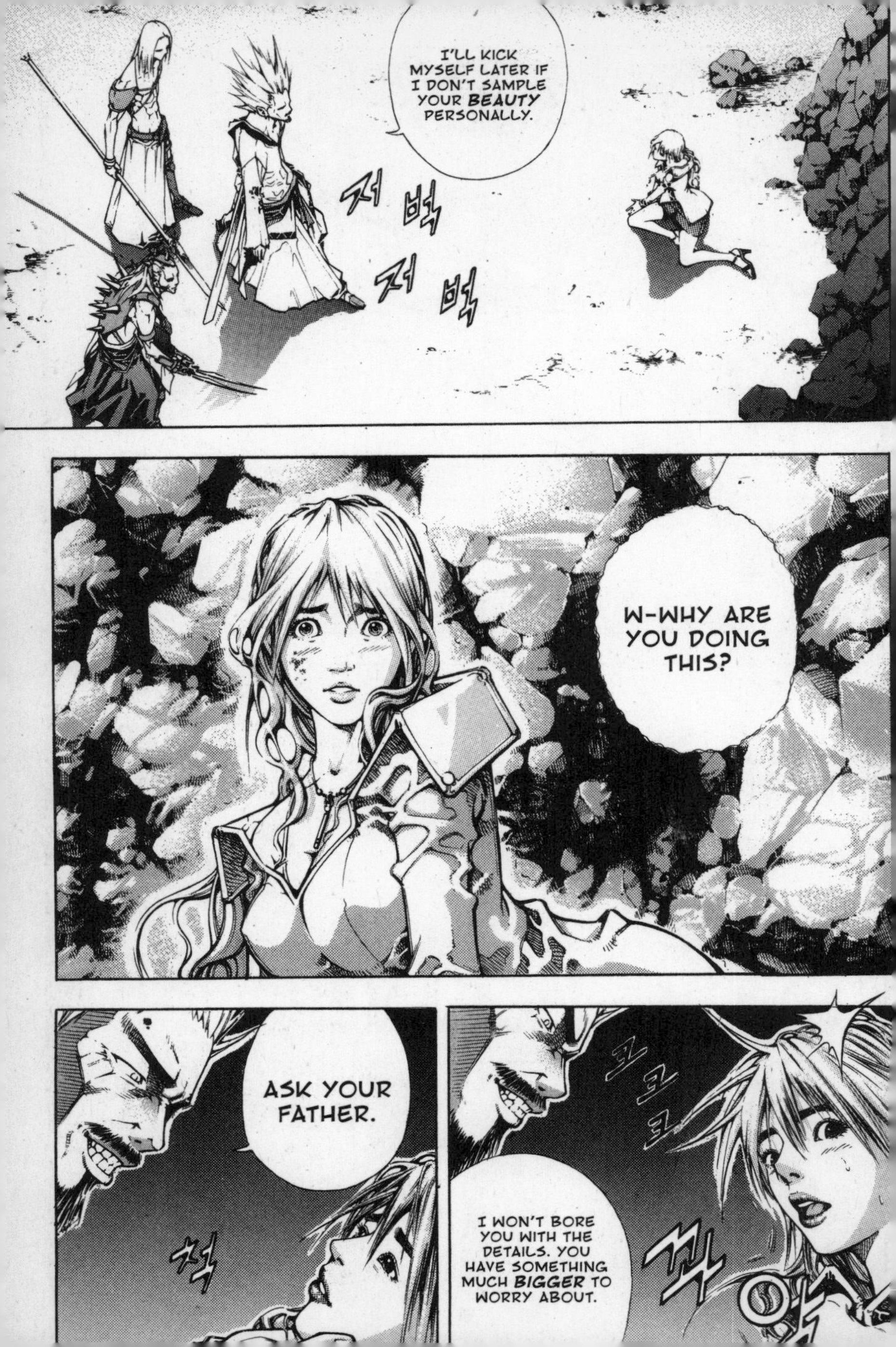
I'LL KICK MYSELF LATER IF I DON'T SAMPLE YOUR BEAUTY PERSONALLY.
저벅
저벅
W-WHY ARE YOU DOING THIS?
ASK YOUR FATHER.
척
I WON'T BORE YOU WITH THE DETAILS. YOU HAVE SOMETHING MUCH BIGGER TO WORRY ABOUT.

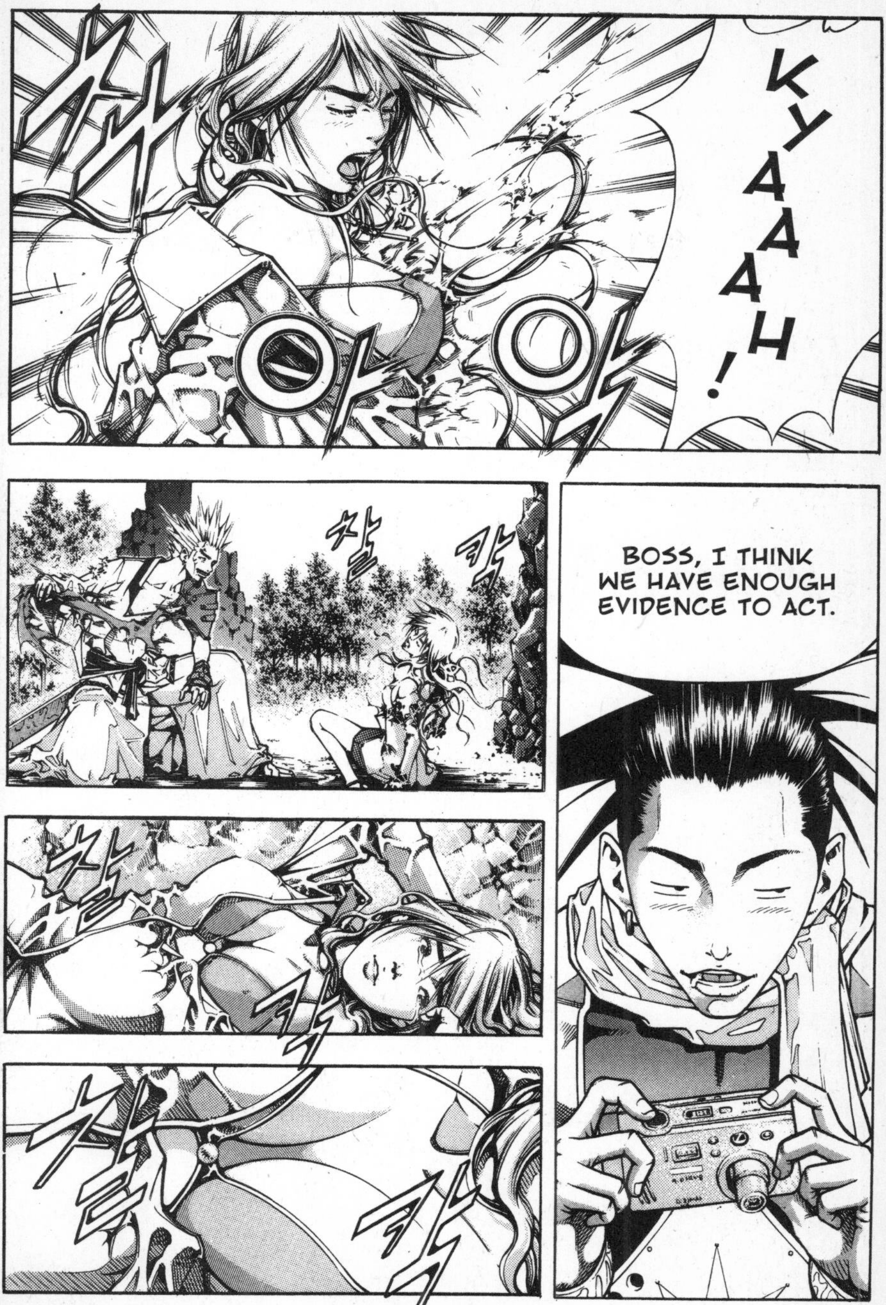
KYAAAH!
BOSS, I THINK WE HAVE ENOUGH EVIDENCE TO ACT.

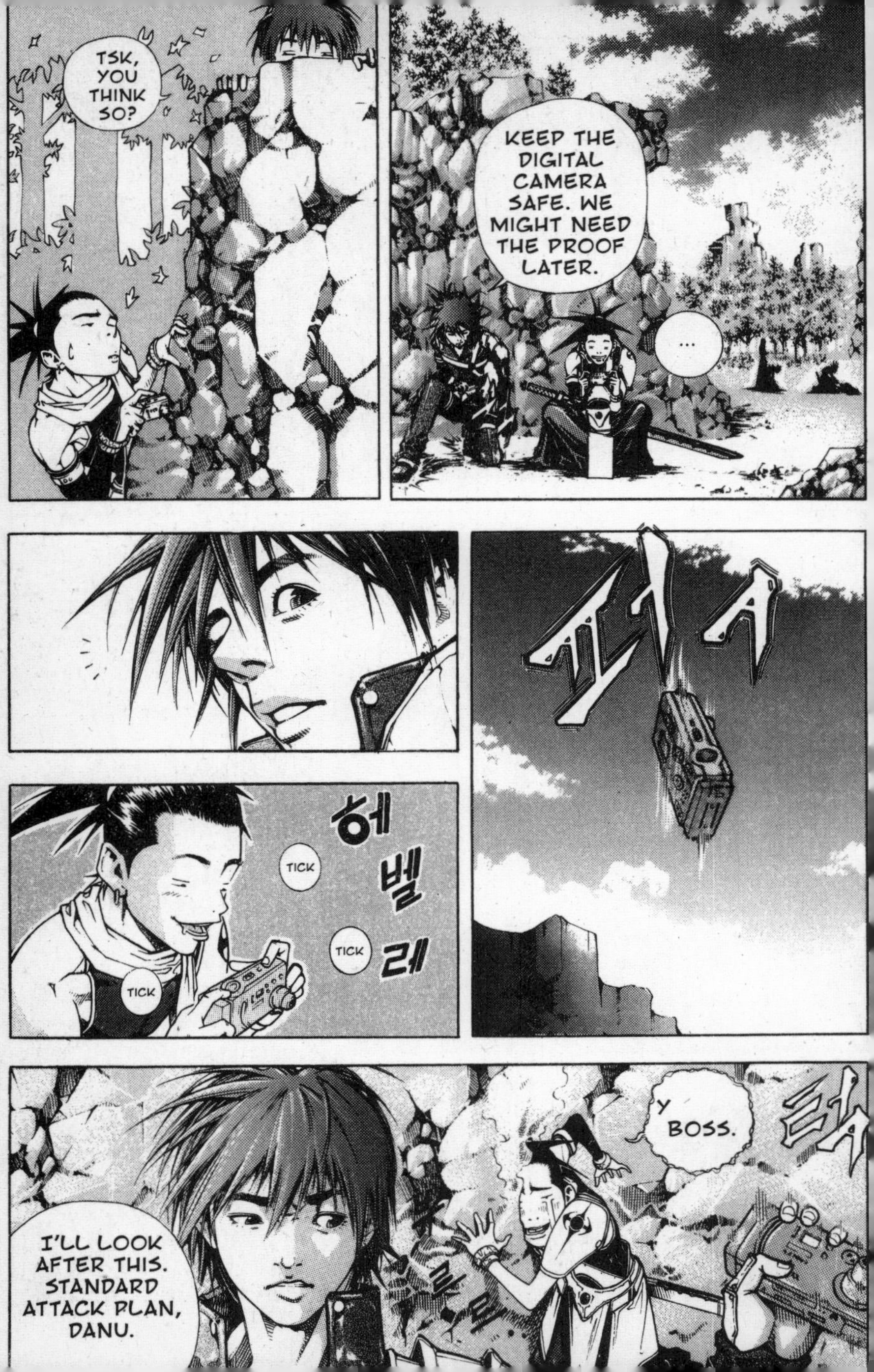
TSK, YOU THINK SO?
KEEP THE DIGITAL CAMERA SAFE. WE MIGHT NEED THE PROOF LATER.
...
TICK
TICK
TICK
헤벨레
Y BOSS.
I'LL LOOK AFTER THIS. STANDARD ATTACK PLAN, DANU.

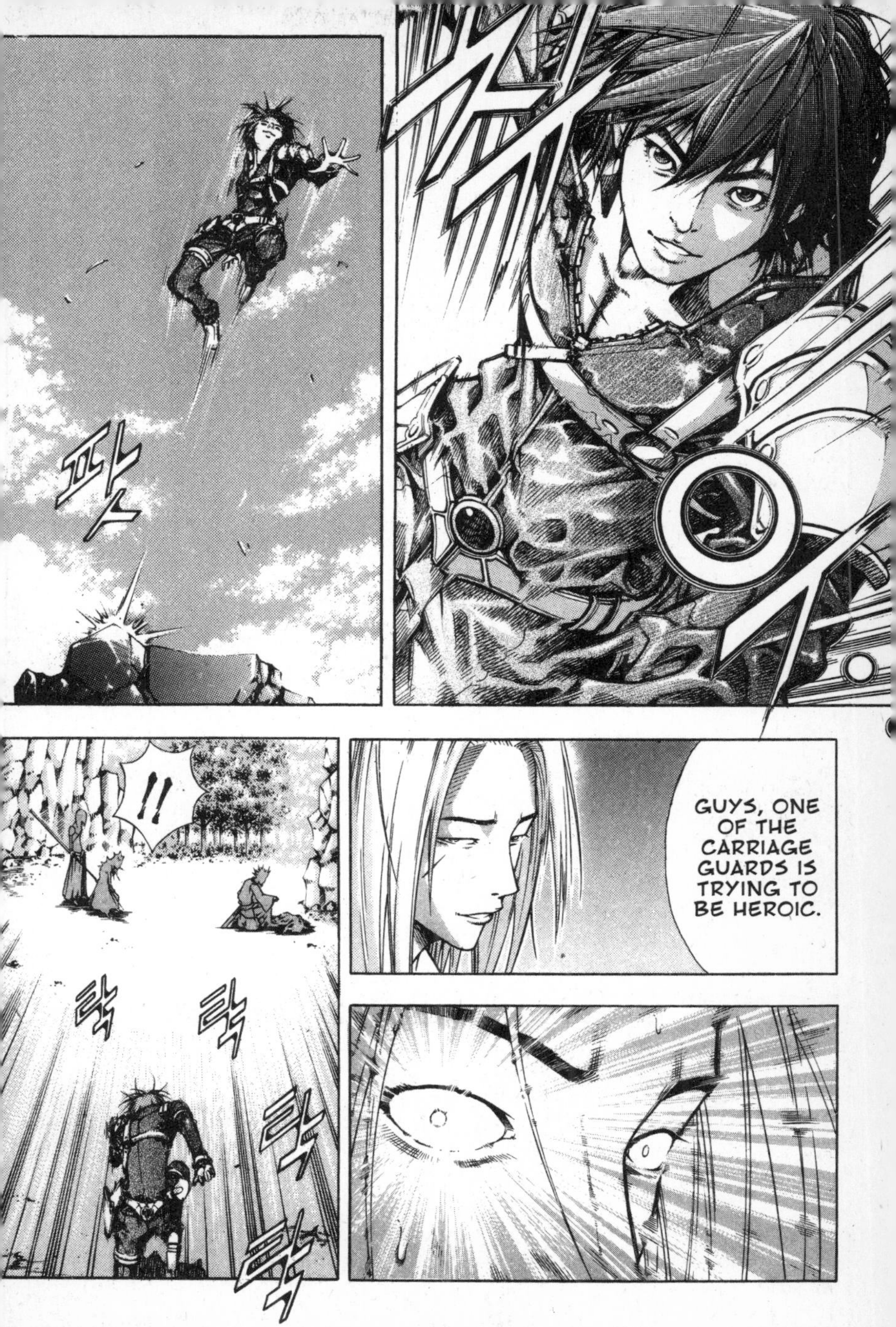
!!
GUYS, ONE OF THE CARRIAGE GUARDS IS TRYING TO BE HEROIC.

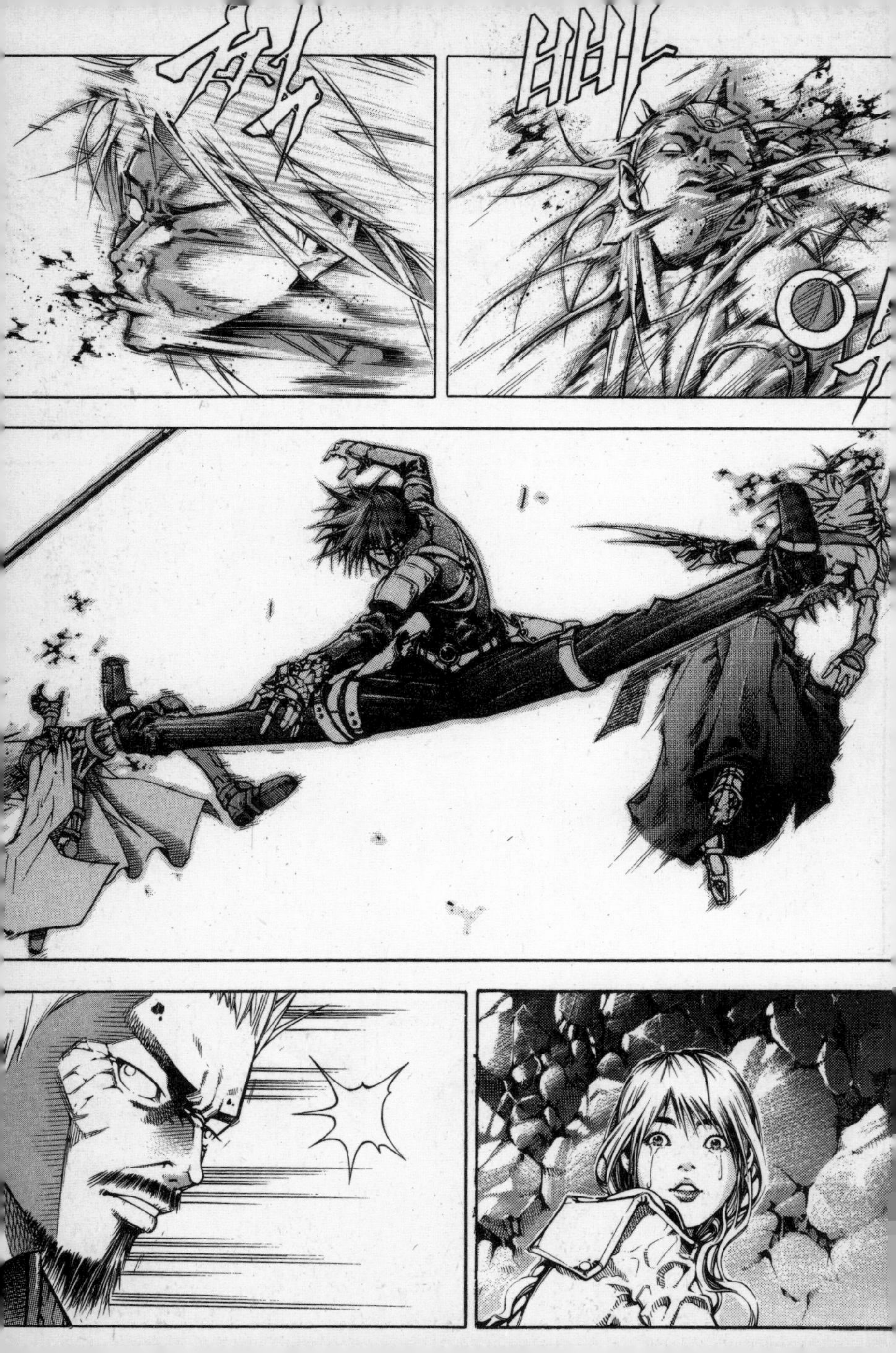

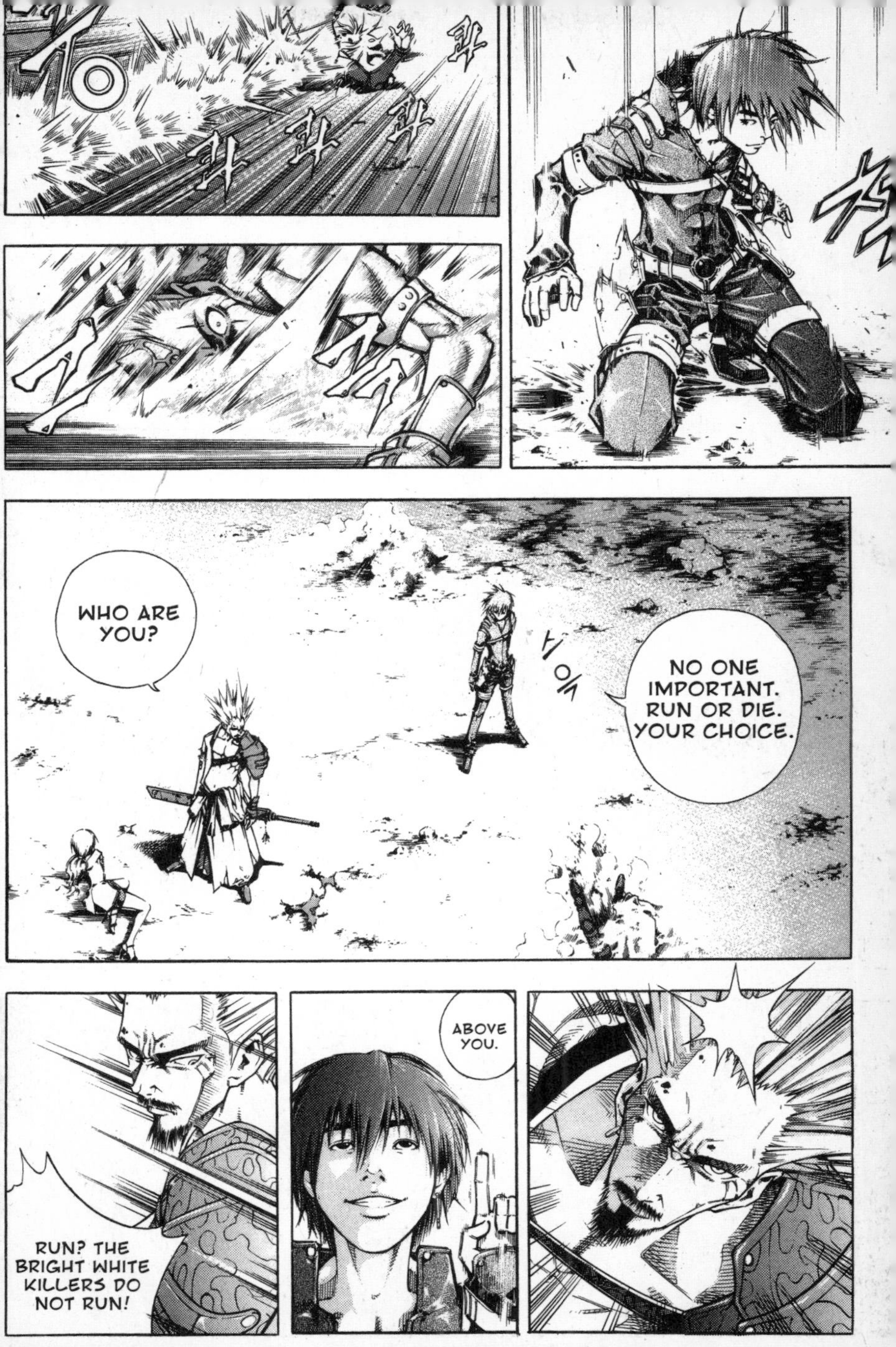
WHO ARE YOU?
NO ONE IMPORTANT. RUN OR DIE. YOUR CHOICE.
RUN? THE BRIGHT WHITE KILLERS DO NOT RUN!
ABOVE YOU.

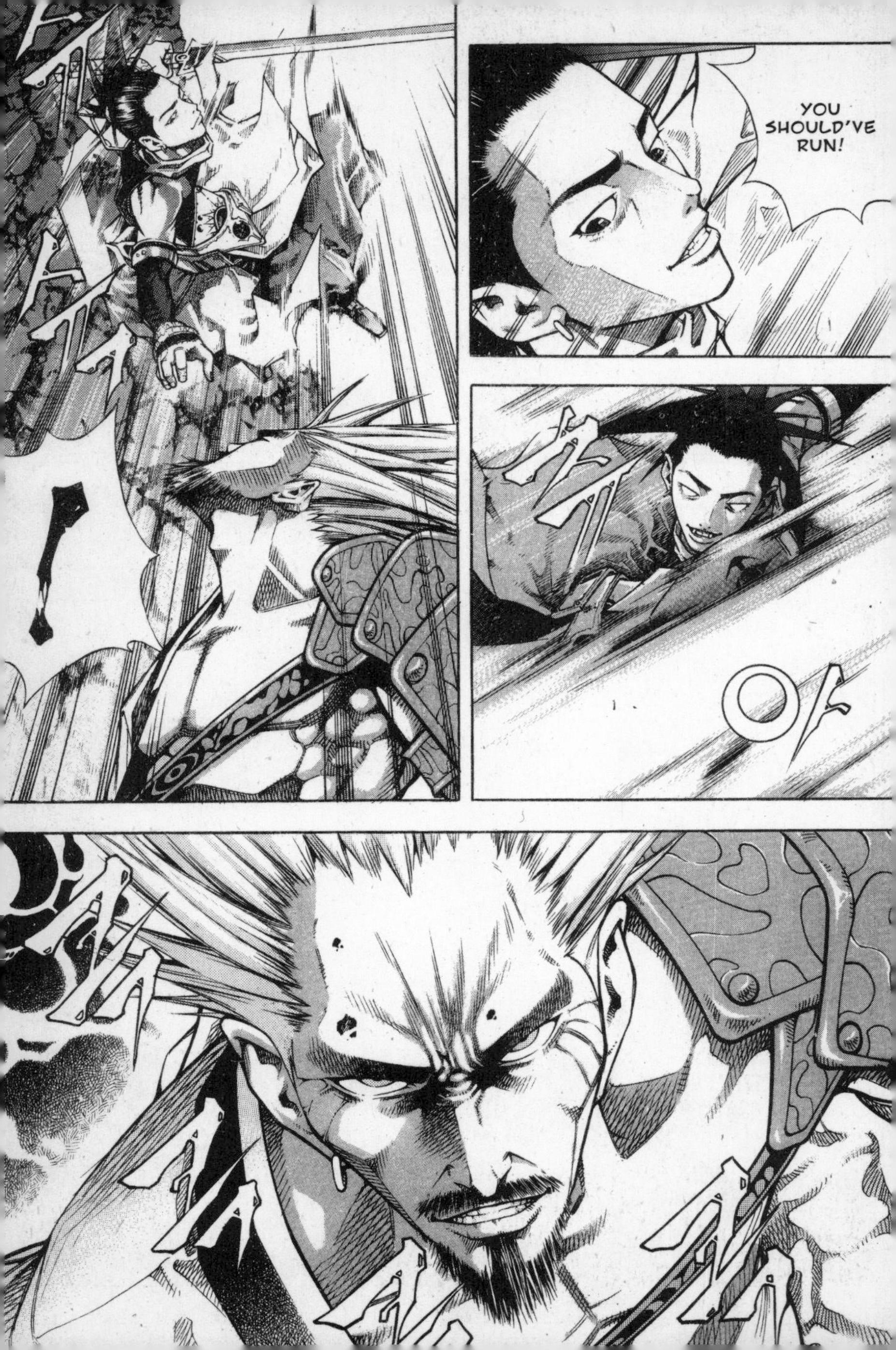
YOU SHOULD'VE RUN!

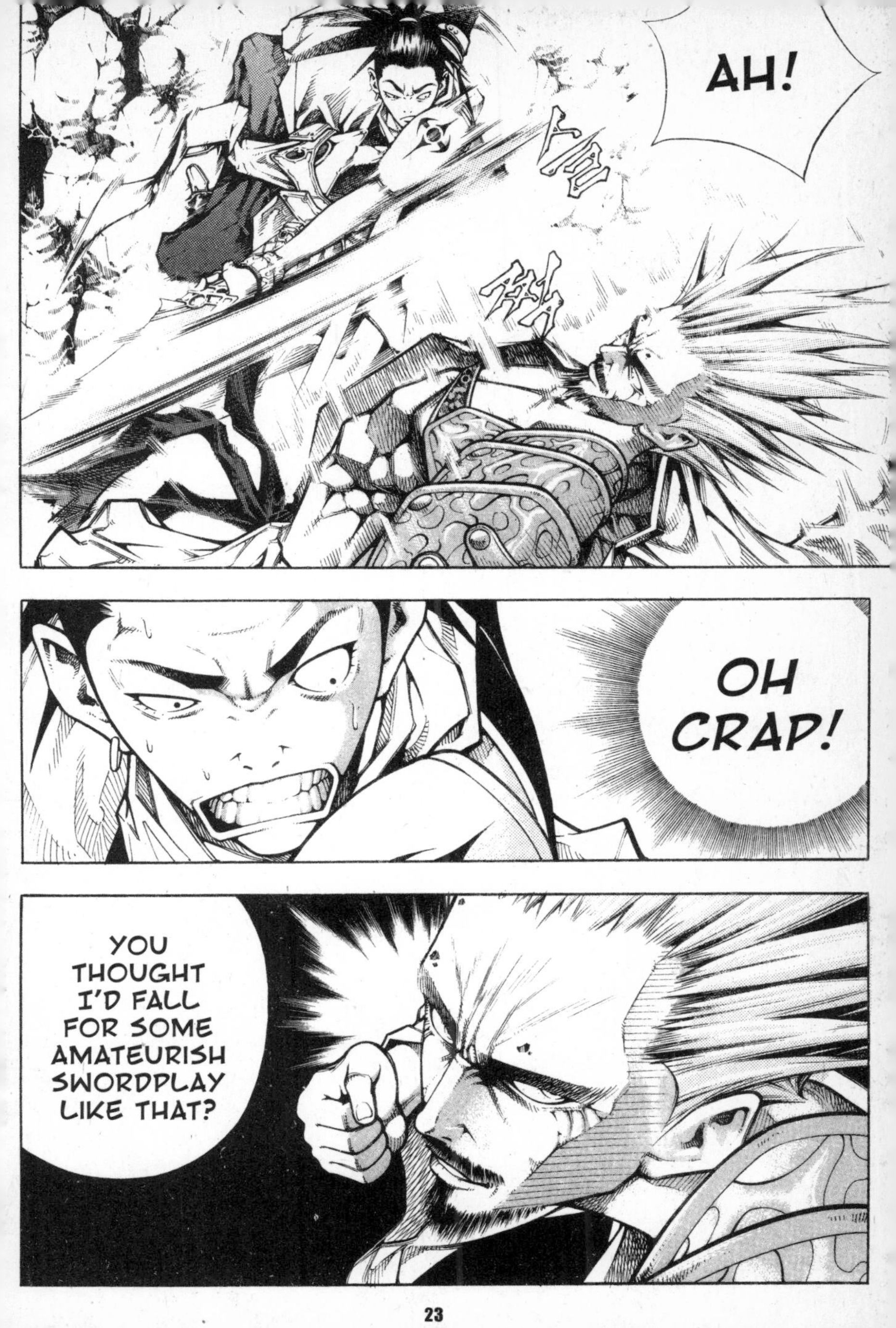
AH!
OH CRAP!
YOU THOUGHT I'D FALL FOR SOME AMATEURISH SWORDPLAY LIKE THAT?

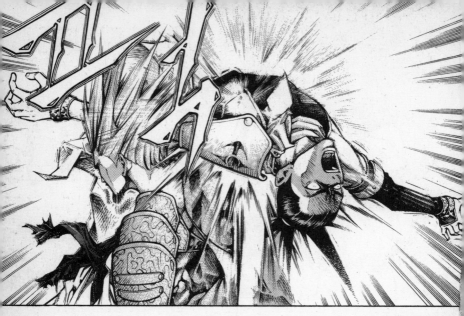

KUH!

WOW, HE'S GOING PRETTY HIGH UP...

......

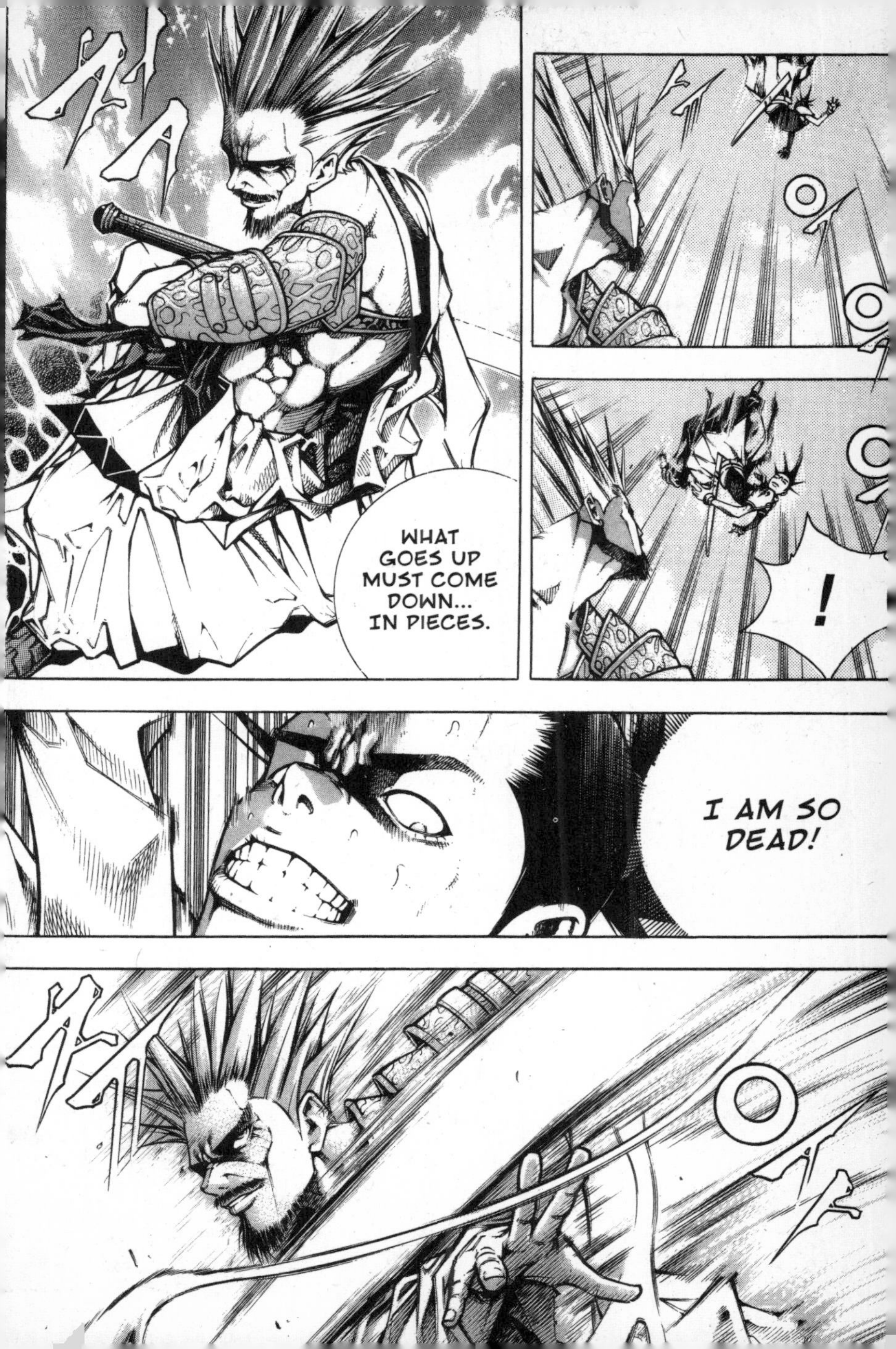
WHAT GOES UP MUST COME DOWN... IN PIECES.
!
I AM SO DEAD!

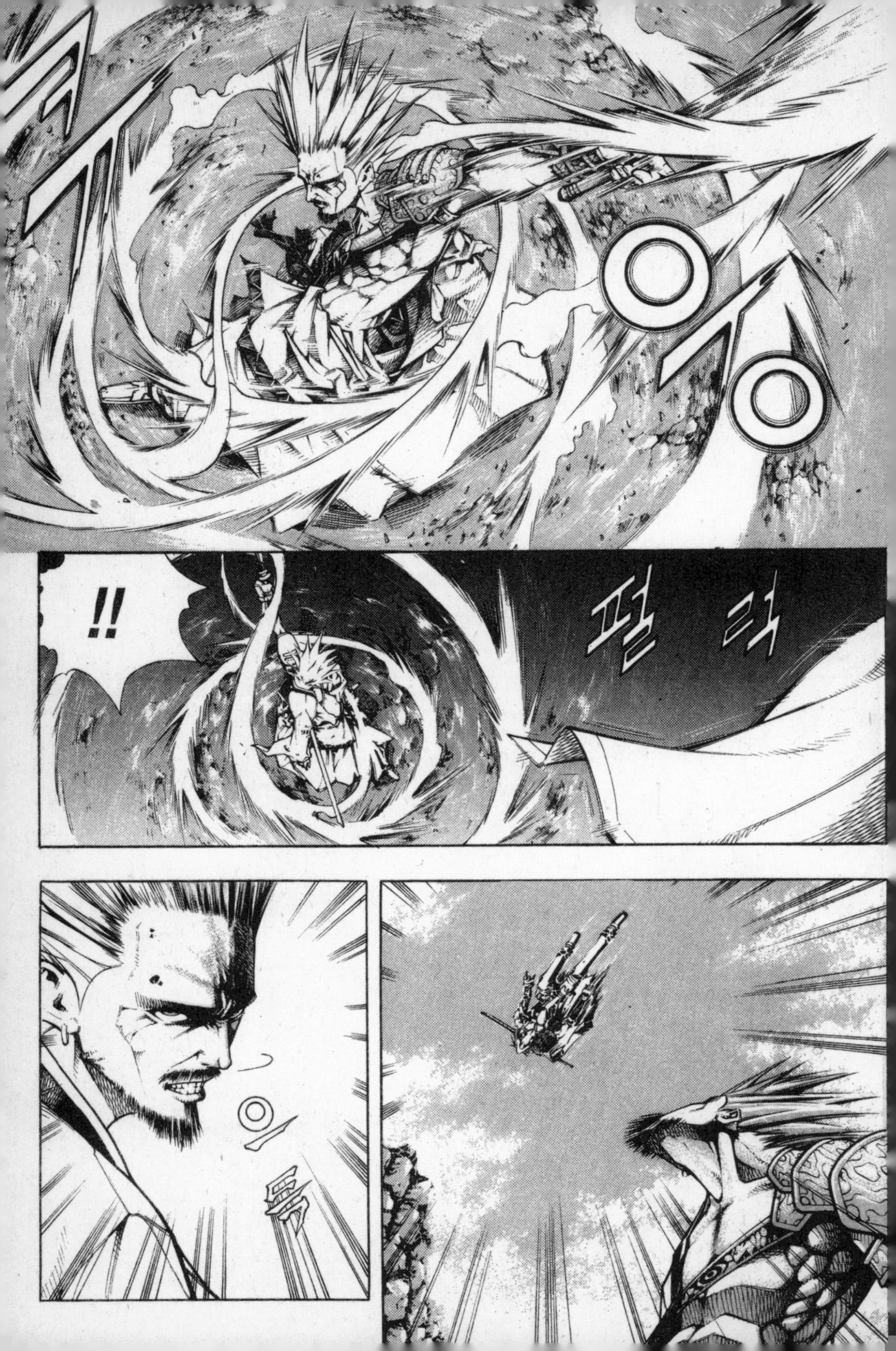
!!
펄럭

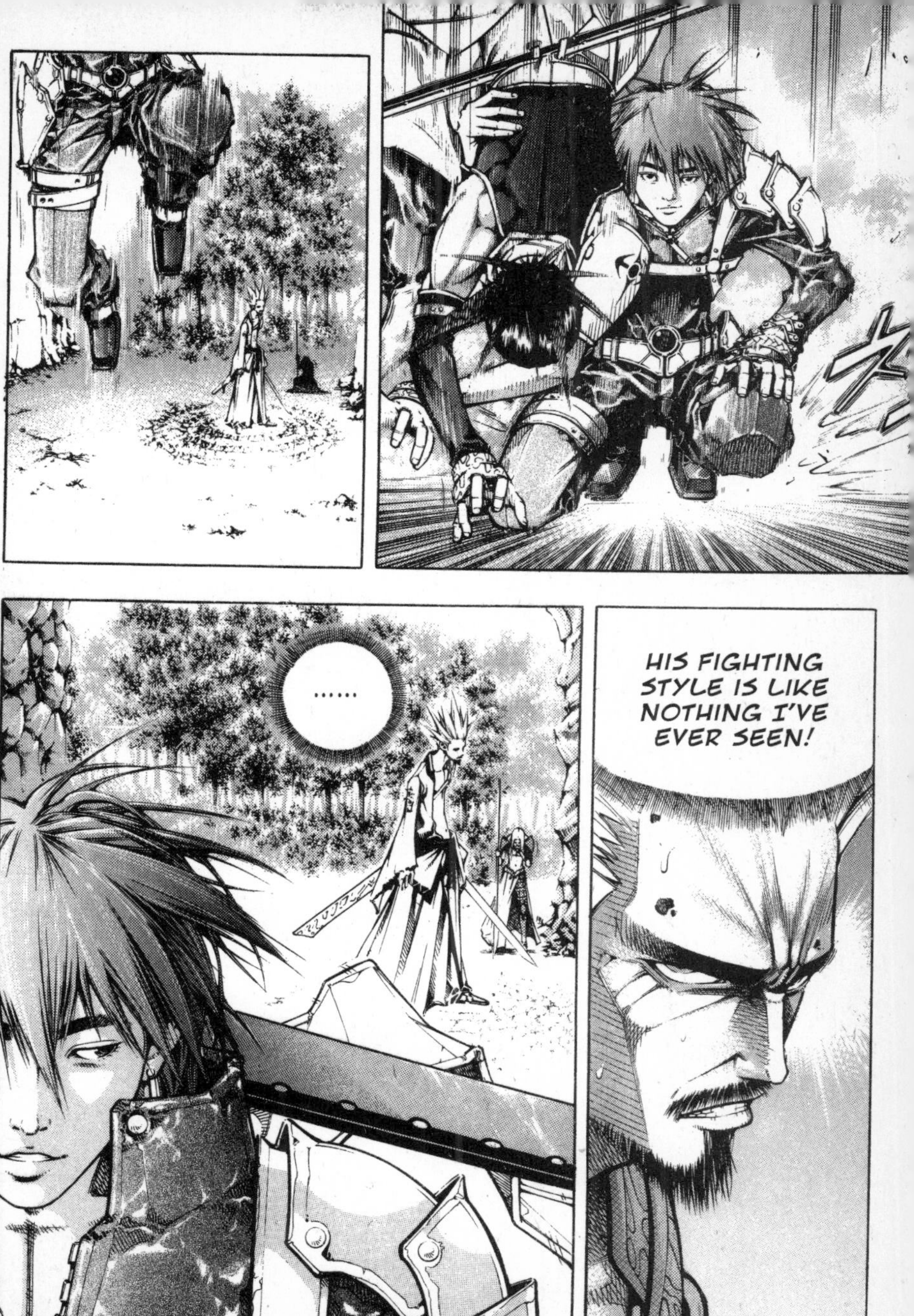

......
HIS FIGHTING STYLE IS LIKE NOTHING I'VE EVER SEEN!

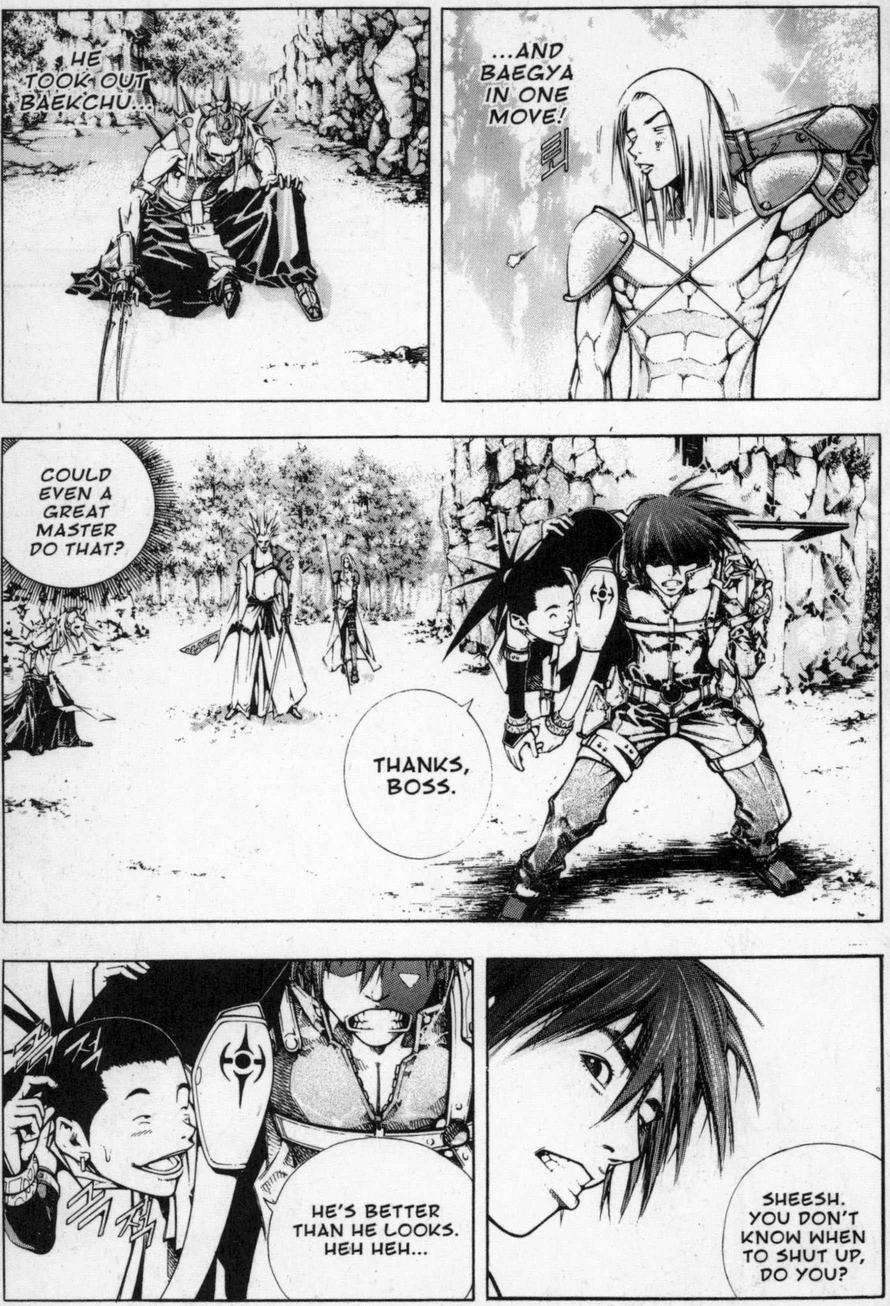
HE TOOK OUT BAEKCHU...
...AND BAEGYA IN ONE MOVE!
COULD EVEN A GREAT MASTER DO THAT?
THANKS, BOSS.
HE'S BETTER THAN HE LOOKS. HEH HEH...
SHEESH. YOU DON'T KNOW WHEN TO SHUT UP, DO YOU?

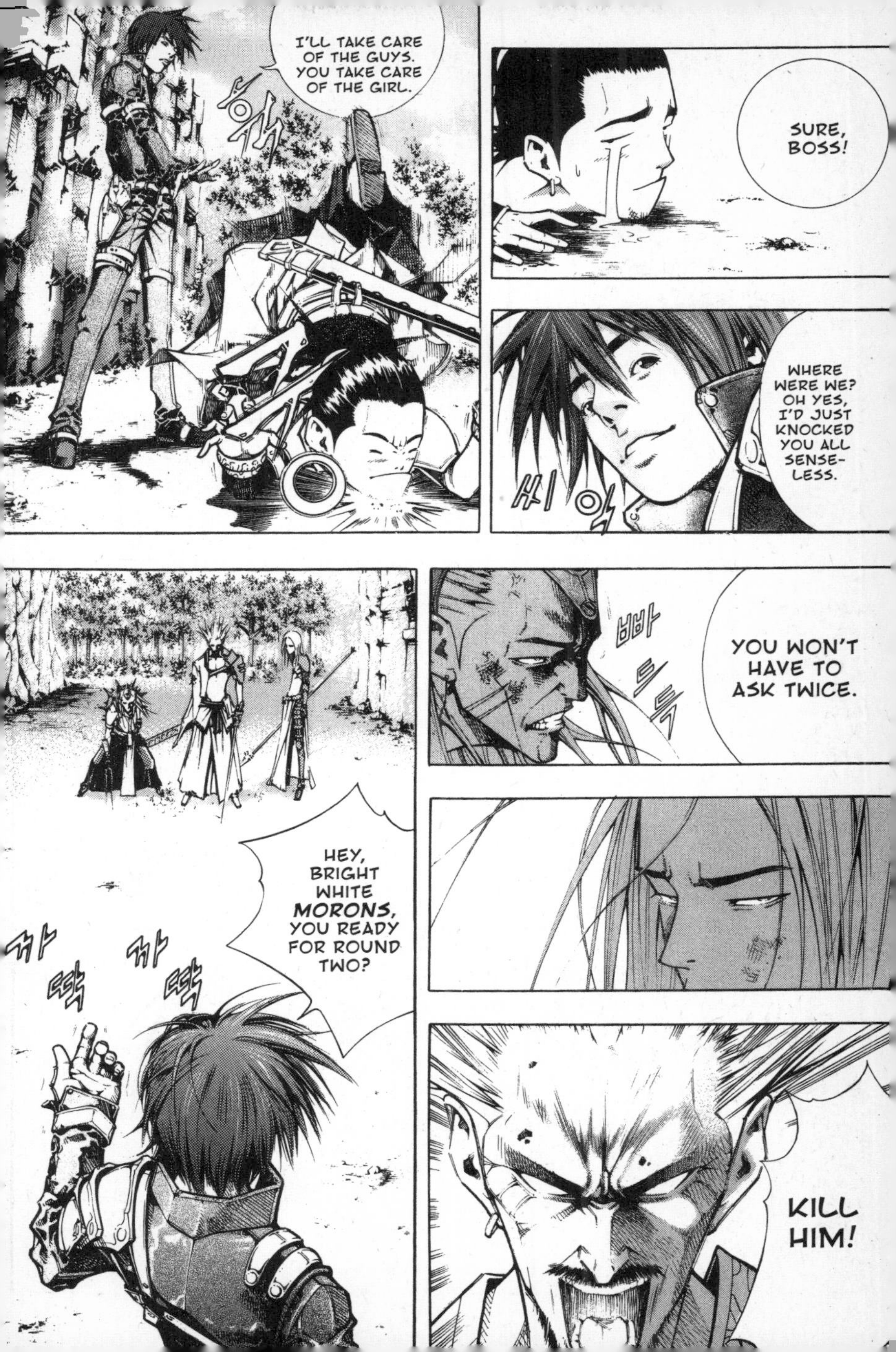
I'LL TAKE CARE OF THE GUYS. YOU TAKE CARE OF THE GIRL.
SURE, BOSS!
WHERE WERE WE? OH YES, I'D JUST KNOCKED YOU ALL SENSE-LESS.
YOU WON'T HAVE TO ASK TWICE.
HEY, BRIGHT WHITE MORONS, YOU READY FOR ROUND TWO?
KILL HIM!

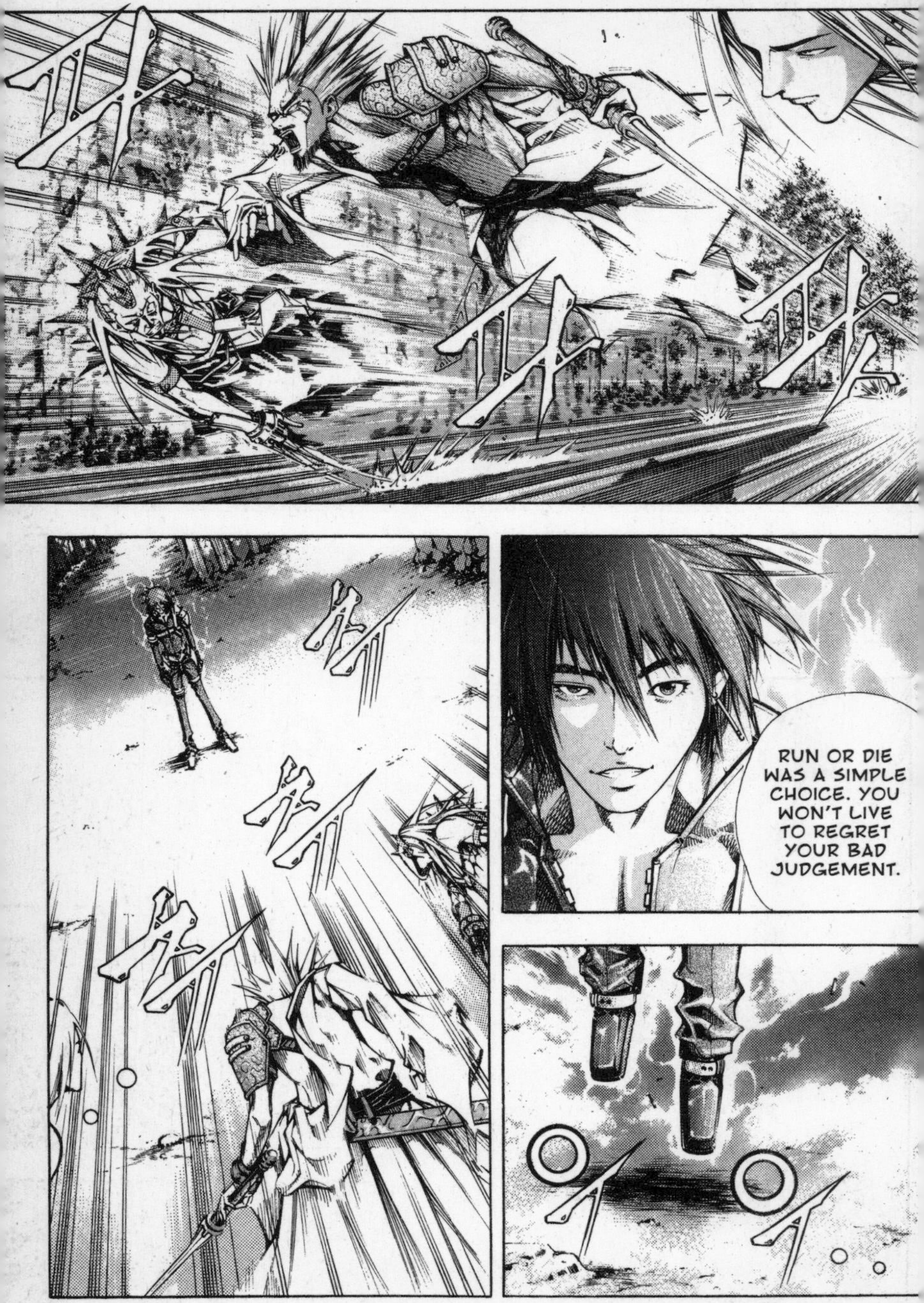
RUN OR DIE WAS A SIMPLE CHOICE. YOU WON'T LIVE TO REGRET YOUR BAD JUDGEMENT.

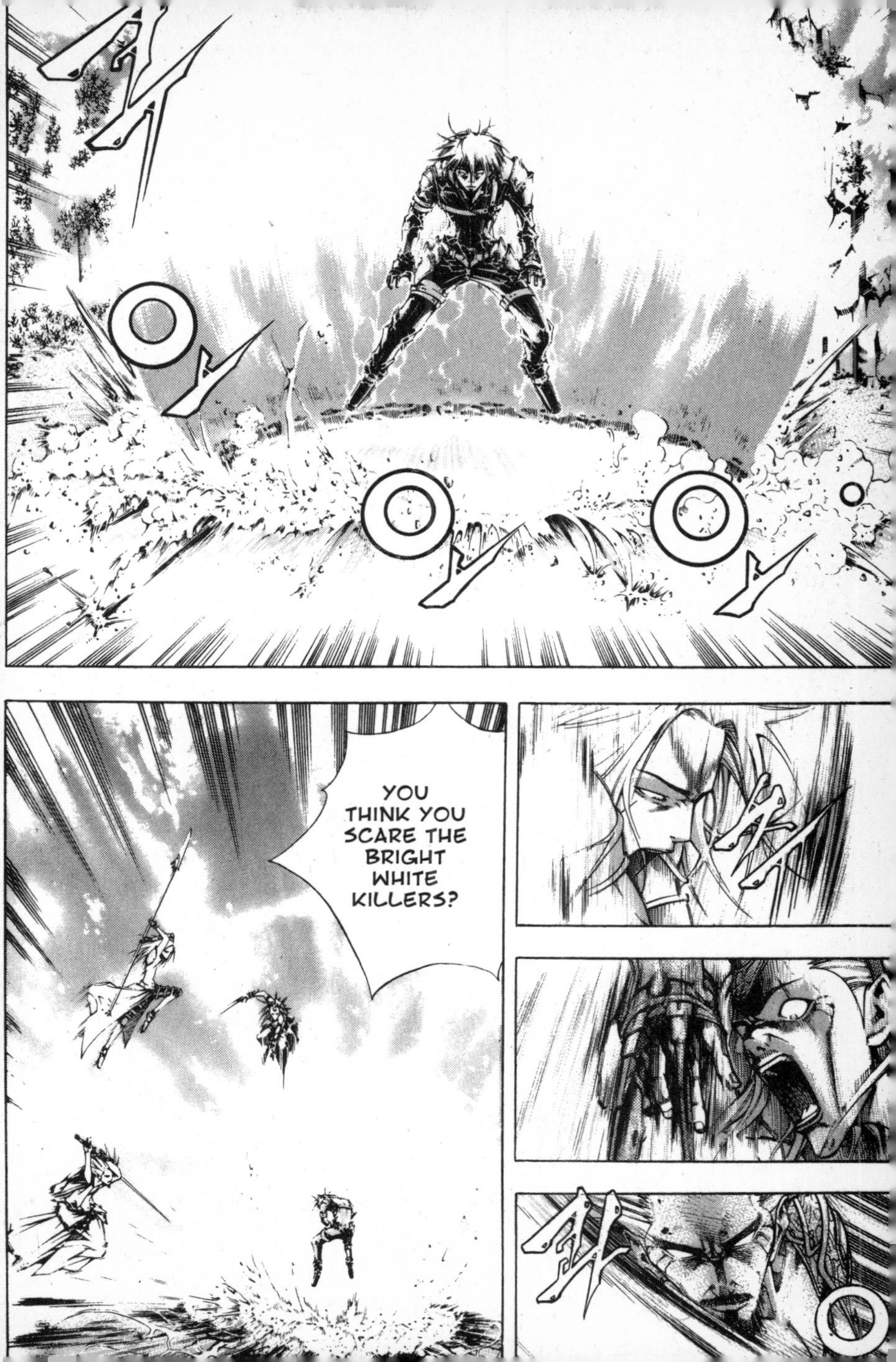
YOU THINK YOU SCARE THE BRIGHT WHITE KILLERS?

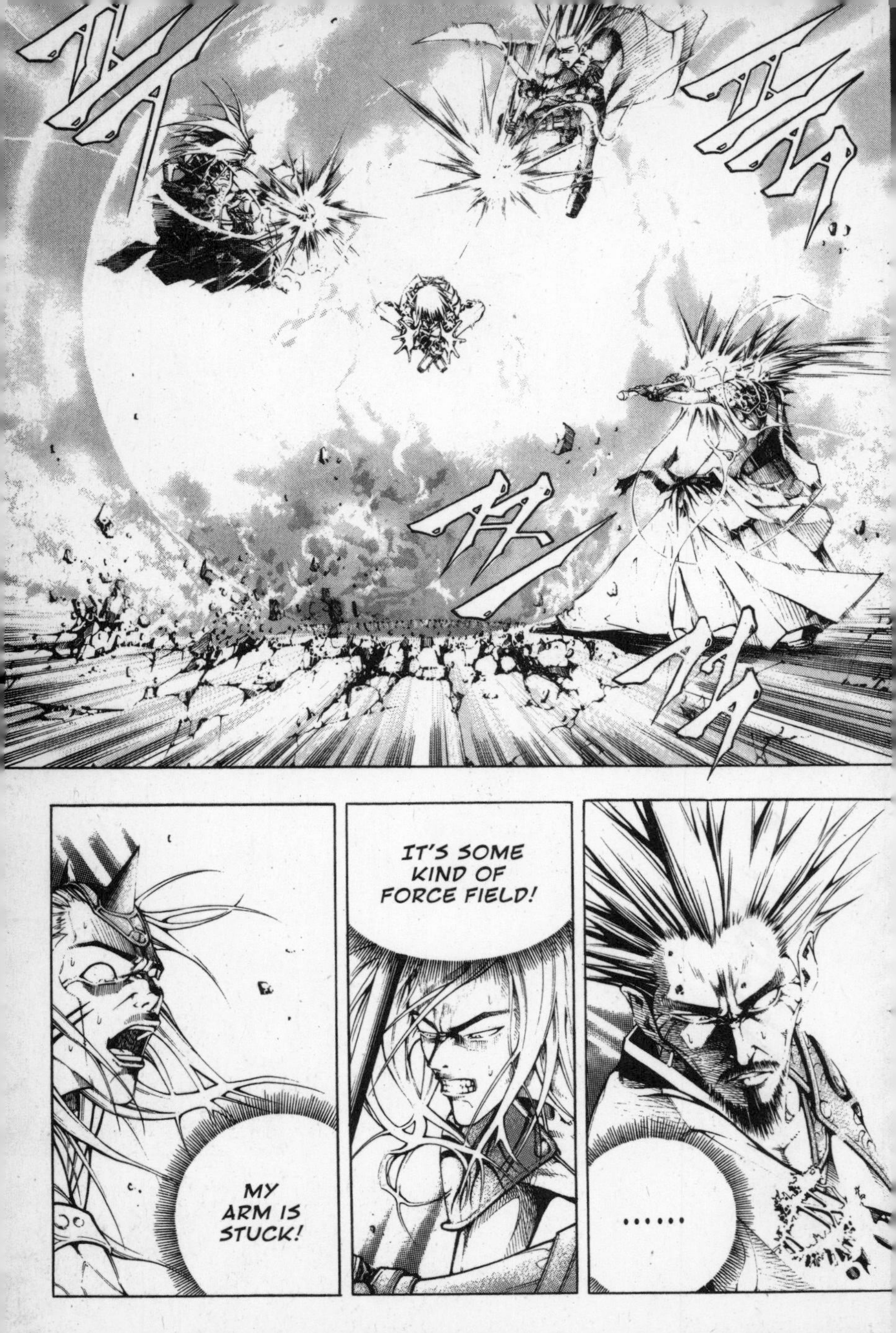
IT'S SOME KIND OF FORCE FIELD!
MY ARM IS STUCK!
......

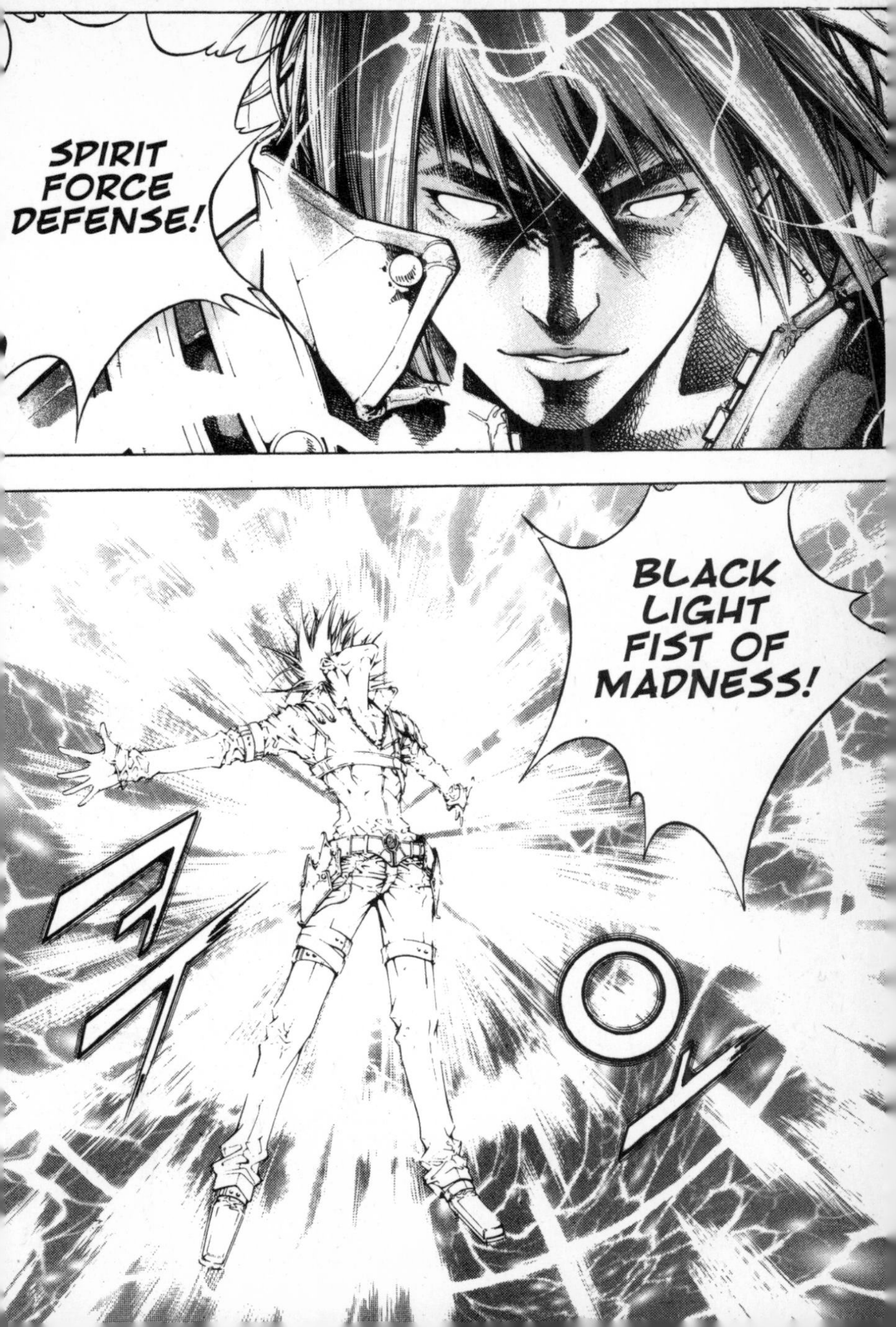
SPIRIT FORCE DEFENSE!
BLACK LIGHT FIST OF MADNESS!

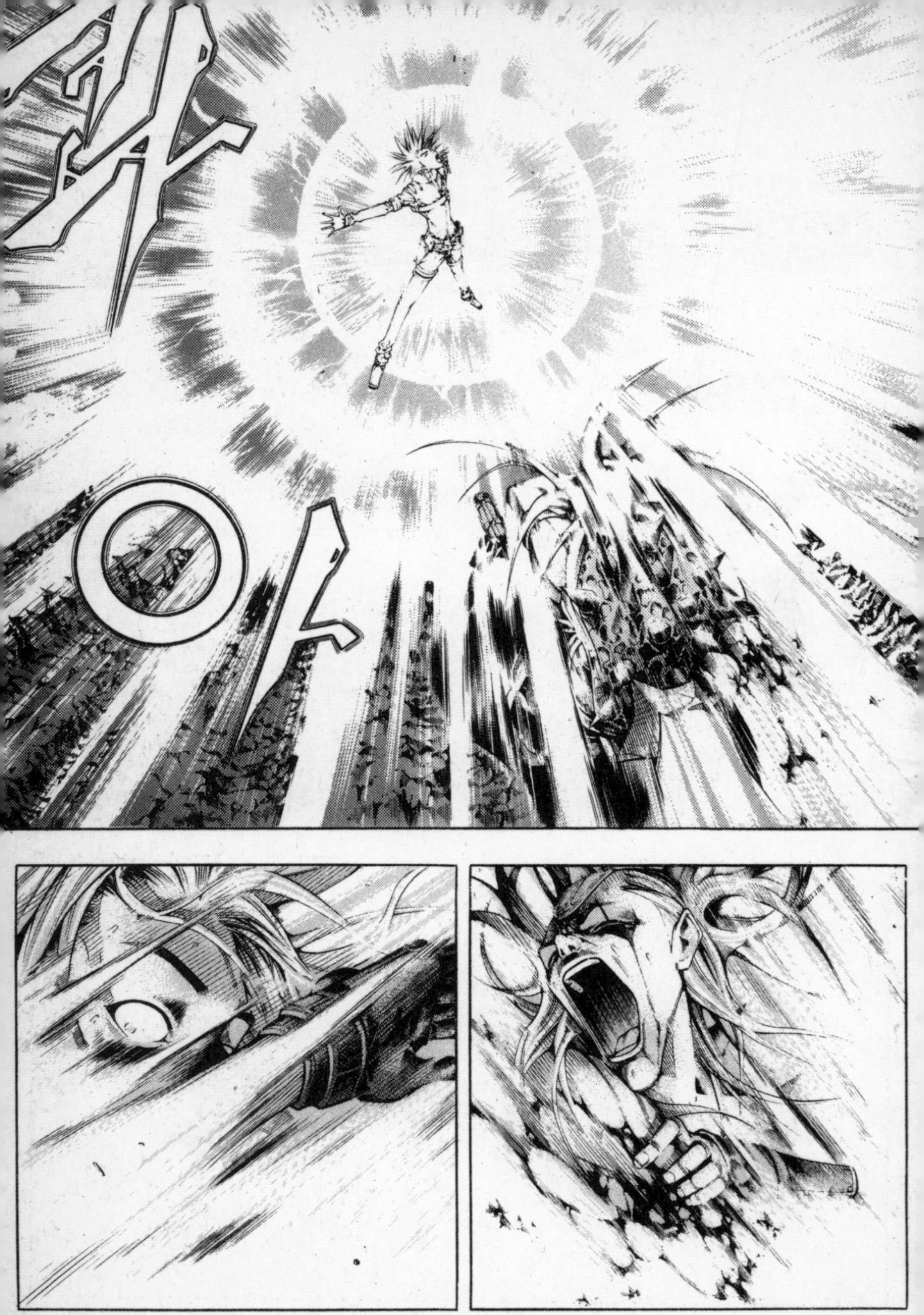

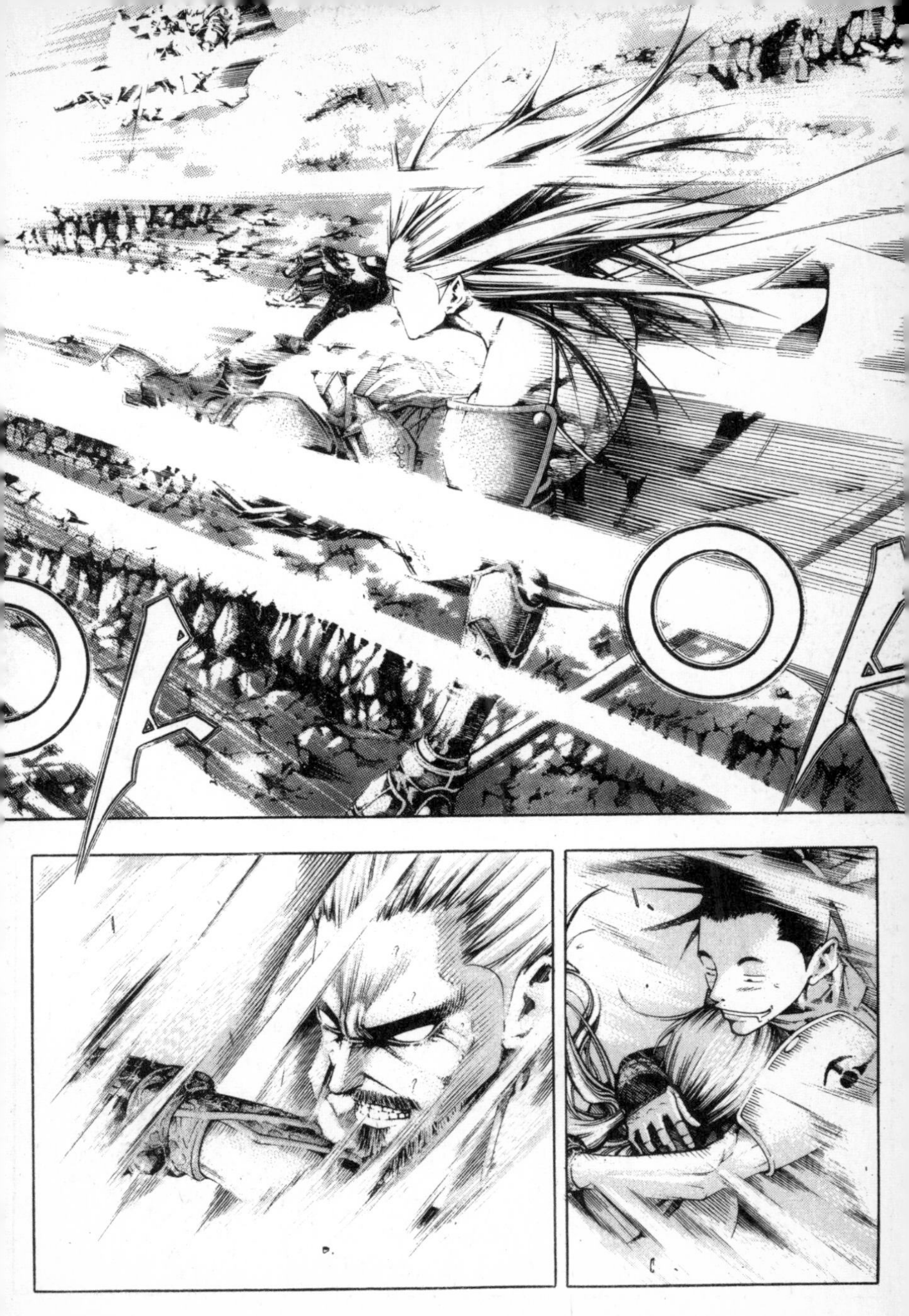

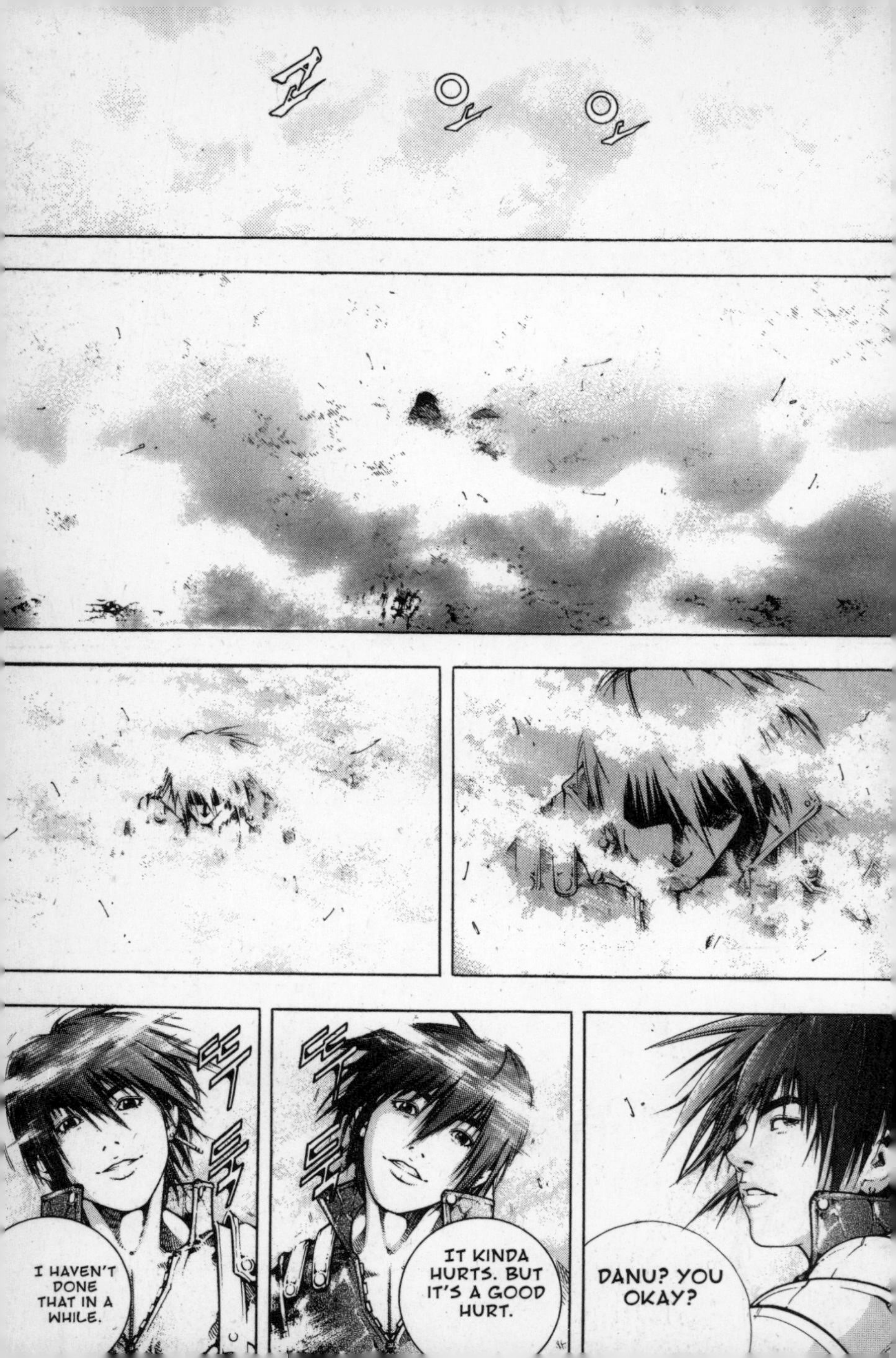
I HAVEN'T DONE THAT IN A WHILE.
IT KINDA HURTS. BUT IT'S A GOOD HURT.
DANU? YOU OKAY?

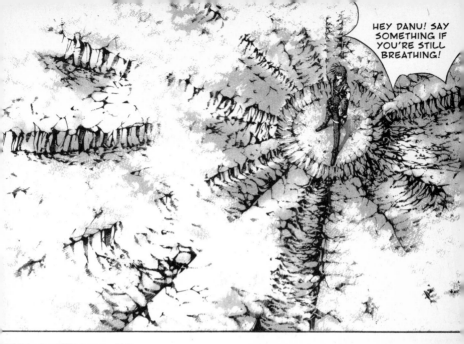

HEY DANU! SAY SOMETHING IF YOU'RE STILL BREATHING!

HI, I'M DANU, YOUR SAVIOR.

I'M SANGHUI, AND YOU DON'T HAVE TO PROTECT ME ANYMORE!

STOP STRUGGLING. STAY UNDER ME, IT'S TOO DANGEROUS TO GET UP...

DANU!

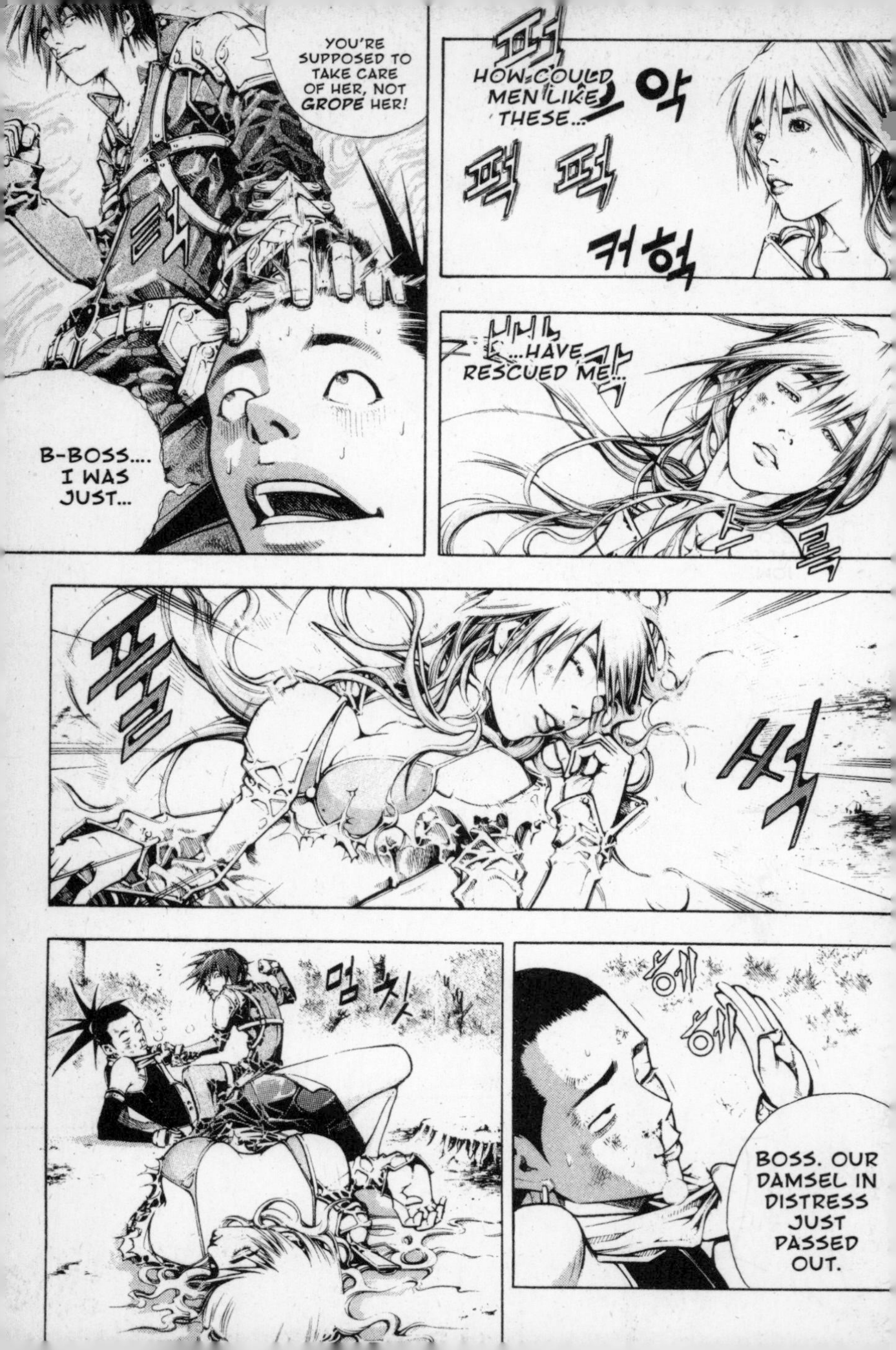
YOU'RE SUPPOSED TO TAKE CARE OF HER, NOT GROPE HER!
B-BOSS.... I WAS JUST...
HOW COULD MEN LIKE THESE...
퍽 퍽
커헉
...HAVE RESCUED ME!...
멈칫
BOSS. OUR DAMSEL IN DISTRESS JUST PASSED OUT.

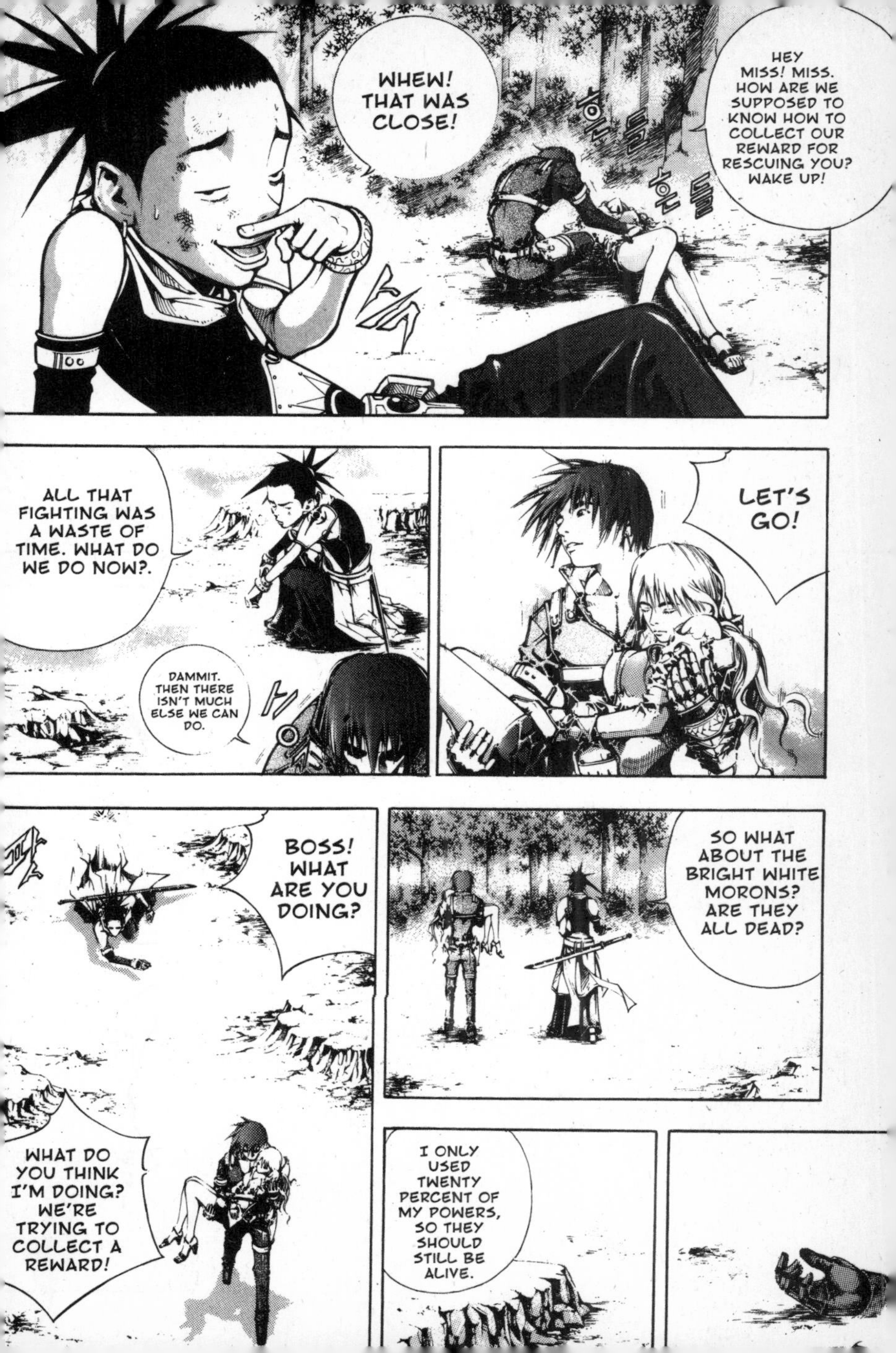
WHEW! THAT WAS CLOSE!
HEY MISS! MISS. HOW ARE WE SUPPOSED TO KNOW HOW TO COLLECT OUR REWARD FOR RESCUING YOU? WAKE UP!
ALL THAT FIGHTING WAS A WASTE OF TIME. WHAT DO WE DO NOW?.
DAMMIT. THEN THERE ISN'T MUCH ELSE WE CAN DO.
LET'S GO!
BOSS! WHAT ARE YOU DOING?
WHAT DO YOU THINK I'M DOING? WE'RE TRYING TO COLLECT A REWARD!
SO WHAT ABOUT THE BRIGHT WHITE MORONS? ARE THEY ALL DEAD?
I ONLY USED TWENTY PERCENT OF MY POWERS, SO THEY SHOULD STILL BE ALIVE.

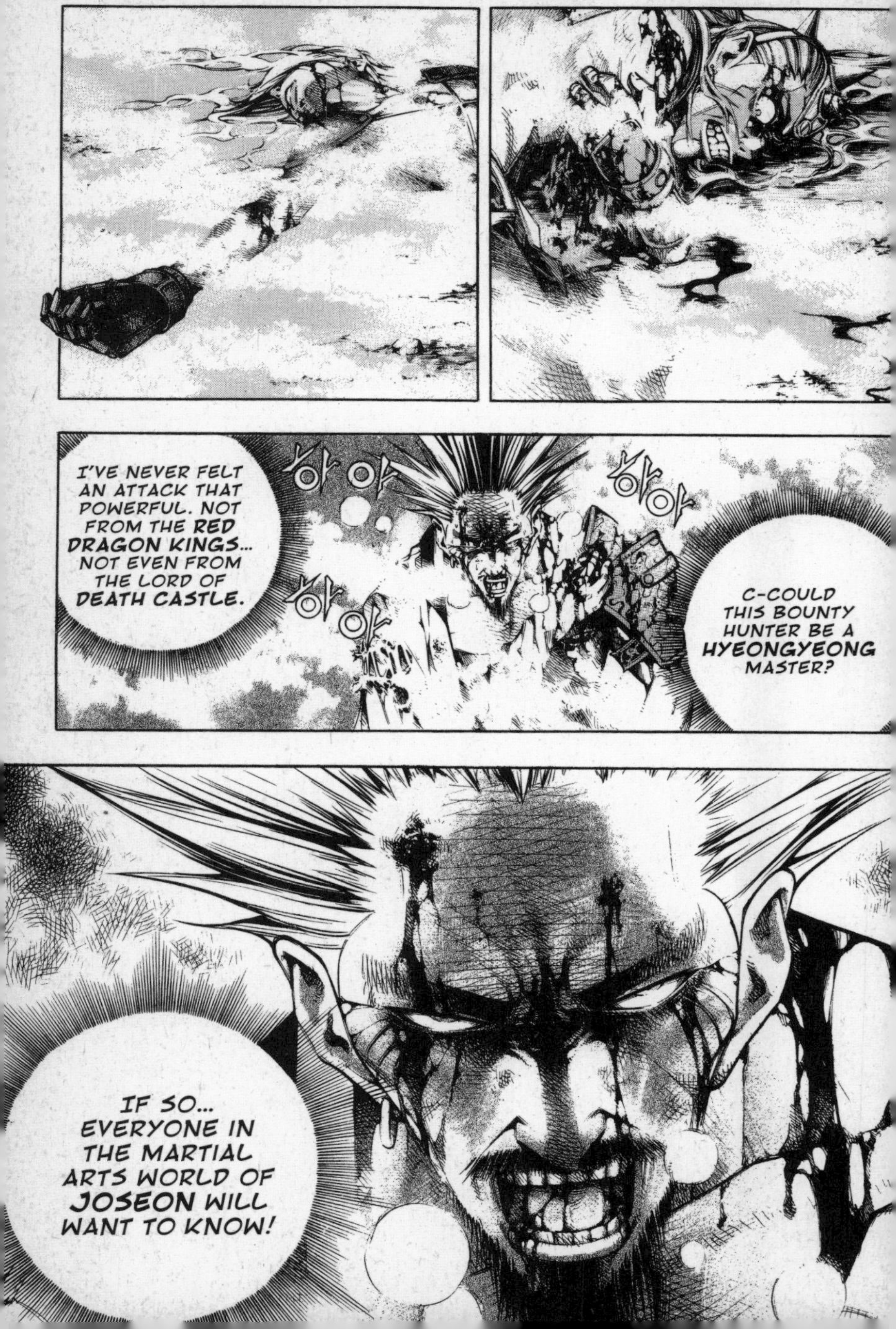
I'VE NEVER FELT AN ATTACK THAT POWERFUL. NOT FROM THE RED DRAGON KINGS... NOT EVEN FROM THE LORD OF DEATH CASTLE.
C-COULD THIS BOUNTY HUNTER BE A HYEONGYEONG MASTER?
IF SO... EVERYONE IN THE MARTIAL ARTS WORLD OF JOSEON WILL WANT TO KNOW!

Chapter 2
Master of Hyeongyeong

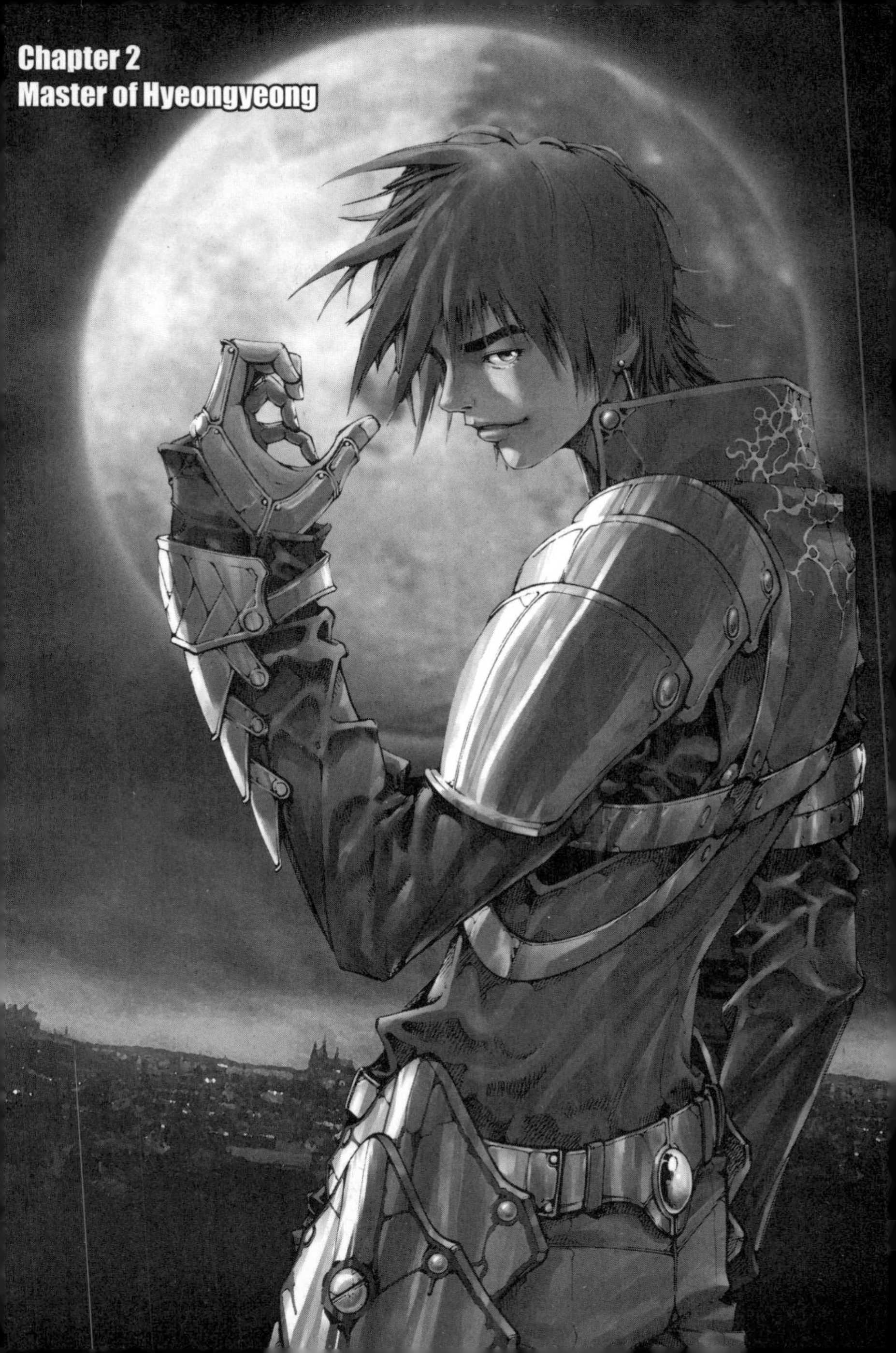

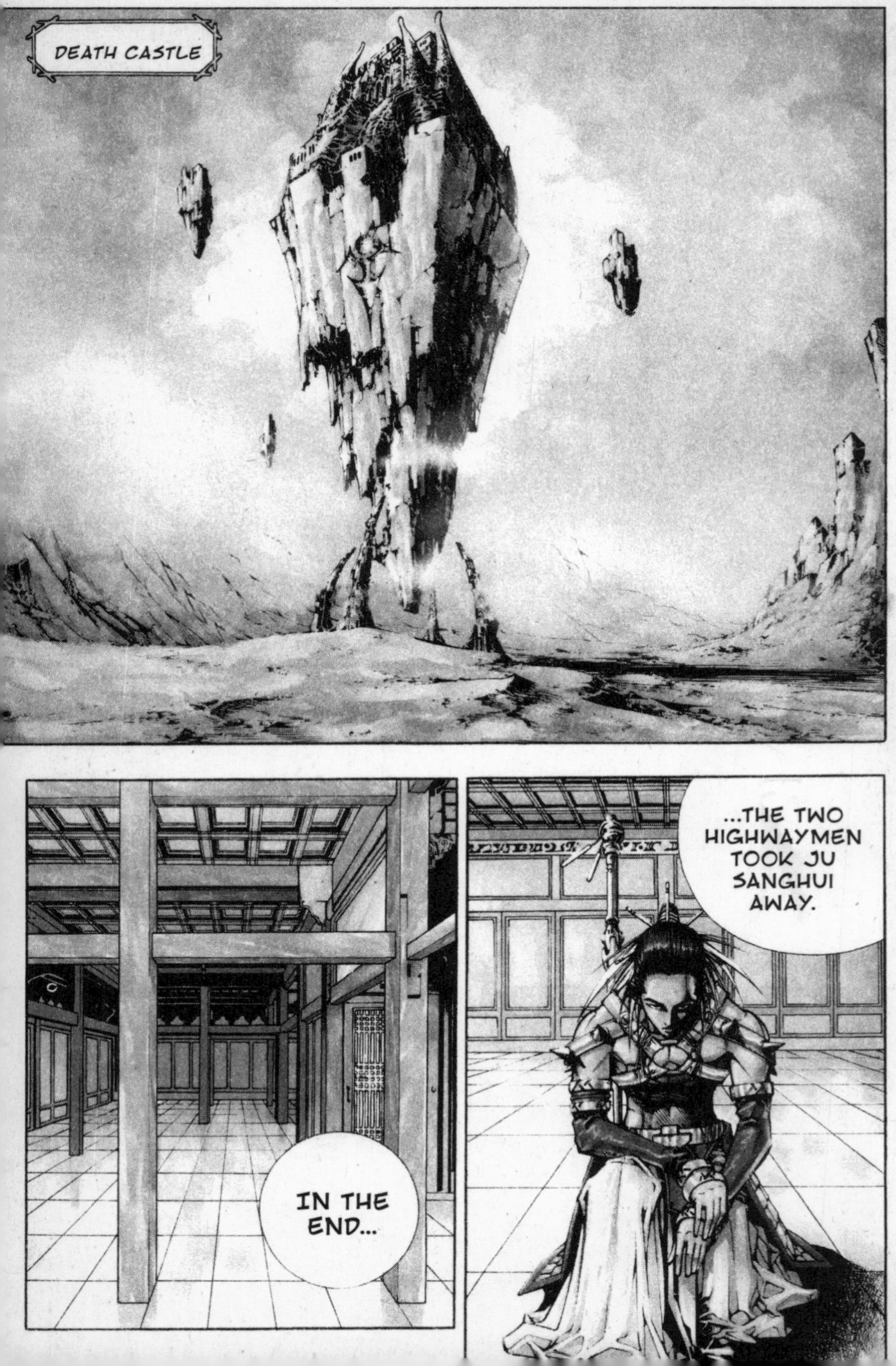
DEATH CASTLE
IN THE END...
...THE TWO HIGHWAYMEN TOOK JU SANGHUI AWAY.

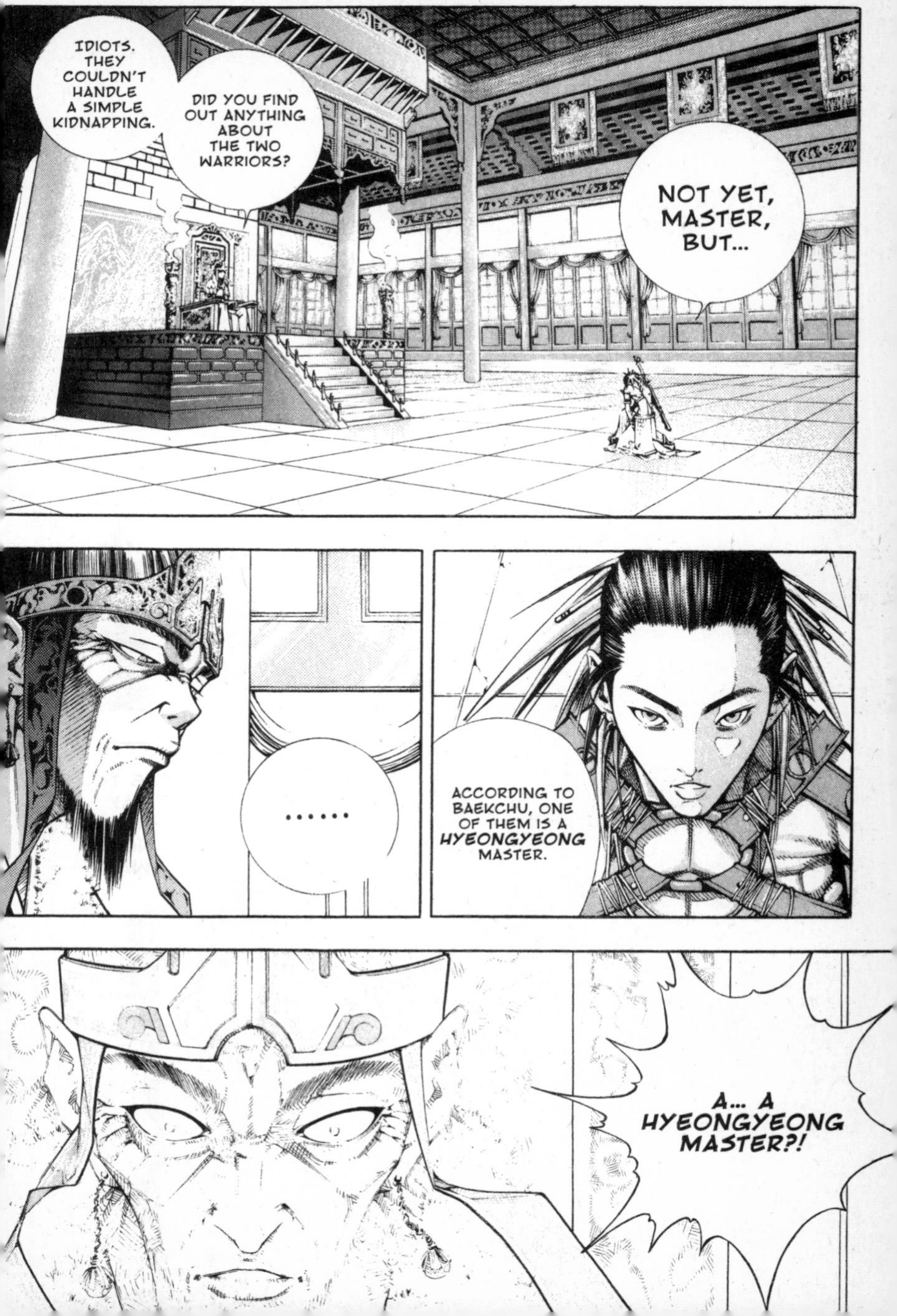
IDIOTS. THEY COULDN'T HANDLE A SIMPLE KIDNAPPING.
DID YOU FIND OUT ANYTHING ABOUT THE TWO WARRIORS?
NOT YET, MASTER, BUT...
......
ACCORDING TO BAEKCHU, ONE OF THEM IS A HYEONGYEONG MASTER.
A... A HYEONGYEONG MASTER?!

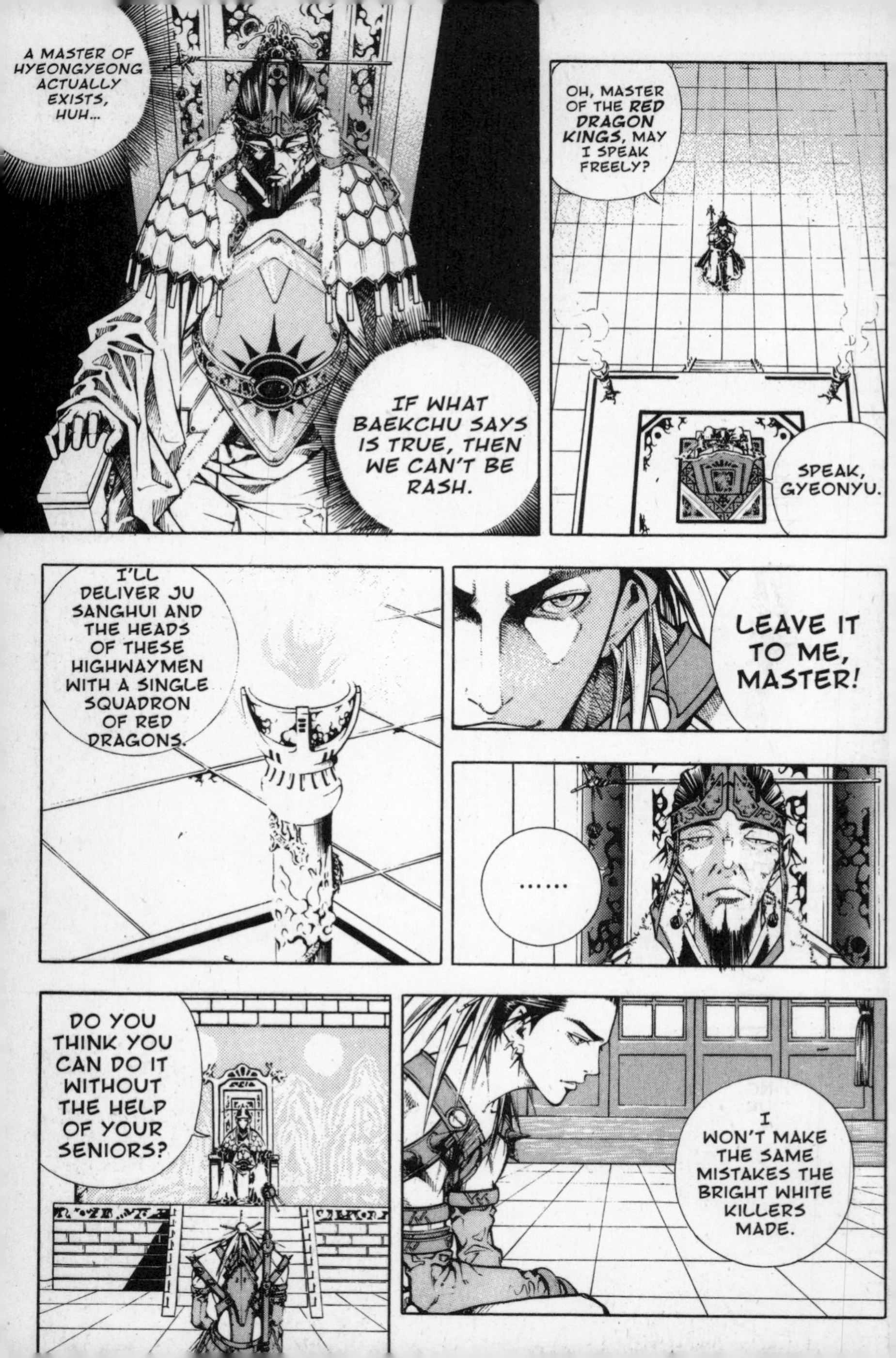
A MASTER OF HYEONGYEONG ACTUALLY EXISTS, HUH...
IF WHAT BAEKCHU SAYS IS TRUE, THEN WE CAN'T BE RASH.
OH, MASTER OF THE RED DRAGON KINGS, MAY I SPEAK FREELY?
SPEAK, GYEONYU.
I'LL DELIVER JU SANGHUI AND THE HEADS OF THESE HIGHWAYMEN WITH A SINGLE SQUADRON OF RED DRAGONS.
LEAVE IT TO ME, MASTER!
......
DO YOU THINK YOU CAN DO IT WITHOUT THE HELP OF YOUR SENIORS?
I WON'T MAKE THE SAME MISTAKES THE BRIGHT WHITE KILLERS MADE.

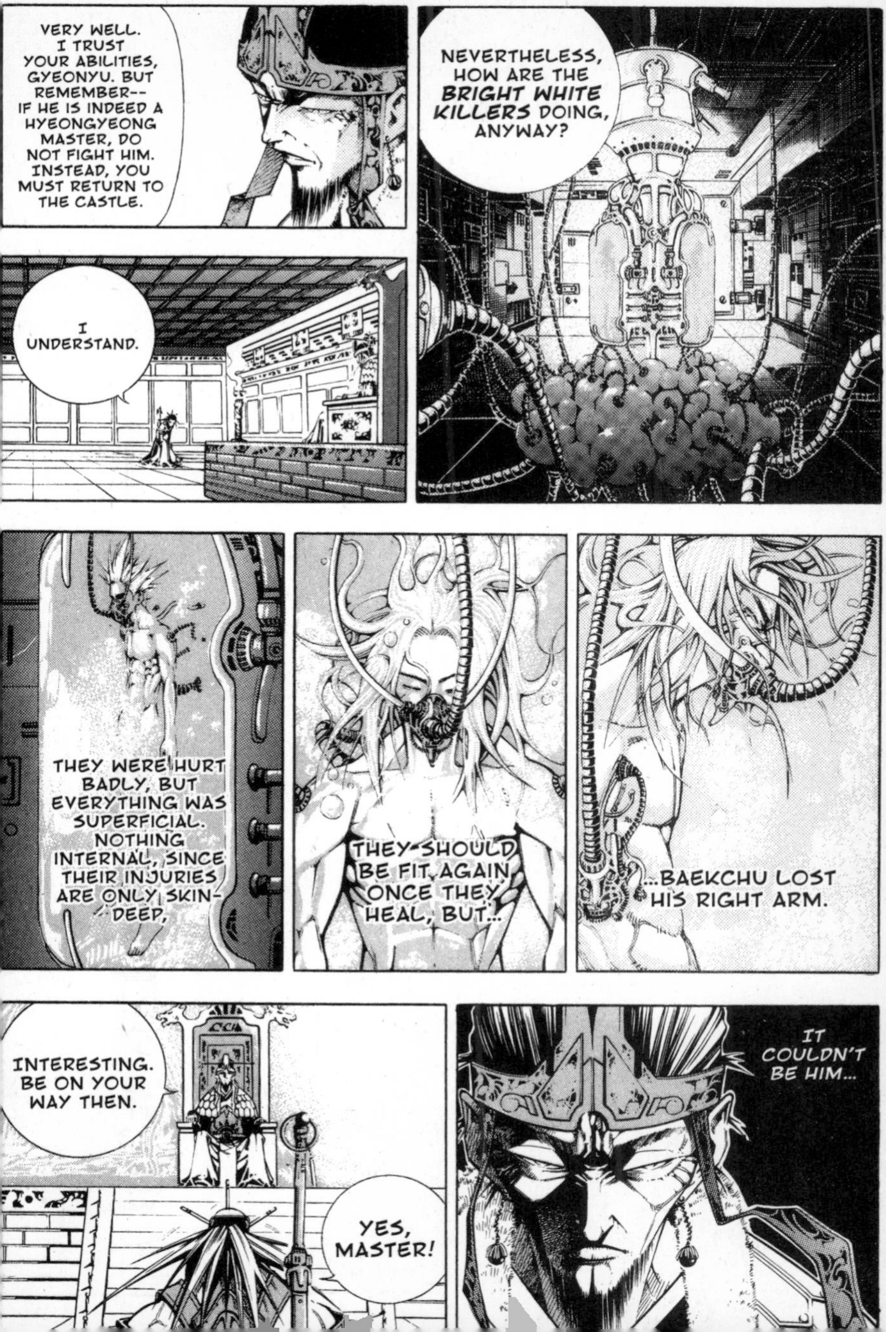
VERY WELL. I TRUST YOUR ABILITIES, GYEONYU. BUT REMEMBER-- IF HE IS INDEED A HYEONGYEONG MASTER, DO NOT FIGHT HIM. INSTEAD, YOU MUST RETURN TO THE CASTLE.
I UNDERSTAND.
NEVERTHELESS, HOW ARE THE BRIGHT WHITE KILLERS DOING, ANYWAY?
THEY WERE HURT BADLY, BUT EVERYTHING WAS SUPERFICIAL. NOTHING INTERNAL, SINCE THEIR INJURIES ARE ONLY SKIN-DEEP,
THEY SHOULD BE FIT AGAIN ONCE THEY HEAL, BUT...
...BAEKCHU LOST HIS RIGHT ARM.
INTERESTING. BE ON YOUR WAY THEN.
YES, MASTER!
IT COULDN'T BE HIM...

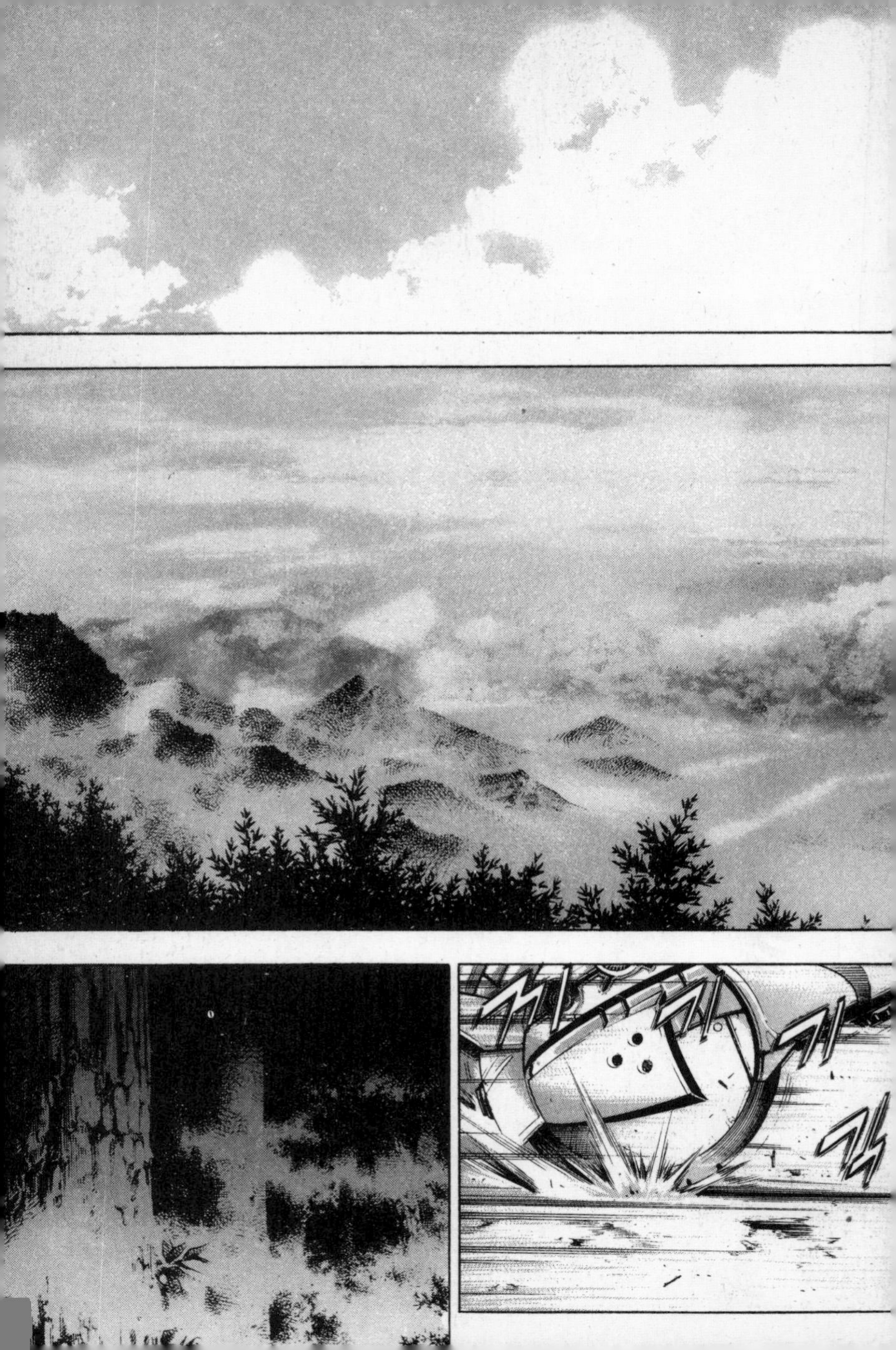

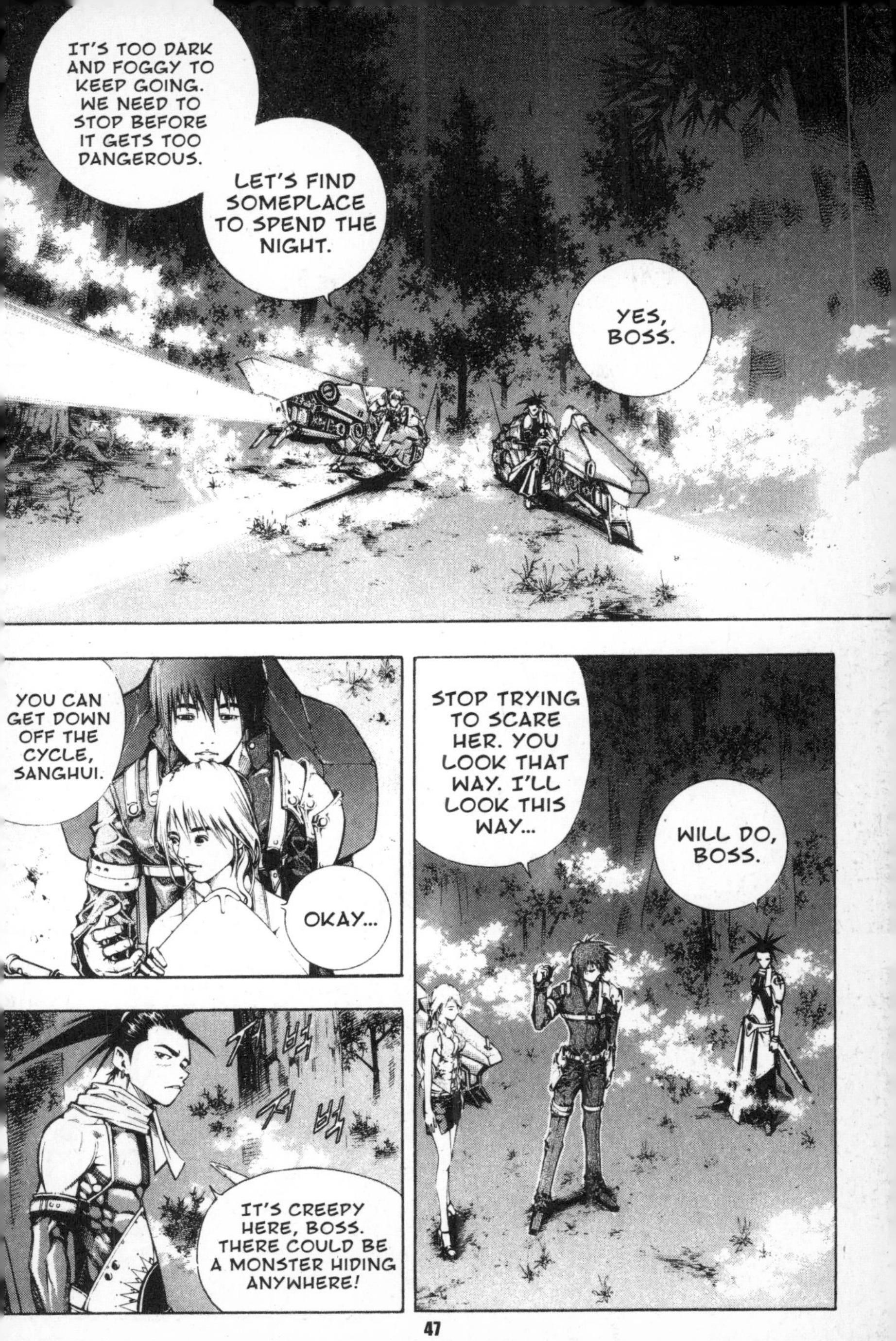
IT'S TOO DARK AND FOGGY TO KEEP GOING. WE NEED TO STOP BEFORE IT GETS TOO DANGEROUS.
LET'S FIND SOMEPLACE TO SPEND THE NIGHT.
YES, BOSS.
YOU CAN GET DOWN OFF THE CYCLE, SANGHUI.
OKAY...
IT'S CREEPY HERE, BOSS. THERE COULD BE A MONSTER HIDING ANYWHERE!
STOP TRYING TO SCARE HER. YOU LOOK THAT WAY. I'LL LOOK THIS WAY...
WILL DO, BOSS.

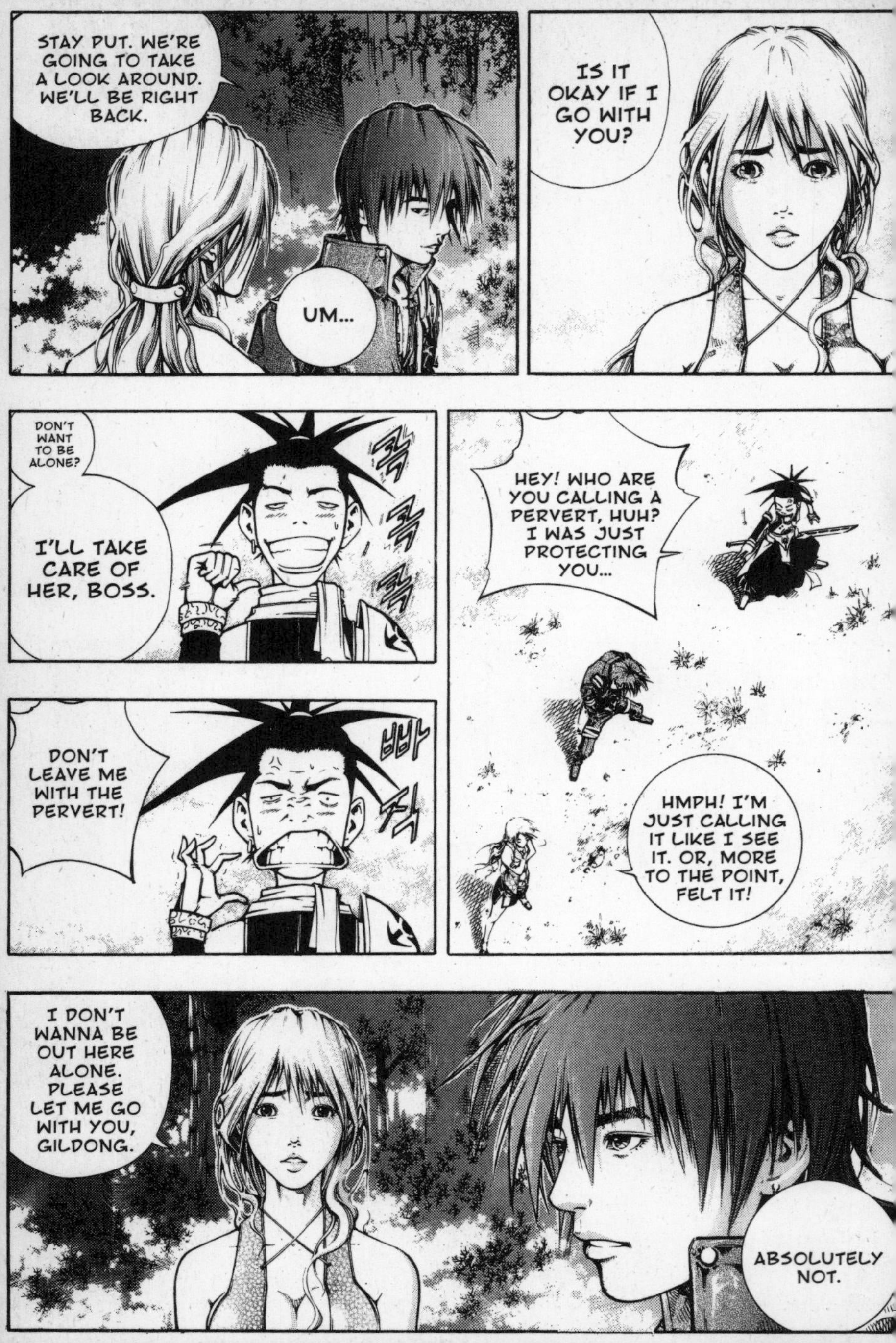
STAY PUT. WE'RE GOING TO TAKE A LOOK AROUND. WE'LL BE RIGHT BACK.
UM...
IS IT OKAY IF I GO WITH YOU?
DON'T WANT TO BE ALONE?
I'LL TAKE CARE OF HER, BOSS.
DON'T LEAVE ME WITH THE PERVERT!
HEY! WHO ARE YOU CALLING A PERVERT, HUH? I WAS JUST PROTECTING YOU...
HMPH! I'M JUST CALLING IT LIKE I SEE IT. OR, MORE TO THE POINT, FELT IT!
I DON'T WANNA BE OUT HERE ALONE. PLEASE LET ME GO WITH YOU, GILDONG.
ABSOLUTELY NOT.

I CAN'T RISK TAKING YOU OUT INTO A DARK FOGGY NIGHT WHEN YOU CAN'T SEE TWO FEET IN FRONT OF YOU.

I UNDERSTAND YOU'RE SCARED, BUT WE WON'T BE LONG.

I'LL BE RIGHT BACK.

YES...

ANY DAY NOW, DANU.

YES, BOSS.

HAVE FUN ON YOUR OWN, TEASE!

GOODBYE. TINY.

I JUST CAN'T FIGURE IT OUT.

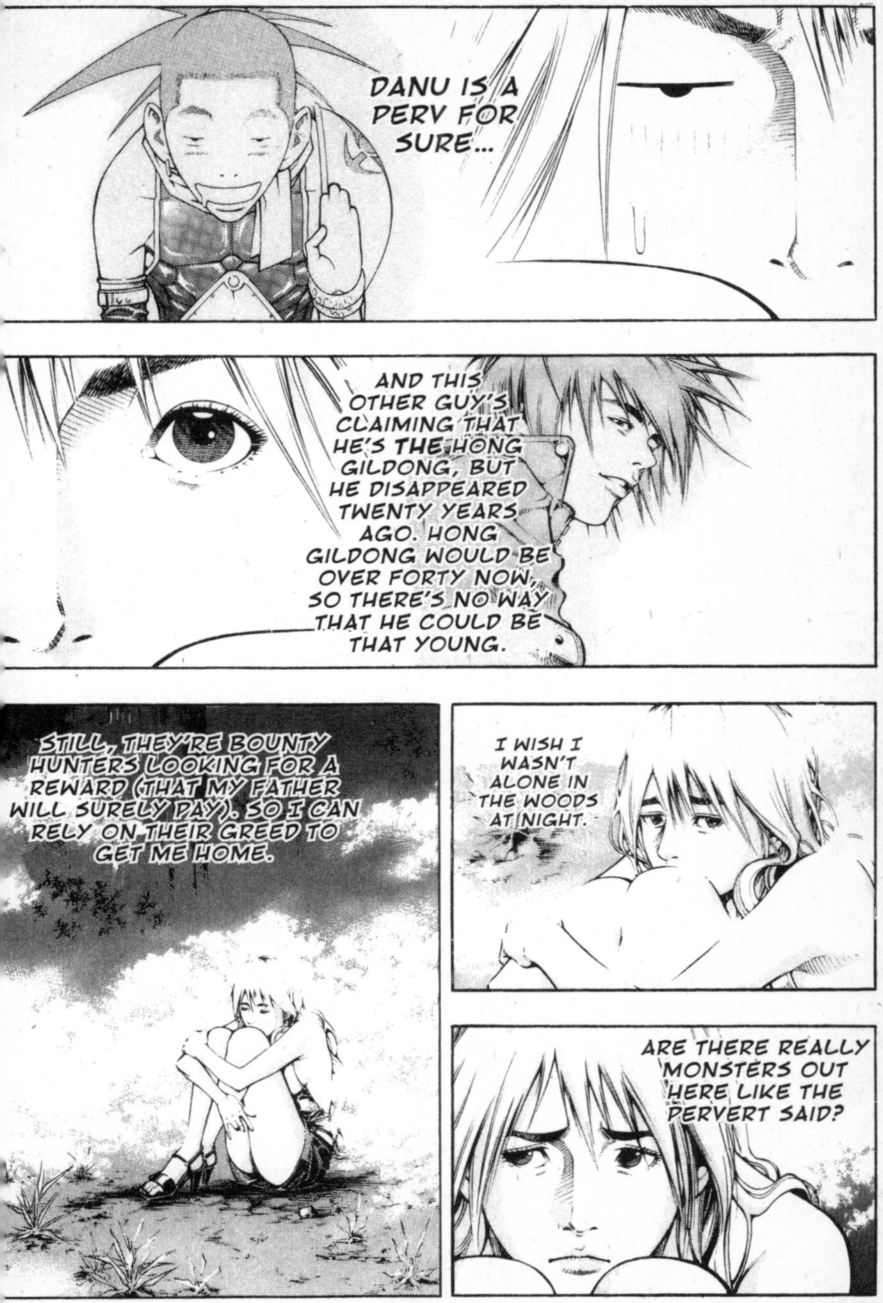
DANU IS A PERV FOR SURE...
AND THIS OTHER GUY'S CLAIMING THAT HE'S THE HONG GILDONG, BUT HE DISAPPEARED TWENTY YEARS AGO. HONG GILDONG WOULD BE OVER FORTY NOW, SO THERE'S NO WAY THAT HE COULD BE THAT YOUNG.
STILL, THEY'RE BOUNTY HUNTERS LOOKING FOR A REWARD (THAT MY FATHER WILL SURELY PAY). SO I CAN RELY ON THEIR GREED TO GET ME HOME.
I WISH I WASN'T ALONE IN THE WOODS AT NIGHT.
ARE THERE REALLY MONSTERS OUT HERE LIKE THE PERVERT SAID?

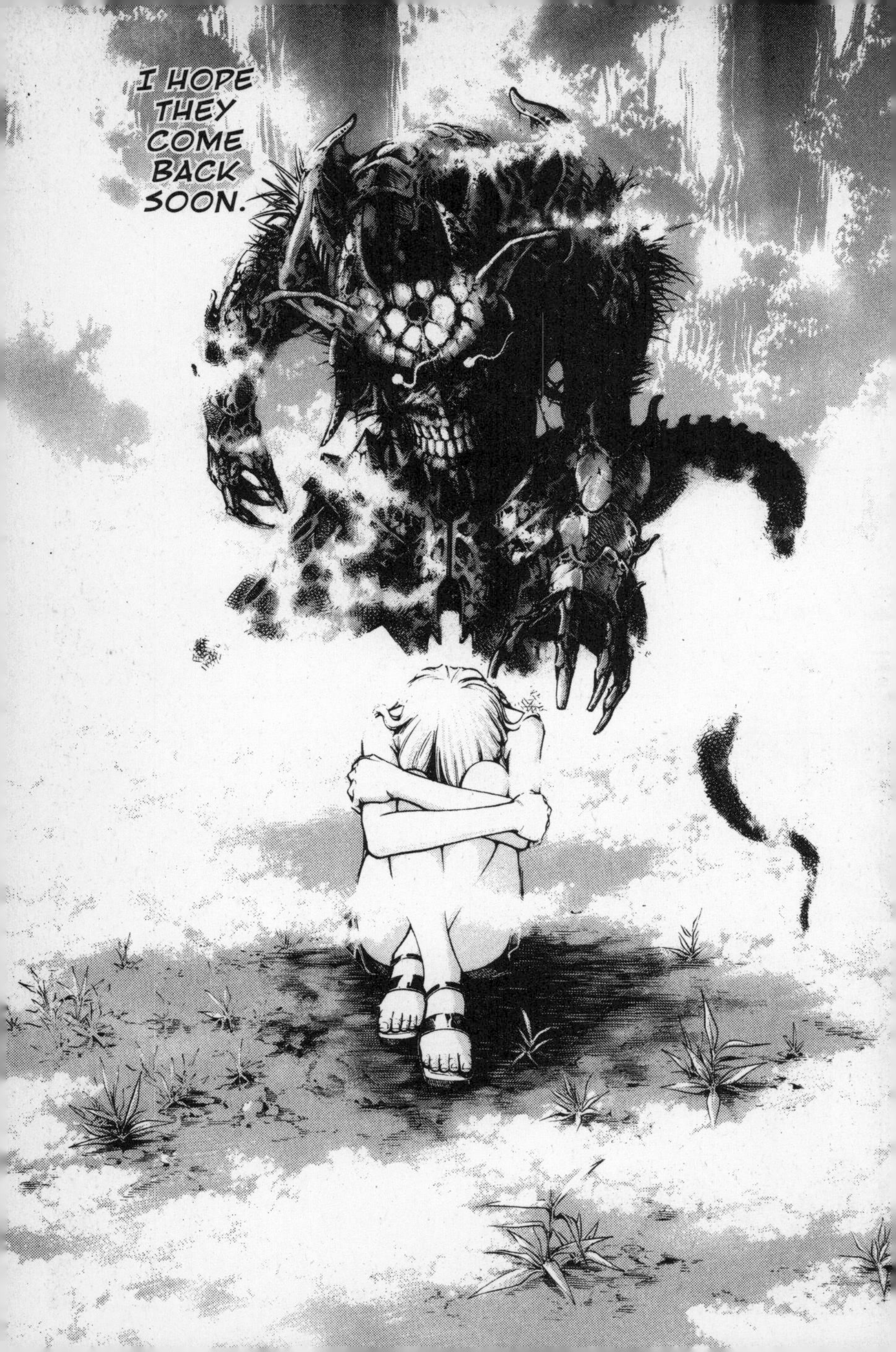
I HOPE THEY COME BACK SOON.

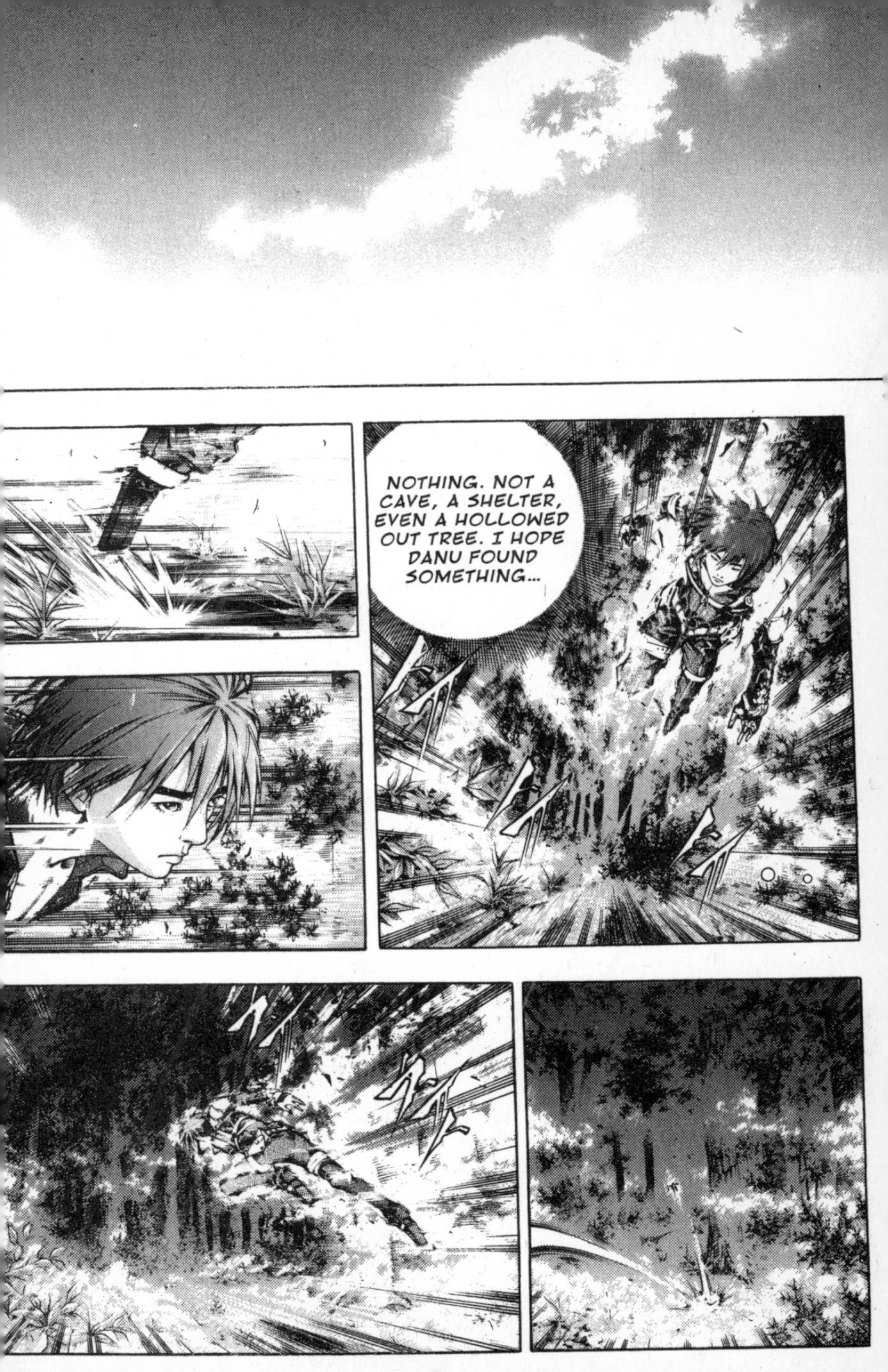
NOTHING. NOT A CAVE, A SHELTER, EVEN A HOLLOWED OUT TREE. I HOPE DANU FOUND SOMETHING...

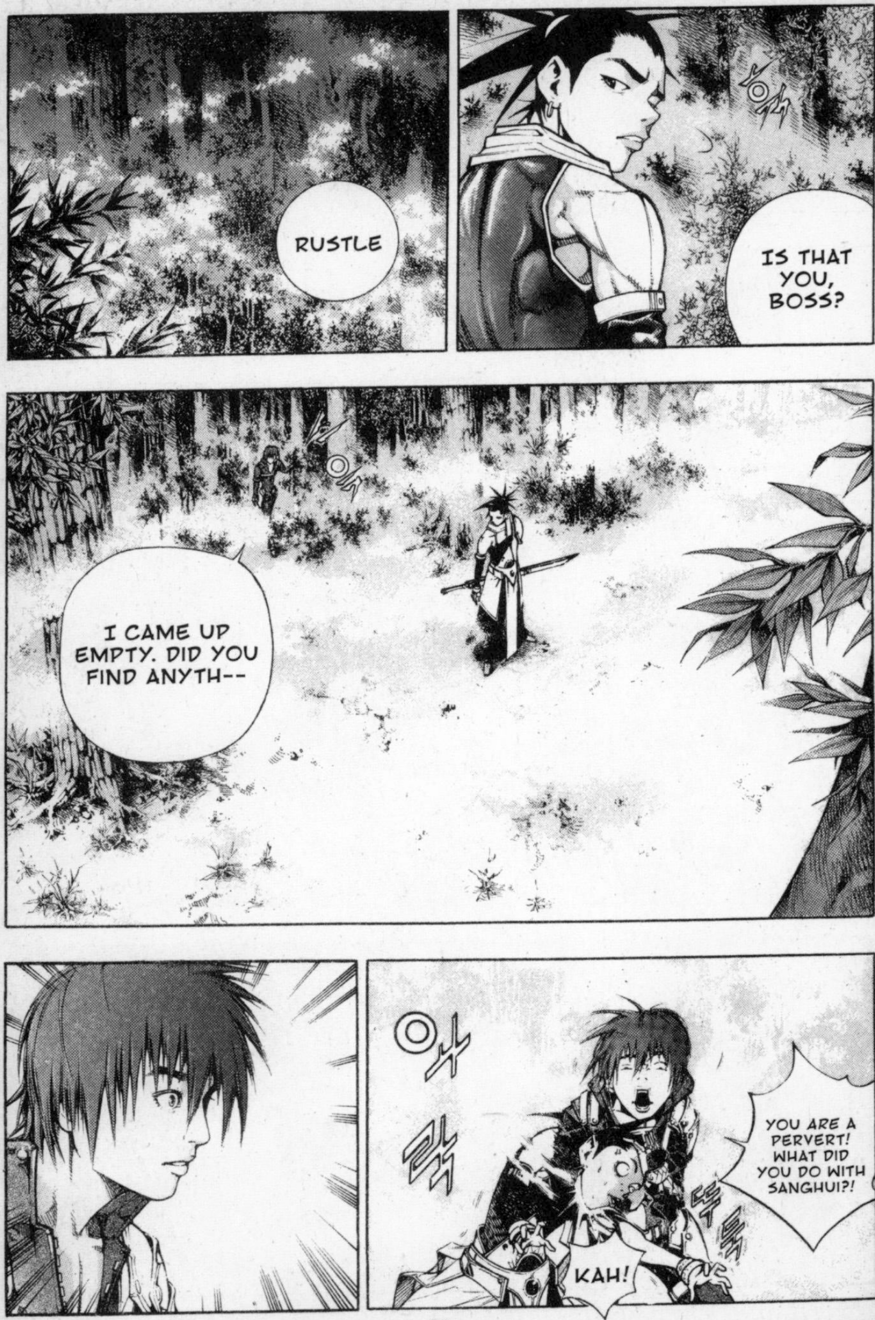

RUSTLE
IS THAT YOU, BOSS?
I CAME UP EMPTY. DID YOU FIND ANYTH--
YOU ARE A PERVERT! WHAT DID YOU DO WITH SANGHUI?!
KAH!

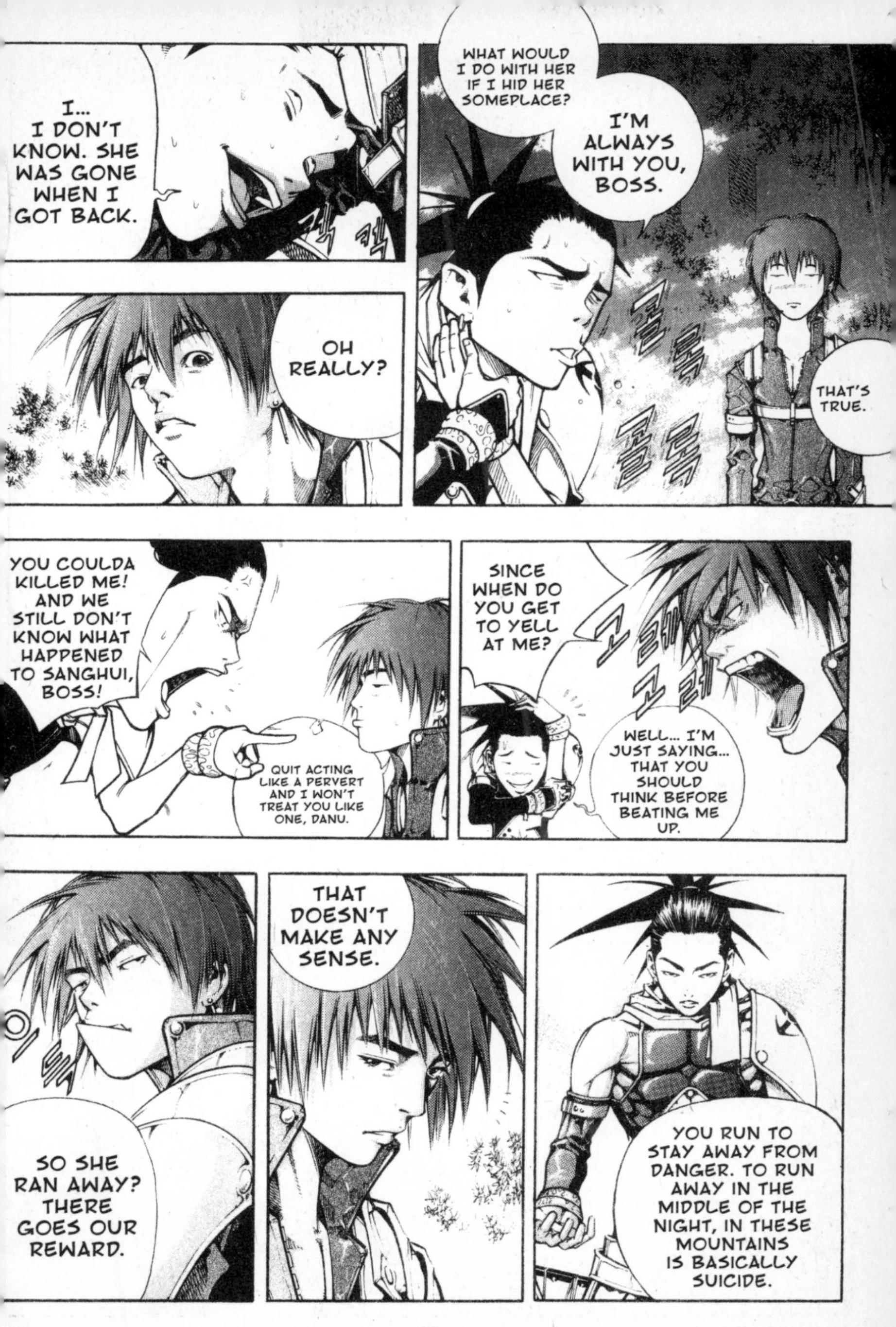
I... I DON'T KNOW. SHE WAS GONE WHEN I GOT BACK.
WHAT WOULD I DO WITH HER IF I HID HER SOMEPLACE?
I'M ALWAYS WITH YOU, BOSS.
OH REALLY?
THAT'S TRUE.
YOU COULDA KILLED ME! AND WE STILL DON'T KNOW WHAT HAPPENED TO SANGHUI, BOSS!
QUIT ACTING LIKE A PERVERT AND I WON'T TREAT YOU LIKE ONE, DANU.
SINCE WHEN DO YOU GET TO YELL AT ME?
WELL... I'M JUST SAYING... THAT YOU SHOULD THINK BEFORE BEATING ME UP.
SO SHE RAN AWAY? THERE GOES OUR REWARD.
THAT DOESN'T MAKE ANY SENSE.
YOU RUN TO STAY AWAY FROM DANGER. TO RUN AWAY IN THE MIDDLE OF THE NIGHT, IN THESE MOUNTAINS IS BASICALLY SUICIDE.

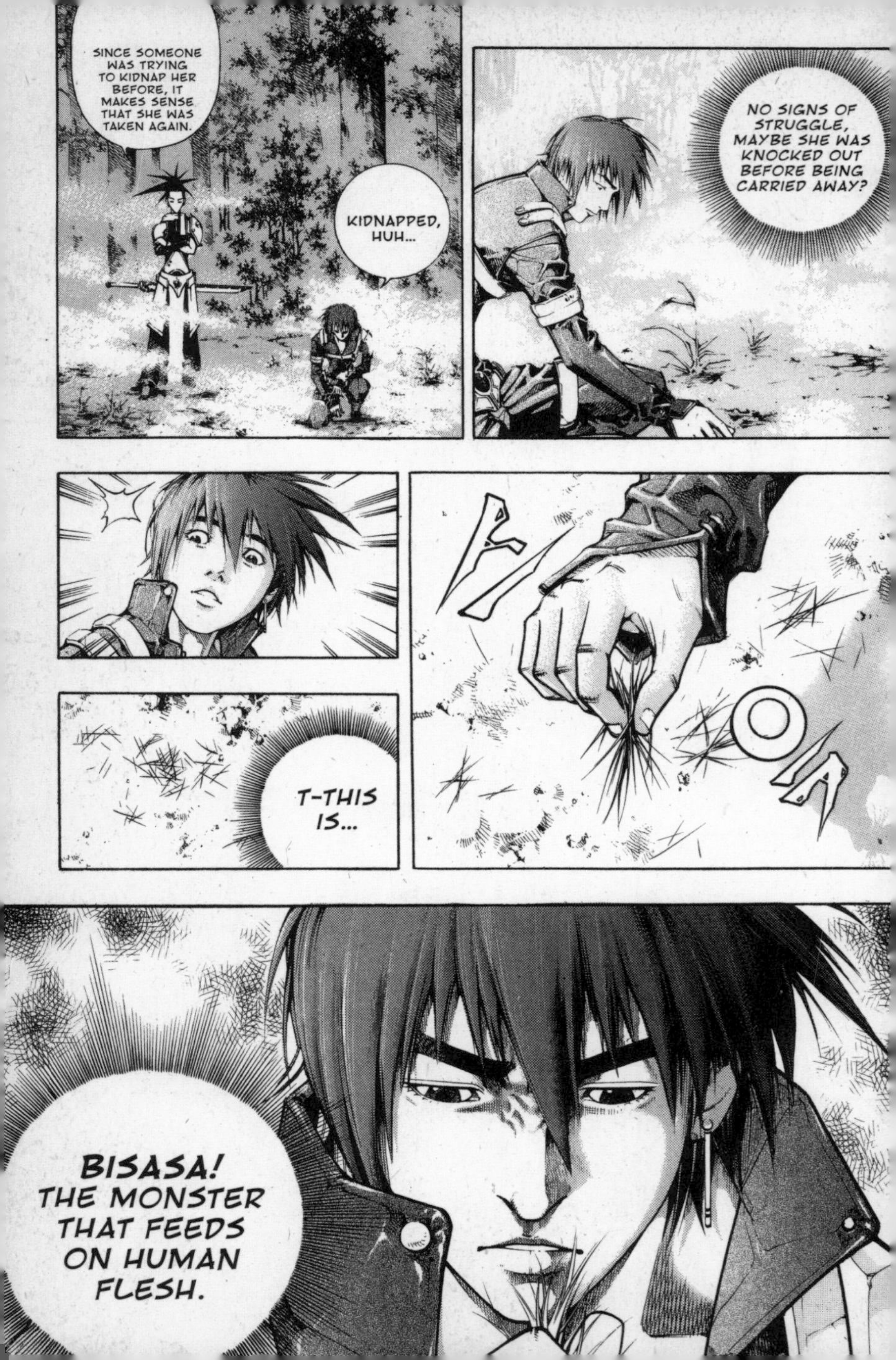
NO SIGNS OF STRUGGLE, MAYBE SHE WAS KNOCKED OUT BEFORE BEING CARRIED AWAY?
SINCE SOMEONE WAS TRYING TO KIDNAP HER BEFORE, IT MAKES SENSE THAT SHE WAS TAKEN AGAIN.
KIDNAPPED, HUH...
T-THIS IS...
BISASA! THE MONSTER THAT FEEDS ON HUMAN FLESH.

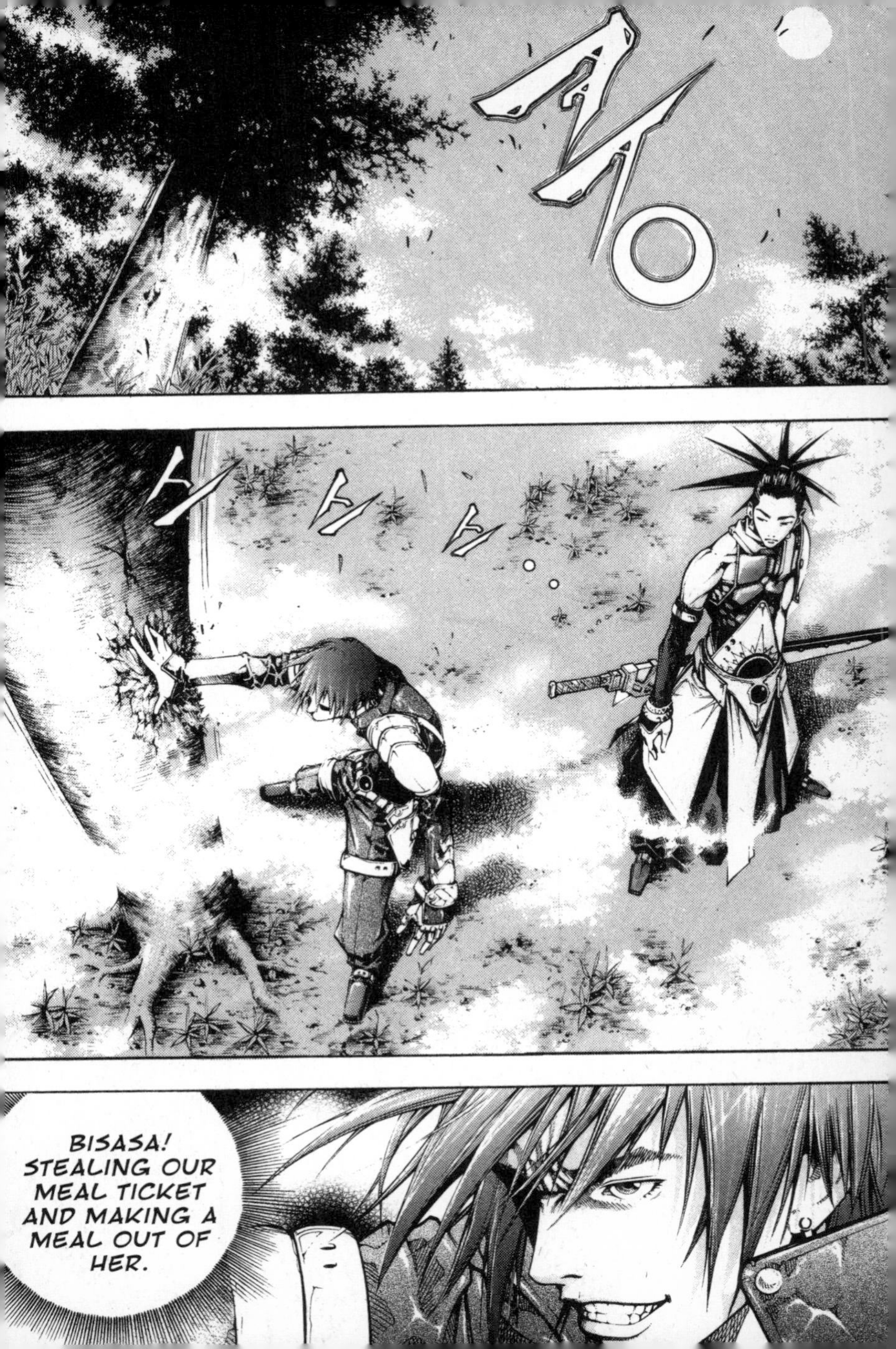
BISASA! STEALING OUR MEAL TICKET AND MAKING A MEAL OUT OF HER.

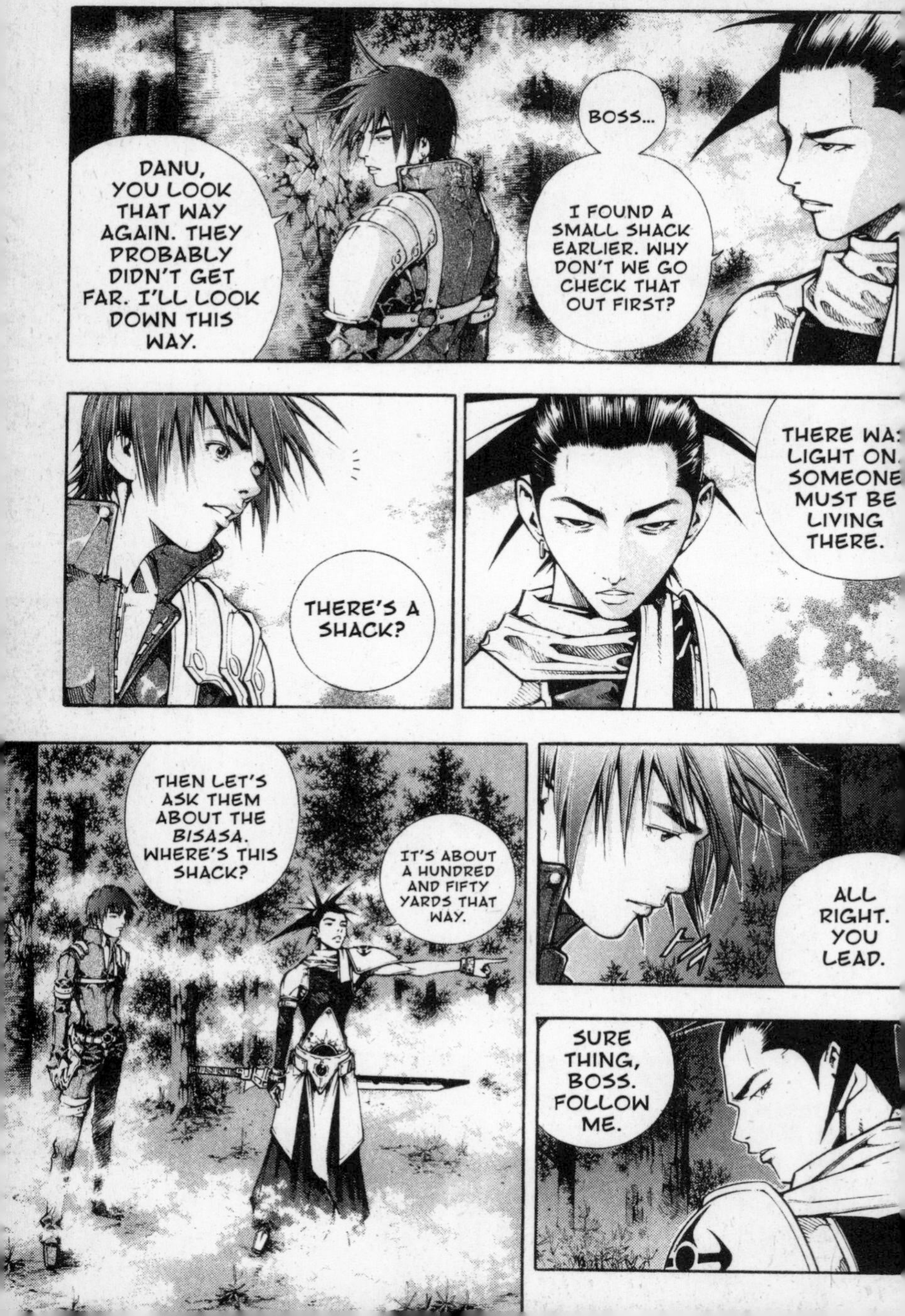
DANU, YOU LOOK THAT WAY AGAIN. THEY PROBABLY DIDN'T GET FAR. I'LL LOOK DOWN THIS WAY.
BOSS...
I FOUND A SMALL SHACK EARLIER. WHY DON'T WE GO CHECK THAT OUT FIRST?
THERE'S A SHACK?
THERE WA: LIGHT ON. SOMEONE MUST BE LIVING THERE.
THEN LET'S ASK THEM ABOUT THE *BISASA*. WHERE'S THIS SHACK?
IT'S ABOUT A HUNDRED AND FIFTY YARDS THAT WAY.
ALL RIGHT. YOU LEAD.
SURE THING, BOSS. FOLLOW ME.

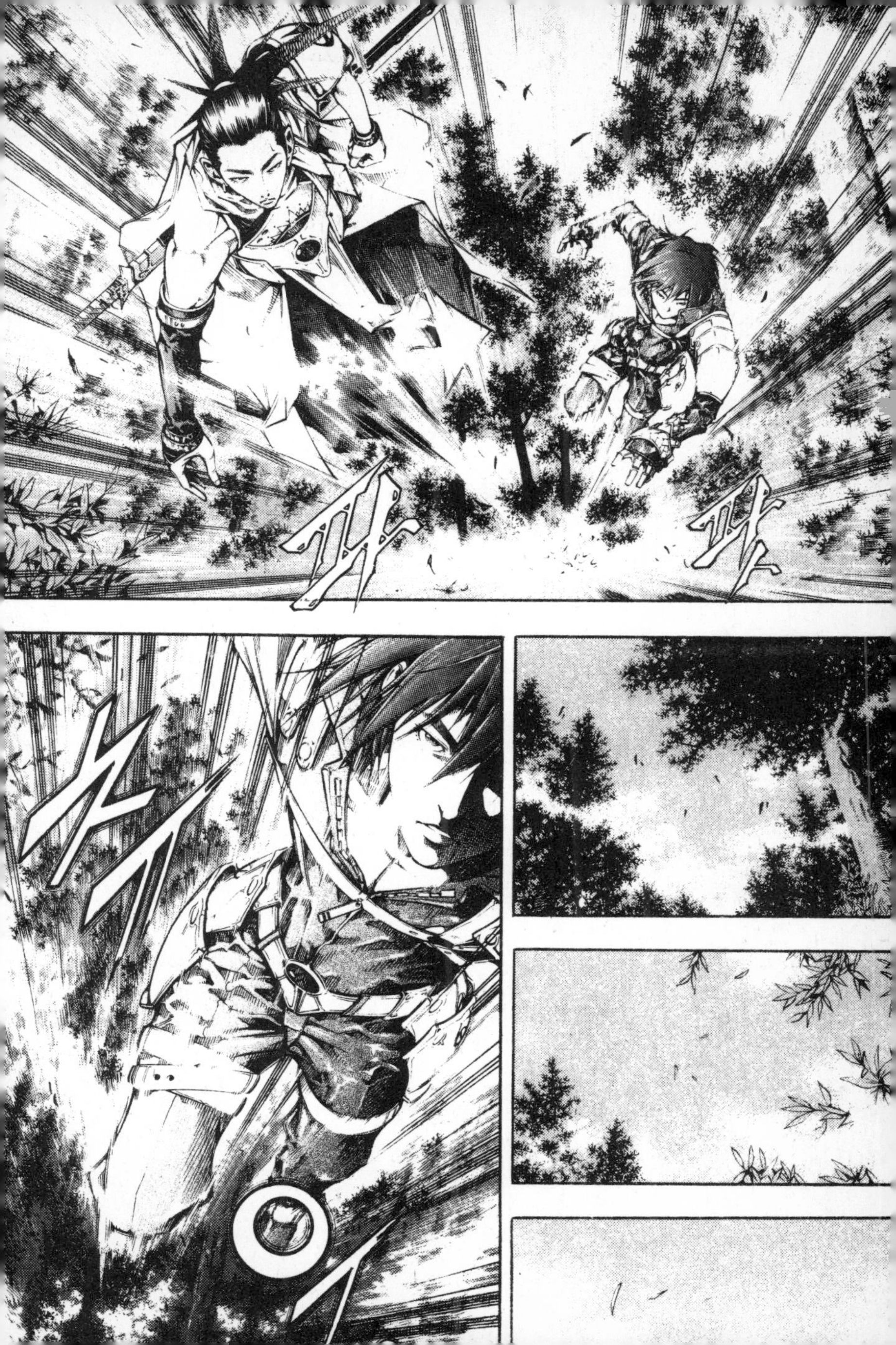

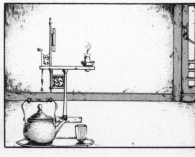

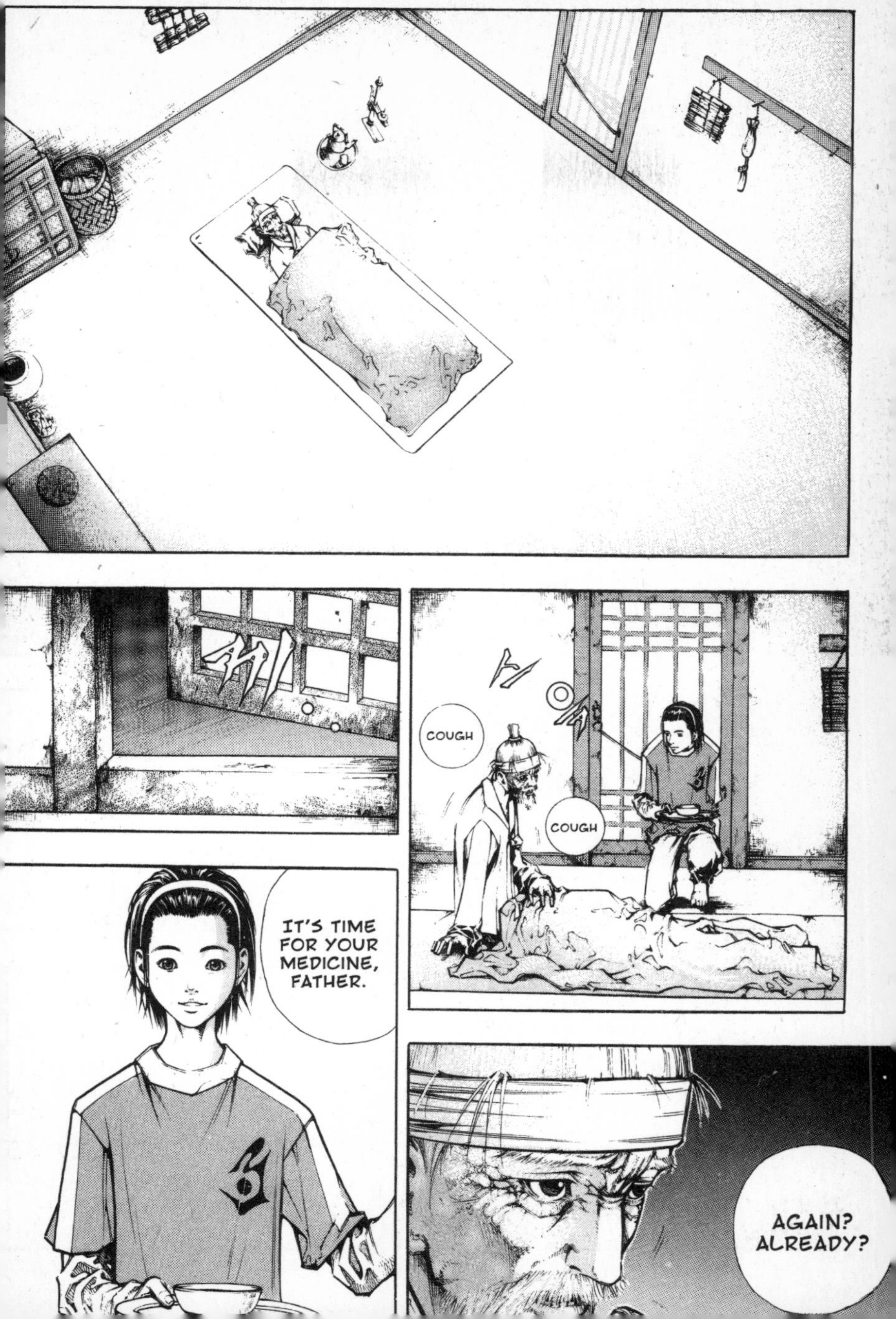
COUGH
COUGH
IT'S TIME FOR YOUR MEDICINE, FATHER.
AGAIN? ALREADY?

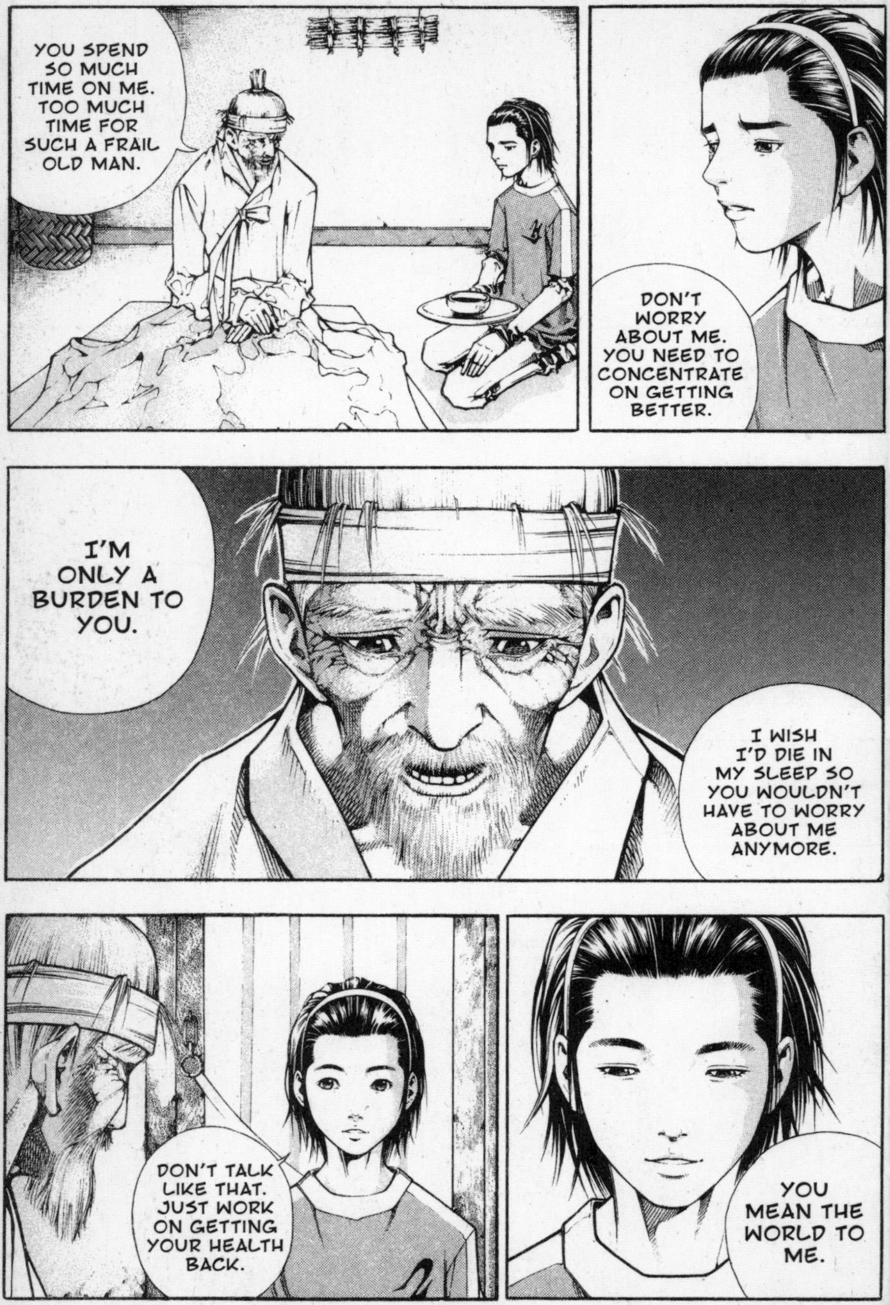
YOU SPEND SO MUCH TIME ON ME. TOO MUCH TIME FOR SUCH A FRAIL OLD MAN.
DON'T WORRY ABOUT ME. YOU NEED TO CONCENTRATE ON GETTING BETTER.
I'M ONLY A BURDEN TO YOU.
I WISH I'D DIE IN MY SLEEP SO YOU WOULDN'T HAVE TO WORRY ABOUT ME ANYMORE.
DON'T TALK LIKE THAT. JUST WORK ON GETTING YOUR HEALTH BACK.
YOU MEAN THE WORLD TO ME.

ANYONE HOME? HELLO?

SOMEONE IS HERE. WHY DON'T YOU GET THE DOOR?

WHO IS IT?

SORRY TO BOTHER YOU SO LATE. I JUST HAD A QUICK QUESTION.

DO YOU KNOW ANYTHING ABOUT THE *BISASA* IN THESE WOODS?

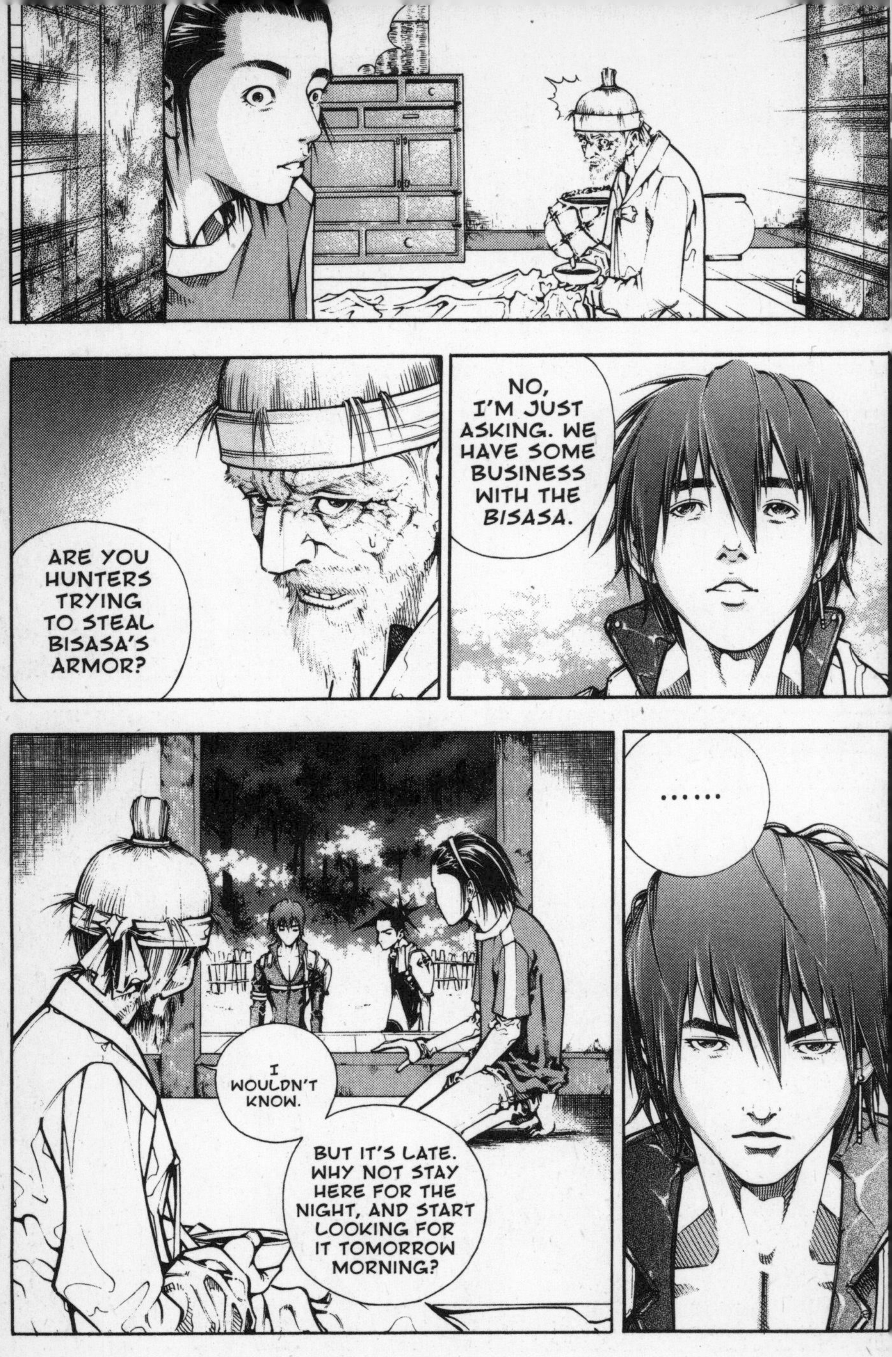
ARE YOU HUNTERS TRYING TO STEAL BISASA'S ARMOR?
NO, I'M JUST ASKING. WE HAVE SOME BUSINESS WITH THE *BISASA*.
I WOULDN'T KNOW.
BUT IT'S LATE. WHY NOT STAY HERE FOR THE NIGHT, AND START LOOKING FOR IT TOMORROW MORNING?
......

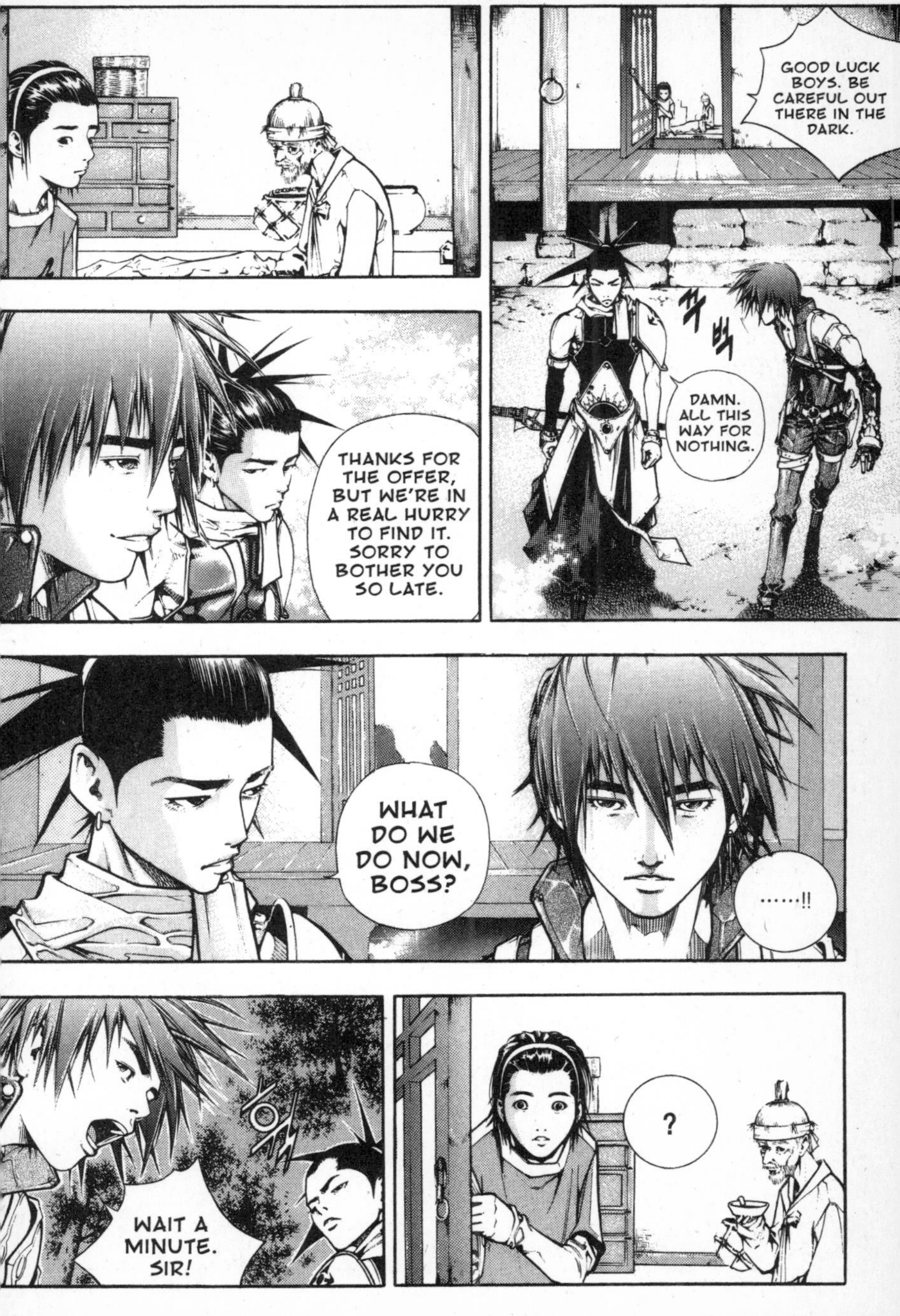
THANKS FOR THE OFFER, BUT WE'RE IN A REAL HURRY TO FIND IT. SORRY TO BOTHER YOU SO LATE.
GOOD LUCK BOYS. BE CAREFUL OUT THERE IN THE DARK.
꾸벅
DAMN. ALL THIS WAY FOR NOTHING.
WHAT DO WE DO NOW, BOSS?
......!!
WAIT A MINUTE. SIR!
?

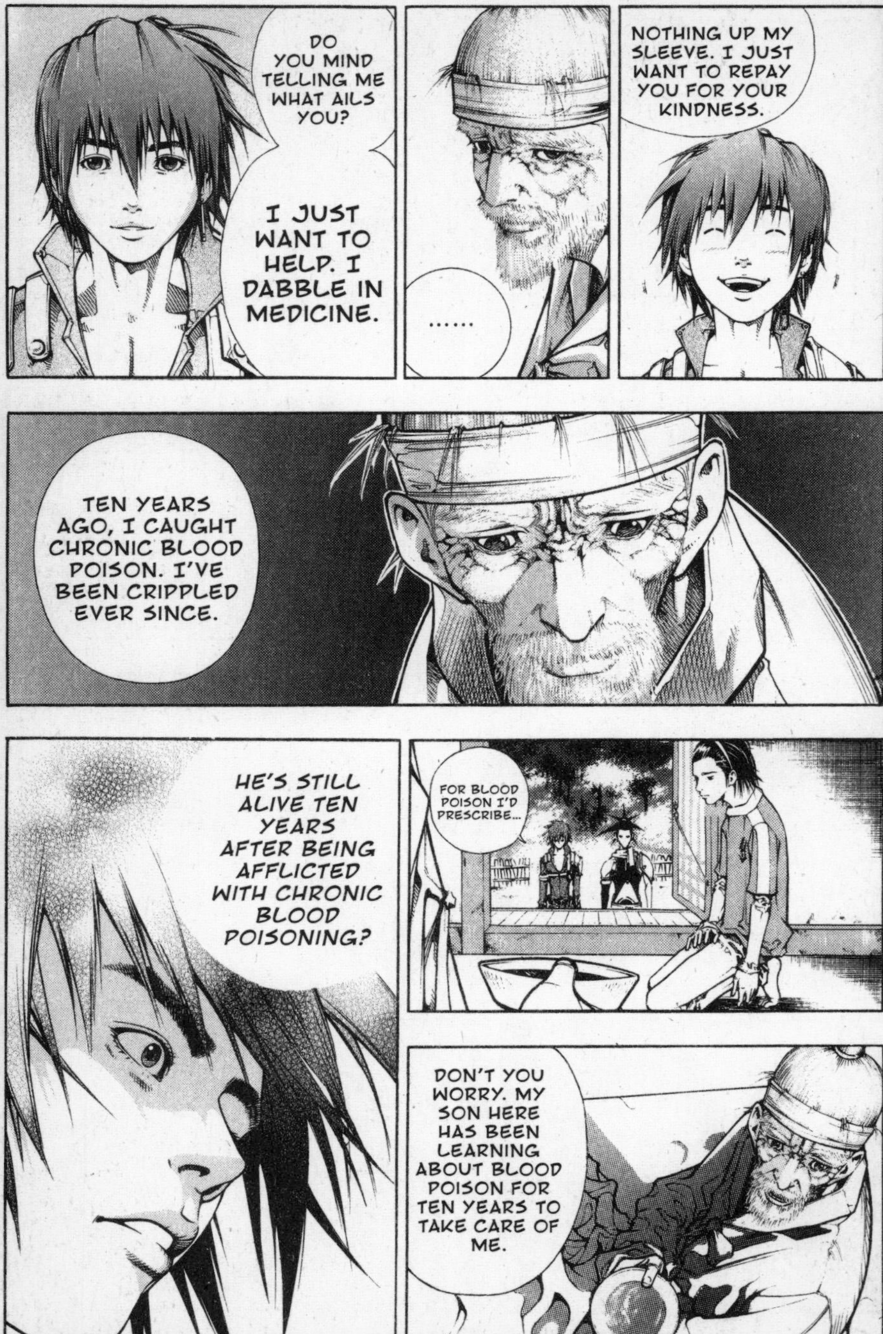
DO YOU MIND TELLING ME WHAT AILS YOU?
I JUST WANT TO HELP. I DABBLE IN MEDICINE.
......
NOTHING UP MY SLEEVE. I JUST WANT TO REPAY YOU FOR YOUR KINDNESS.
TEN YEARS AGO, I CAUGHT CHRONIC BLOOD POISON. I'VE BEEN CRIPPLED EVER SINCE.
HE'S STILL ALIVE TEN YEARS AFTER BEING AFFLICTED WITH CHRONIC BLOOD POISONING?
FOR BLOOD POISON I'D PRESCRIBE...
DON'T YOU WORRY. MY SON HERE HAS BEEN LEARNING ABOUT BLOOD POISON FOR TEN YEARS TO TAKE CARE OF ME.

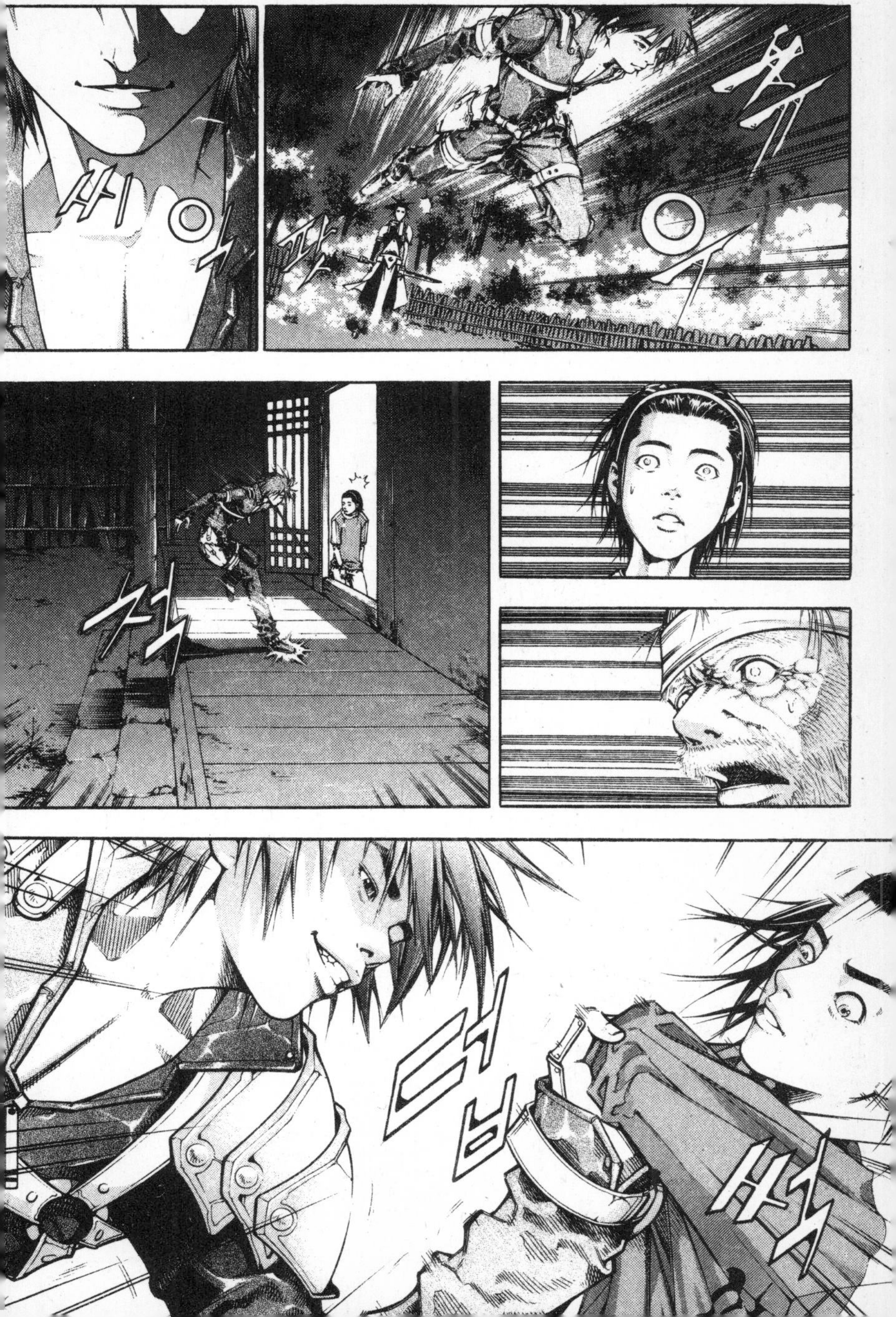

씨익
덥석

......

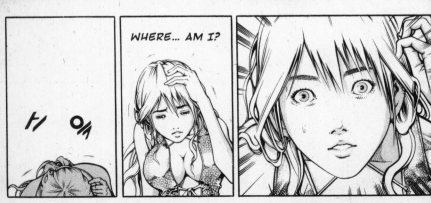

WHERE... AM I?

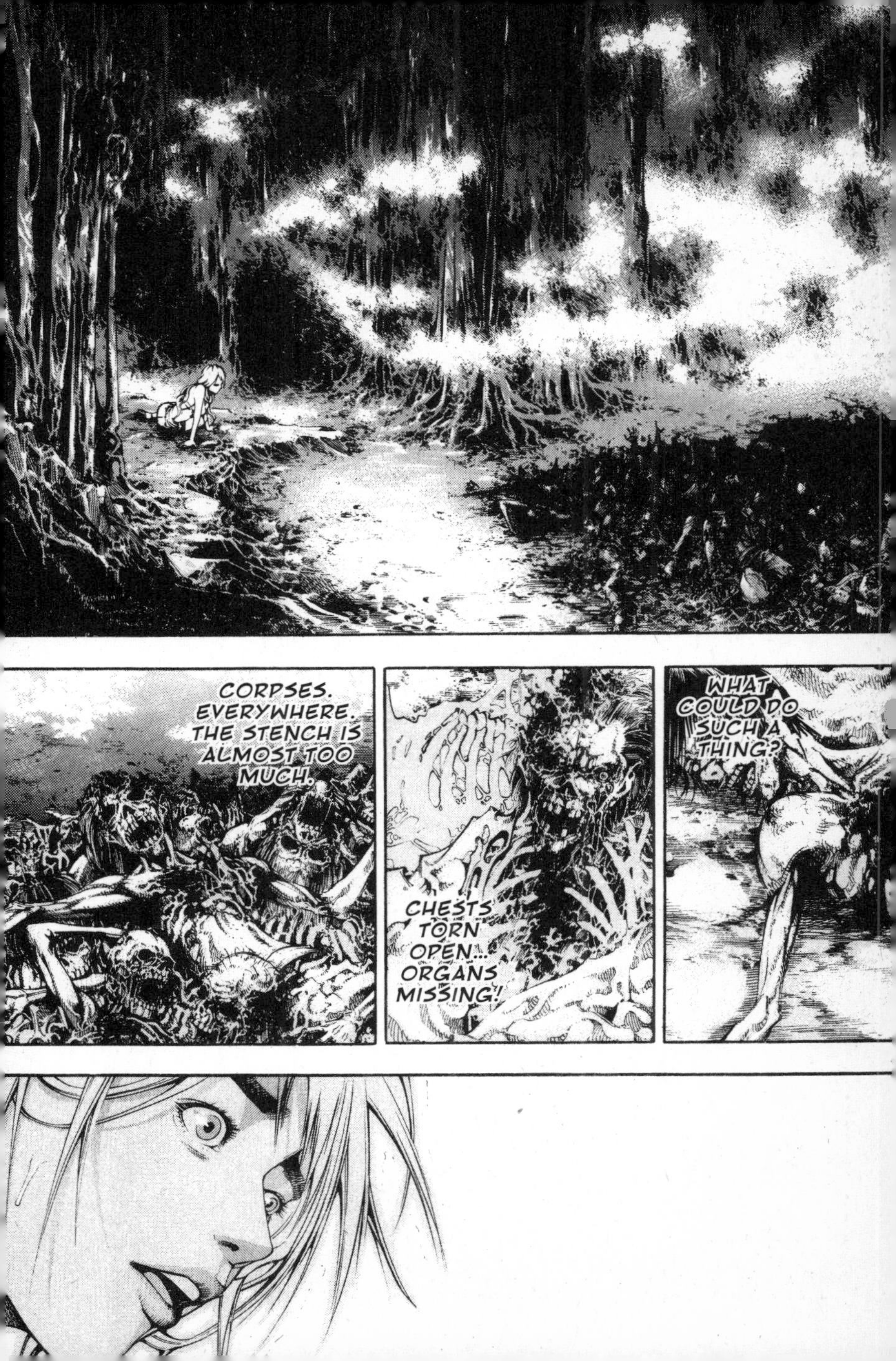
CORPSES. EVERYWHERE. THE STENCH IS ALMOST TOO MUCH.
CHESTS TORN OPEN... ORGANS MISSING!
WHAT COULD DO SUCH A THING?

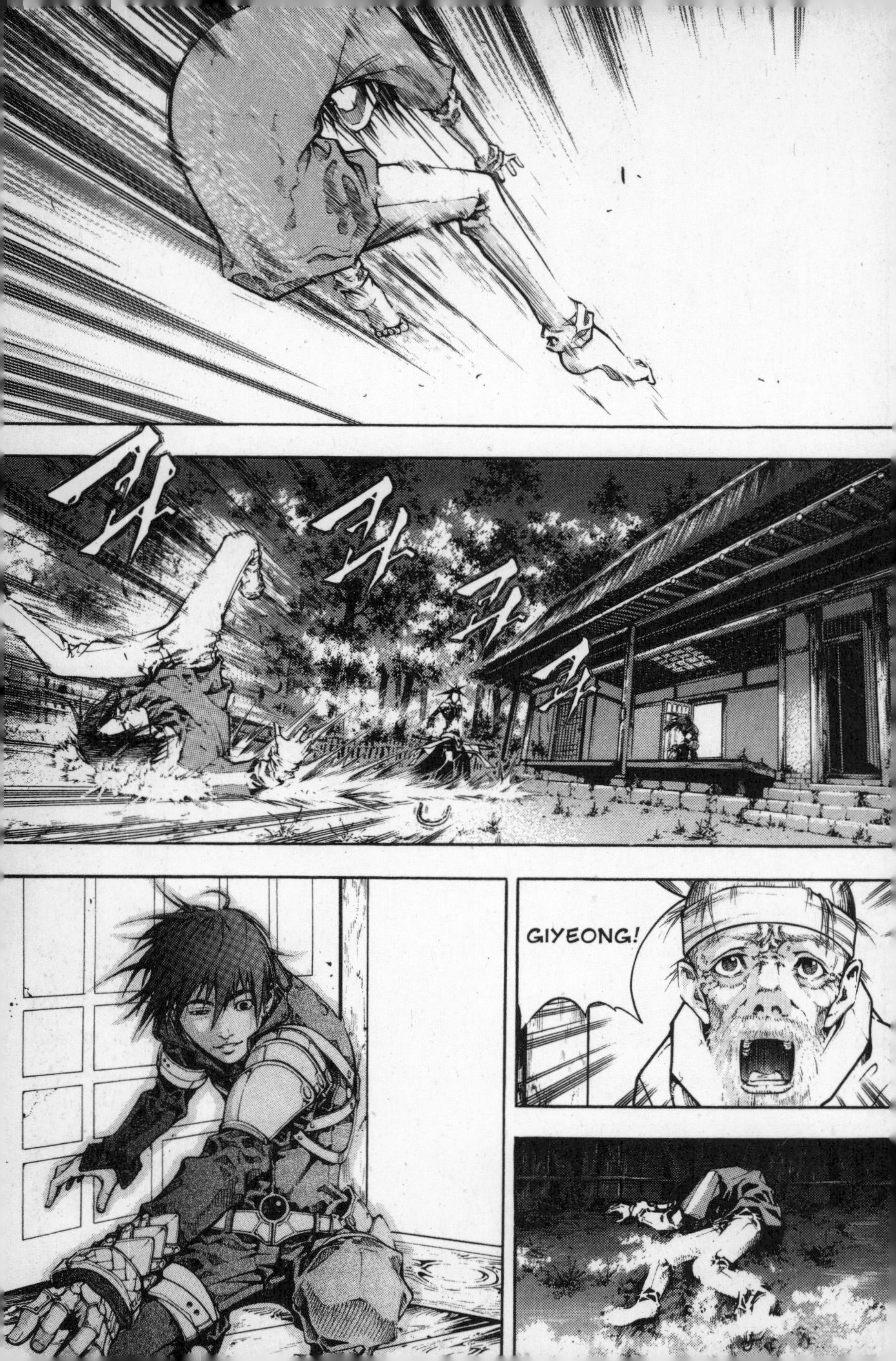
GIYEONG!

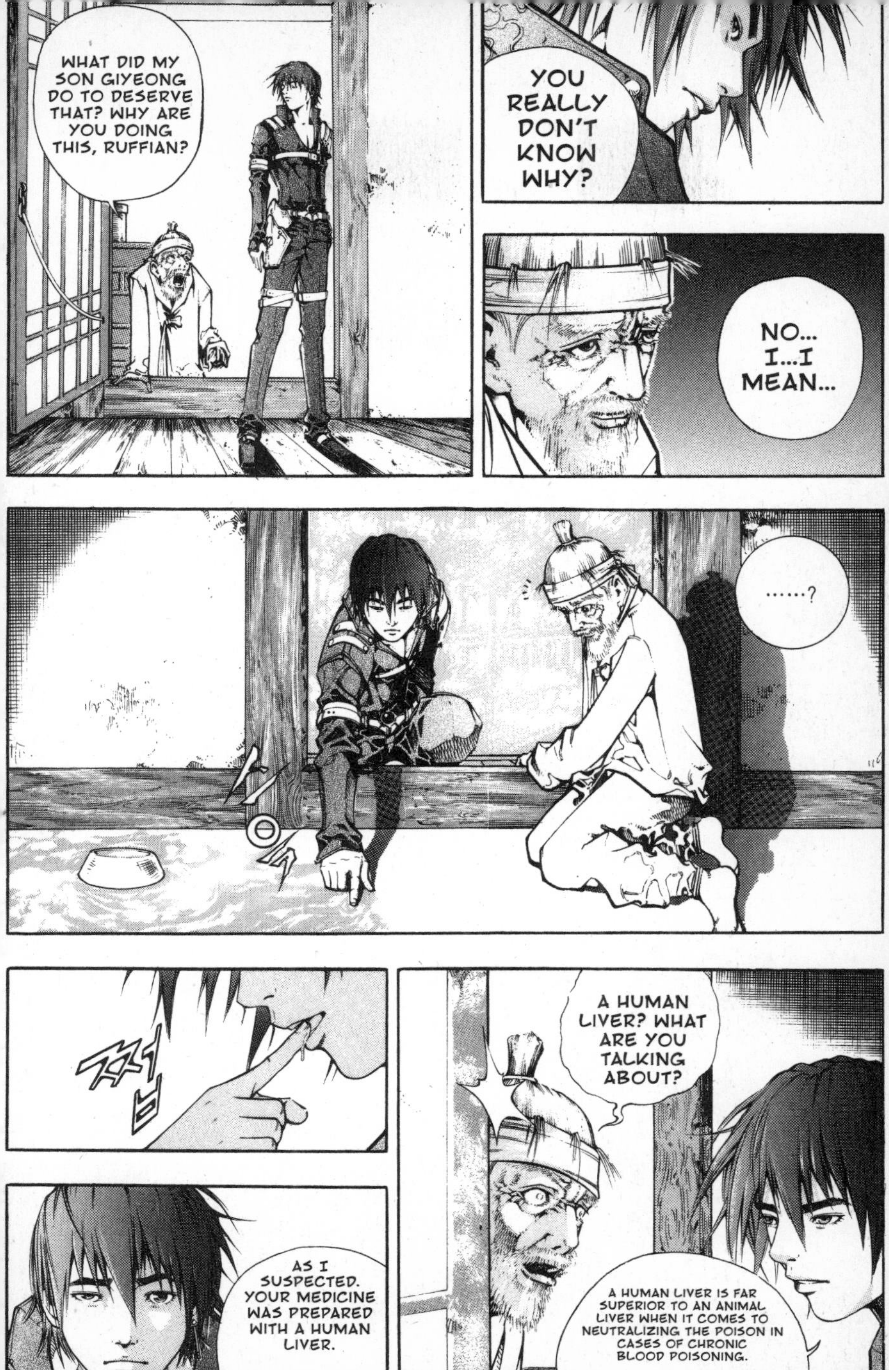
WHAT DID MY SON GIYEONG DO TO DESERVE THAT? WHY ARE YOU DOING THIS, RUFFIAN?
YOU REALLY DON'T KNOW WHY?
NO... I...I MEAN...
......?
A HUMAN LIVER? WHAT ARE YOU TALKING ABOUT?
AS I SUSPECTED. YOUR MEDICINE WAS PREPARED WITH A HUMAN LIVER.
A HUMAN LIVER IS FAR SUPERIOR TO AN ANIMAL LIVER WHEN IT COMES TO NEUTRALIZING THE POISON IN CASES OF CHRONIC BLOOD POISONING.

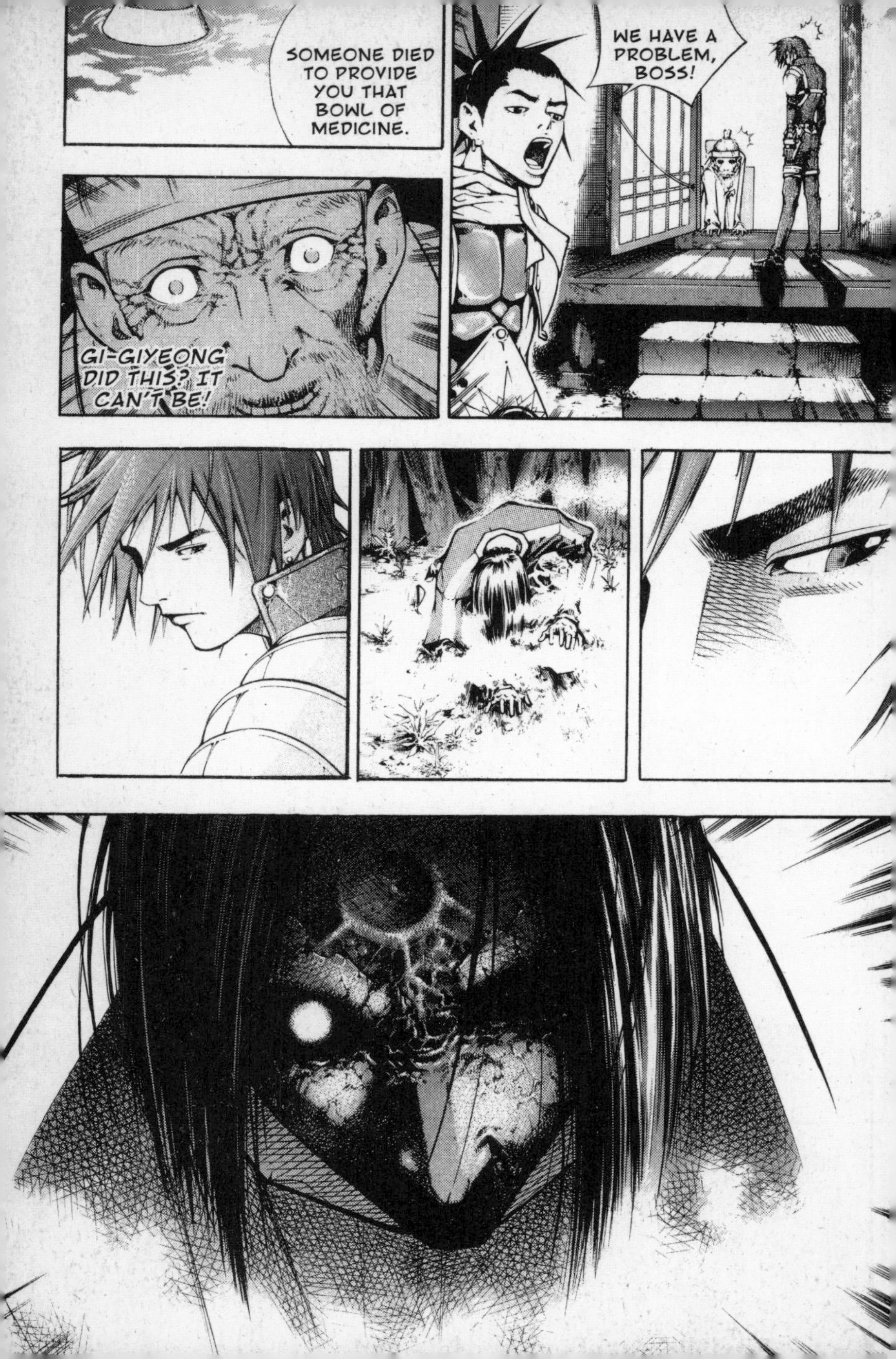
WE HAVE A PROBLEM, BOSS!
SOMEONE DIED TO PROVIDE YOU THAT BOWL OF MEDICINE.
GI-GIYEONG DID THIS? IT CAN'T BE!

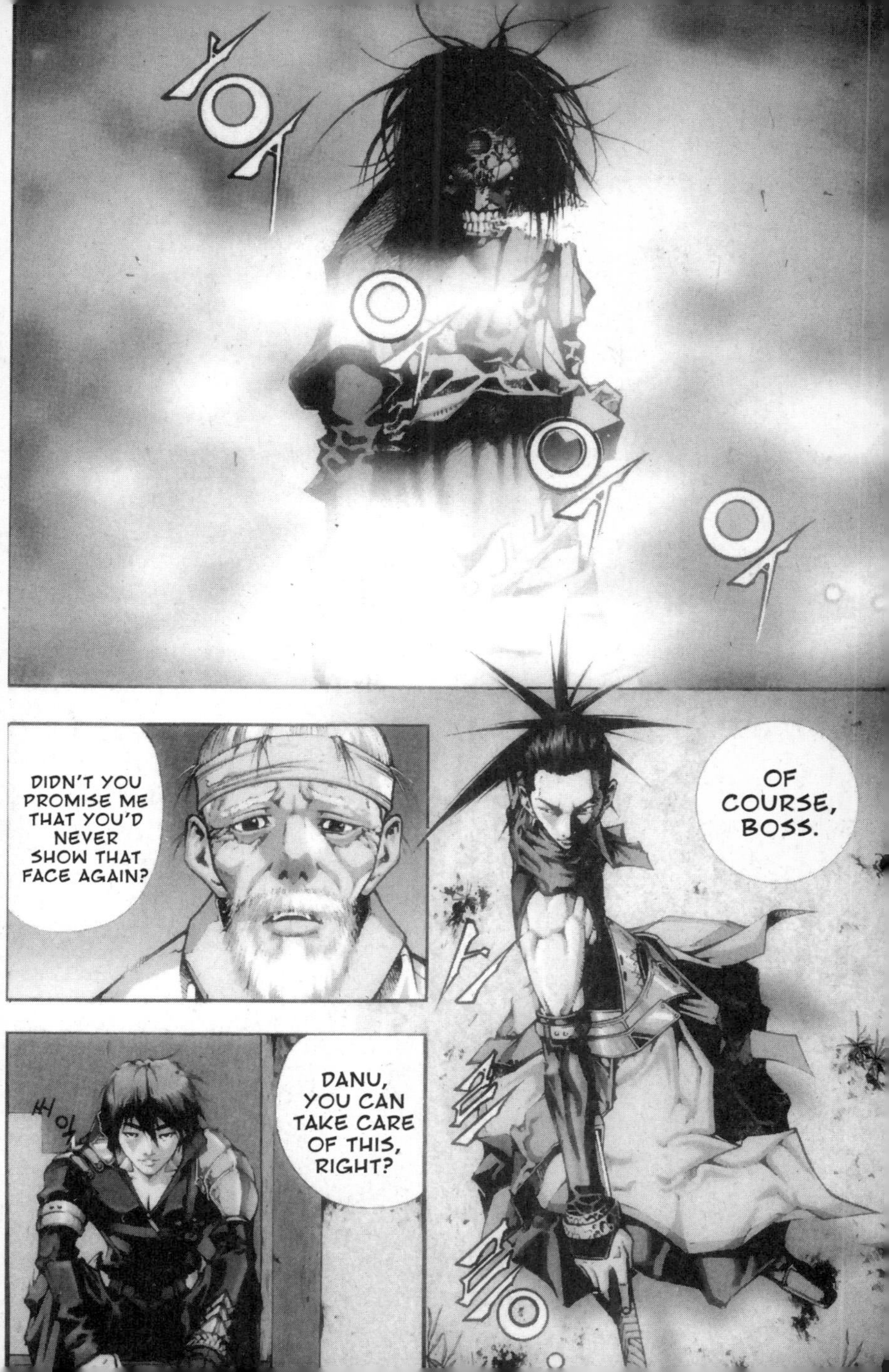
OF COURSE, BOSS.
DIDN'T YOU PROMISE ME THAT YOU'D NEVER SHOW THAT FACE AGAIN?
DANU, YOU CAN TAKE CARE OF THIS, RIGHT?

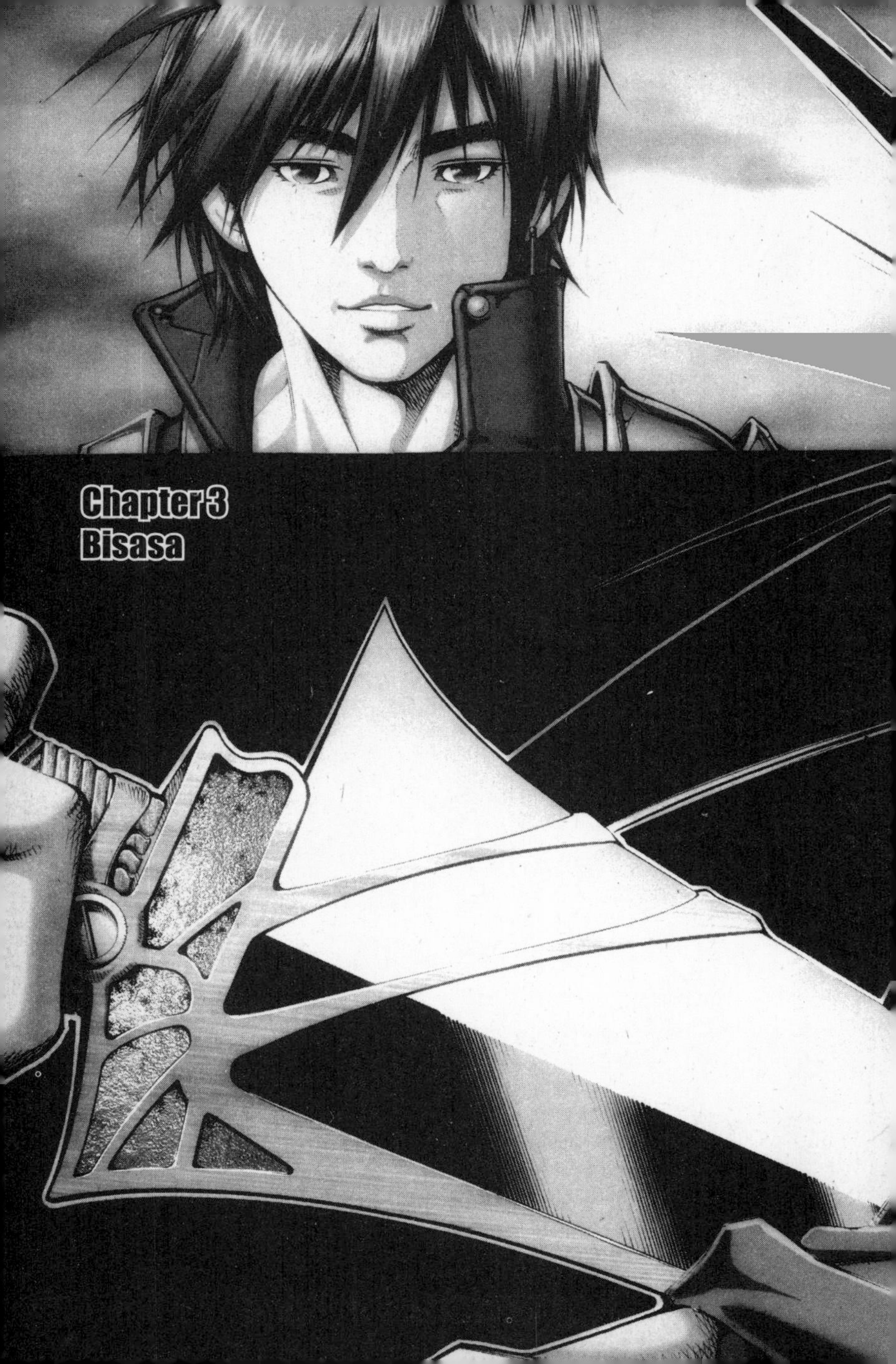
Chapter 3
Bisasa

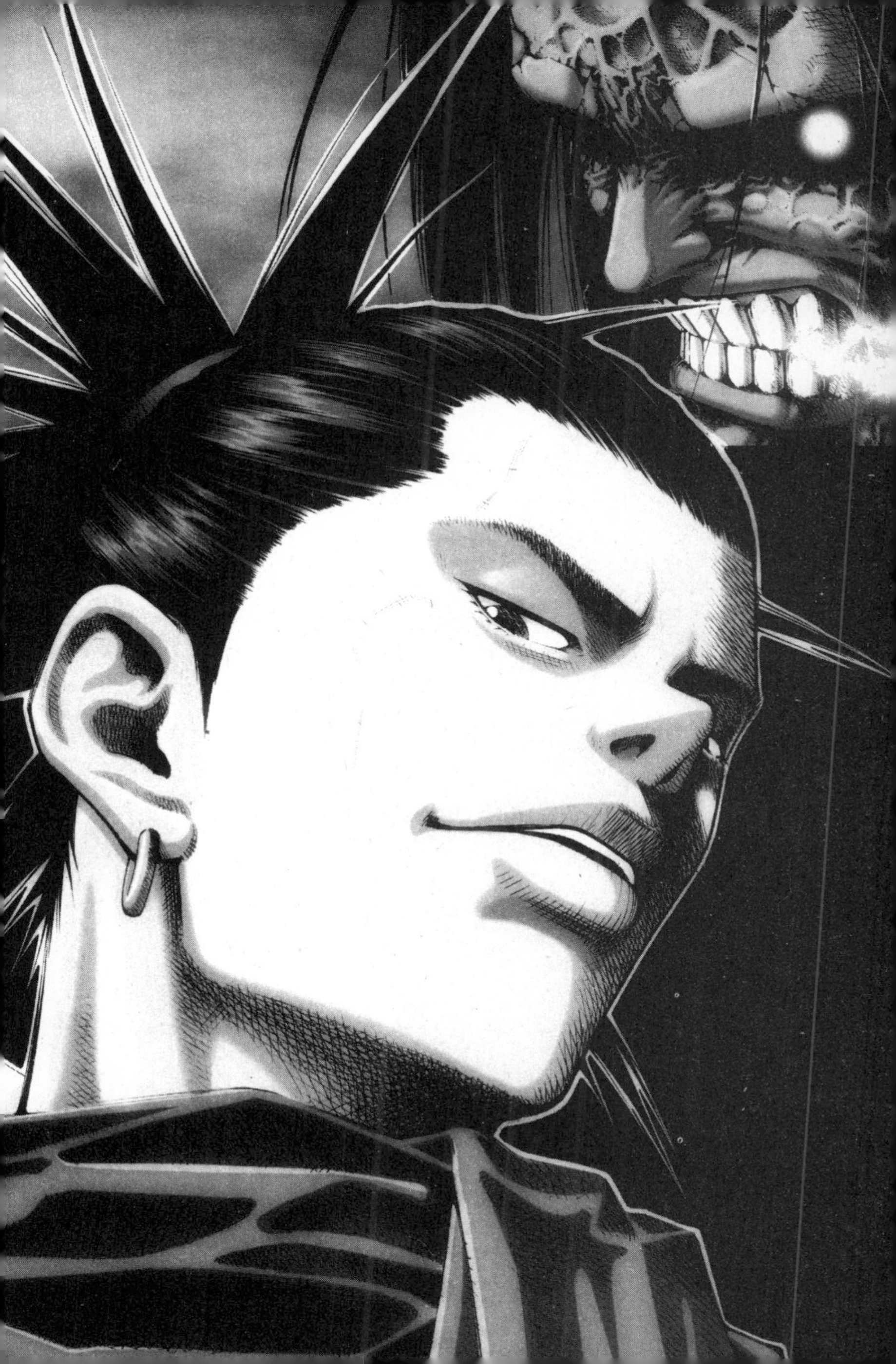

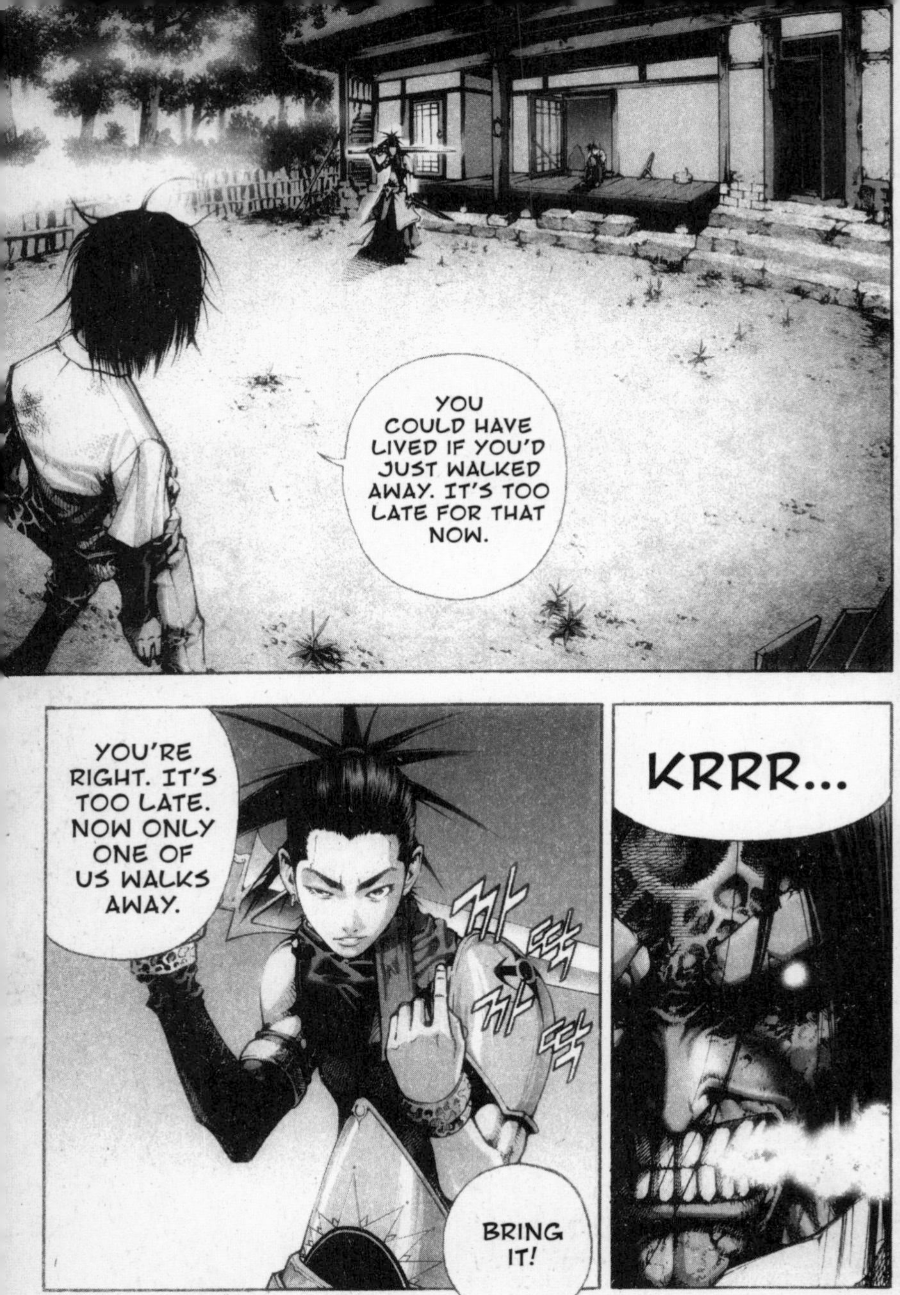
YOU COULD HAVE LIVED IF YOU'D JUST WALKED AWAY. IT'S TOO LATE FOR THAT NOW.
YOU'RE RIGHT. IT'S TOO LATE. NOW ONLY ONE OF US WALKS AWAY.
BRING IT!
KRRR...

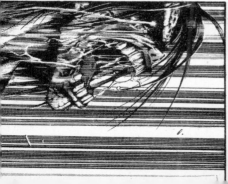

YOU'RE FAST...

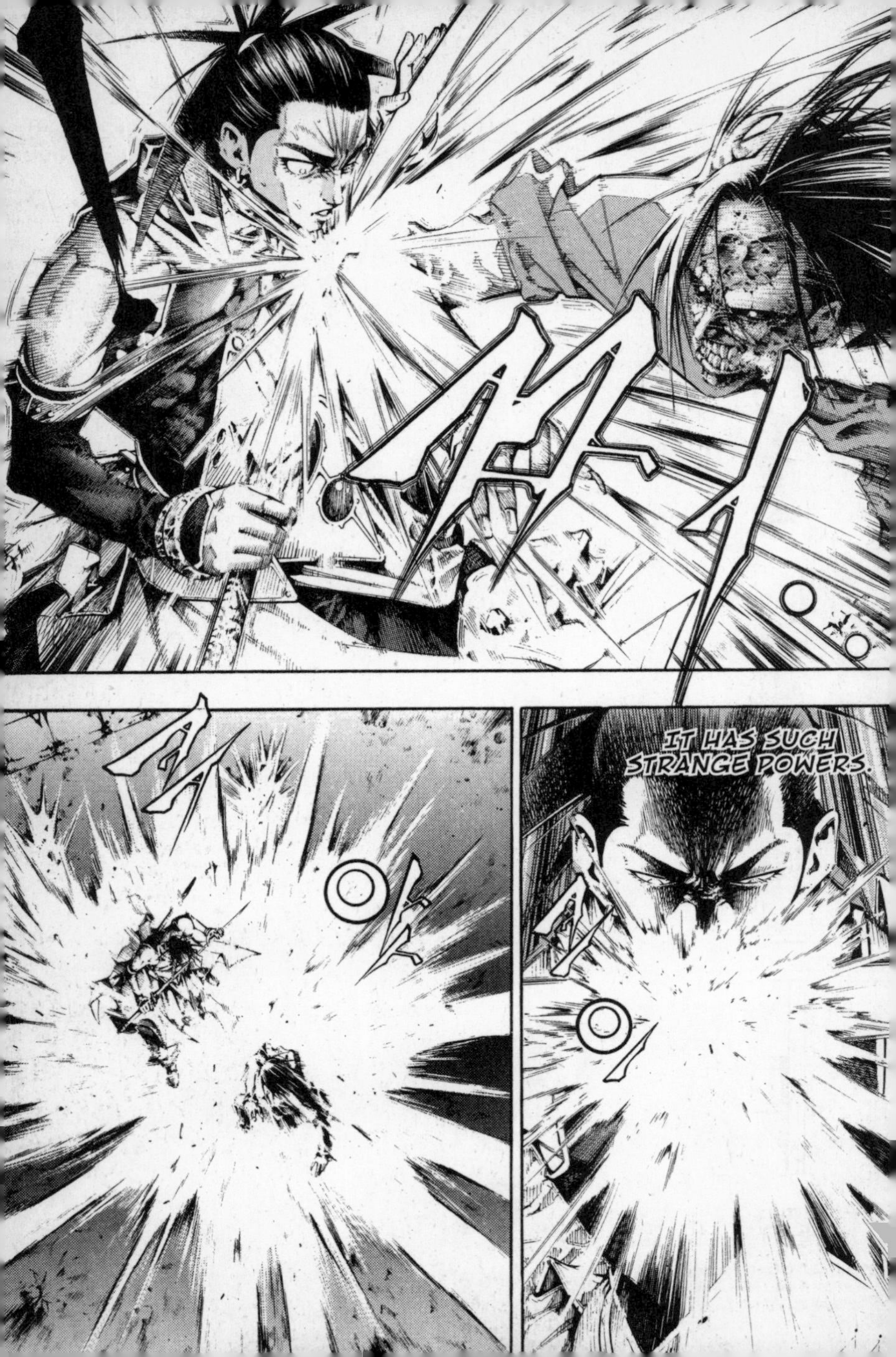
IT HAS SUCH
STRANGE POWERS.

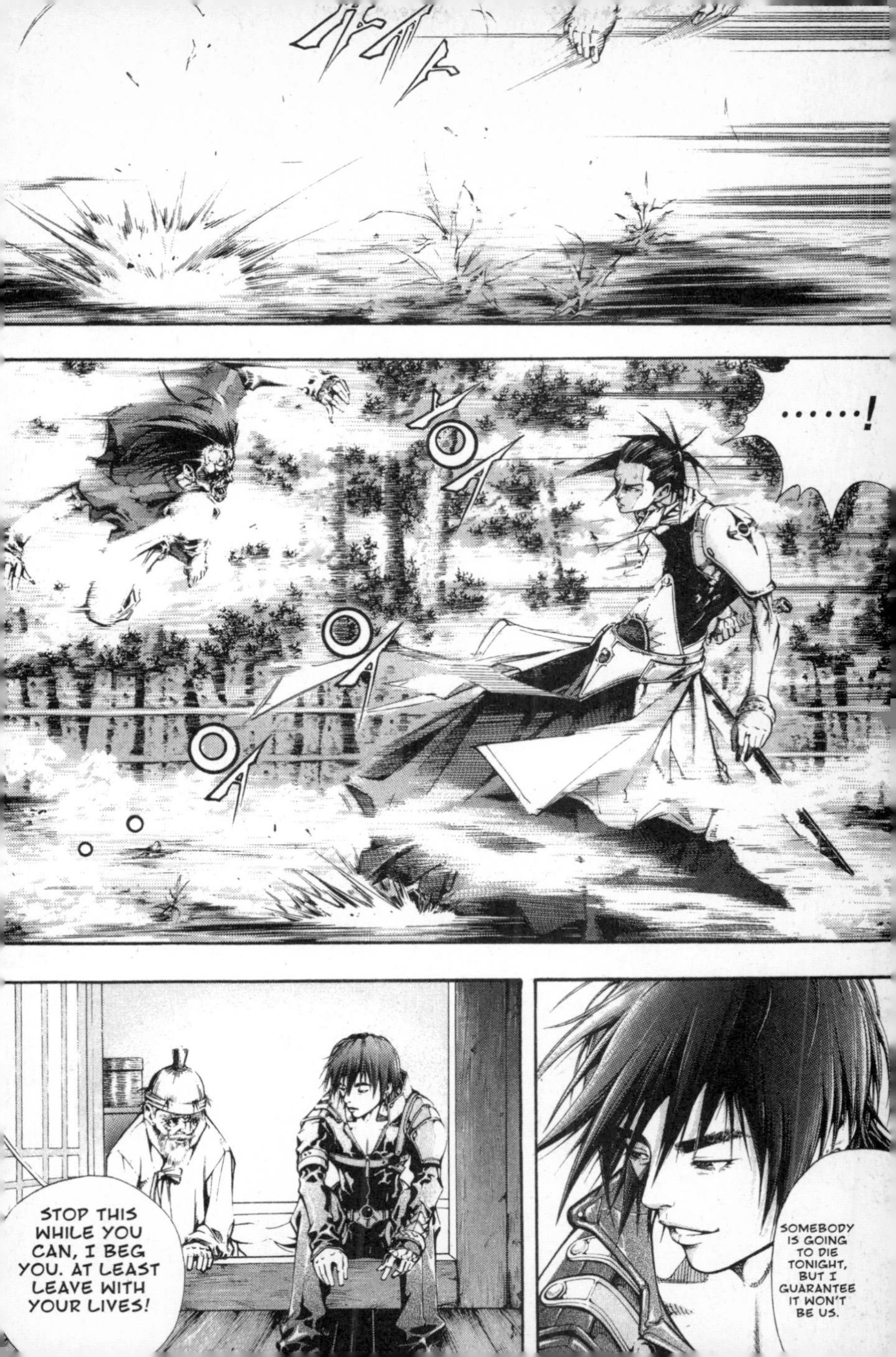
......!
STOP THIS WHILE YOU CAN, I BEG YOU. AT LEAST LEAVE WITH YOUR LIVES!
SOMEBODY IS GOING TO DIE TONIGHT, BUT I GUARANTEE IT WON'T BE US.

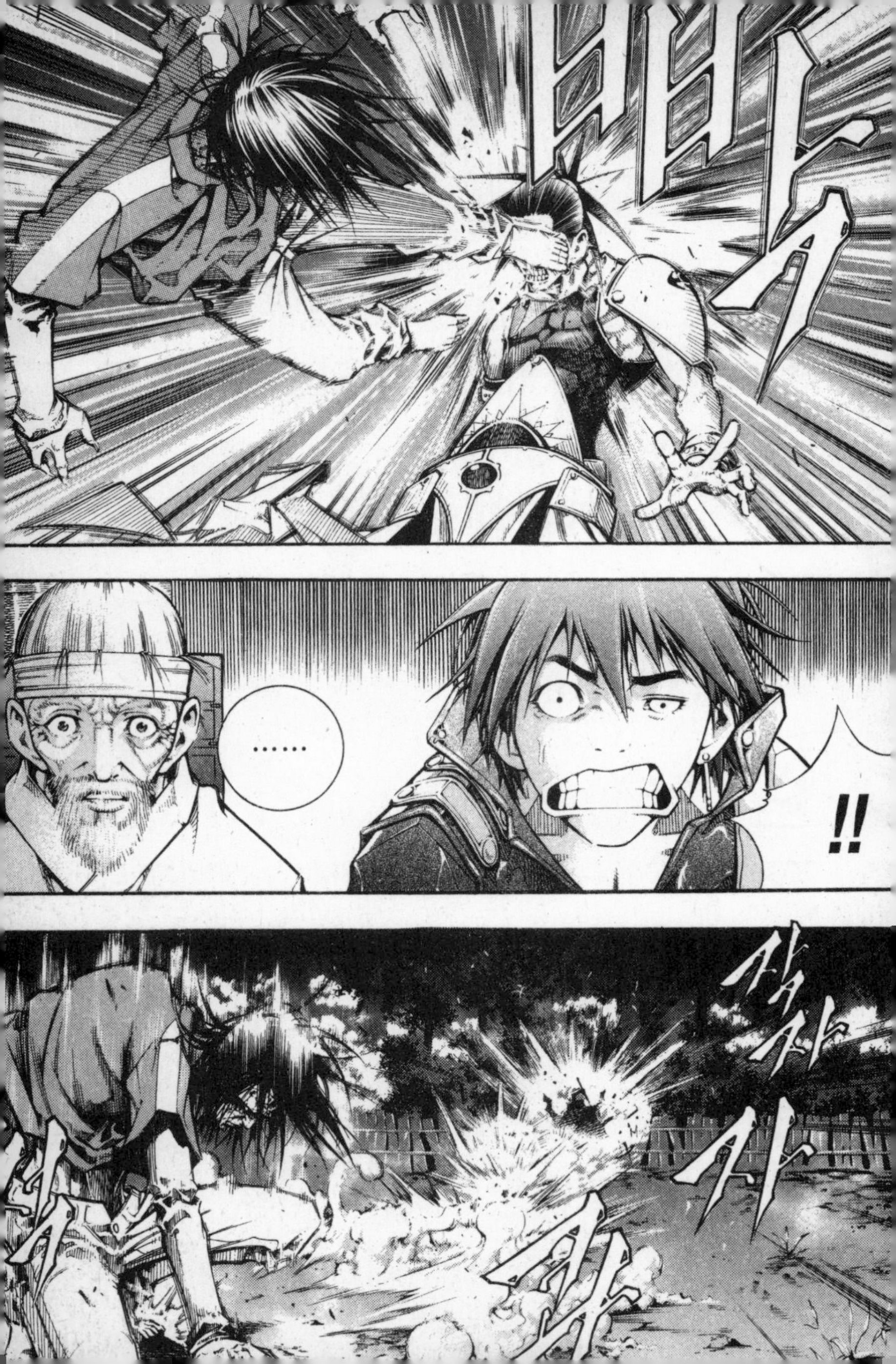

......
!!

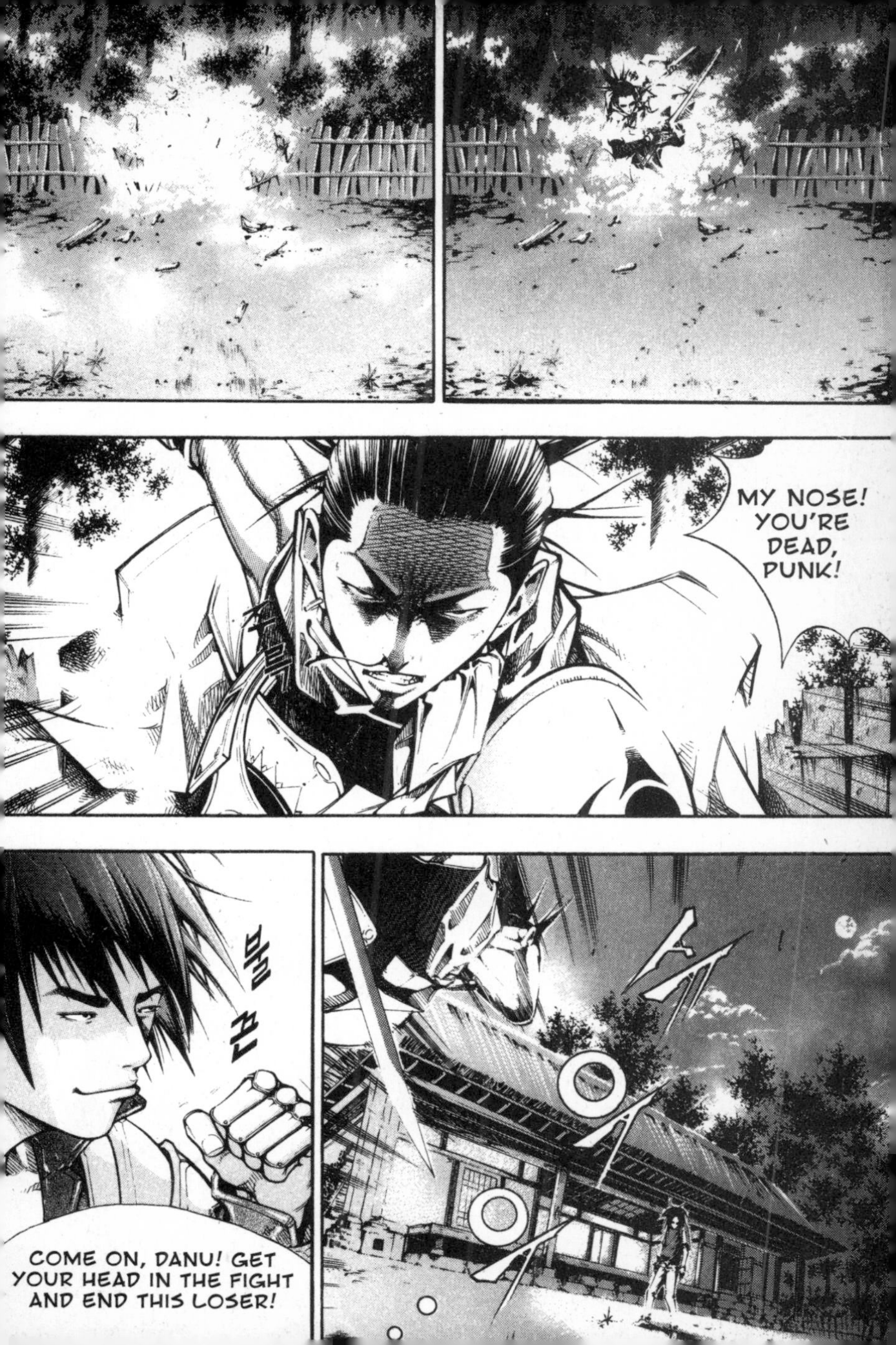
MY NOSE! YOU'RE DEAD, PUNK!
불끈
COME ON, DANU! GET YOUR HEAD IN THE FIGHT AND END THIS LOSER!

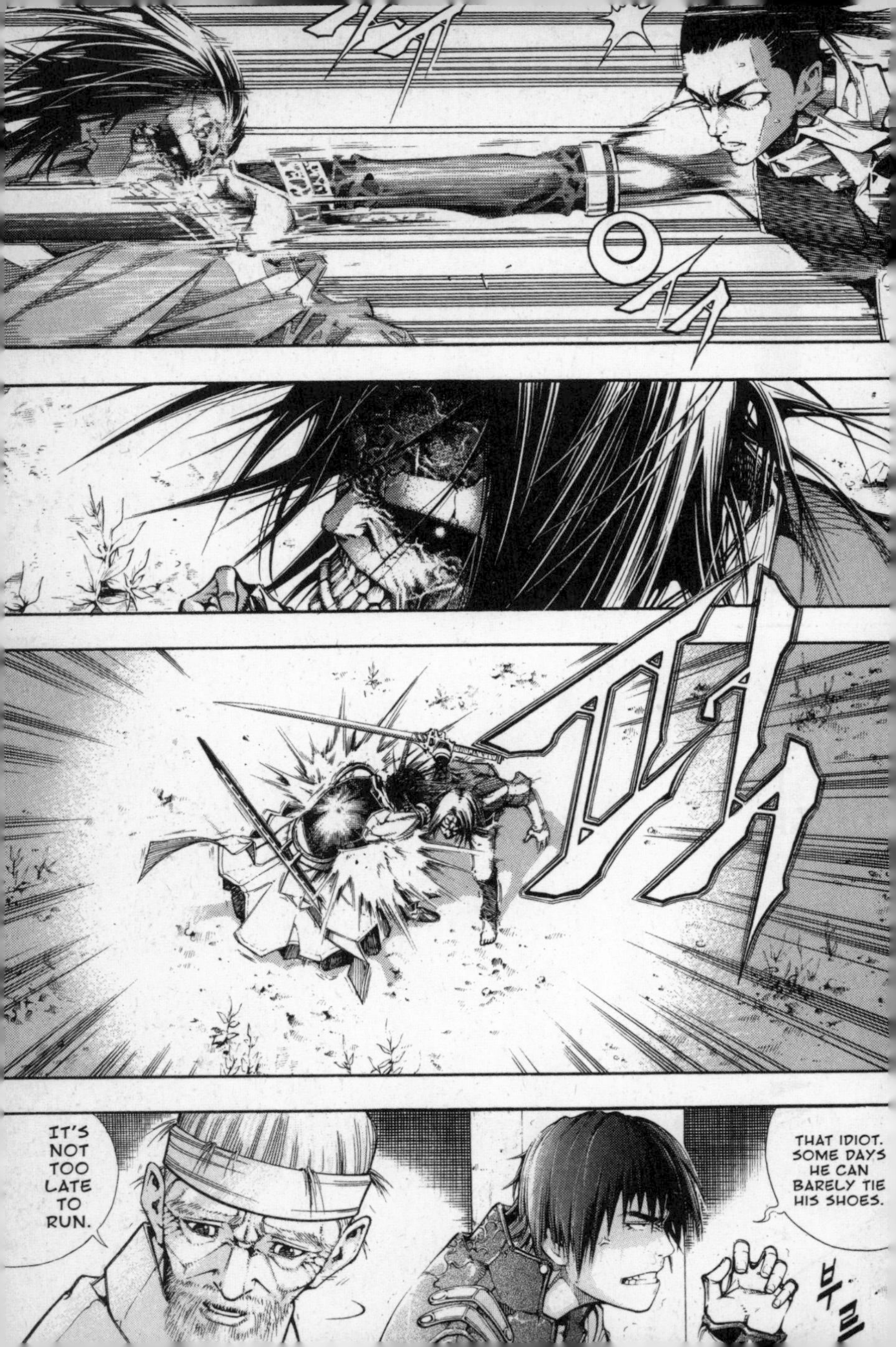
IT'S NOT TOO LATE TO RUN.
THAT IDIOT. SOME DAYS HE CAN BARELY TIE HIS SHOES.

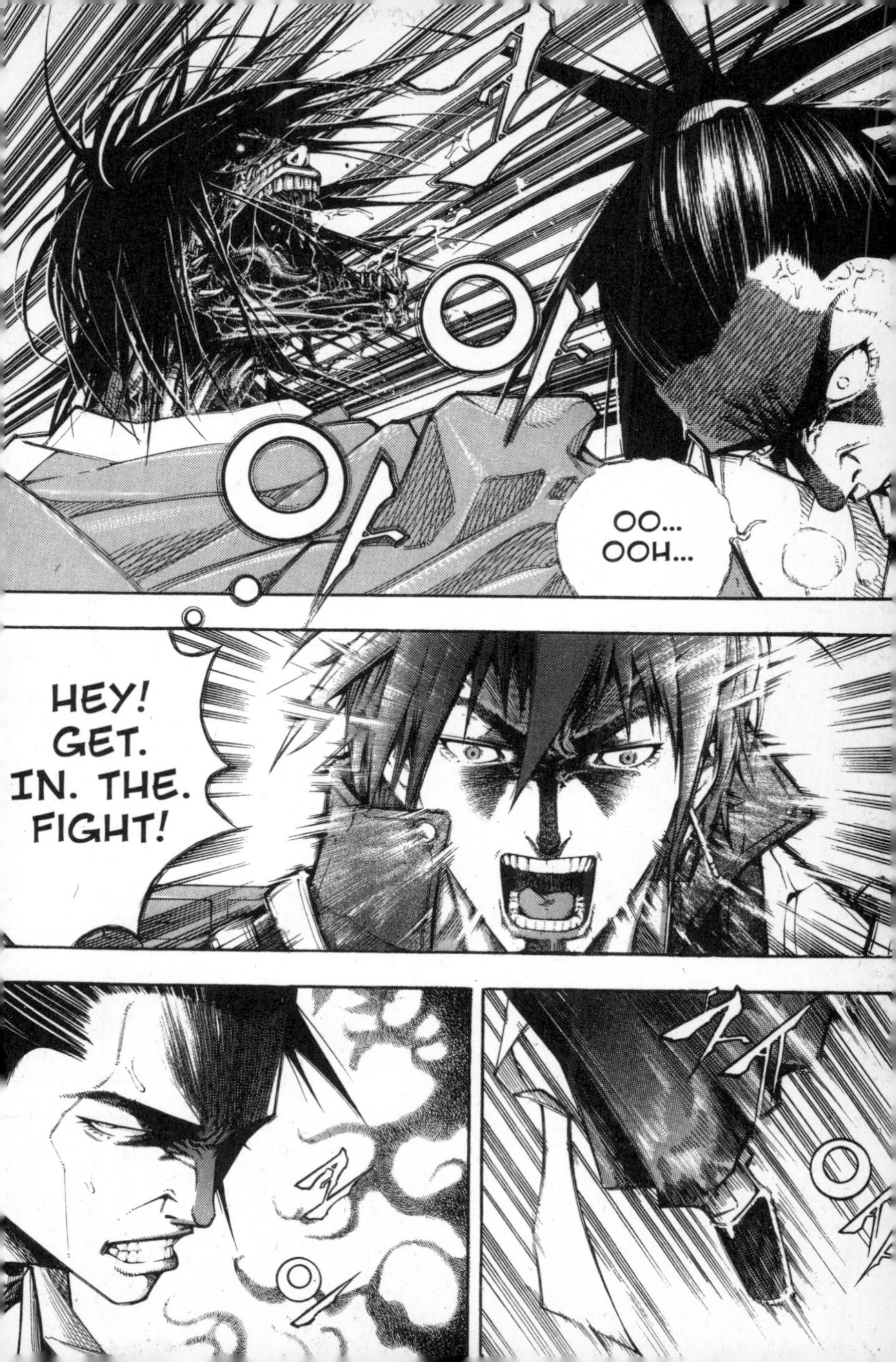
OO...
OOH...
HEY! GET. IN. THE. FIGHT!

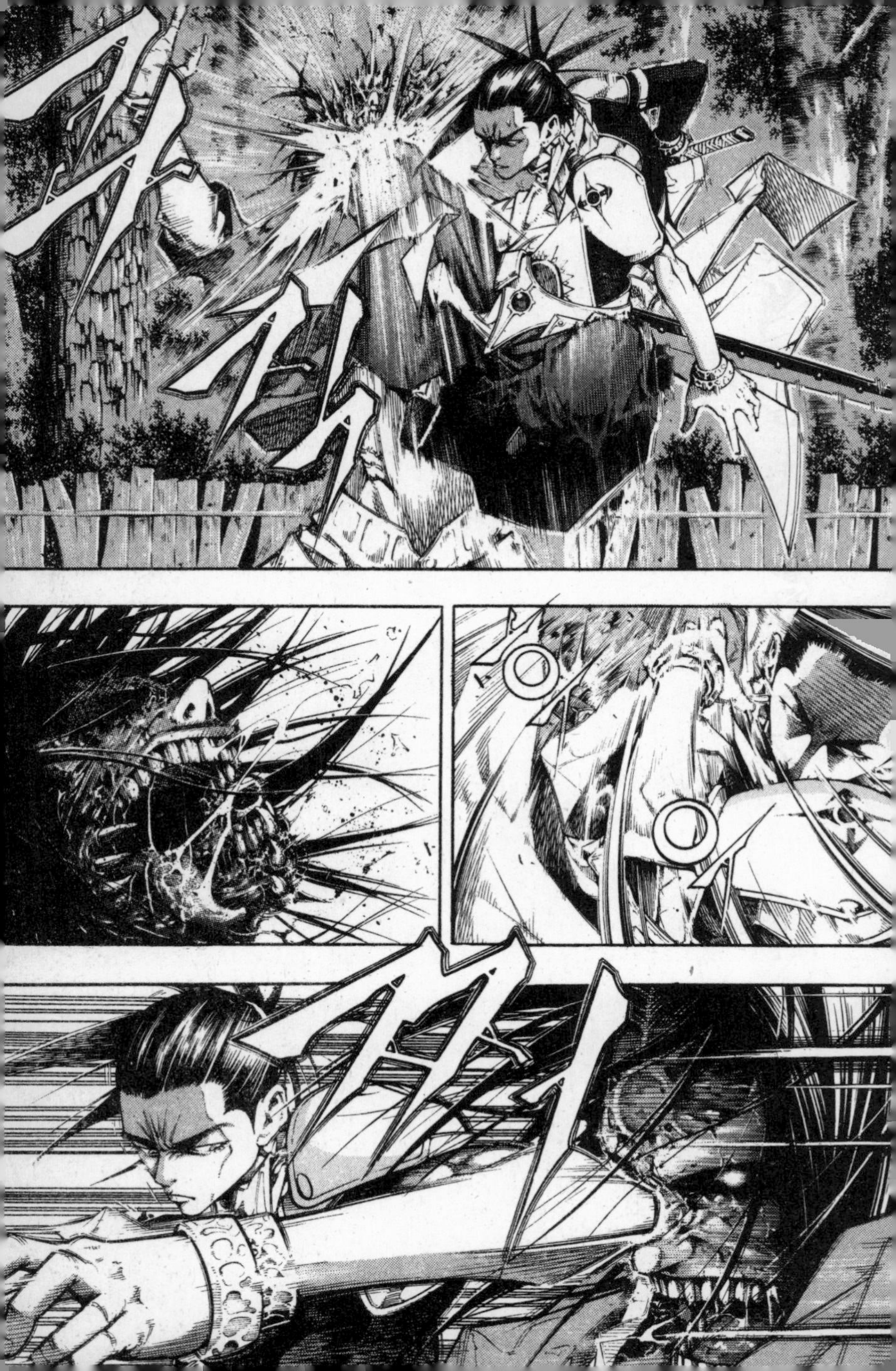

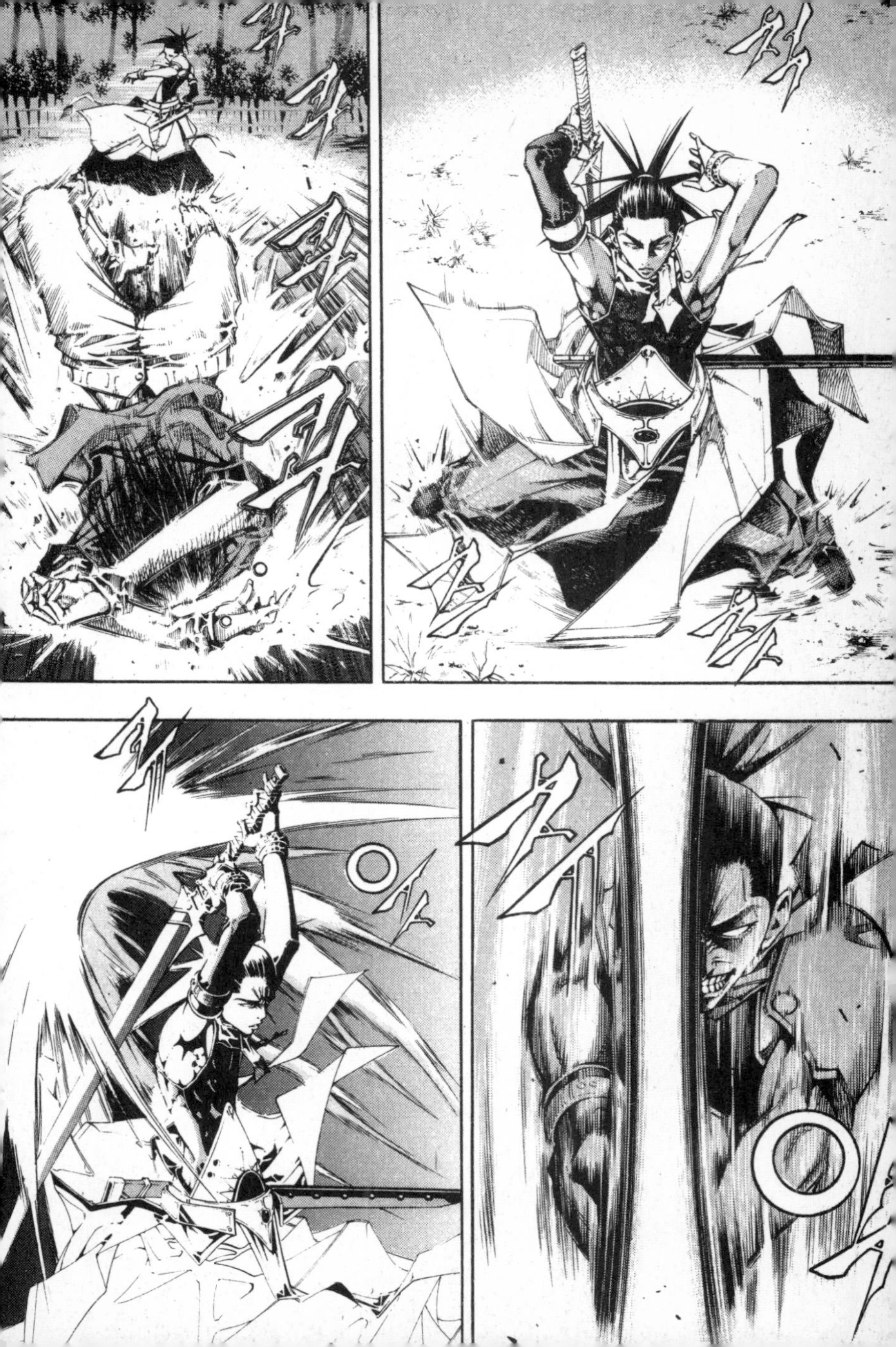

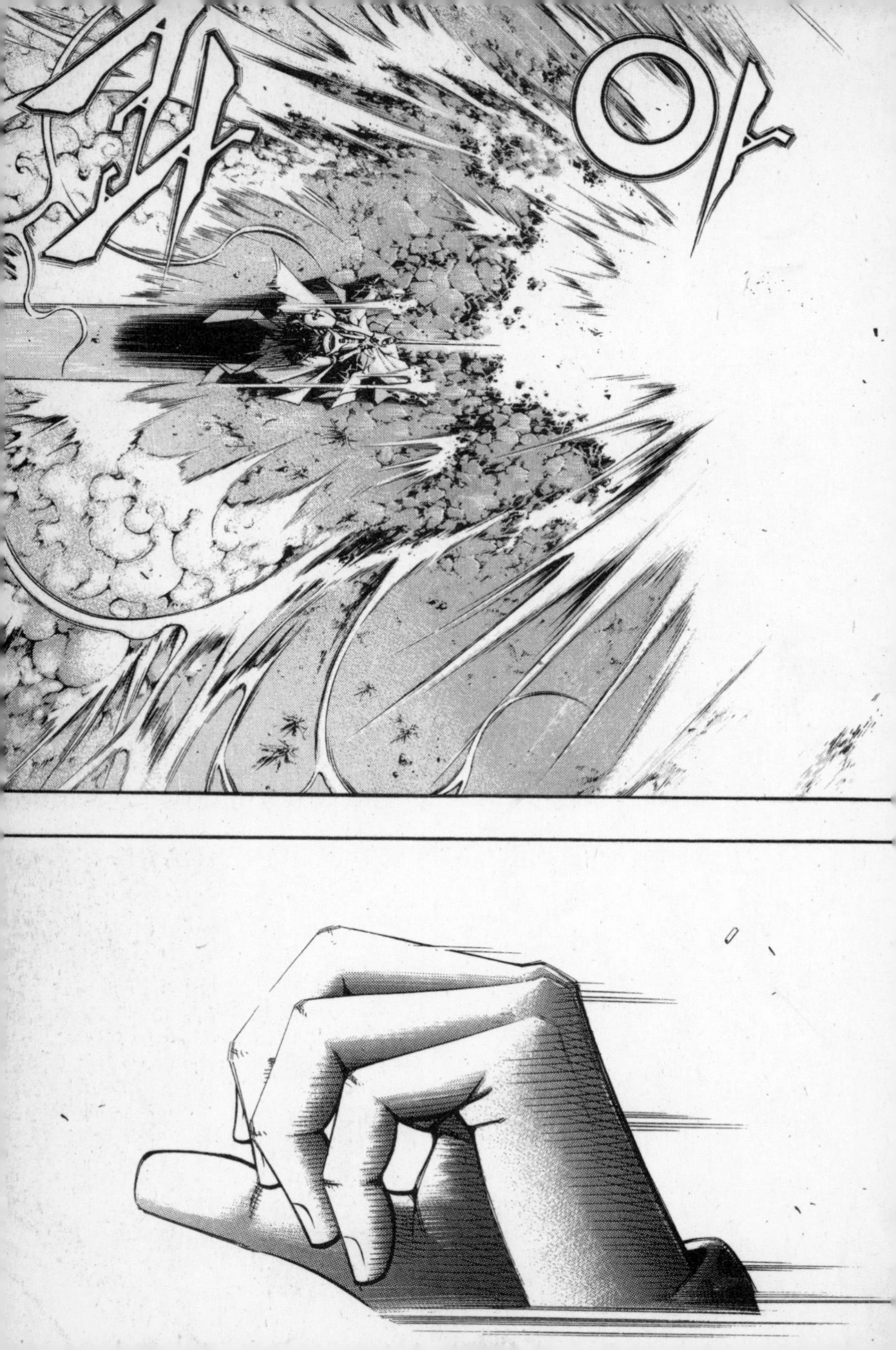

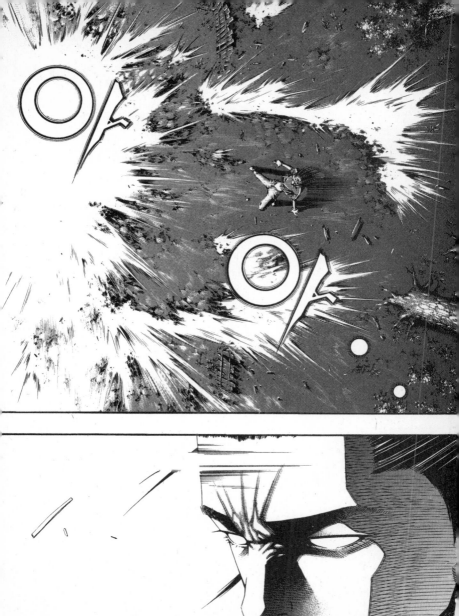

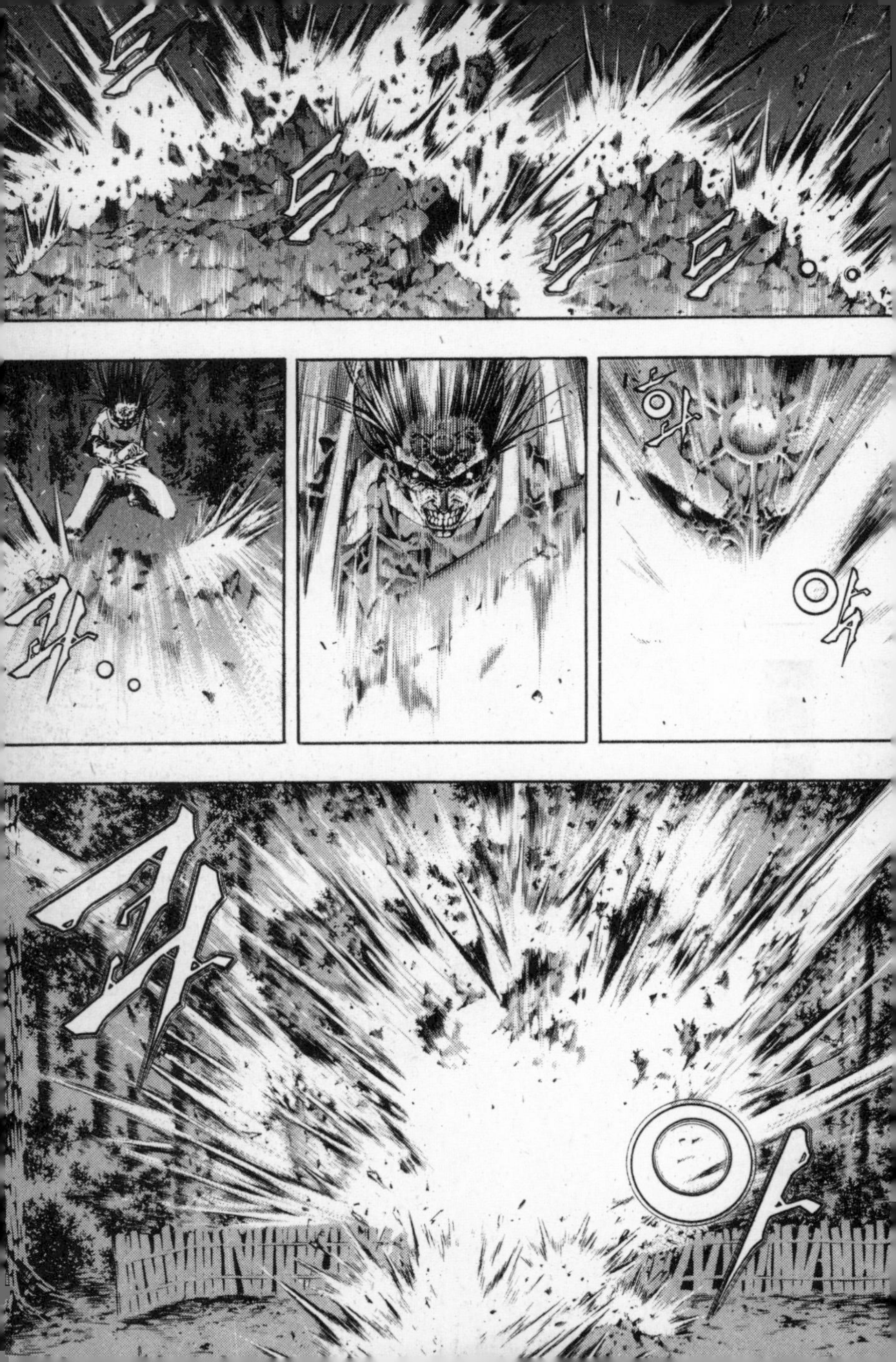
드드드드...

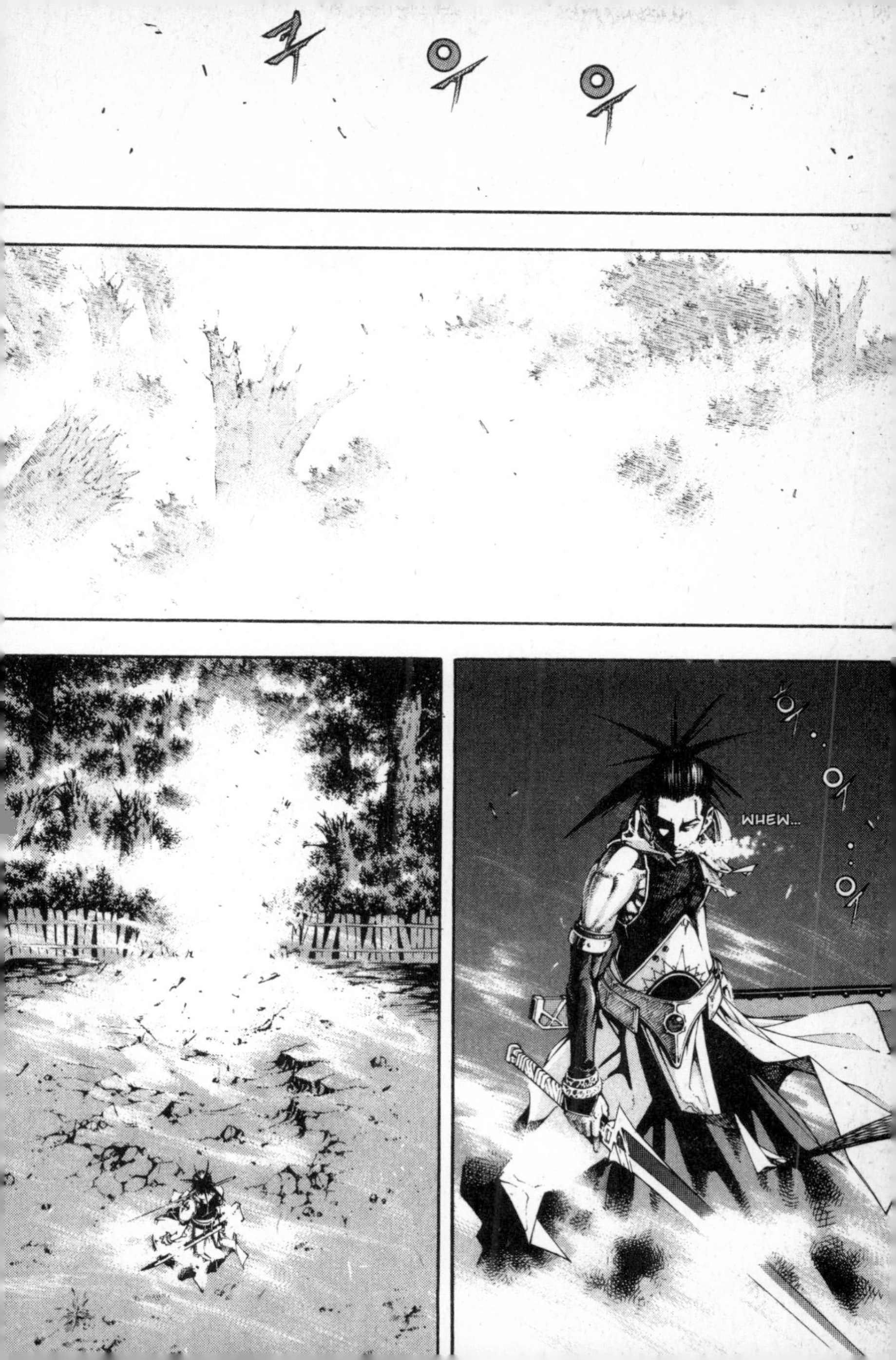
쿠우우
WHEW...
우..우..우

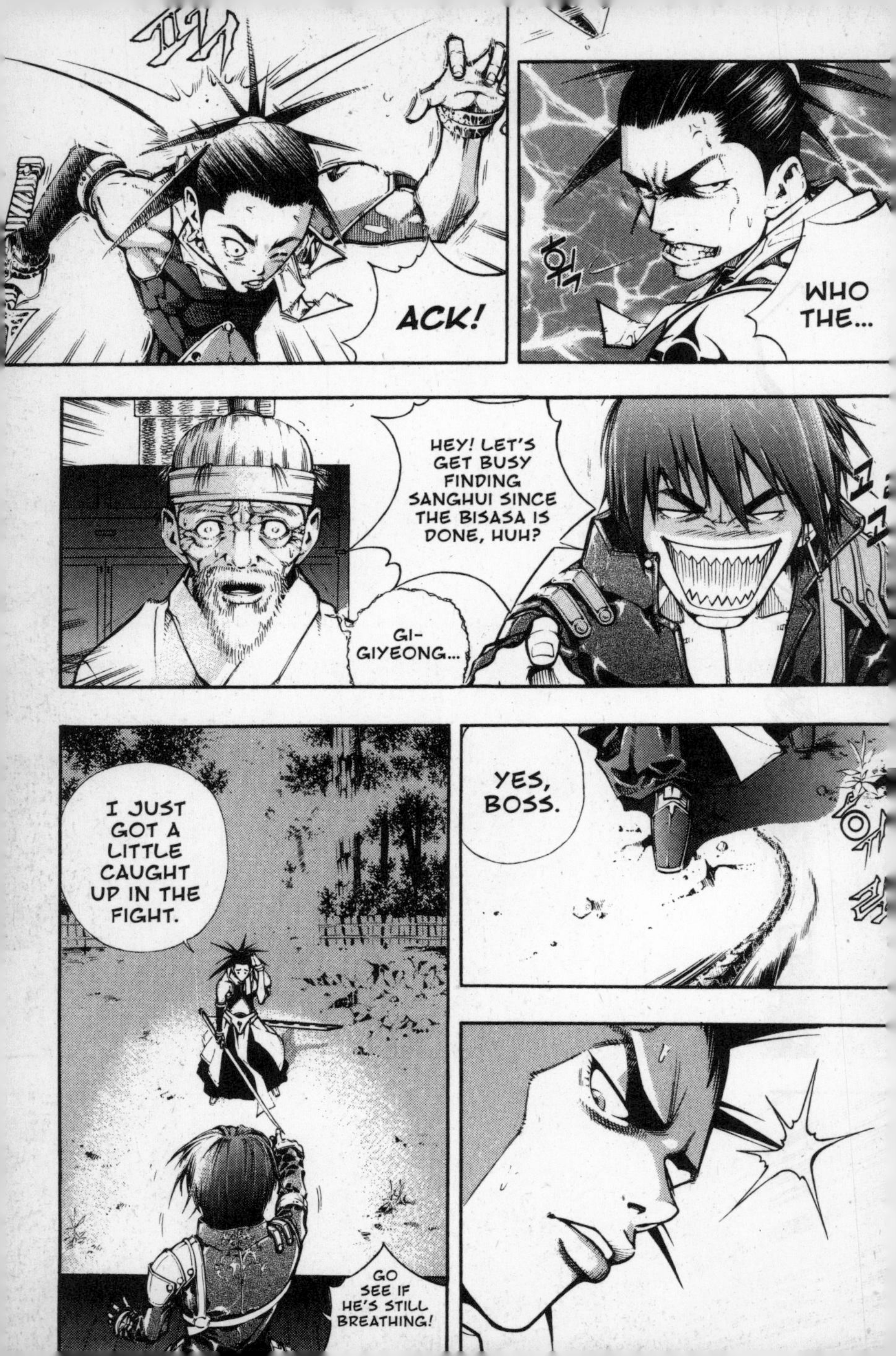

ACK!
WHO THE...
HEY! LET'S GET BUSY FINDING SANGHUI SINCE THE BISASA IS DONE, HUH?
GI-GIYEONG...
I JUST GOT A LITTLE CAUGHT UP IN THE FIGHT.
YES, BOSS.
GO SEE IF HE'S STILL BREATHING!

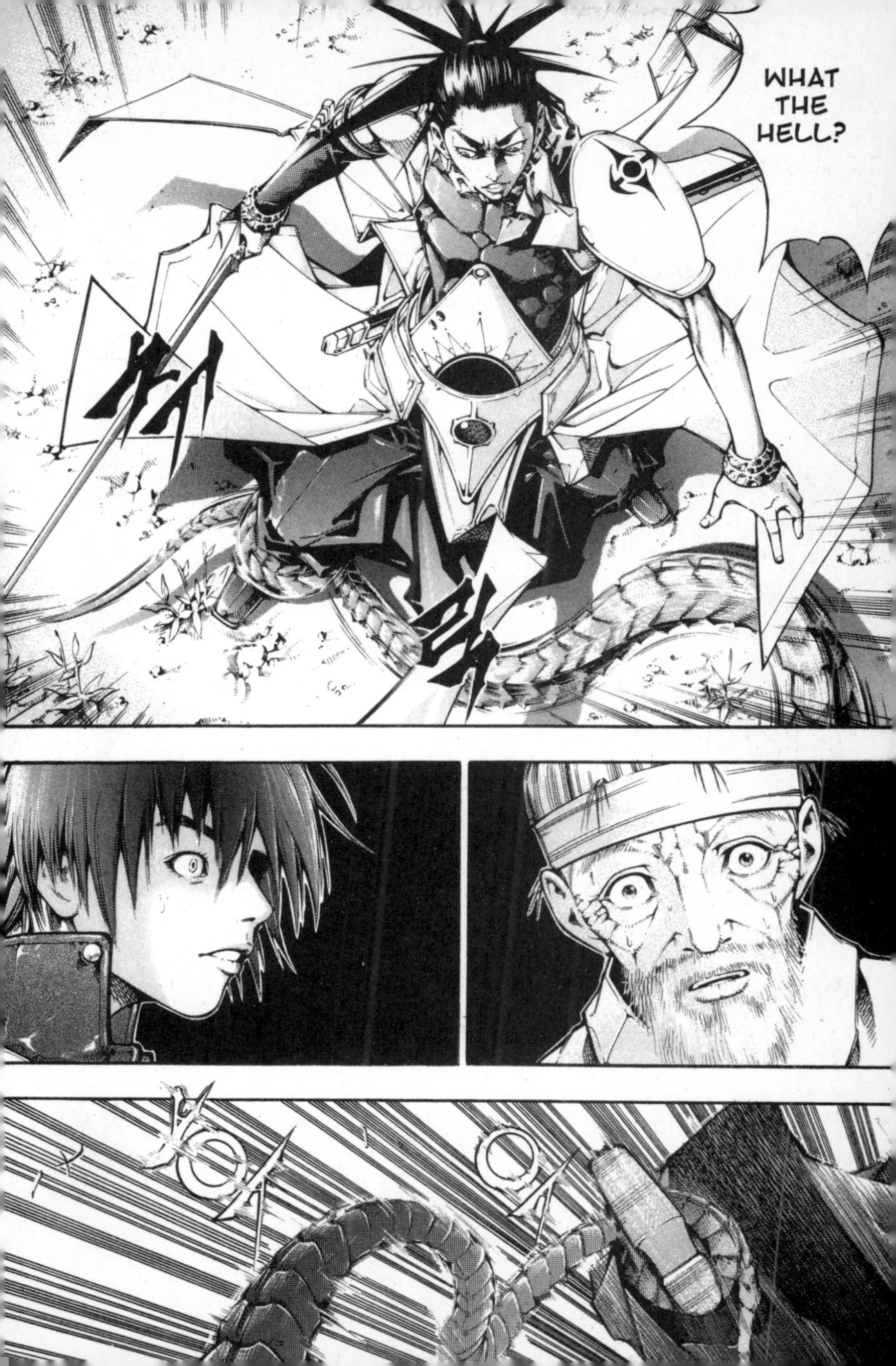
WHAT THE HELL?

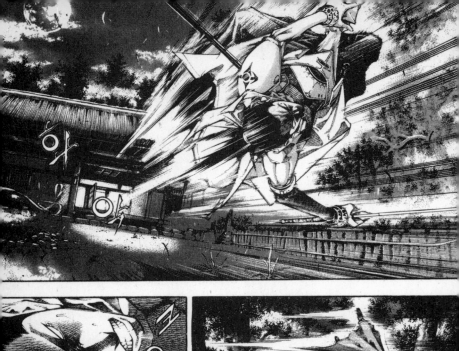

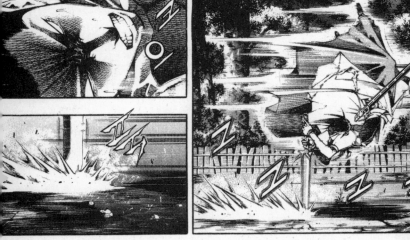

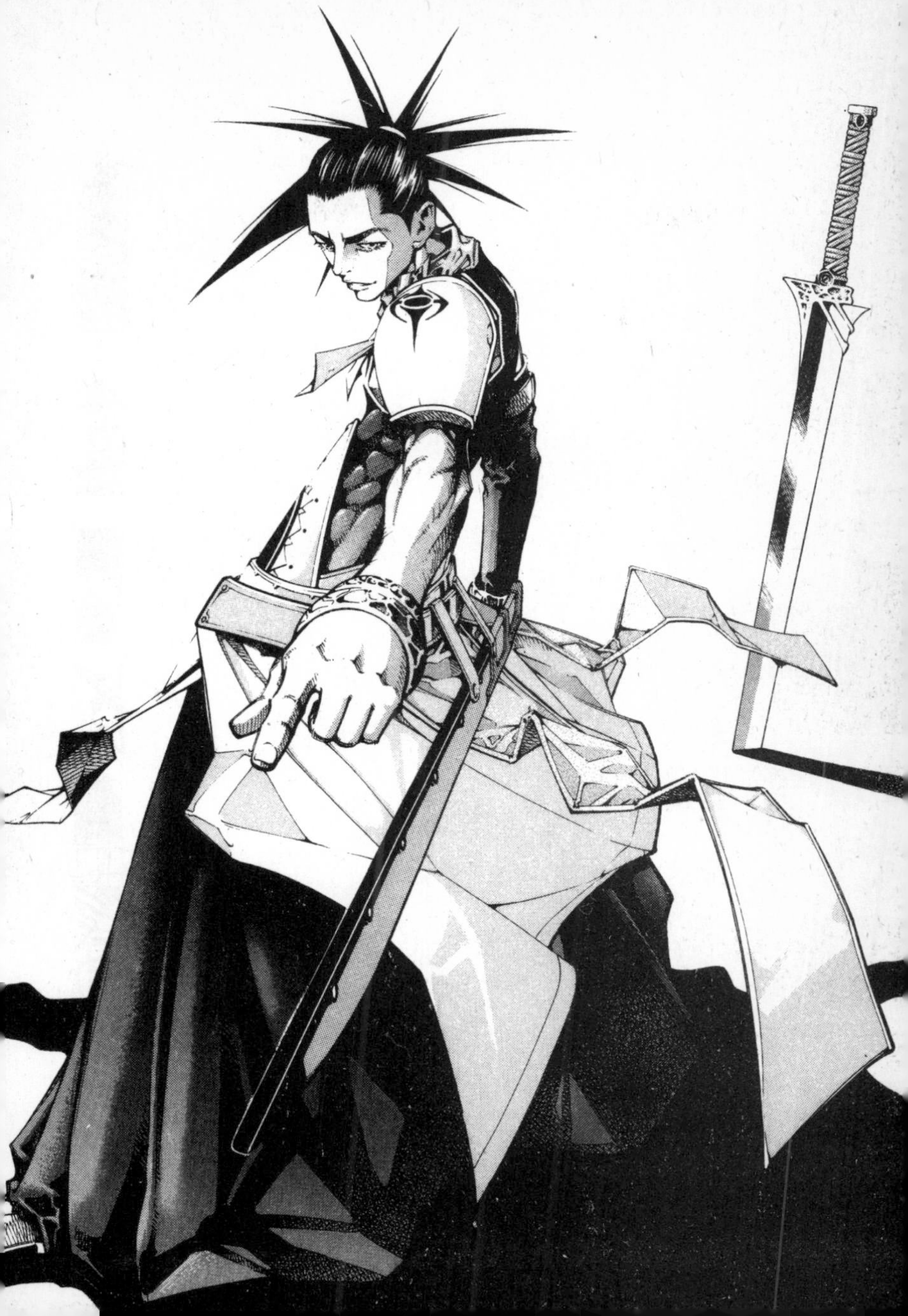

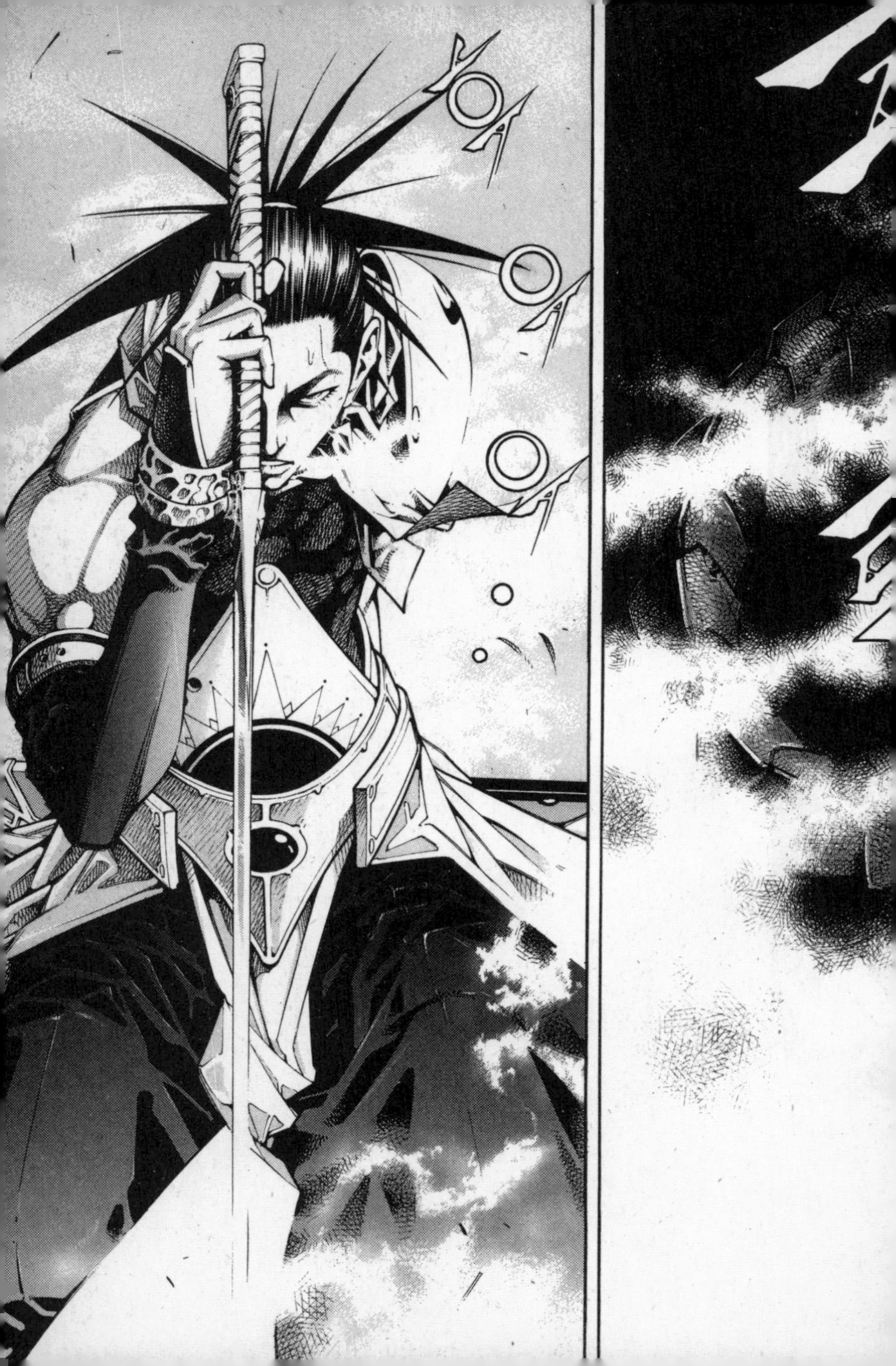

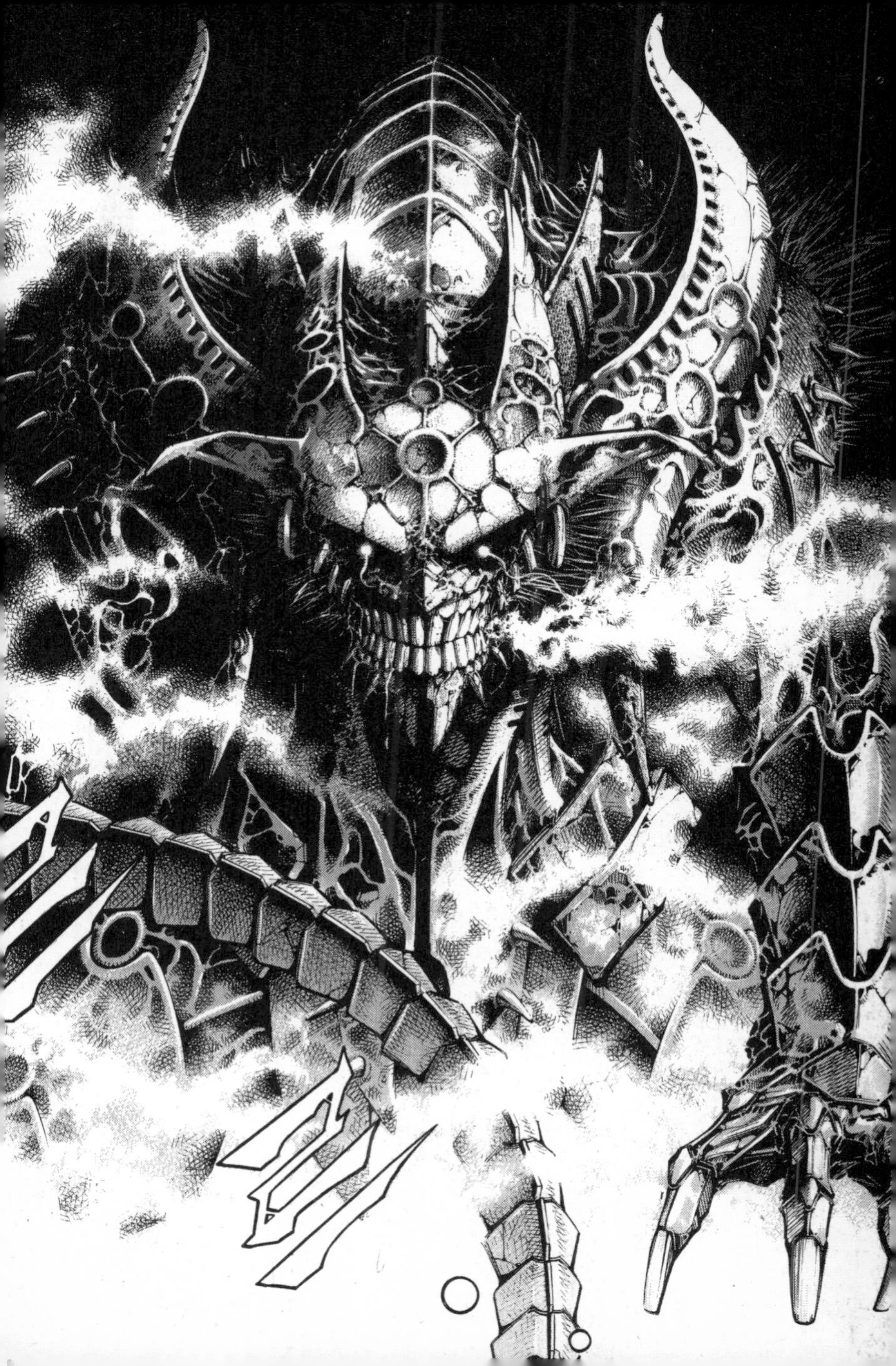

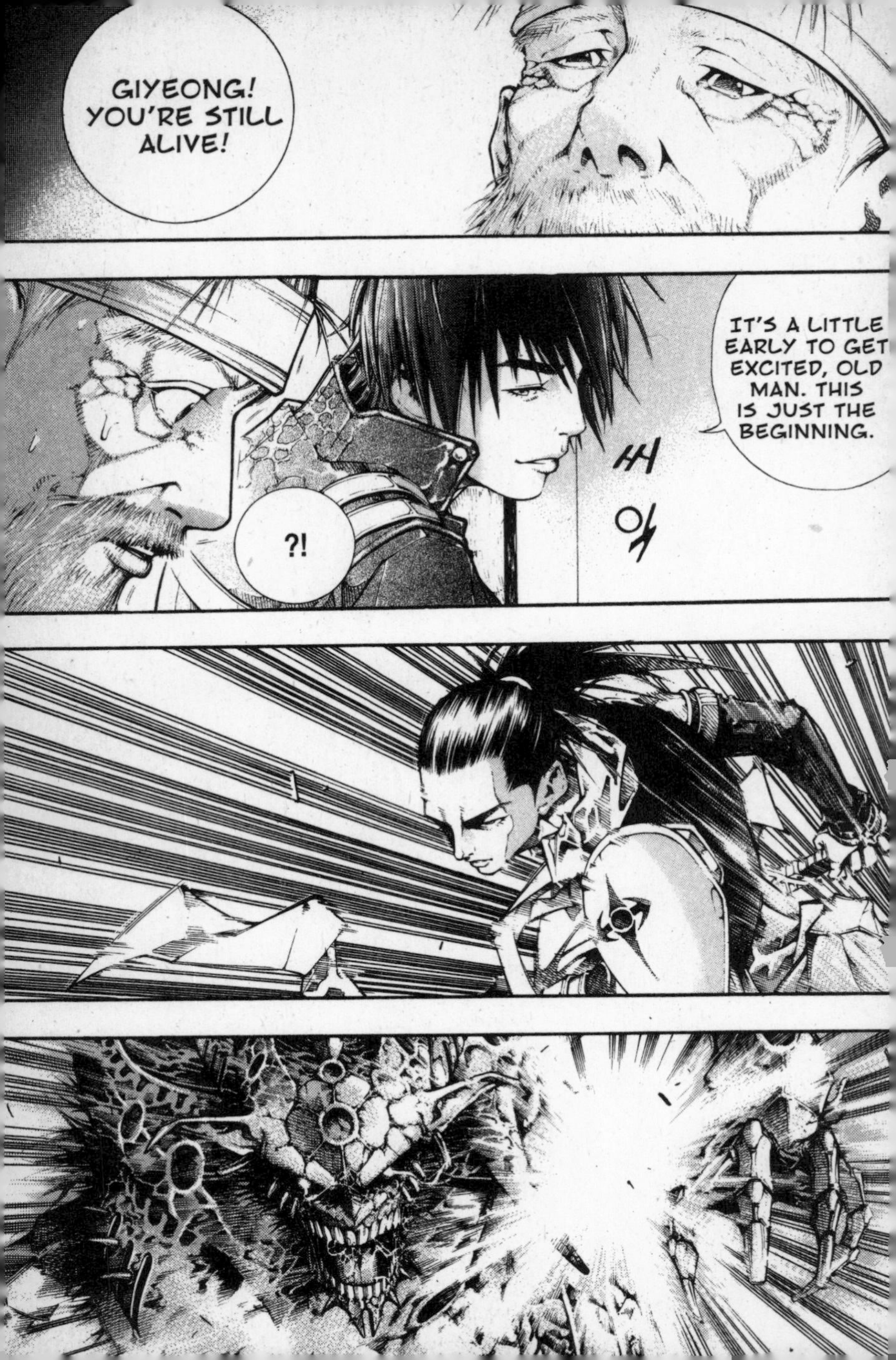
GIYEONG! YOU'RE STILL ALIVE!
?!
IT'S A LITTLE EARLY TO GET EXCITED, OLD MAN. THIS IS JUST THE BEGINNING.

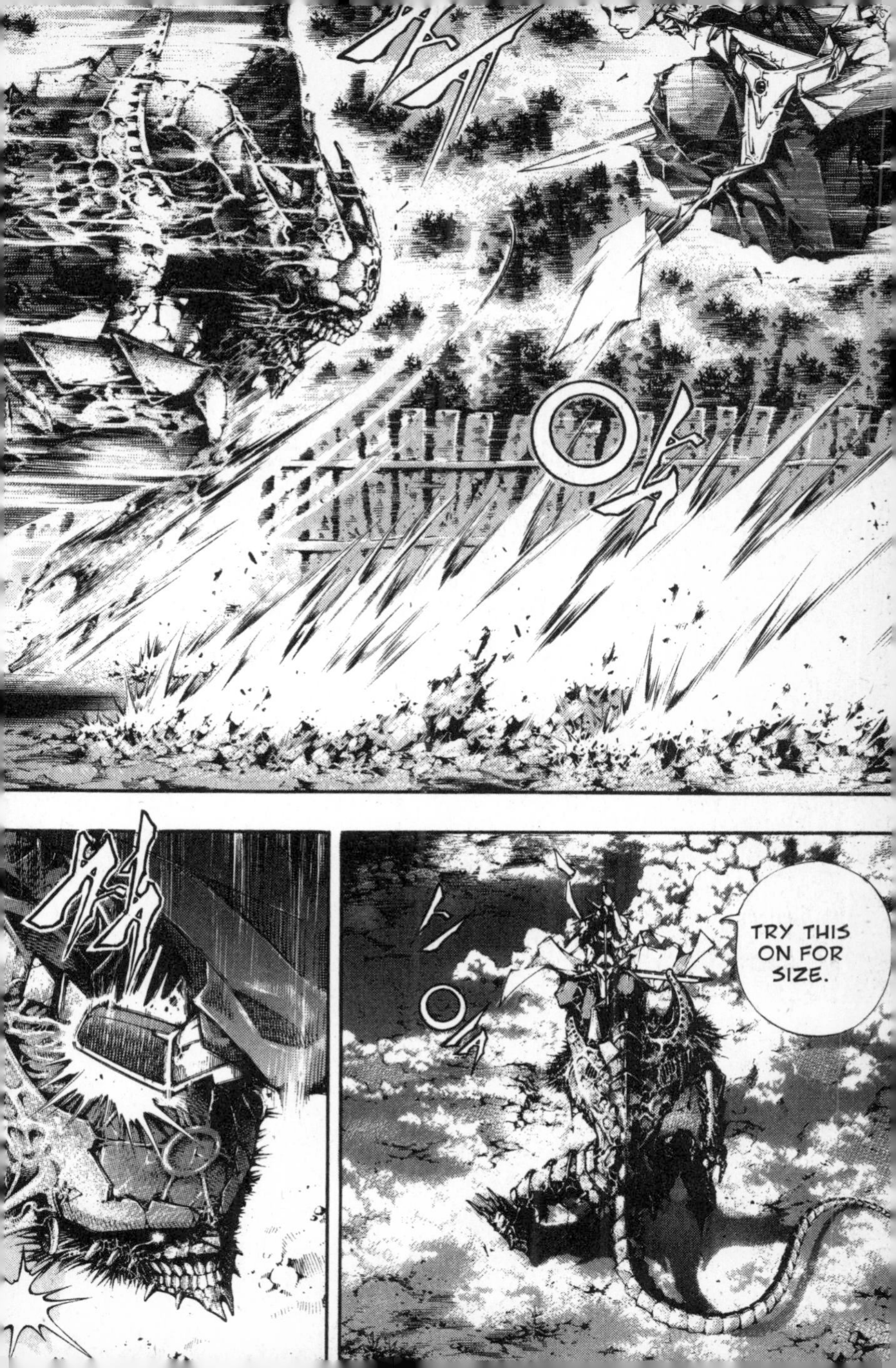
TRY THIS ON FOR SIZE.

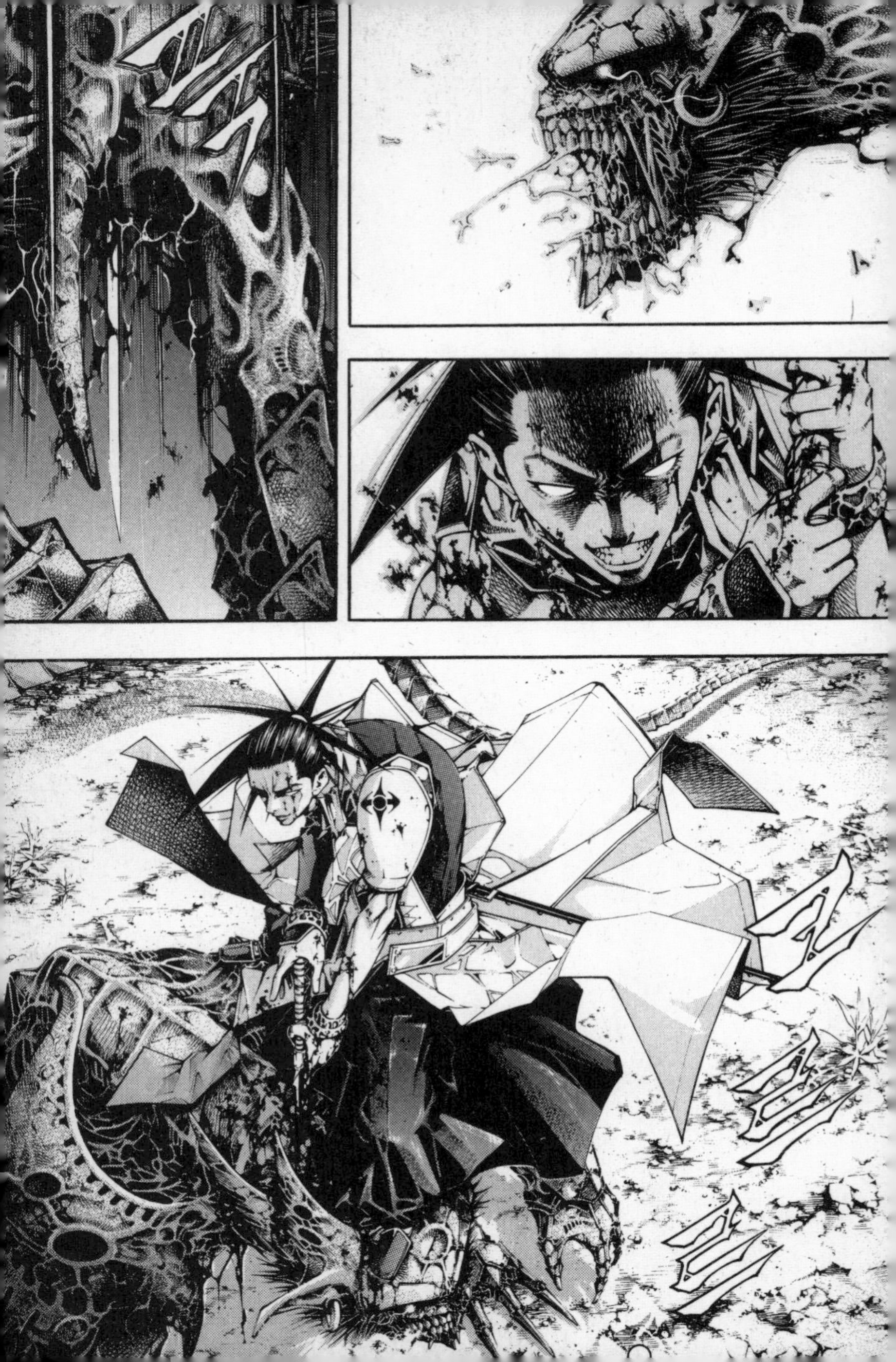

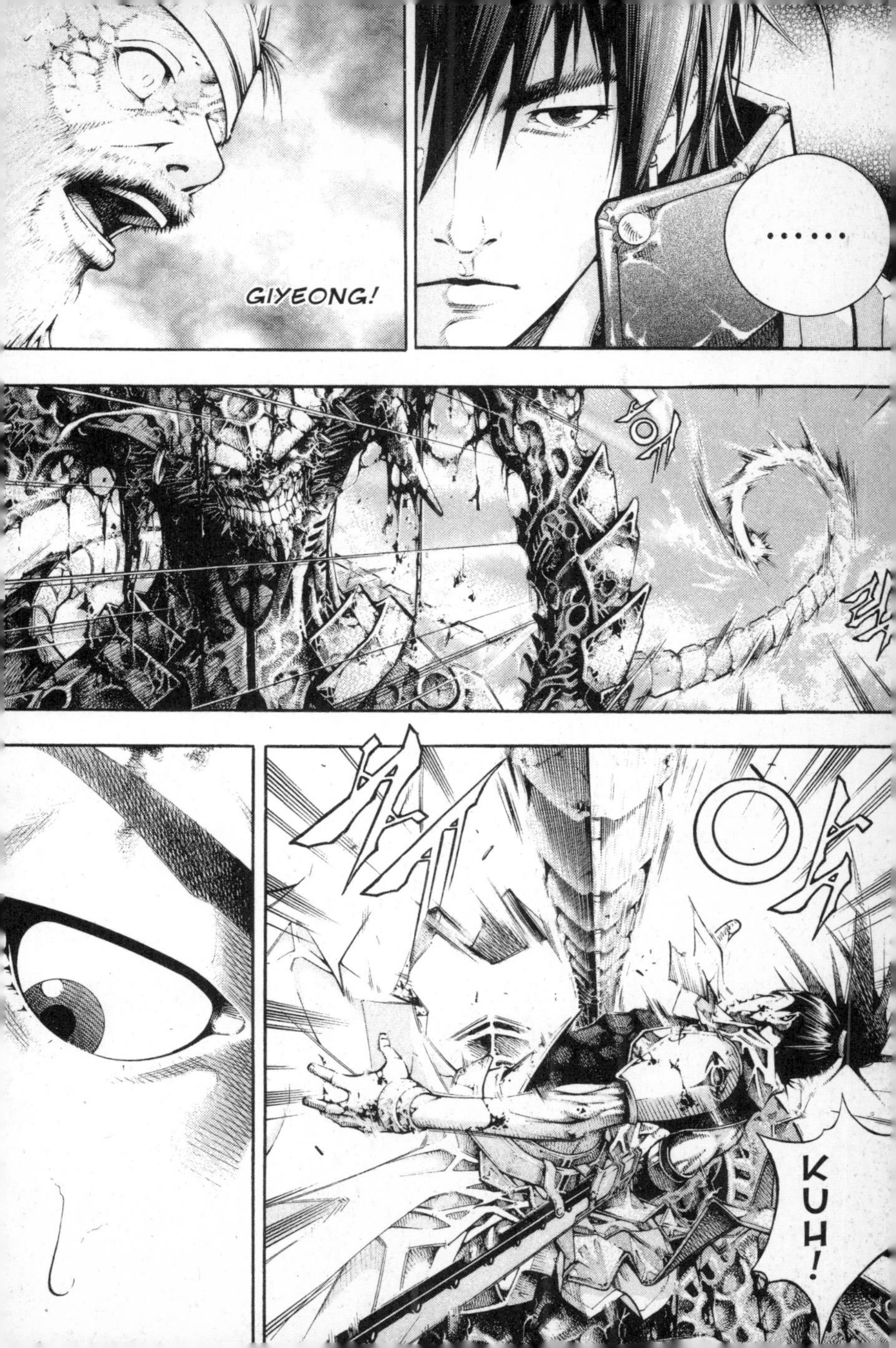
GIYEONG!
......
KUH!

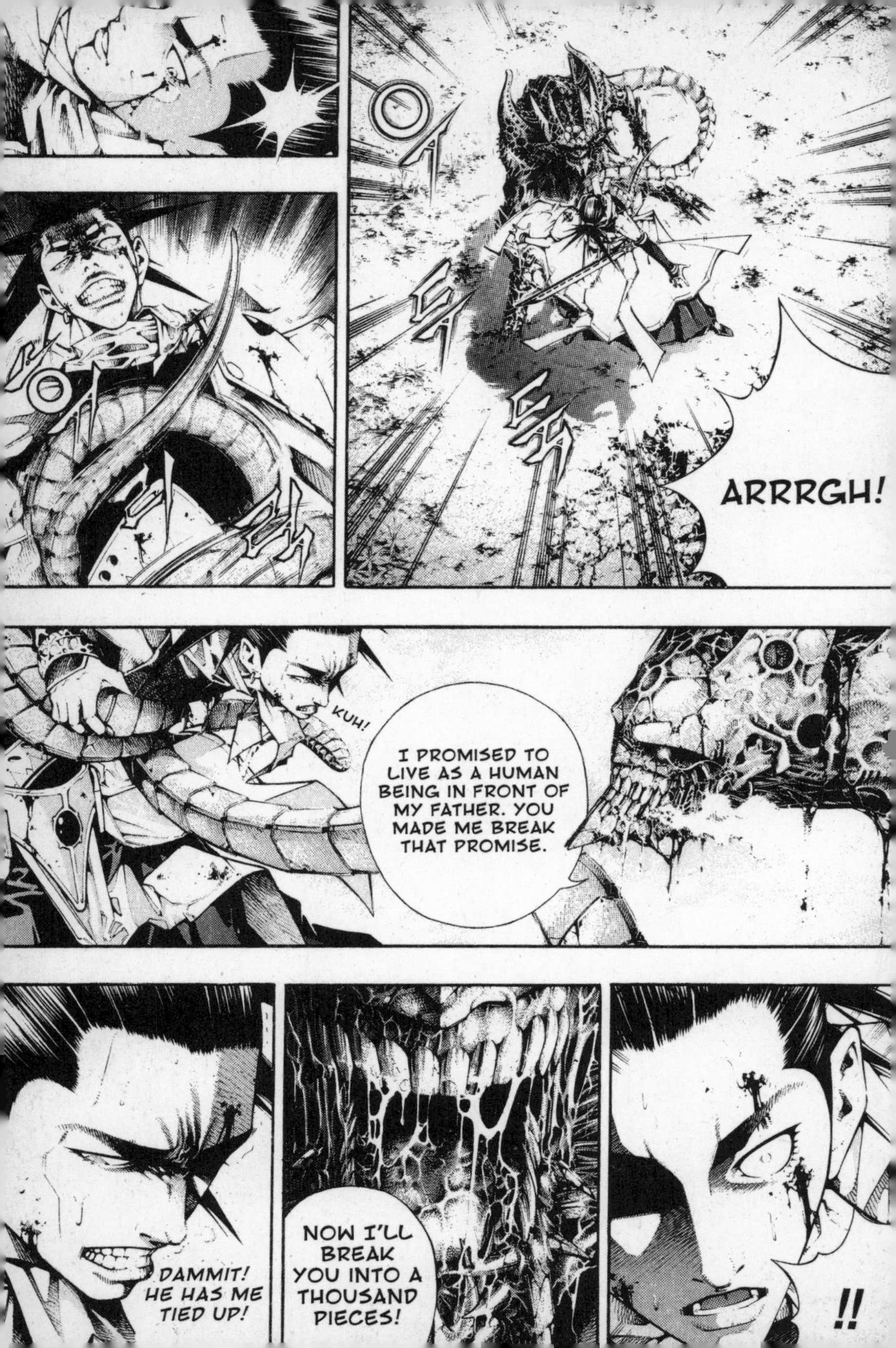

ARRRGH!
I PROMISED TO LIVE AS A HUMAN BEING IN FRONT OF MY FATHER. YOU MADE ME BREAK THAT PROMISE.
KUH!
!!
NOW I'LL BREAK YOU INTO A THOUSAND PIECES!
DAMMIT! HE HAS ME TIED UP!

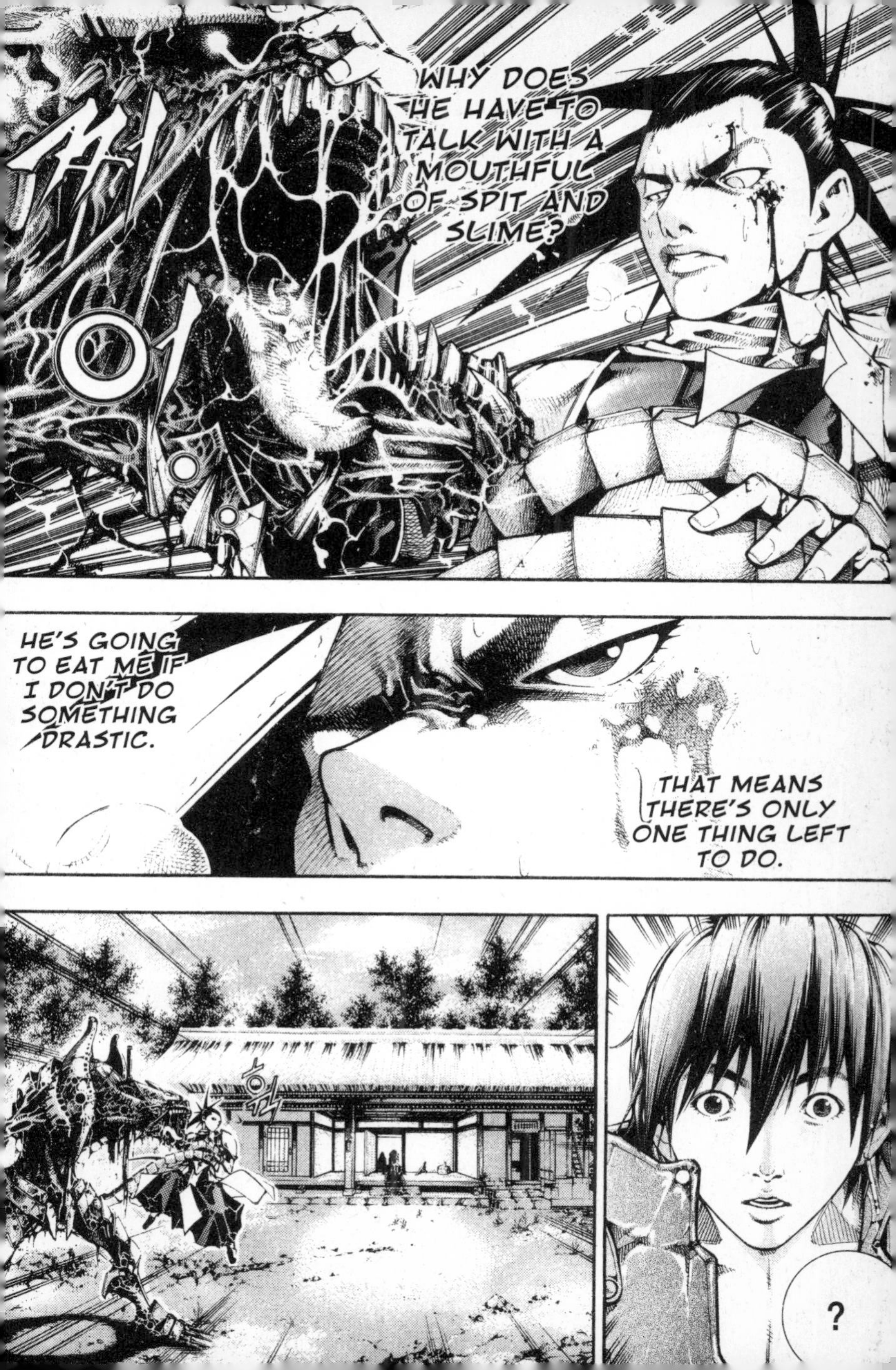
WHY DOES HE HAVE TO TALK WITH A MOUTHFUL OF SPIT AND SLIME?
HE'S GOING TO EAT ME IF I DON'T DO SOMETHING DRASTIC.
THAT MEANS THERE'S ONLY ONE THING LEFT TO DO.
?

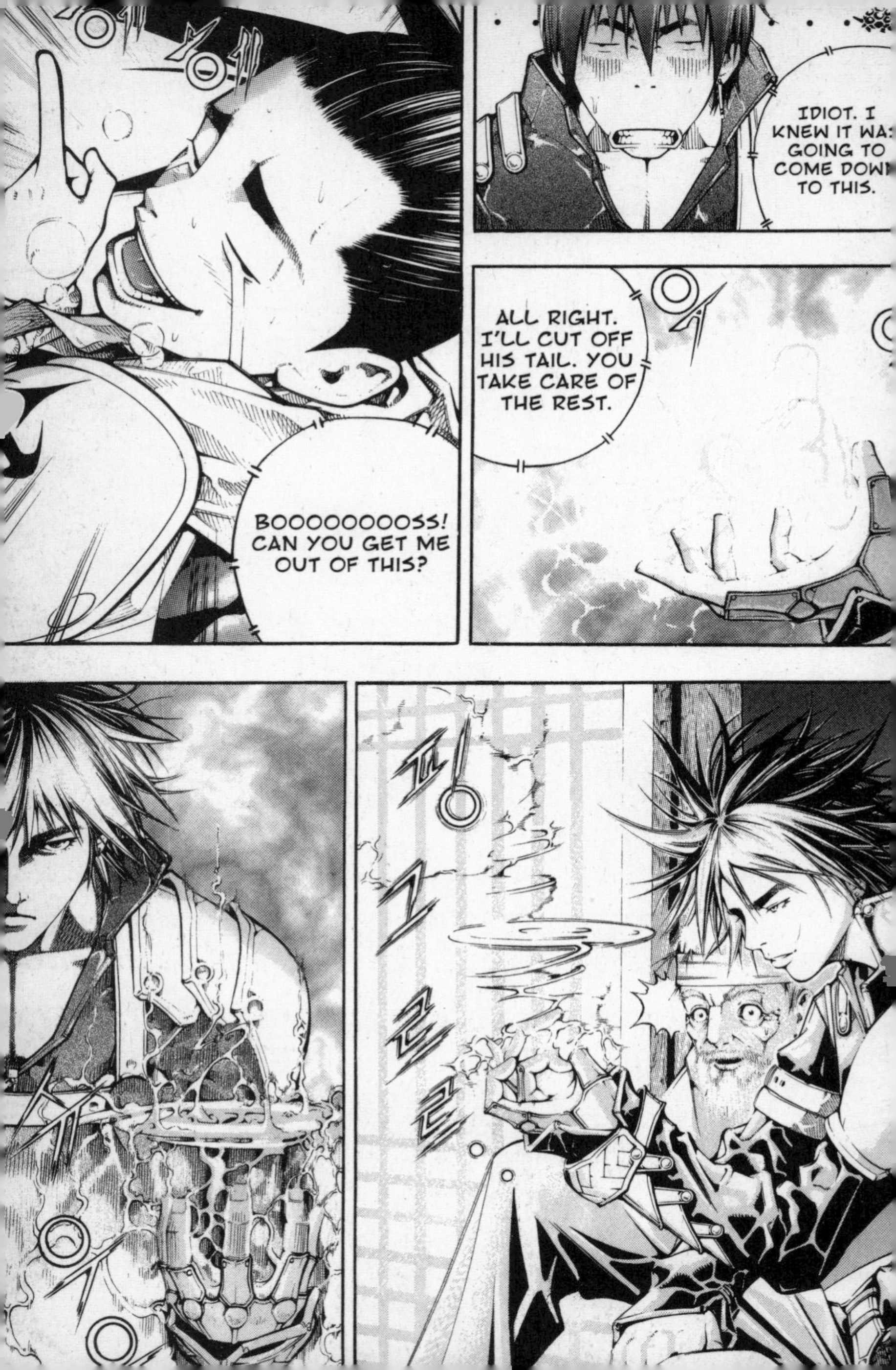
BOOOOOOOOOSS! CAN YOU GET ME OUT OF THIS?
IDIOT. I KNEW IT WA GOING TO COME DOW TO THIS.
ALL RIGHT. I'LL CUT OFF HIS TAIL. YOU TAKE CARE OF THE REST.

GIYEONG!
LOOK OUT!

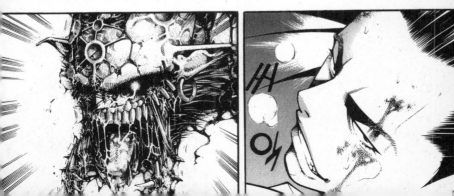

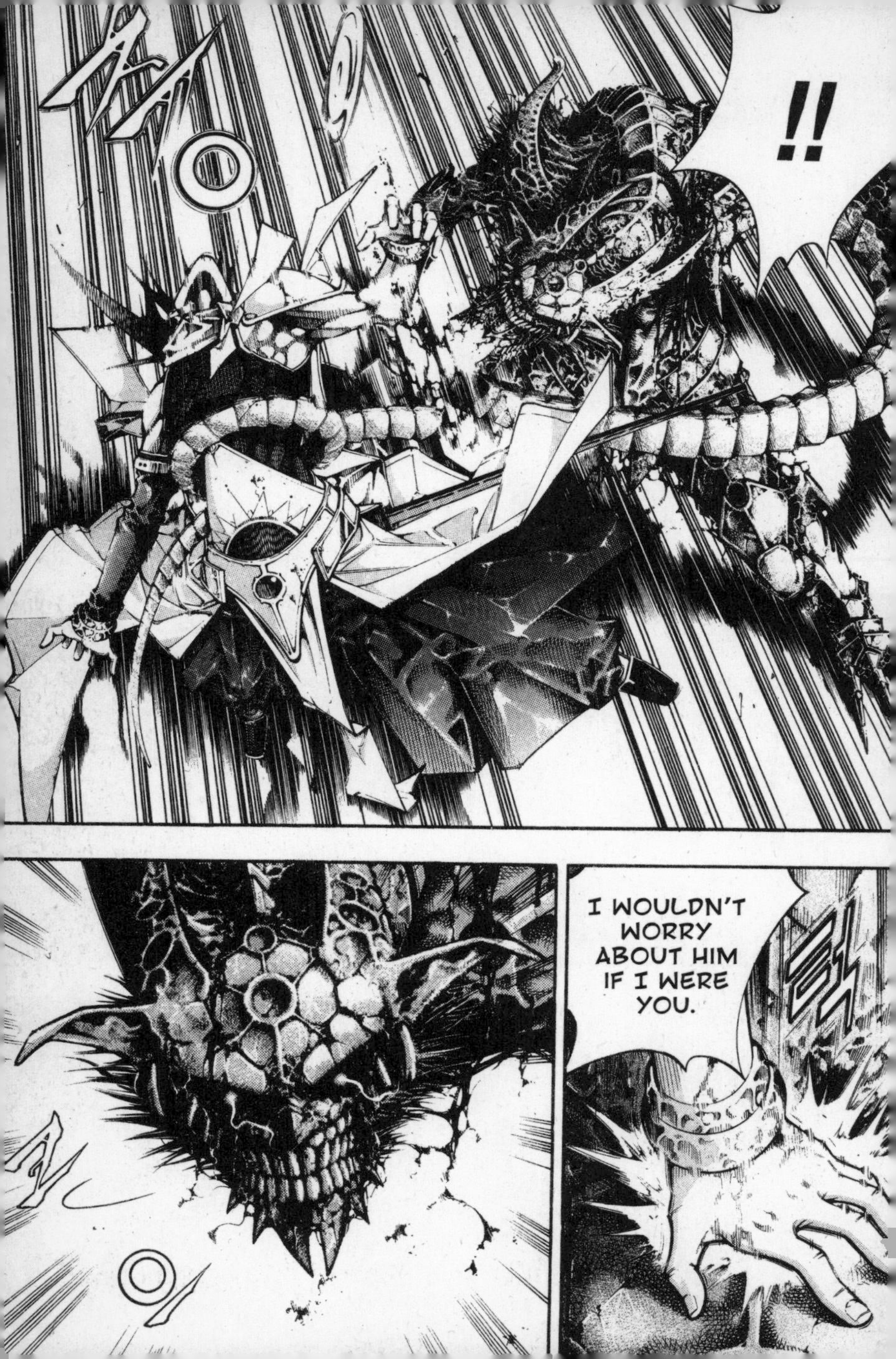
!!
I WOULDN'T WORRY ABOUT HIM IF I WERE YOU.

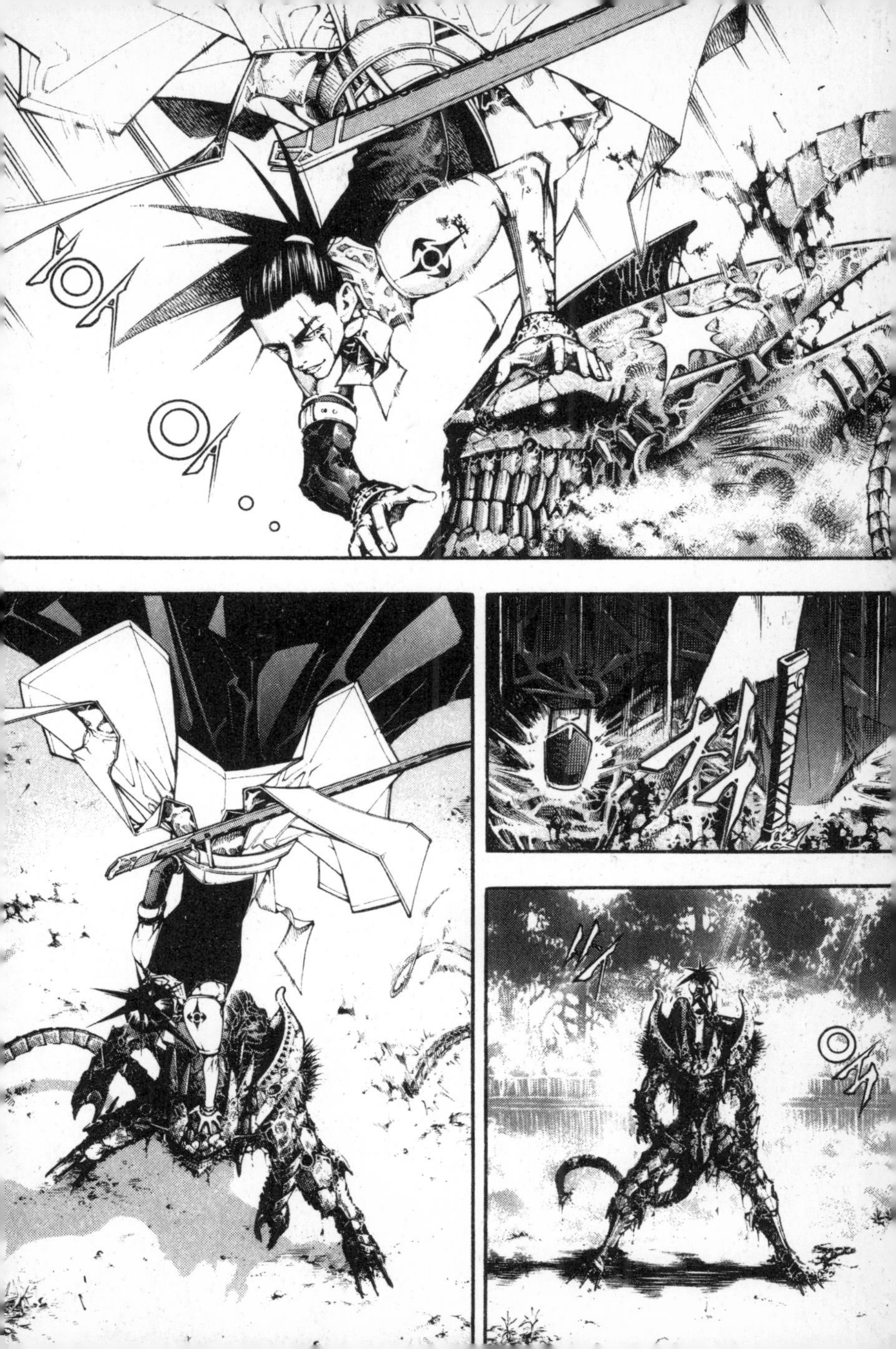

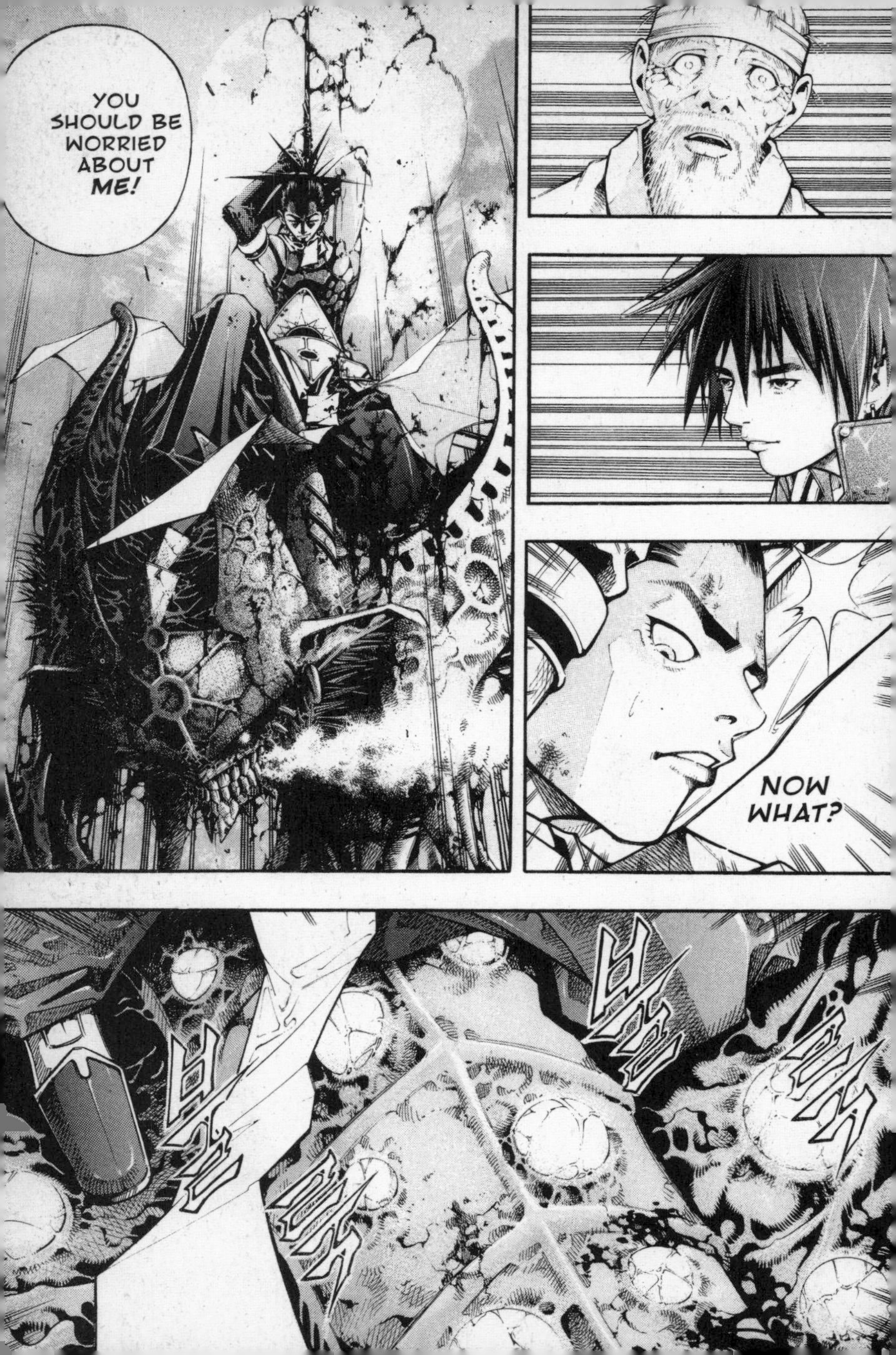
YOU SHOULD BE WORRIED ABOUT ME!
NOW WHAT?

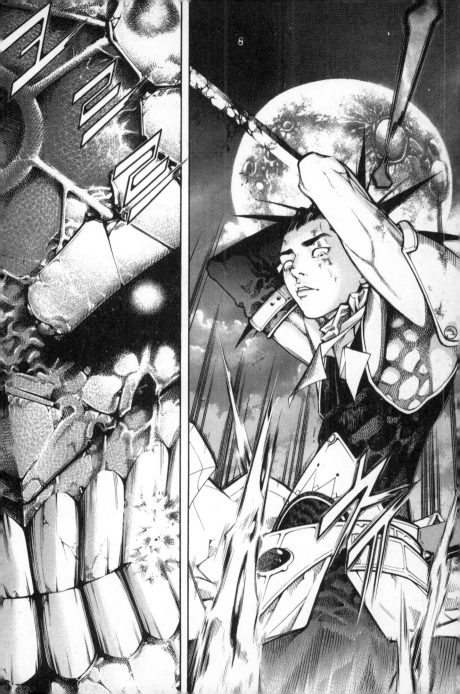

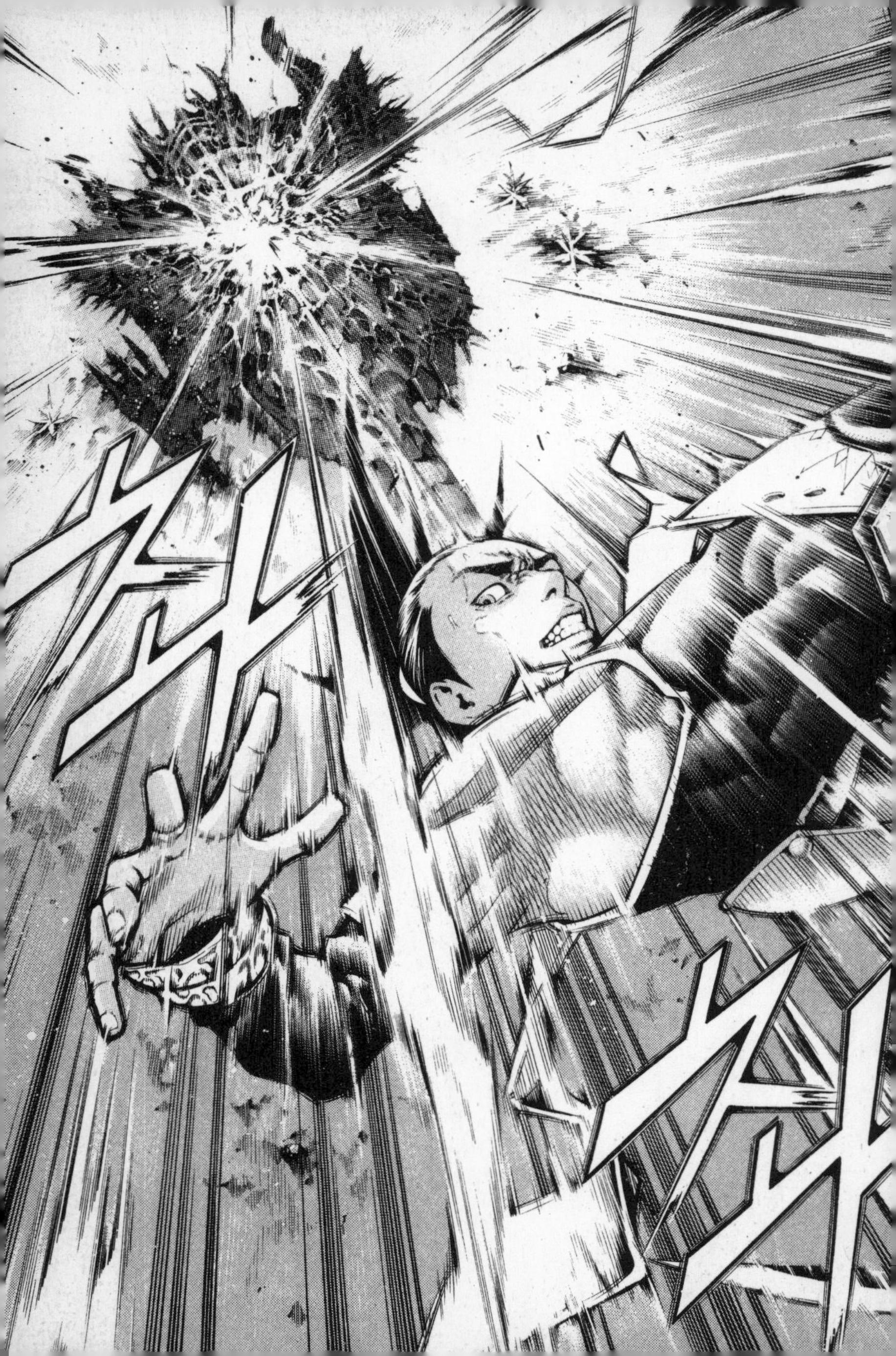

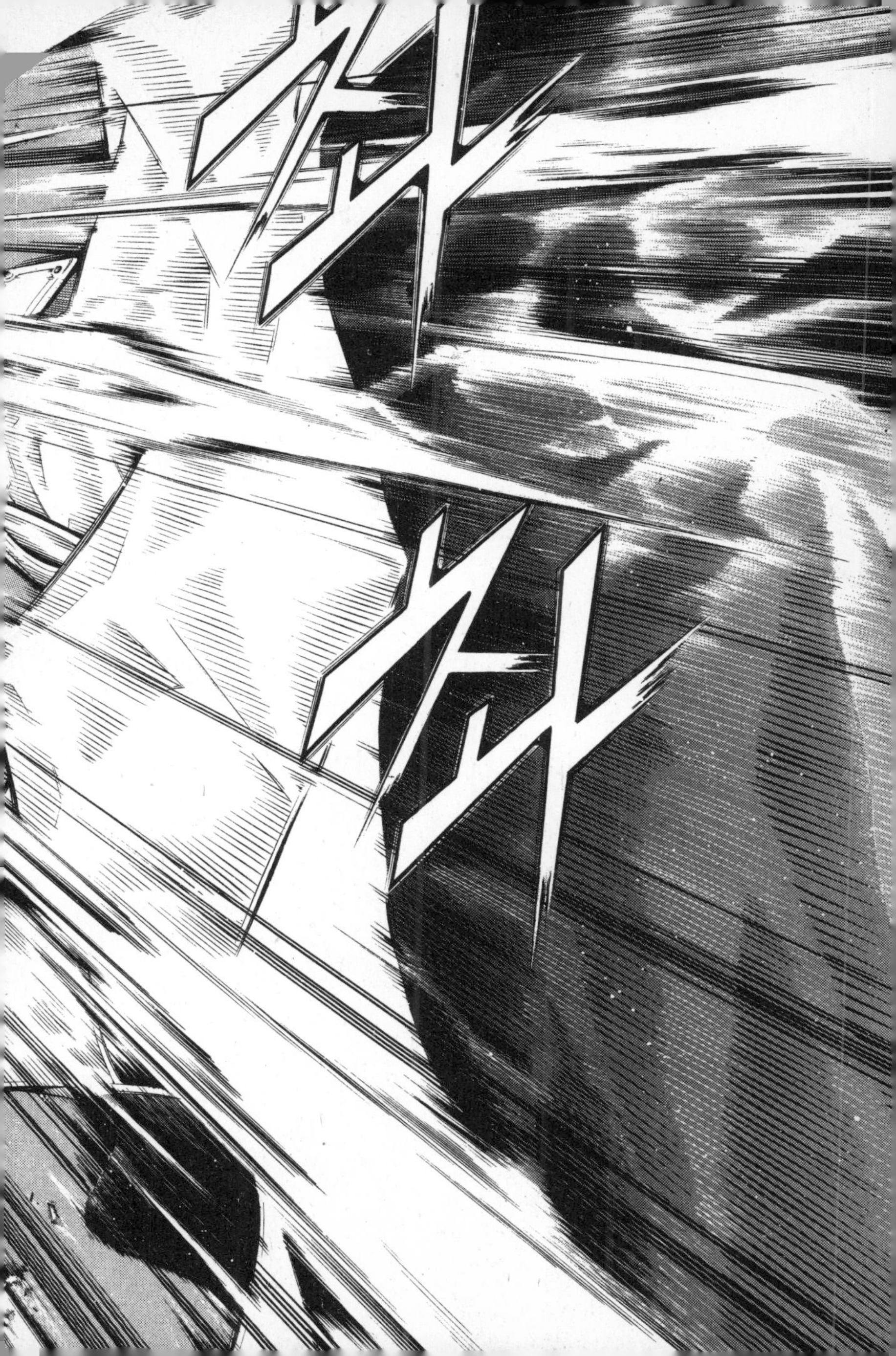

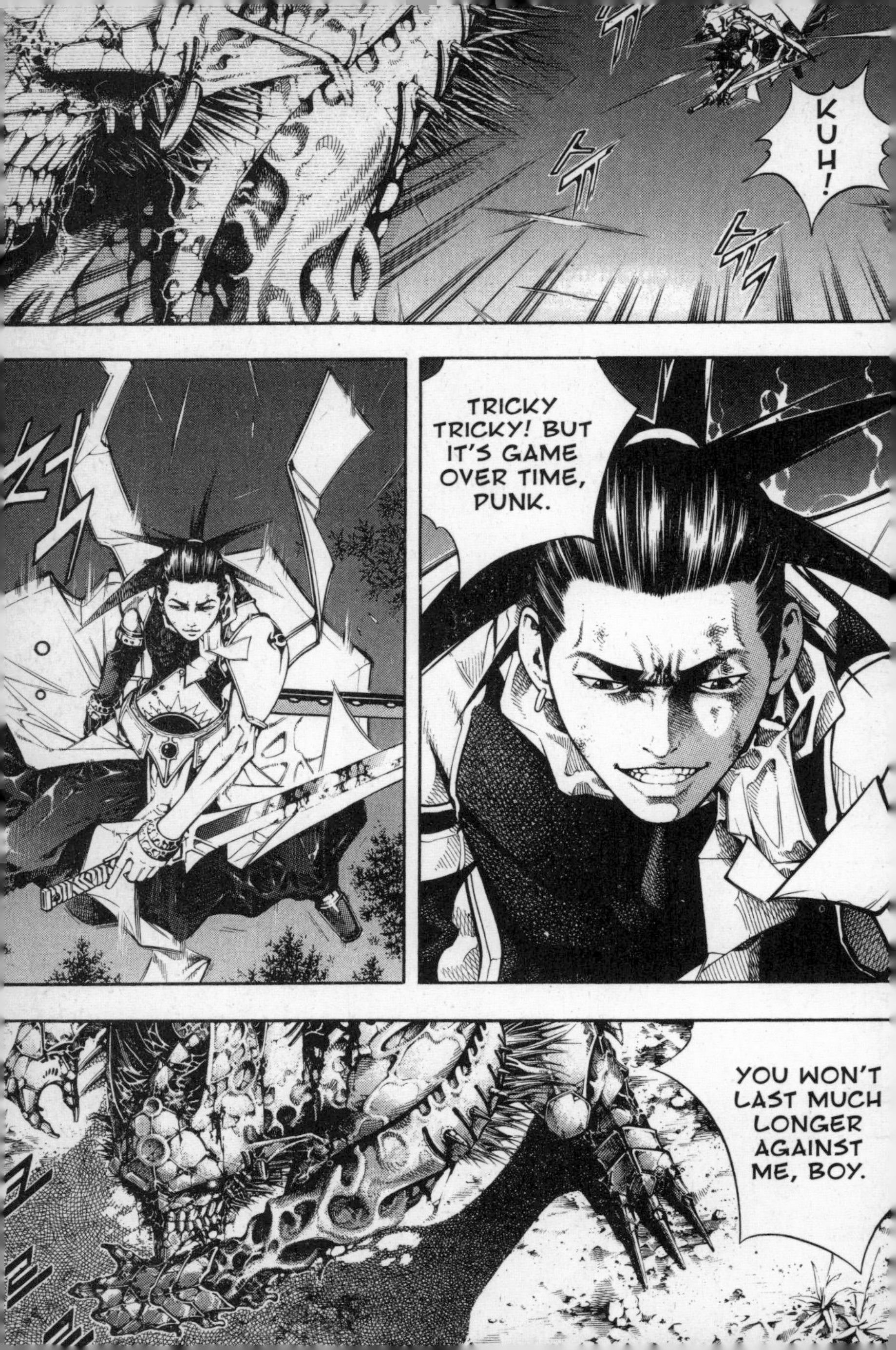
KUH!
TRICKY TRICKY! BUT IT'S GAME OVER TIME, PUNK.
YOU WON'T LAST MUCH LONGER AGAINST ME, BOY.

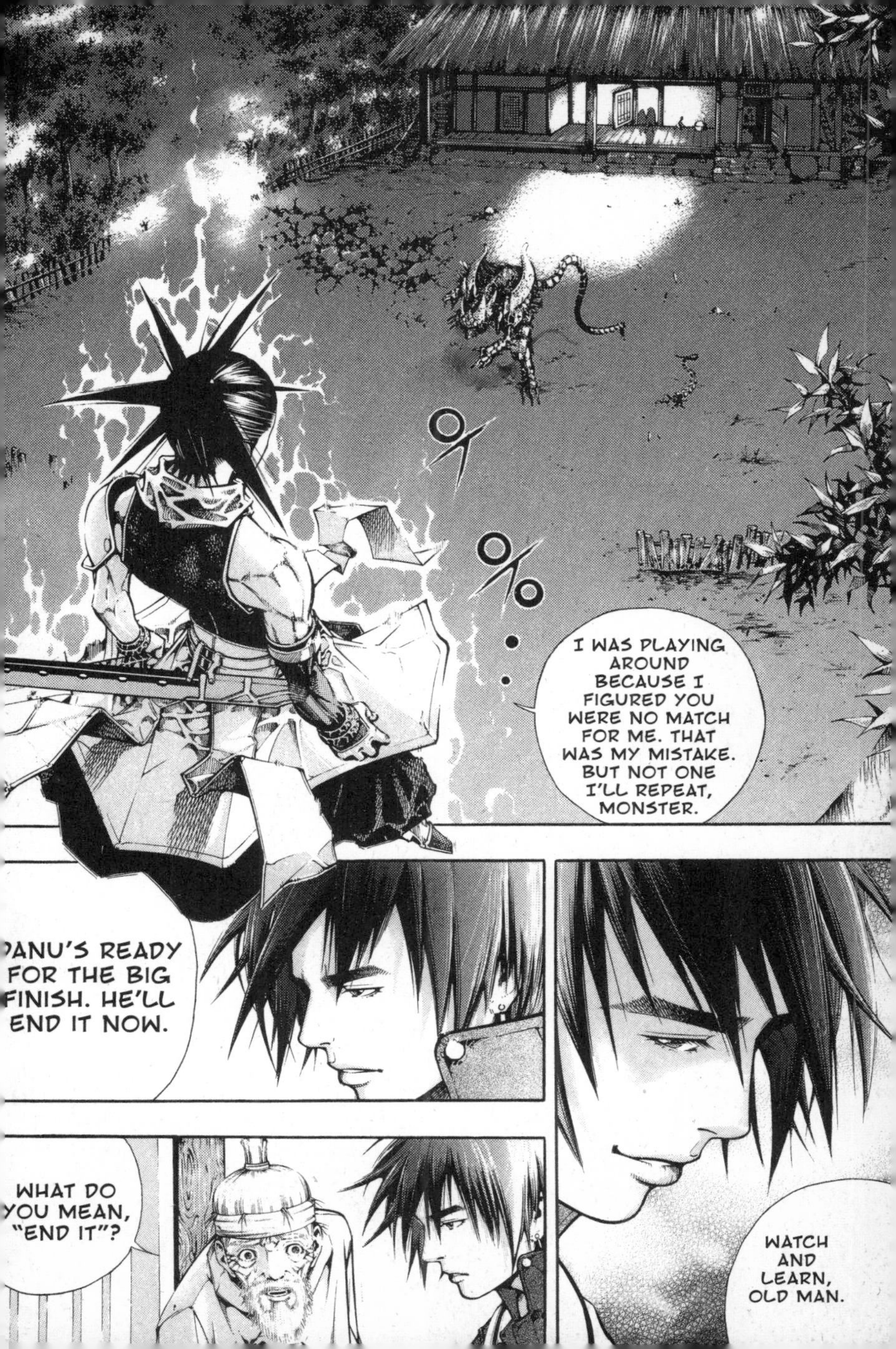
I WAS PLAYING AROUND BECAUSE I FIGURED YOU WERE NO MATCH FOR ME. THAT WAS MY MISTAKE. BUT NOT ONE I'LL REPEAT, MONSTER.
PANU'S READY FOR THE BIG FINISH. HE'LL END IT NOW.
WHAT DO YOU MEAN, "END IT"?
WATCH AND LEARN, OLD MAN.

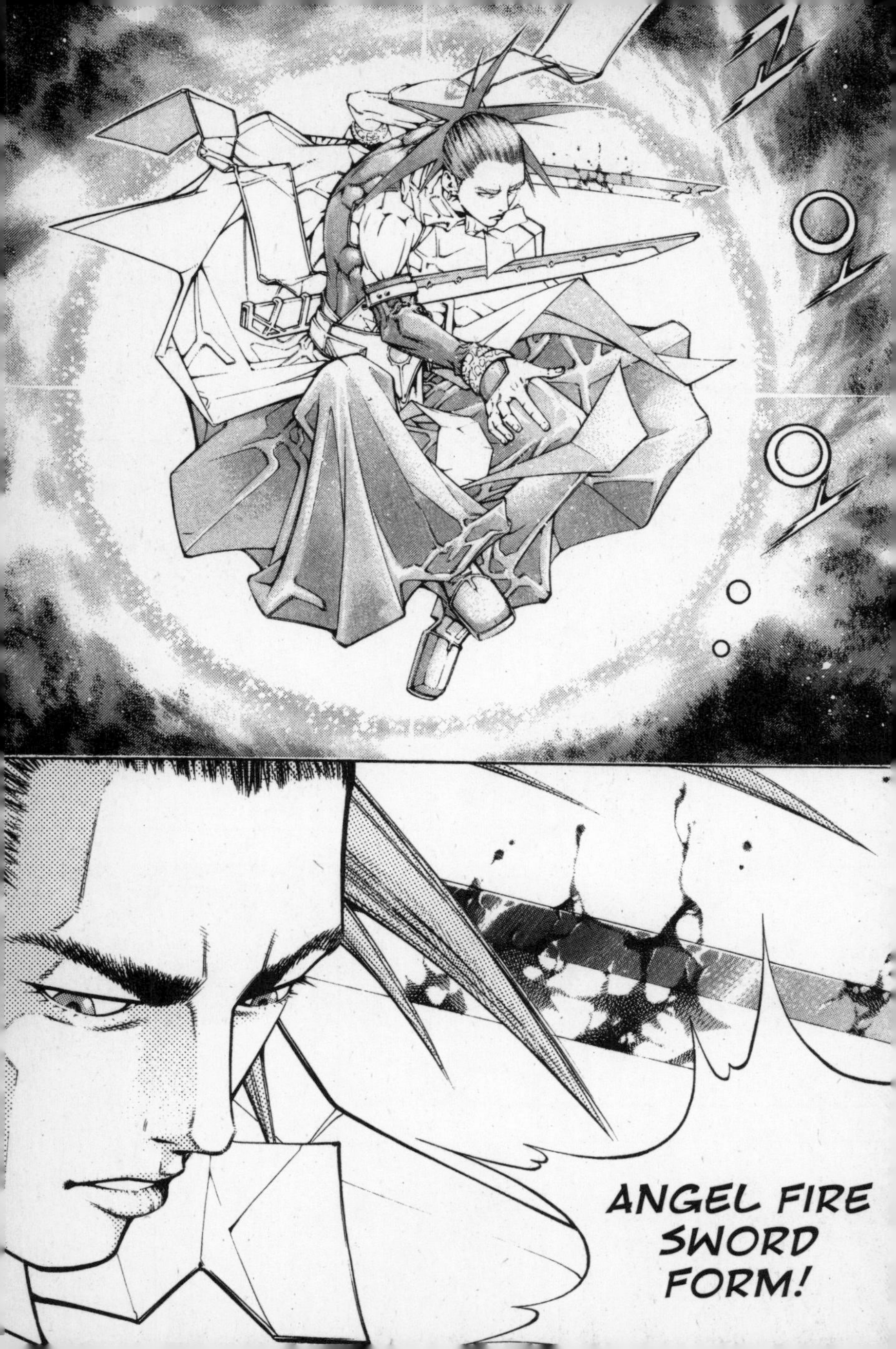
ANGEL FIRE SWORD FORM!

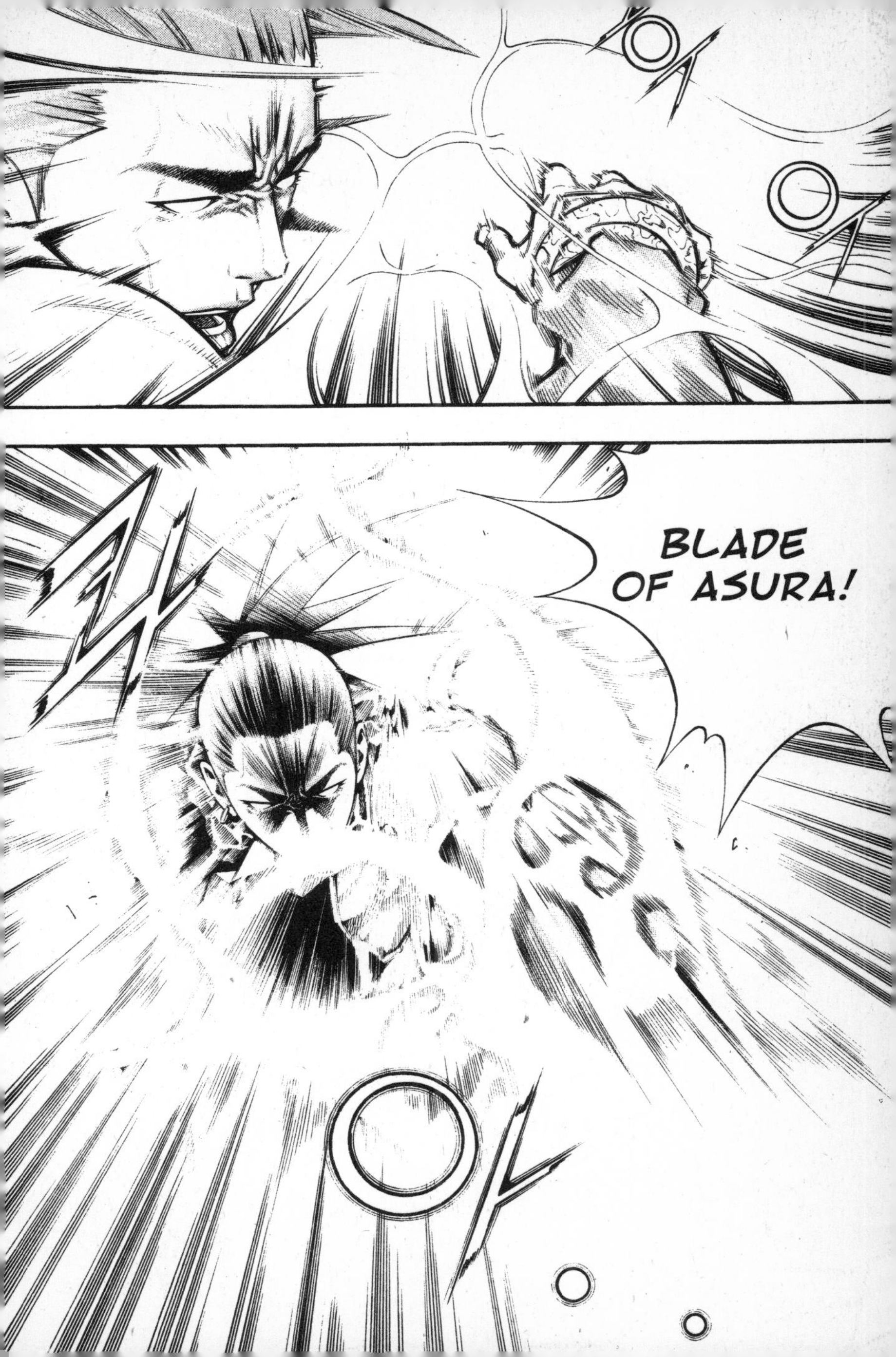
BLADE OF ASURA!

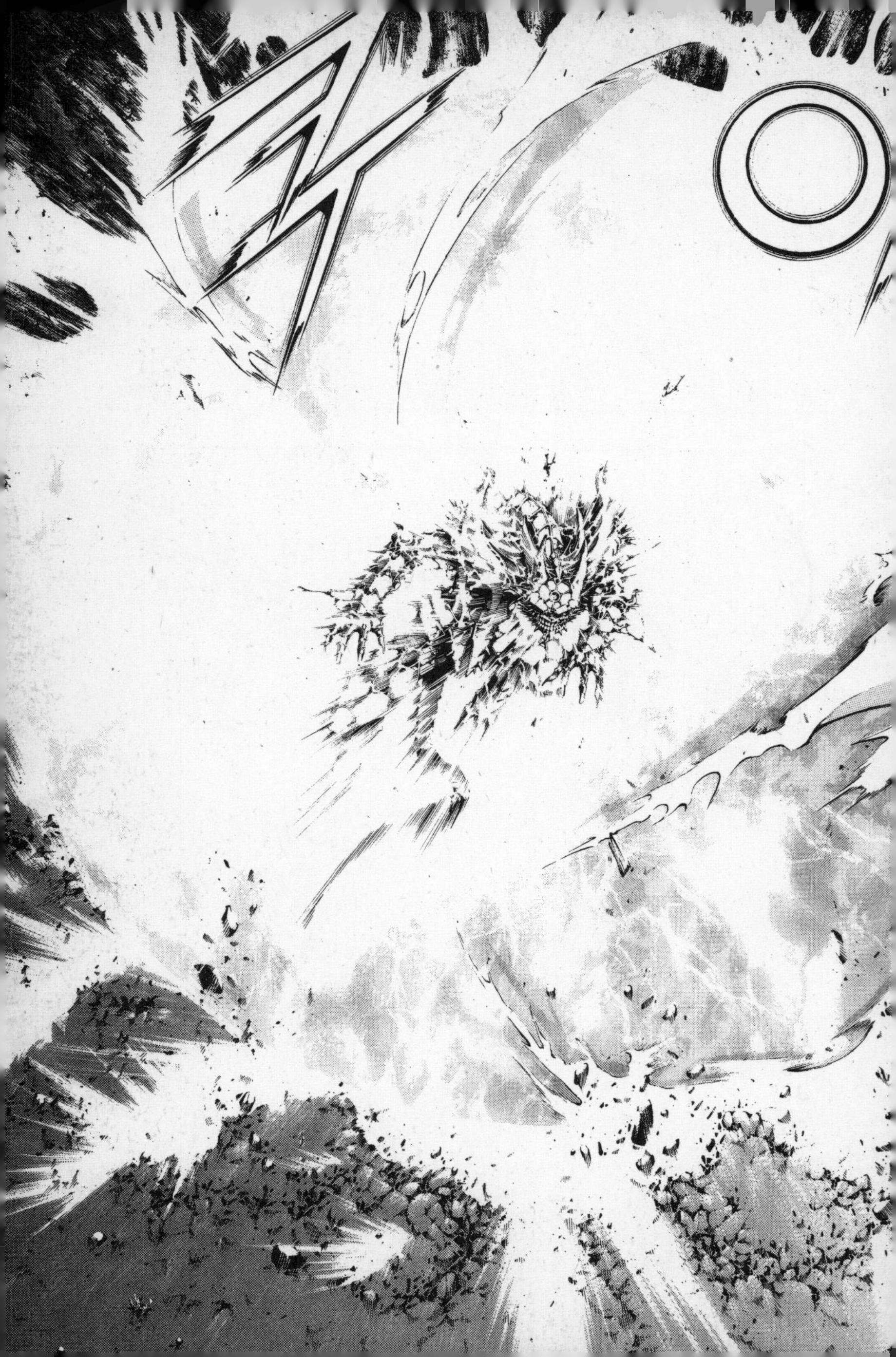

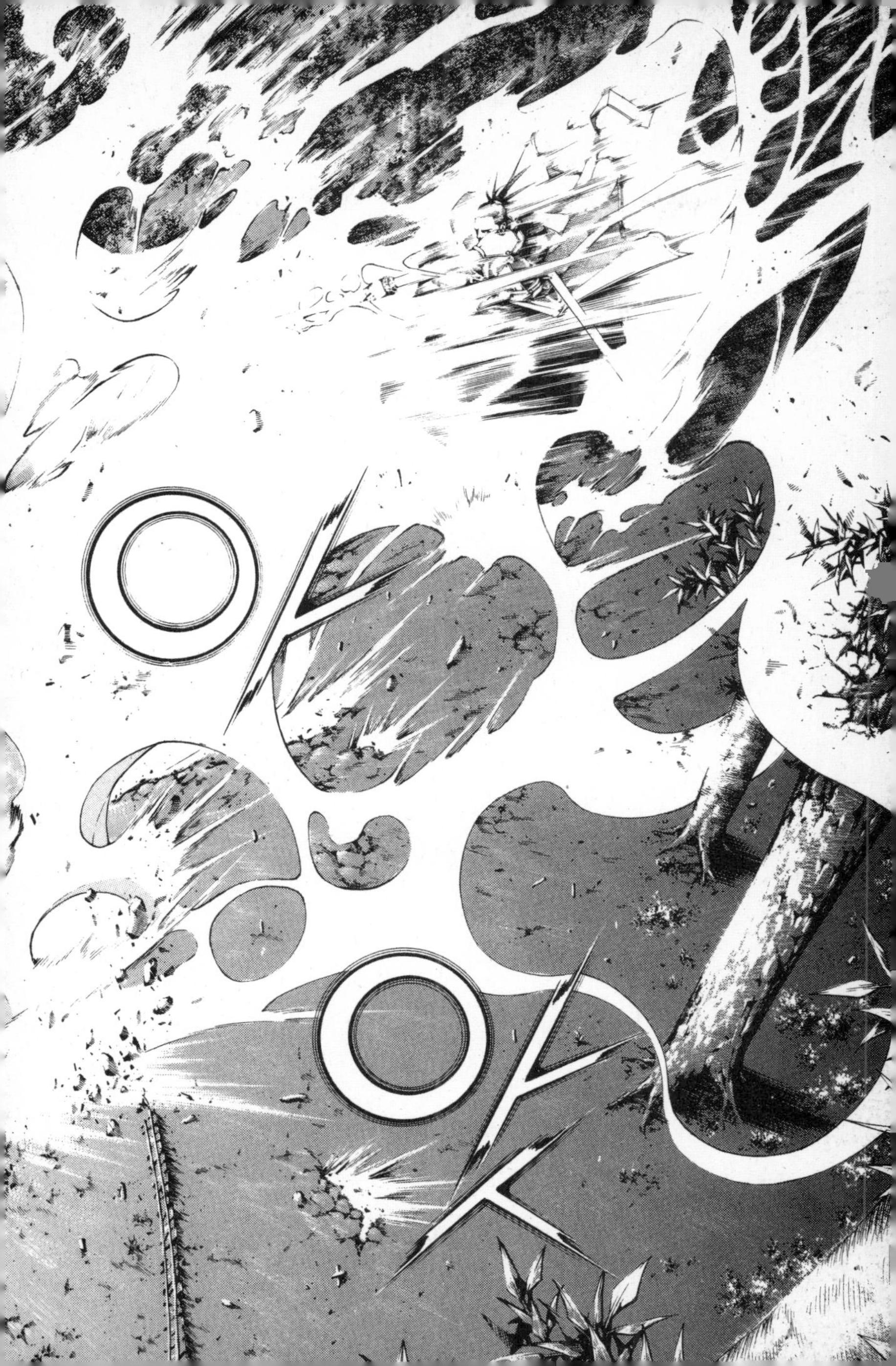

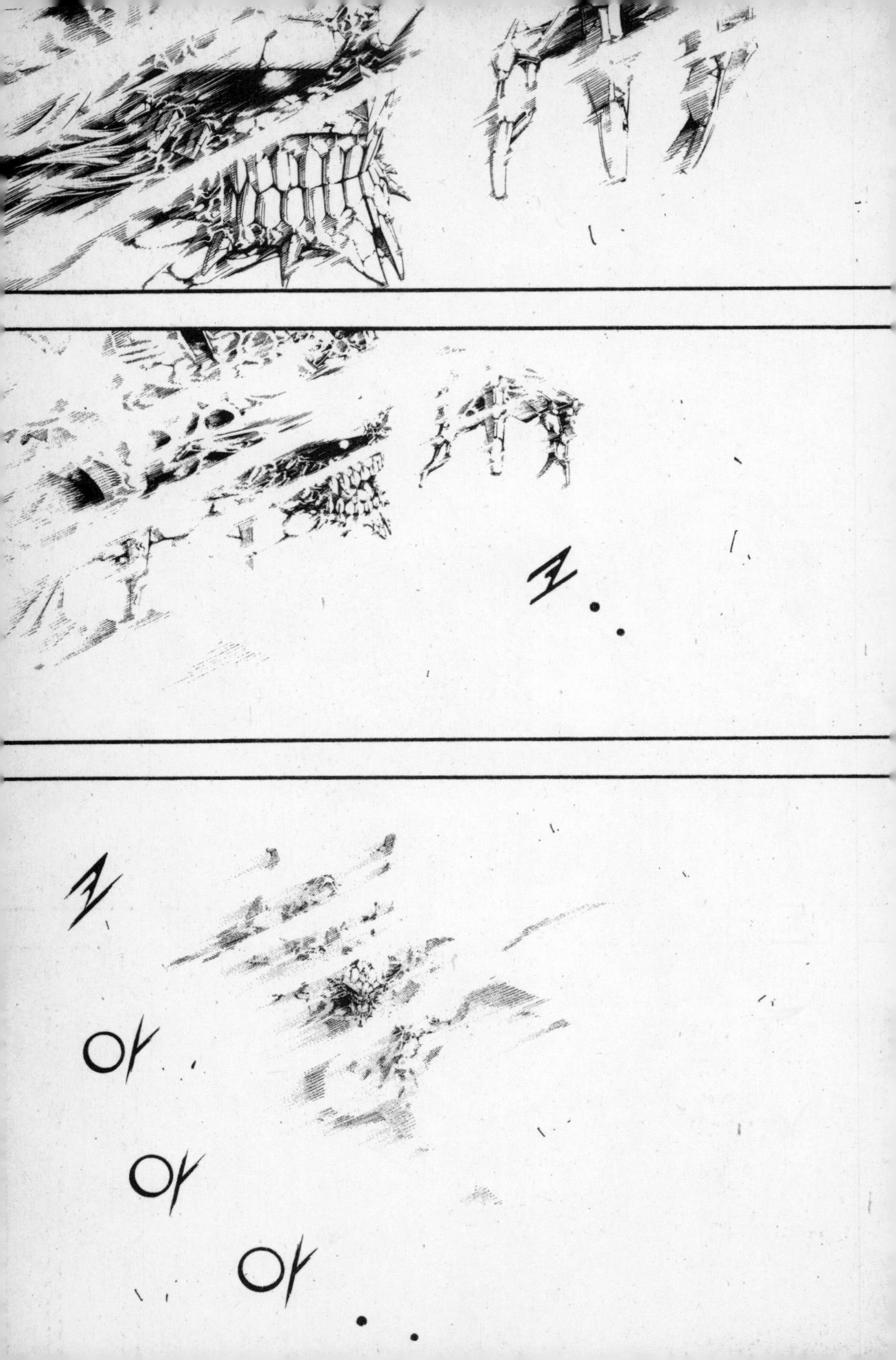

즈..
즈
야..
야
야..

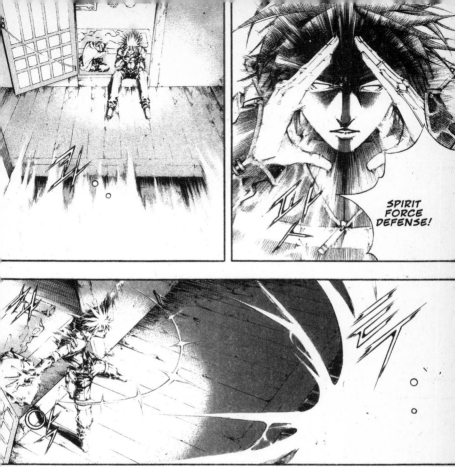

SPIRIT
FORCE
DEFENSE!

......

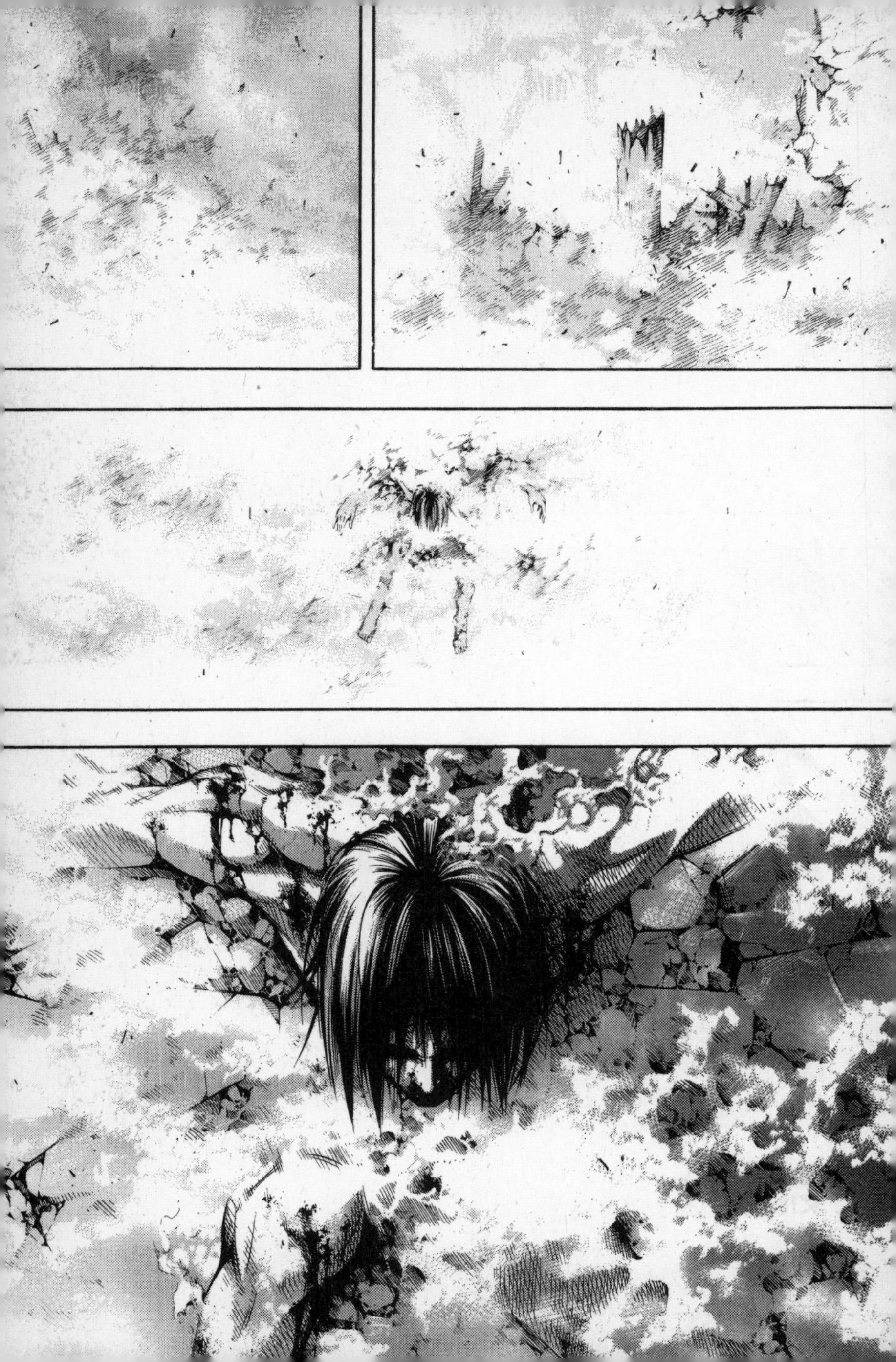

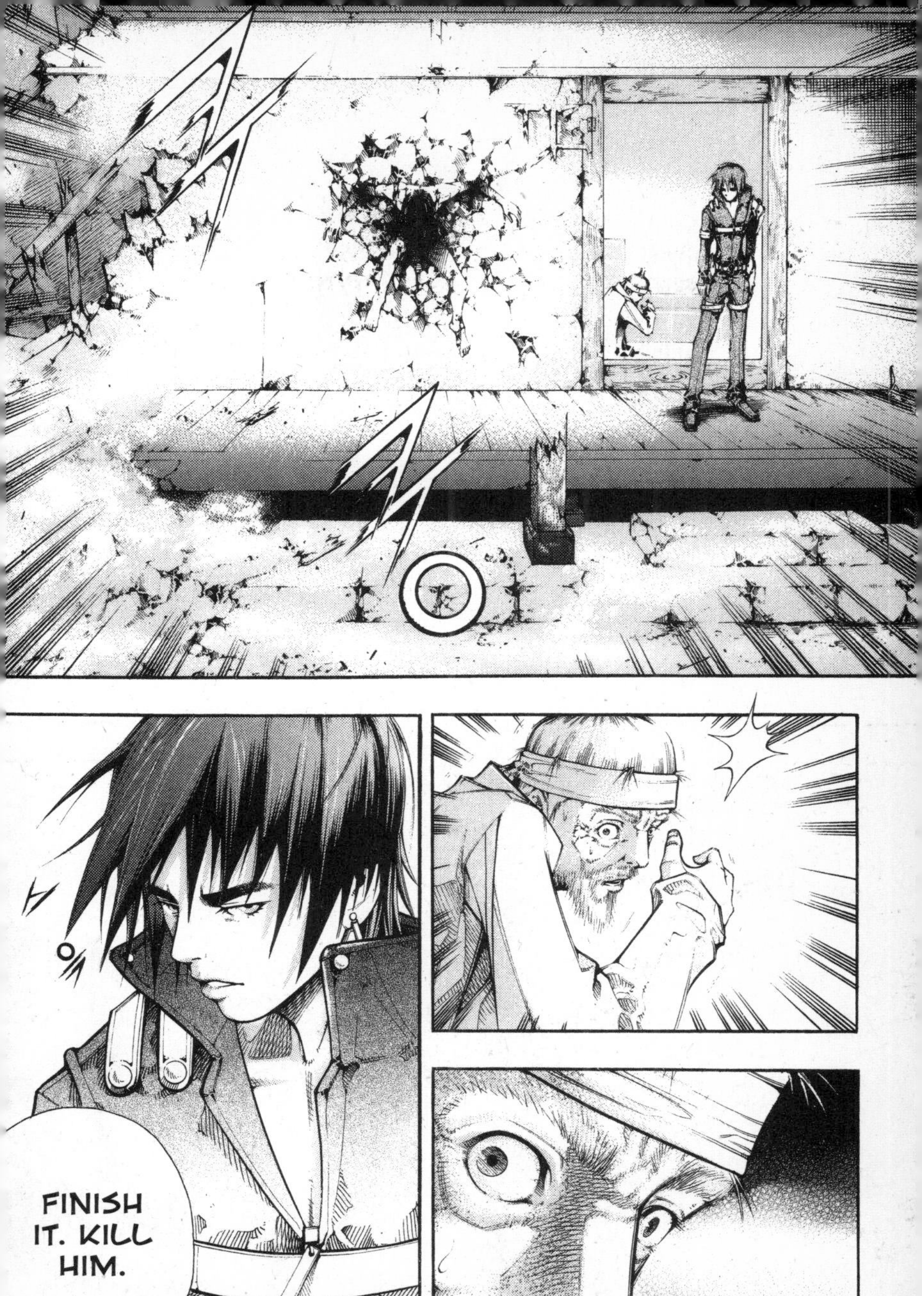
FINISH IT. KILL HIM.

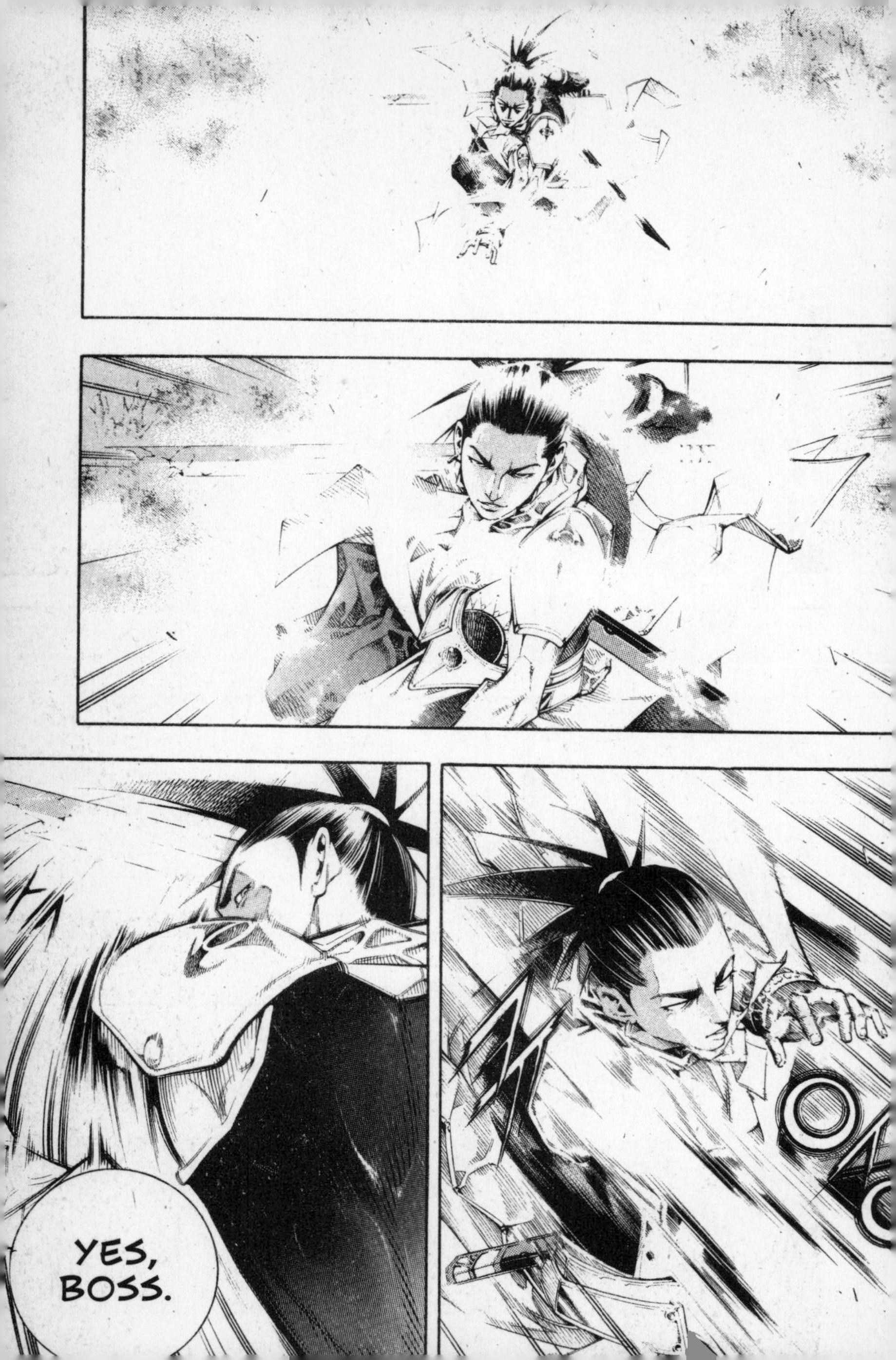
YES, BOSS.

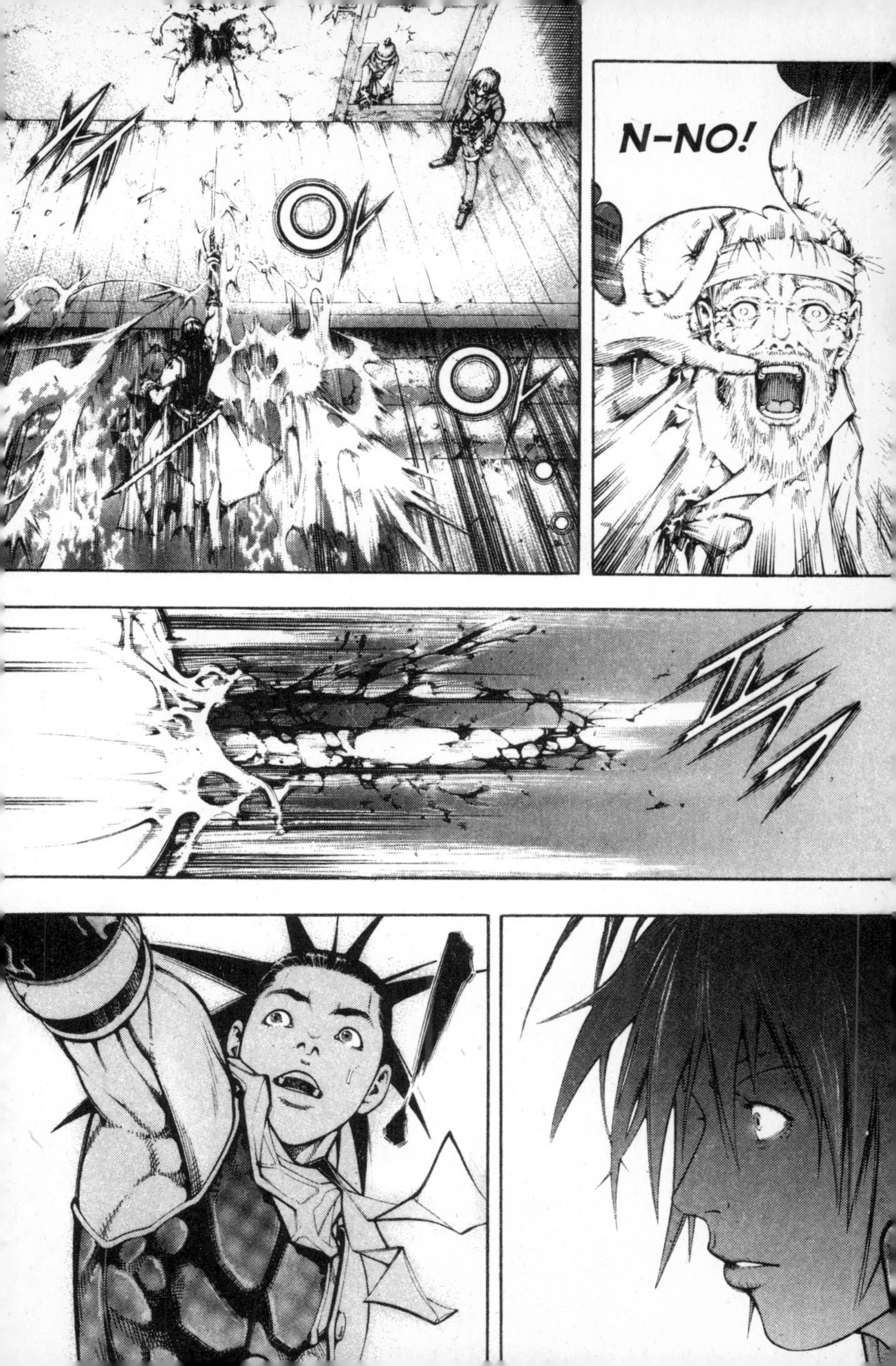
N-NO!

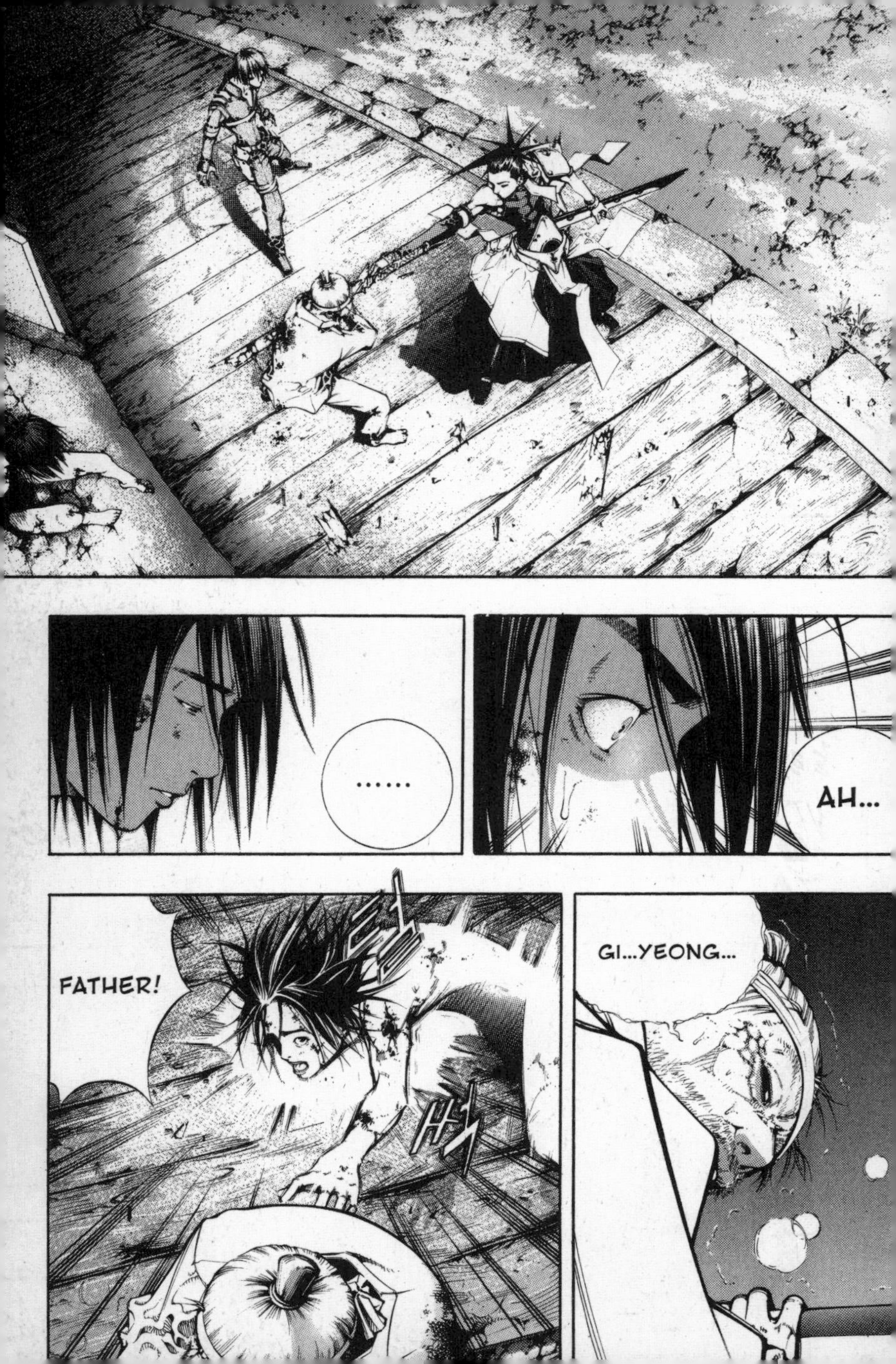

......
AH...
FATHER!
GI...YEONG...

COUGH

COUGH

DON'T PULL THE SWORD OUT. LEAVE IT IN.

I COULDN'T STOP IN TIME, BOSS.

I STOPPED THE BLEEDING, BUT IT WENT RIGHT THROUGH THE ARTERIES. HE WON'T MAKE IT.

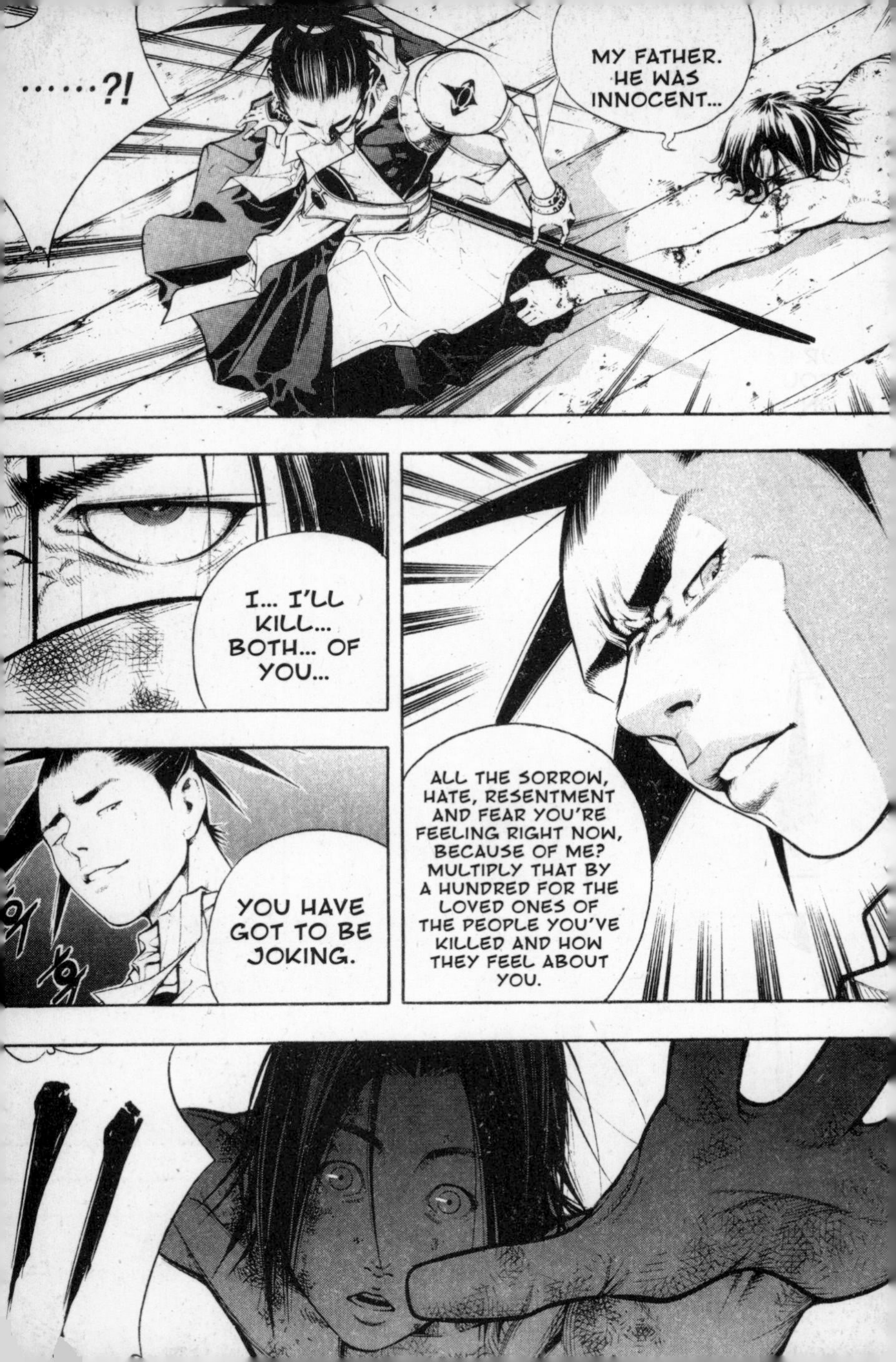
MY FATHER. HE WAS INNOCENT...
......?!
ALL THE SORROW, HATE, RESENTMENT AND FEAR YOU'RE FEELING RIGHT NOW, BECAUSE OF ME? MULTIPLY THAT BY A HUNDRED FOR THE LOVED ONES OF THE PEOPLE YOU'VE KILLED AND HOW THEY FEEL ABOUT YOU.
I... I'LL KILL... BOTH... OF YOU...
YOU HAVE GOT TO BE JOKING.

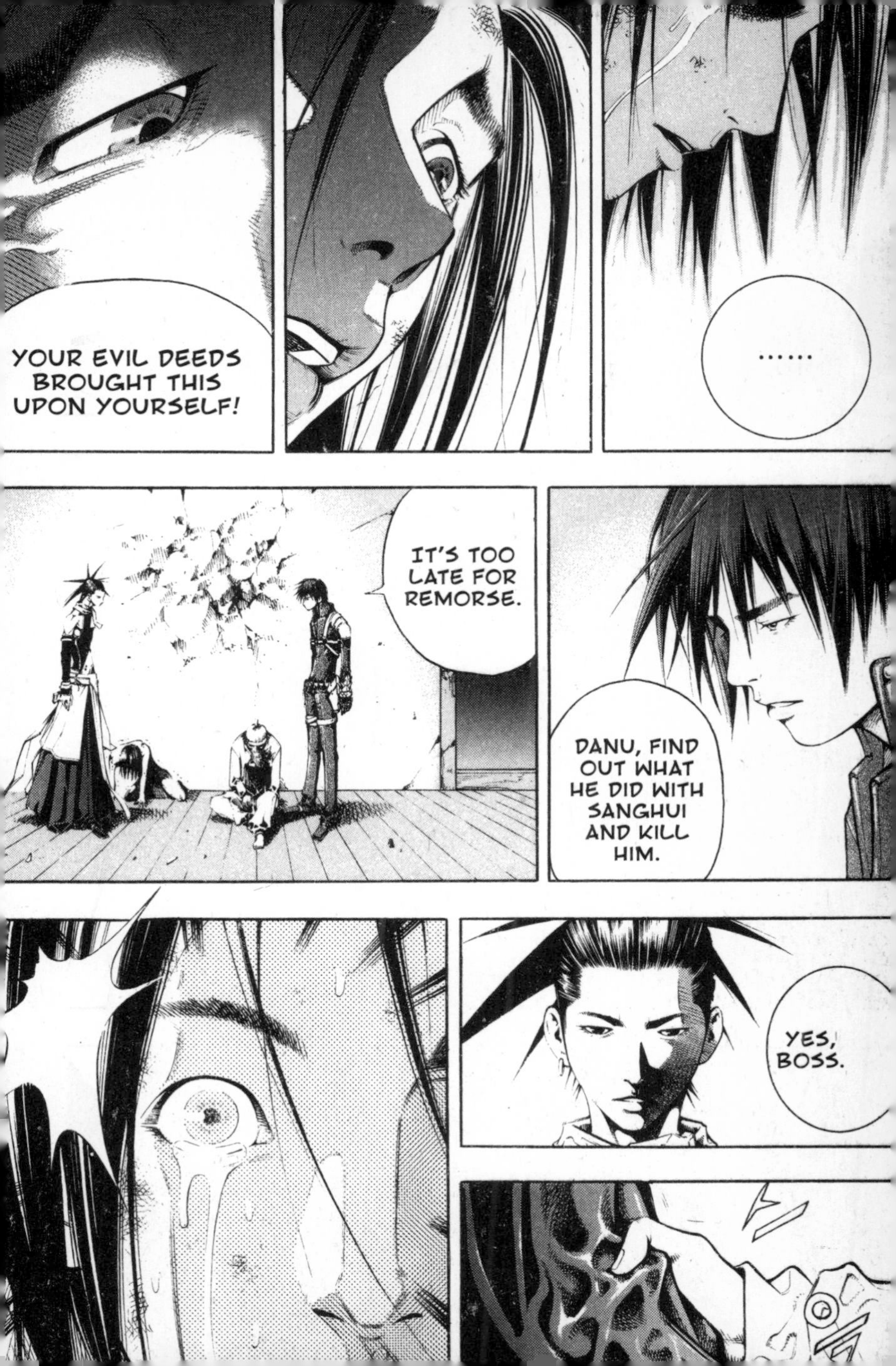
YOUR EVIL DEEDS BROUGHT THIS UPON YOURSELF!
......
IT'S TOO LATE FOR REMORSE.
DANU, FIND OUT WHAT HE DID WITH SANGHUI AND KILL HIM.
YES, BOSS.

PLEASE...
DON'T KILL...
GIYEONG...

ᄆ--

F-FATHER!

I'M SORRY,
FATHER...
THIS IS ALL
BECAUSE
OF ME...

I... I'M JUST
GOING... TO A
PLACE WHERE
I SHOULD'VE...
GONE... LONG...
AGO...

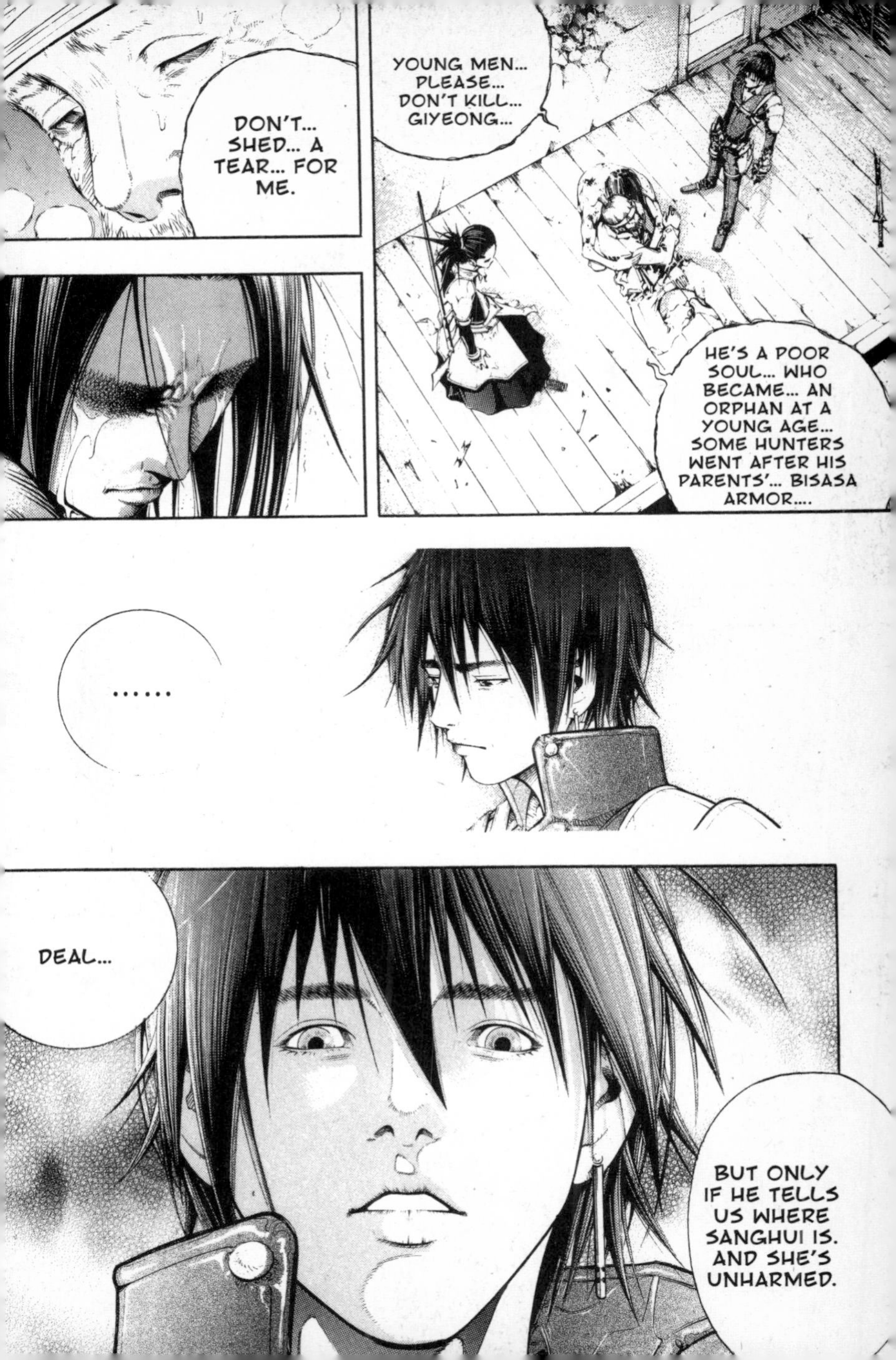
YOUNG MEN... PLEASE... DON'T KILL... GIYEONG...
DON'T... SHED... A TEAR... FOR ME.
HE'S A POOR SOUL... WHO BECAME... AN ORPHAN AT A YOUNG AGE... SOME HUNTERS WENT AFTER HIS PARENTS'... BISASA ARMOR....
......
DEAL...
BUT ONLY IF HE TELLS US WHERE SANGHUI IS. AND SHE'S UNHARMED.

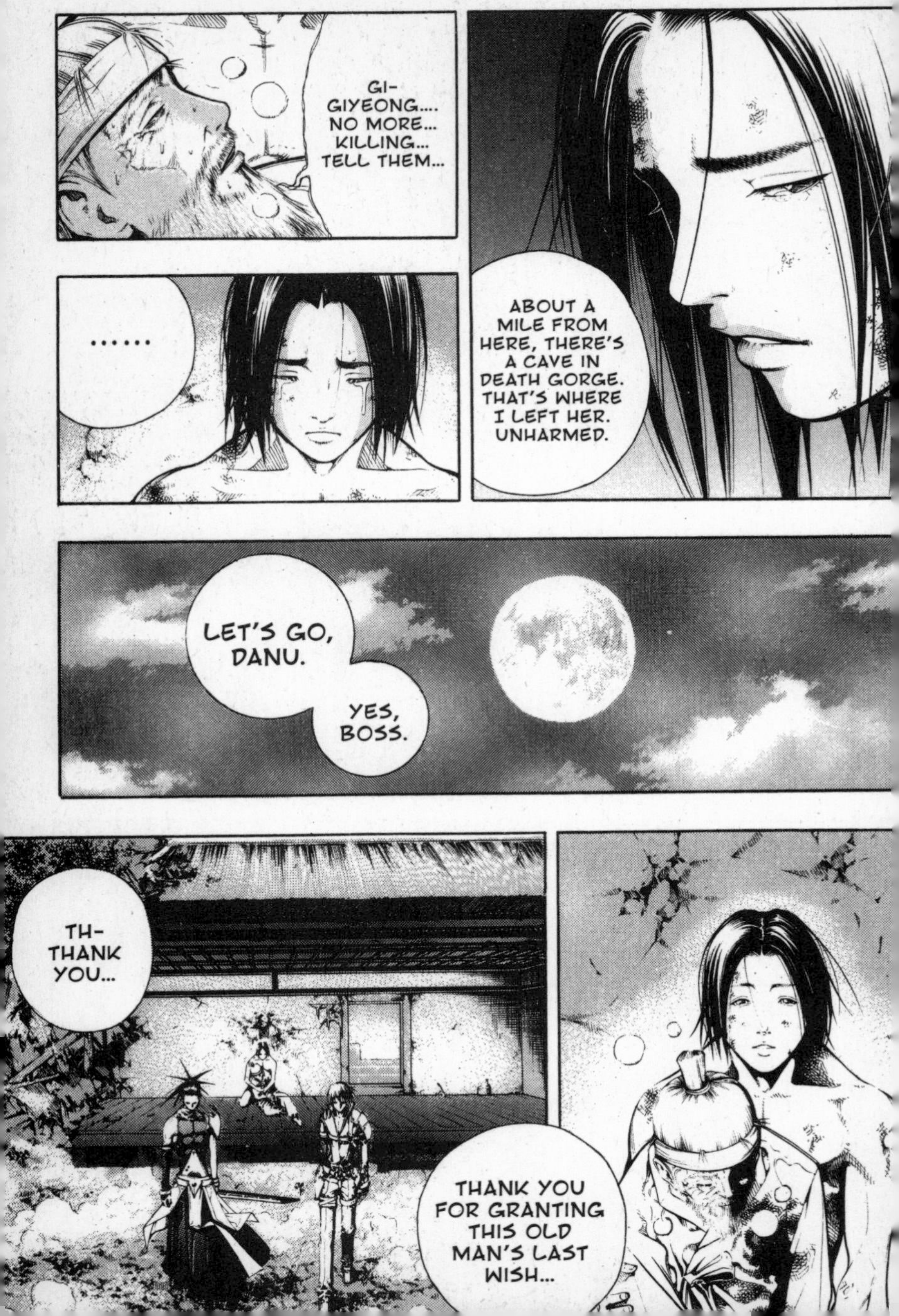
GI-
GIYEONG.... NO MORE... KILLING... TELL THEM...
ABOUT A MILE FROM HERE, THERE'S A CAVE IN DEATH GORGE. THAT'S WHERE I LEFT HER. UNHARMED.
......
LET'S GO, DANU.
YES, BOSS.
TH-
THANK YOU...
THANK YOU FOR GRANTING THIS OLD MAN'S LAST WISH...

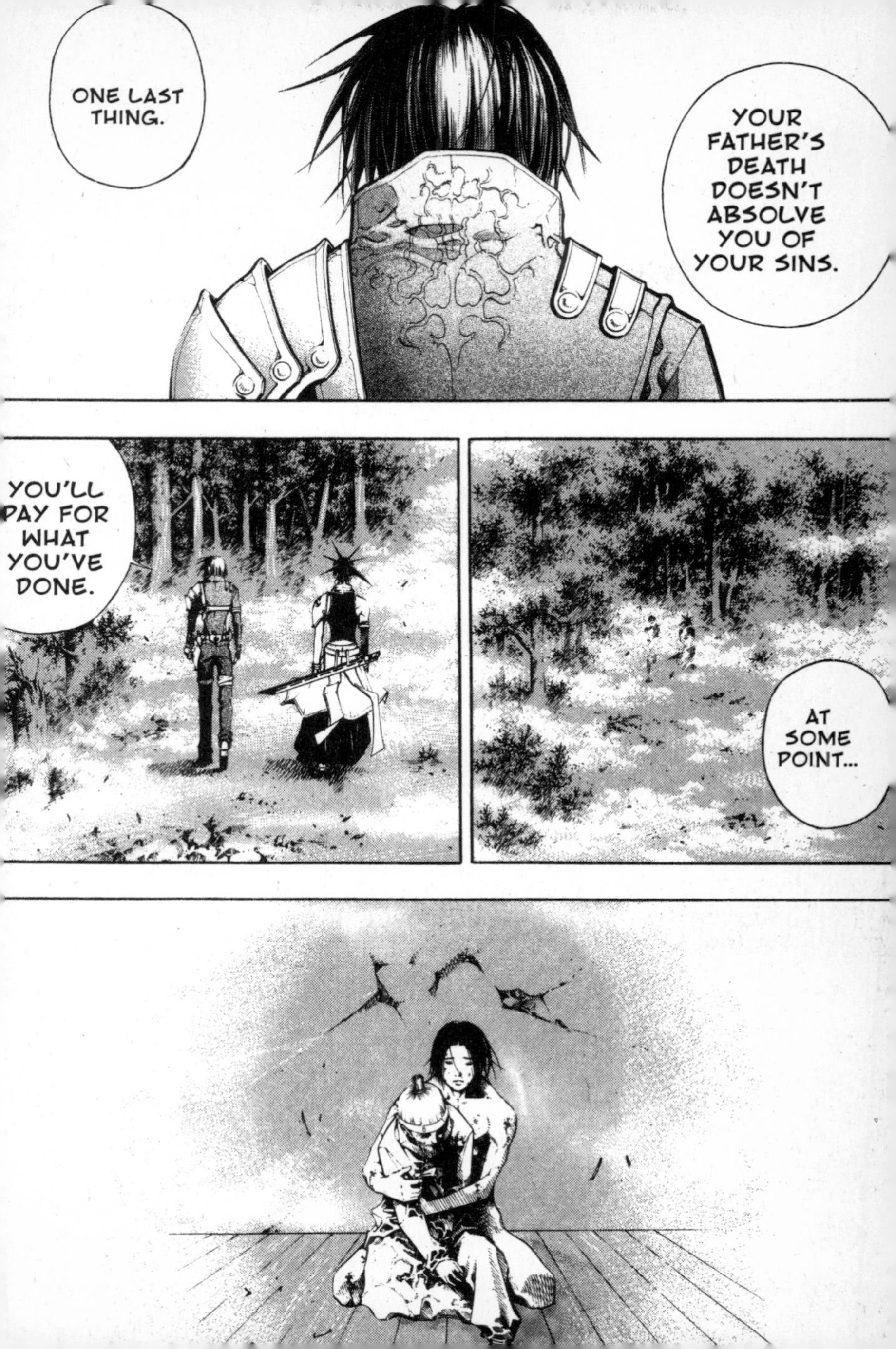
ONE LAST THING.
YOUR FATHER'S DEATH DOESN'T ABSOLVE YOU OF YOUR SINS.
YOU'LL PAY FOR WHAT YOU'VE DONE.
AT SOME POINT...

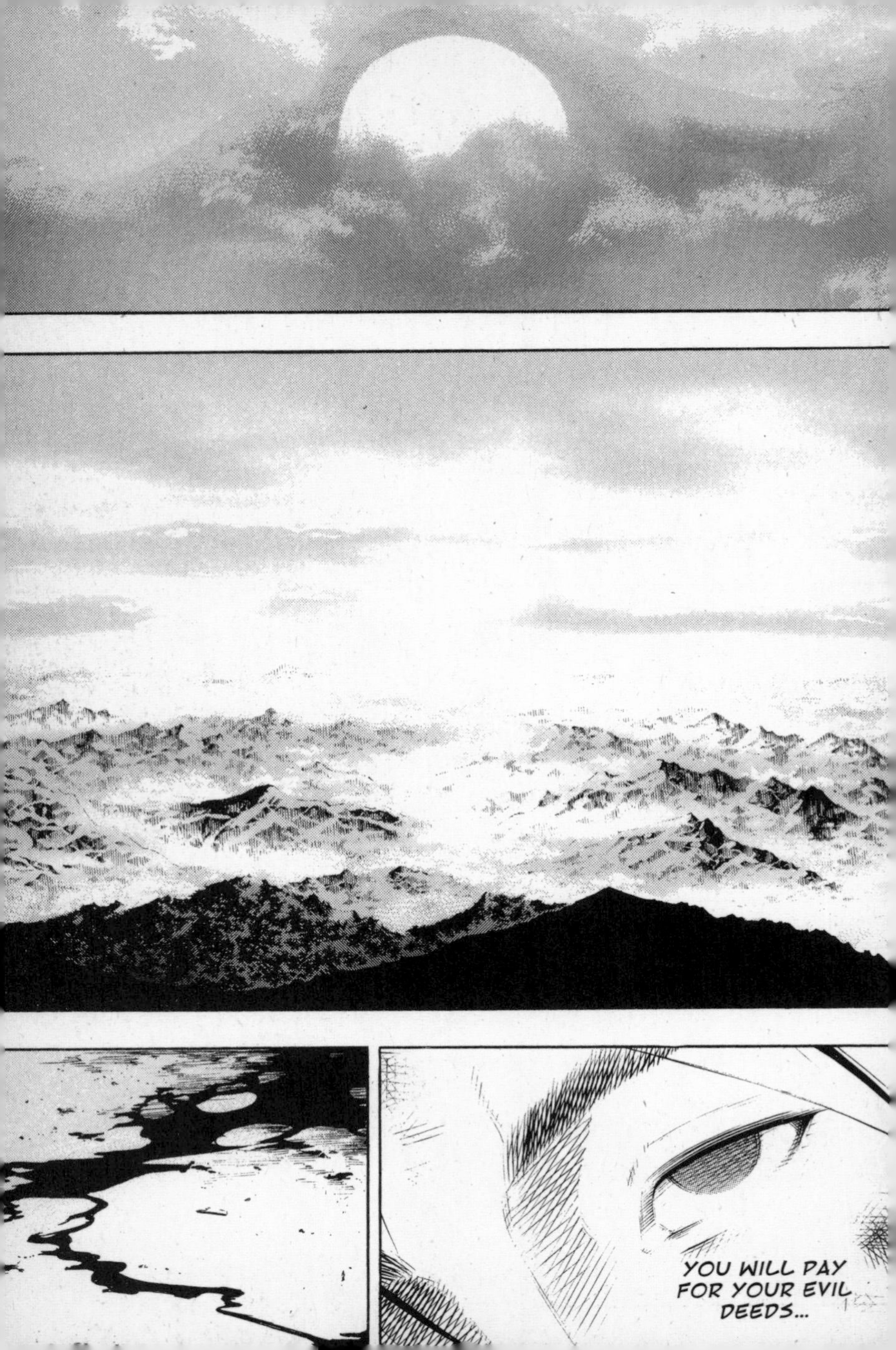
YOU WILL PAY FOR YOUR EVIL DEEDS...

AT SOME
POINT...

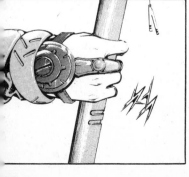

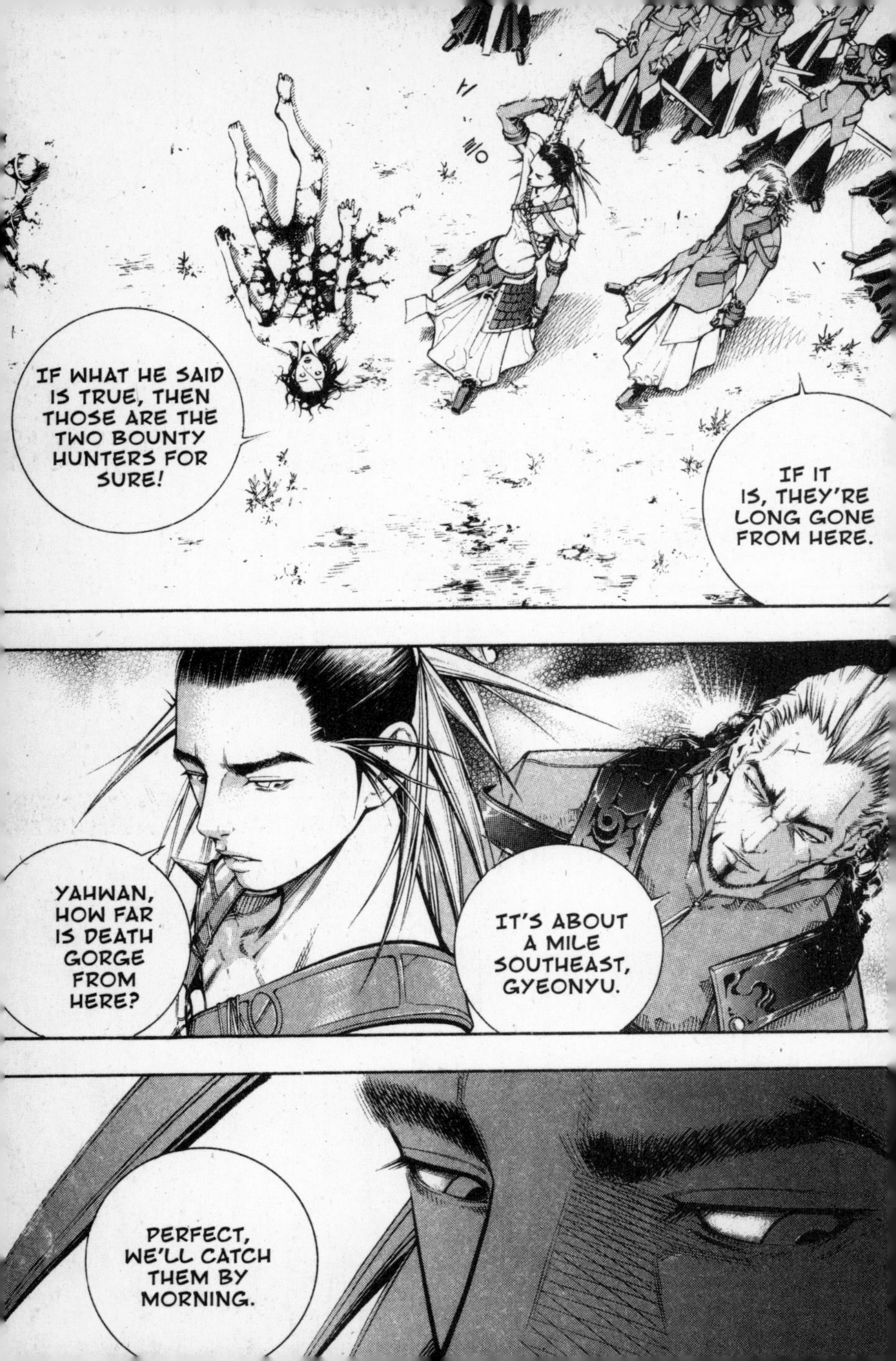
IF WHAT HE SAID IS TRUE, THEN THOSE ARE THE TWO BOUNTY HUNTERS FOR SURE!
IF IT IS, THEY'RE LONG GONE FROM HERE.
YAHWAN, HOW FAR IS DEATH GORGE FROM HERE?
IT'S ABOUT A MILE SOUTHEAST, GYEONYU.
PERFECT, WE'LL CATCH THEM BY MORNING.

Chapter 4
The Fall of Yuldo

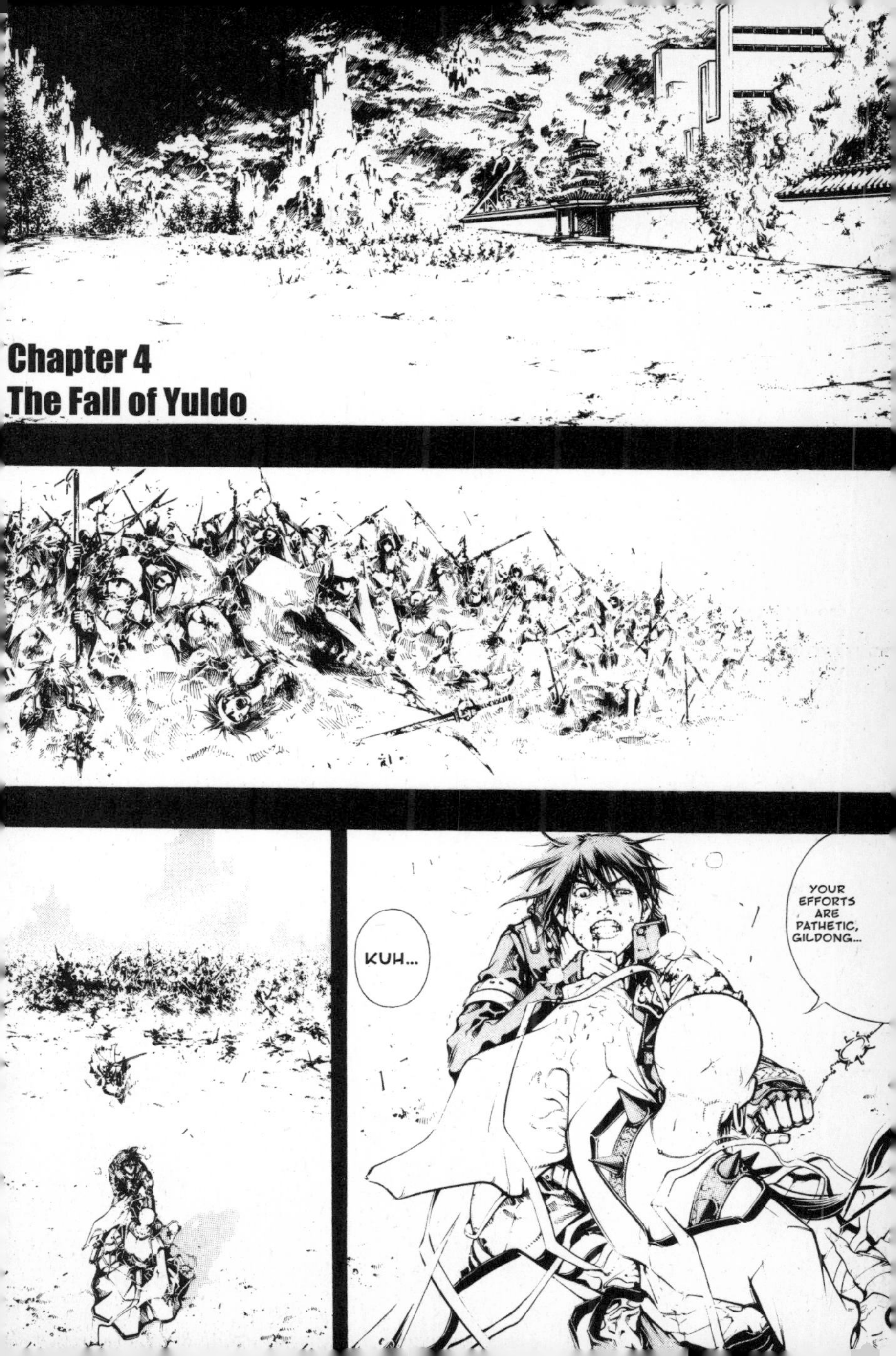
KUH...
YOUR EFFORTS ARE PATHETIC, GILDONG...

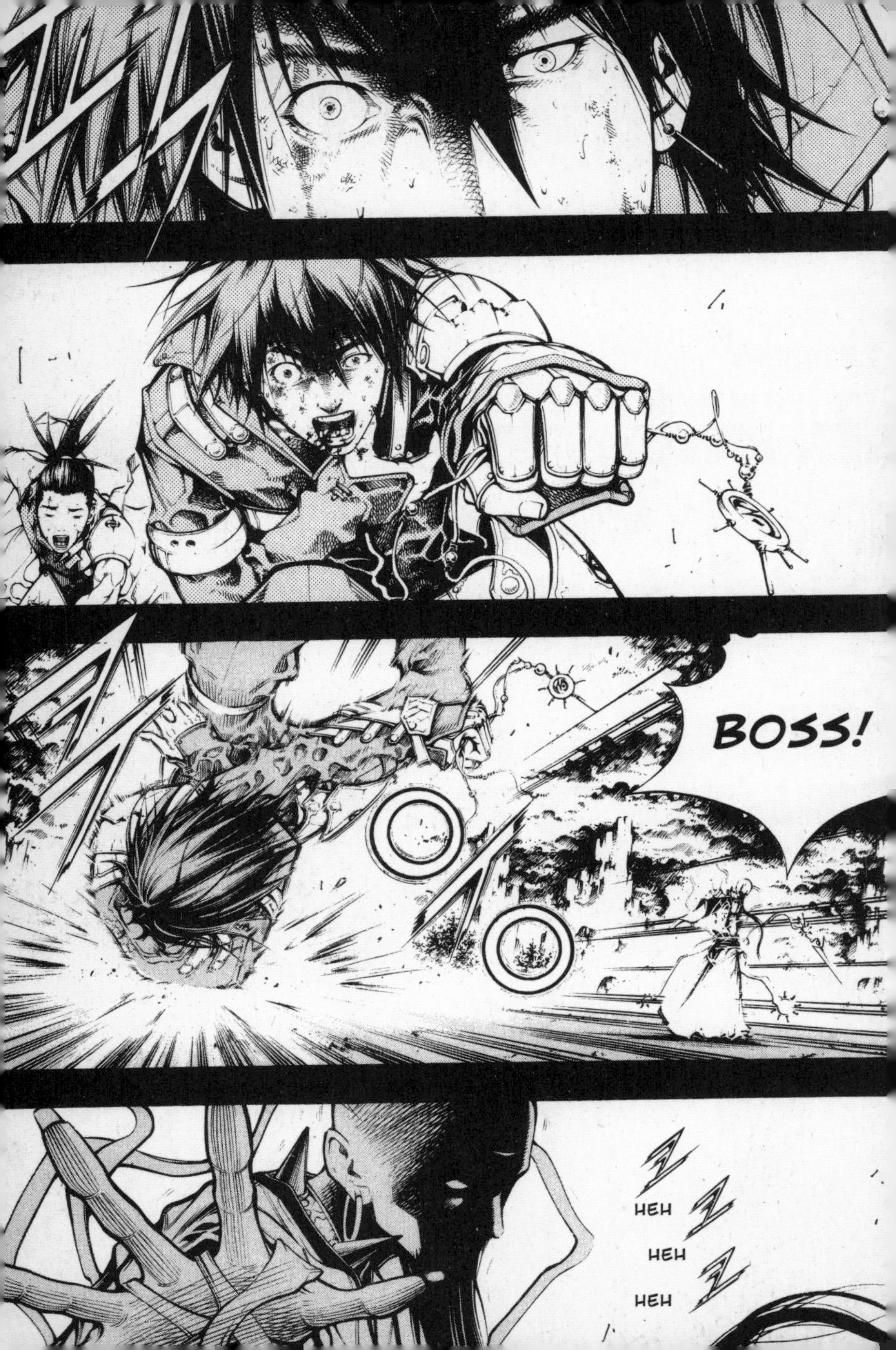
BOSS!
HEH
HEH
HEH

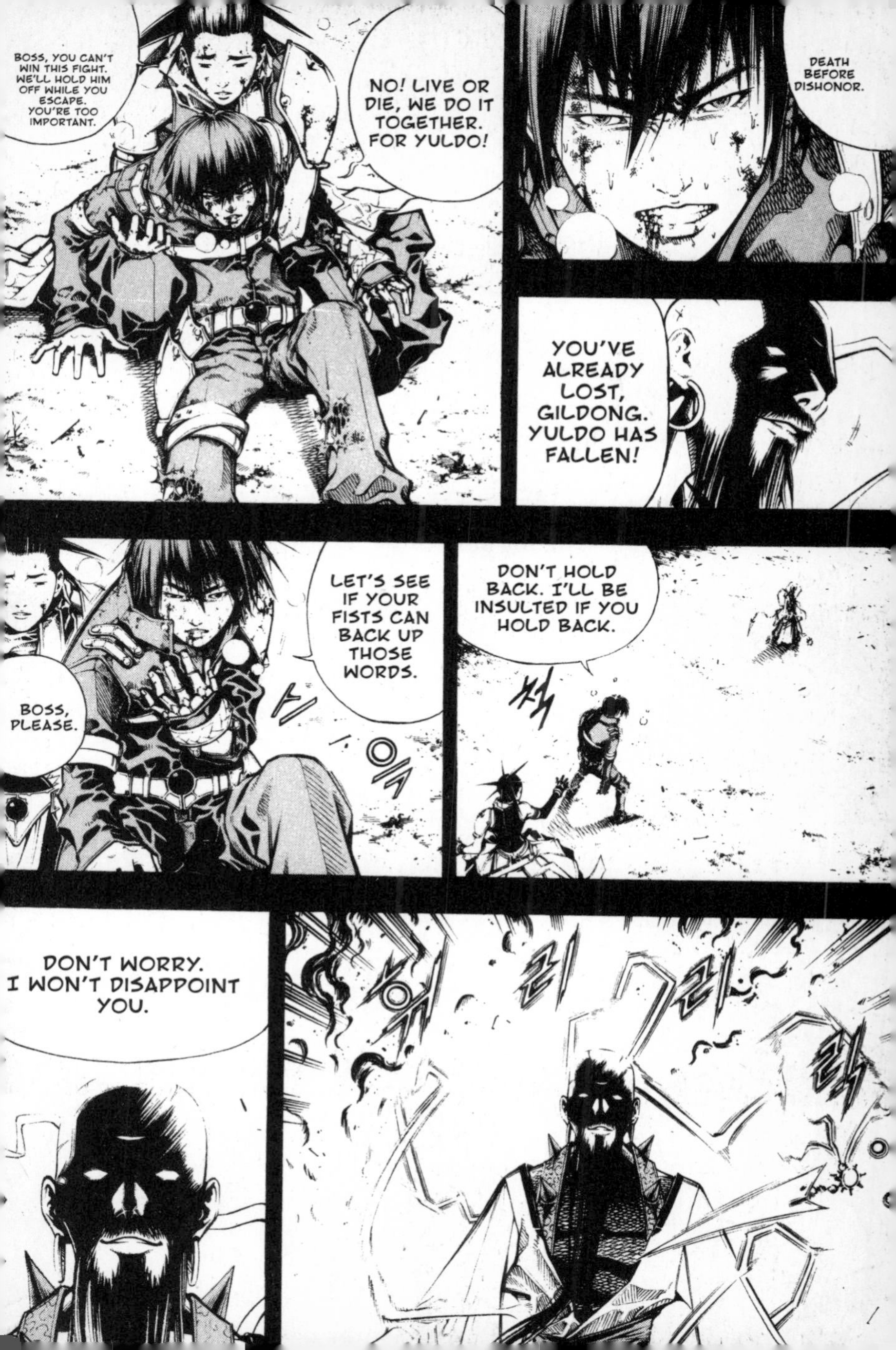
BOSS, YOU CAN'T WIN THIS FIGHT. WE'LL HOLD HIM OFF WHILE YOU ESCAPE. YOU'RE TOO IMPORTANT.
NO! LIVE OR DIE, WE DO IT TOGETHER. FOR YULDO!
DEATH BEFORE DISHONOR.
YOU'VE ALREADY LOST, GILDONG. YULDO HAS FALLEN!
LET'S SEE IF YOUR FISTS CAN BACK UP THOSE WORDS.
BOSS, PLEASE.
DON'T HOLD BACK. I'LL BE INSULTED IF YOU HOLD BACK.
DON'T WORRY. I WON'T DISAPPOINT YOU.

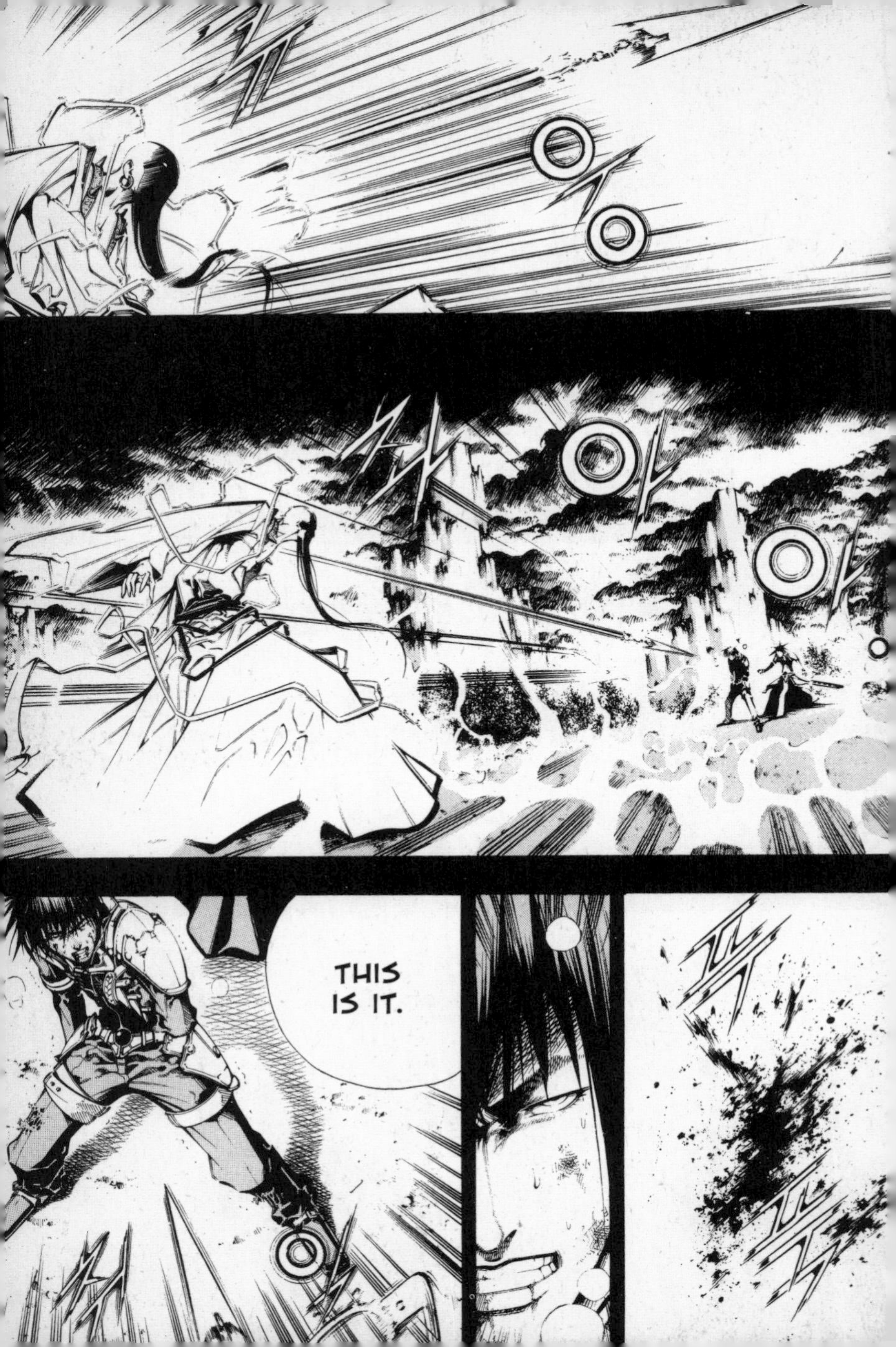
THIS IS IT.

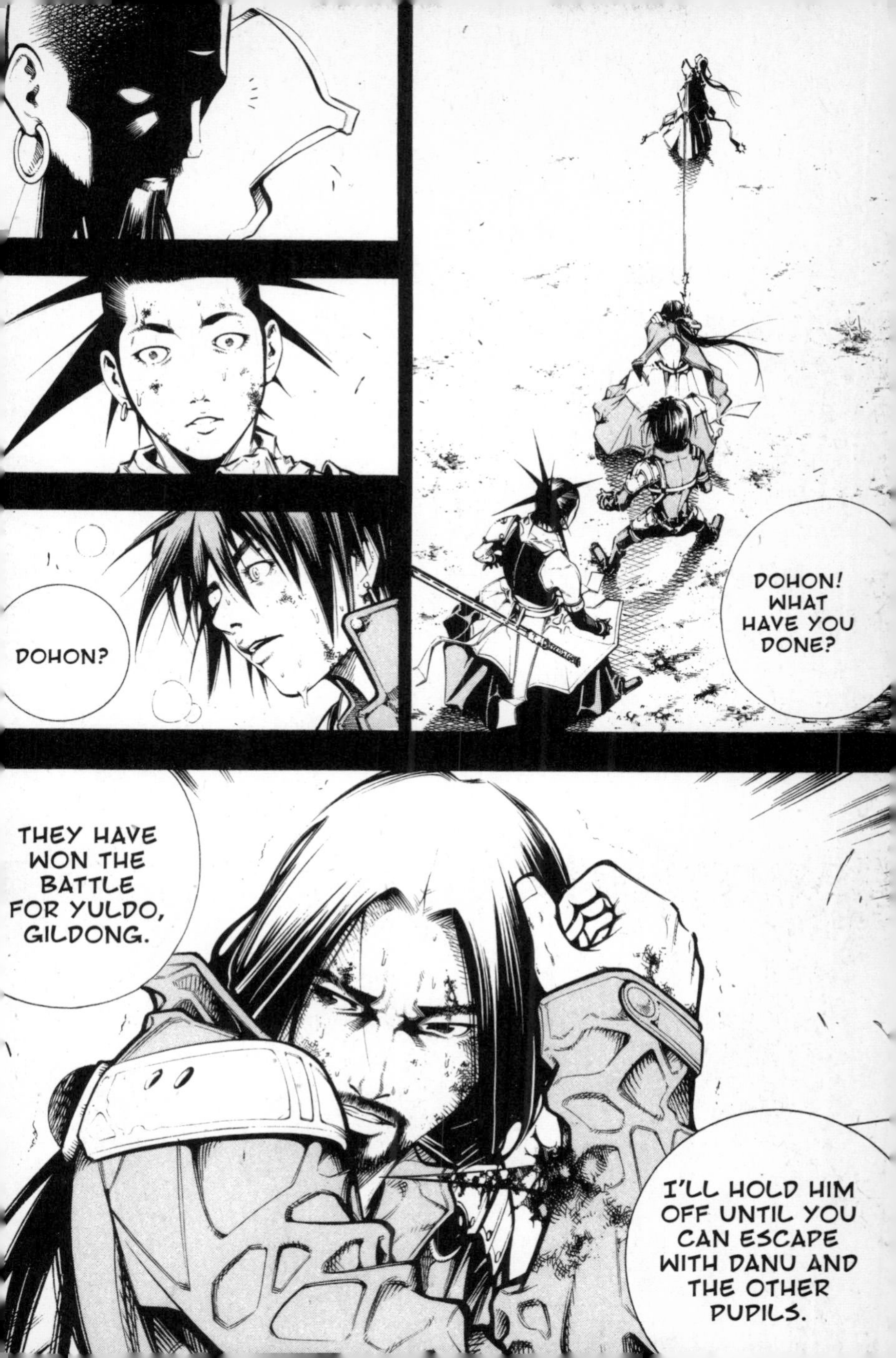
DOHON! WHAT HAVE YOU DONE?
DOHON?
THEY HAVE WON THE BATTLE FOR YULDO, GILDONG.
I'LL HOLD HIM OFF UNTIL YOU CAN ESCAPE WITH DANU AND THE OTHER PUPILS.

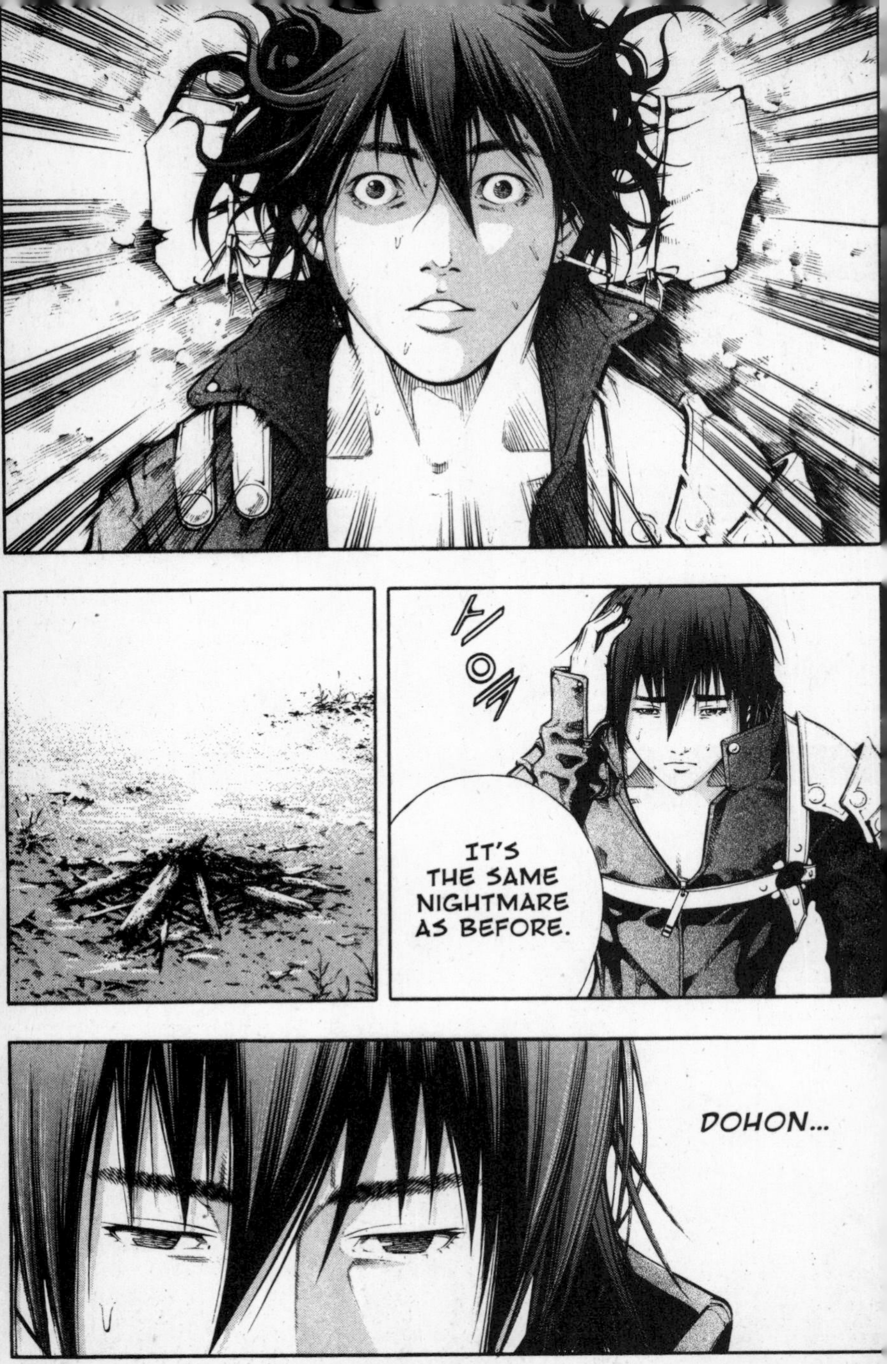
IT'S THE SAME NIGHTMARE AS BEFORE.
DOHON...

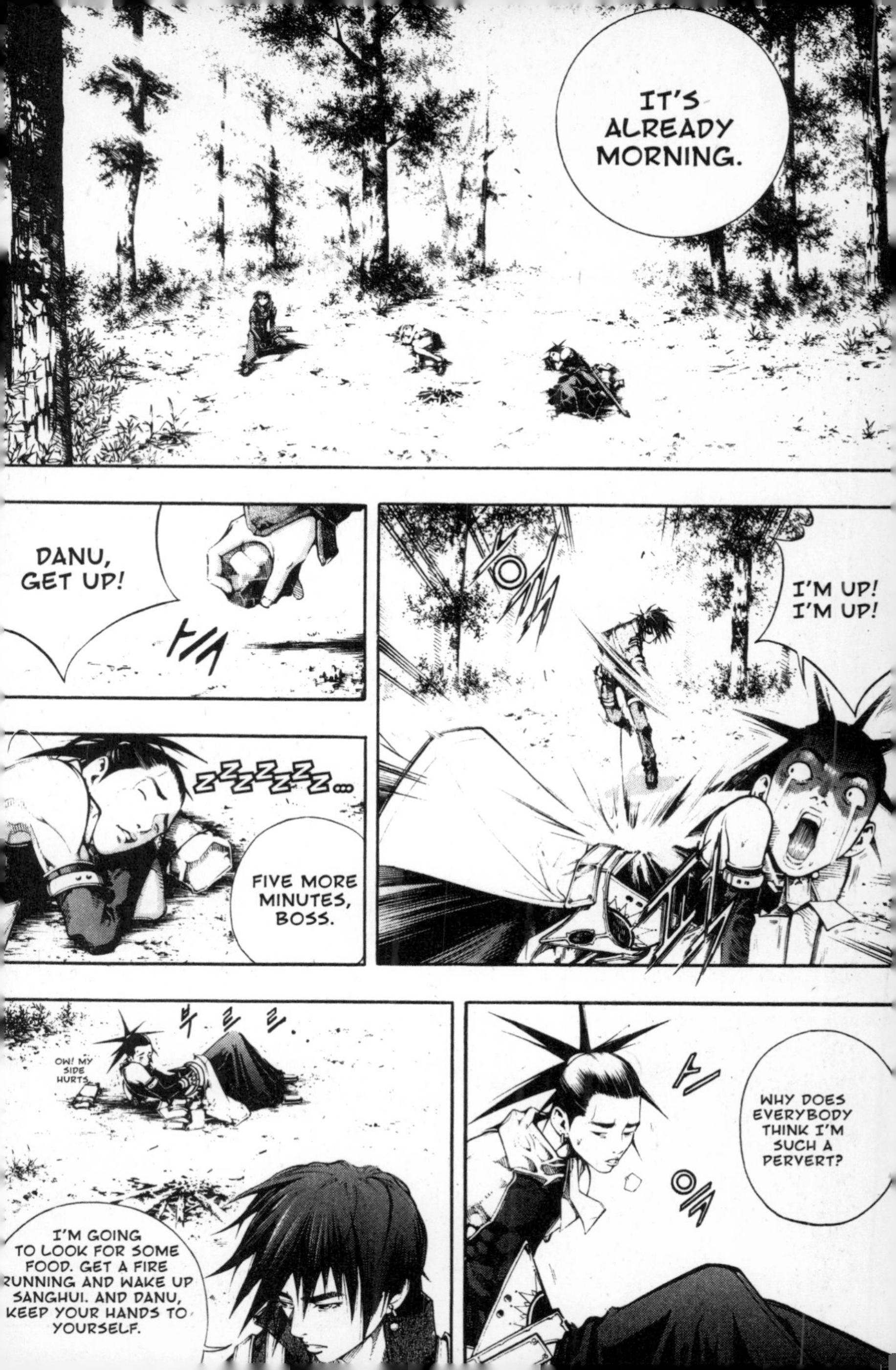
IT'S ALREADY MORNING.
DANU, GET UP!
ZZZZZZZ...
FIVE MORE MINUTES, BOSS.
I'M UP! I'M UP!
부르르.
OW! MY SIDE HURTS
I'M GOING TO LOOK FOR SOME FOOD. GET A FIRE RUNNING AND WAKE UP SANGHUI. AND DANU, KEEP YOUR HANDS TO YOURSELF.
WHY DOES EVERYBODY THINK I'M SUCH A PERVERT?

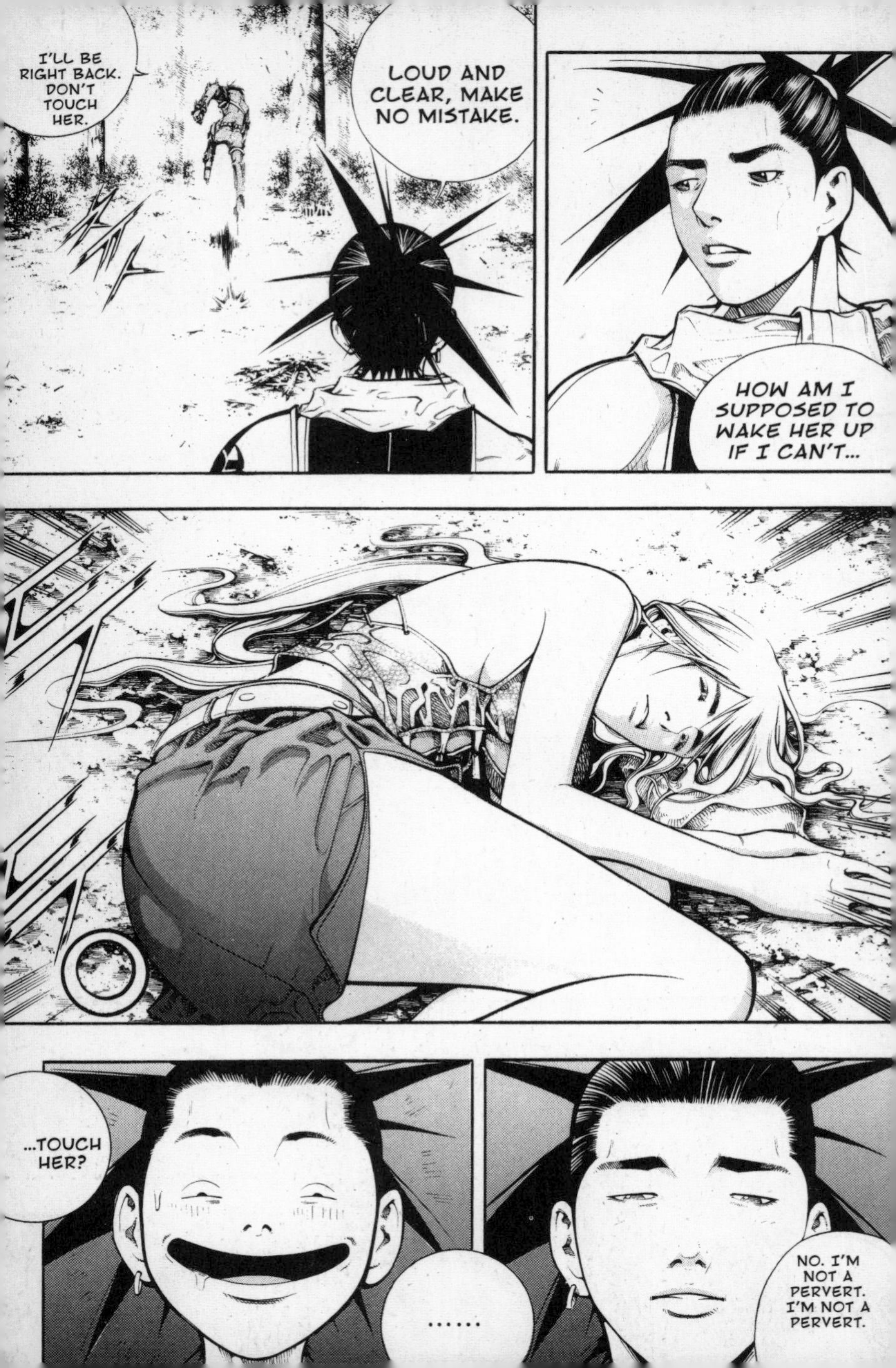
I'LL BE RIGHT BACK. DON'T TOUCH HER.
LOUD AND CLEAR, MAKE NO MISTAKE.
HOW AM I SUPPOSED TO WAKE HER UP IF I CAN'T...
...TOUCH HER?
......
NO. I'M NOT A PERVERT. I'M NOT A PERVERT.

MMM....

BUT I DO HAVE URGES.

POKE

POKE

POKE

......

PLEASE WAKE UP, SANGHUI. I DON'T KNOW WHAT'LL HAPPEN IF I HAVE TO TOUCH YOU.

....

.!!!!....

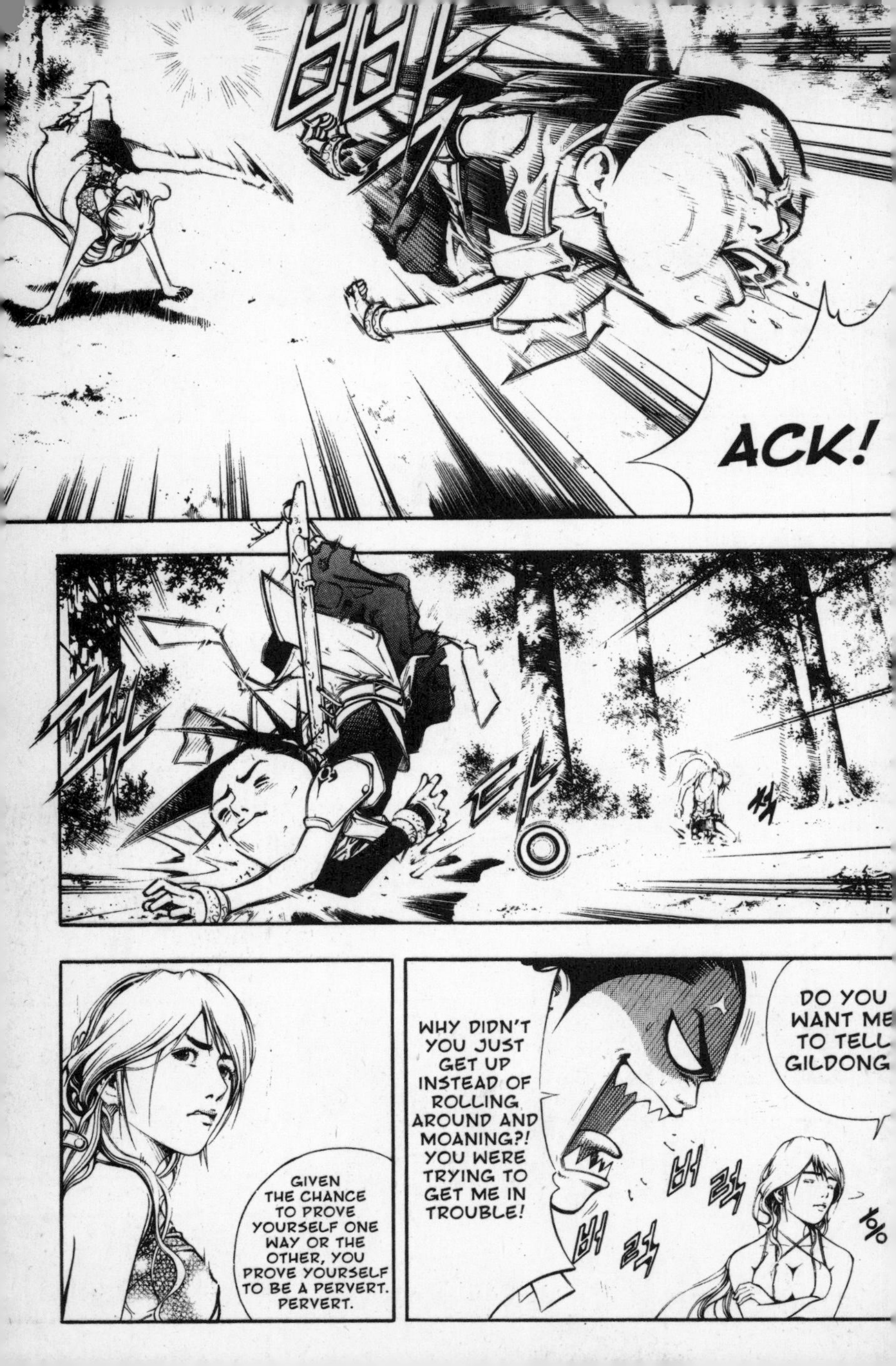
ACK!
GIVEN THE CHANCE TO PROVE YOURSELF ONE WAY OR THE OTHER, YOU PROVE YOURSELF TO BE A PERVERT. PERVERT.
WHY DIDN'T YOU JUST GET UP INSTEAD OF ROLLING AROUND AND MOANING?! YOU WERE TRYING TO GET ME IN TROUBLE!
DO YOU WANT ME TO TELL GILDONG

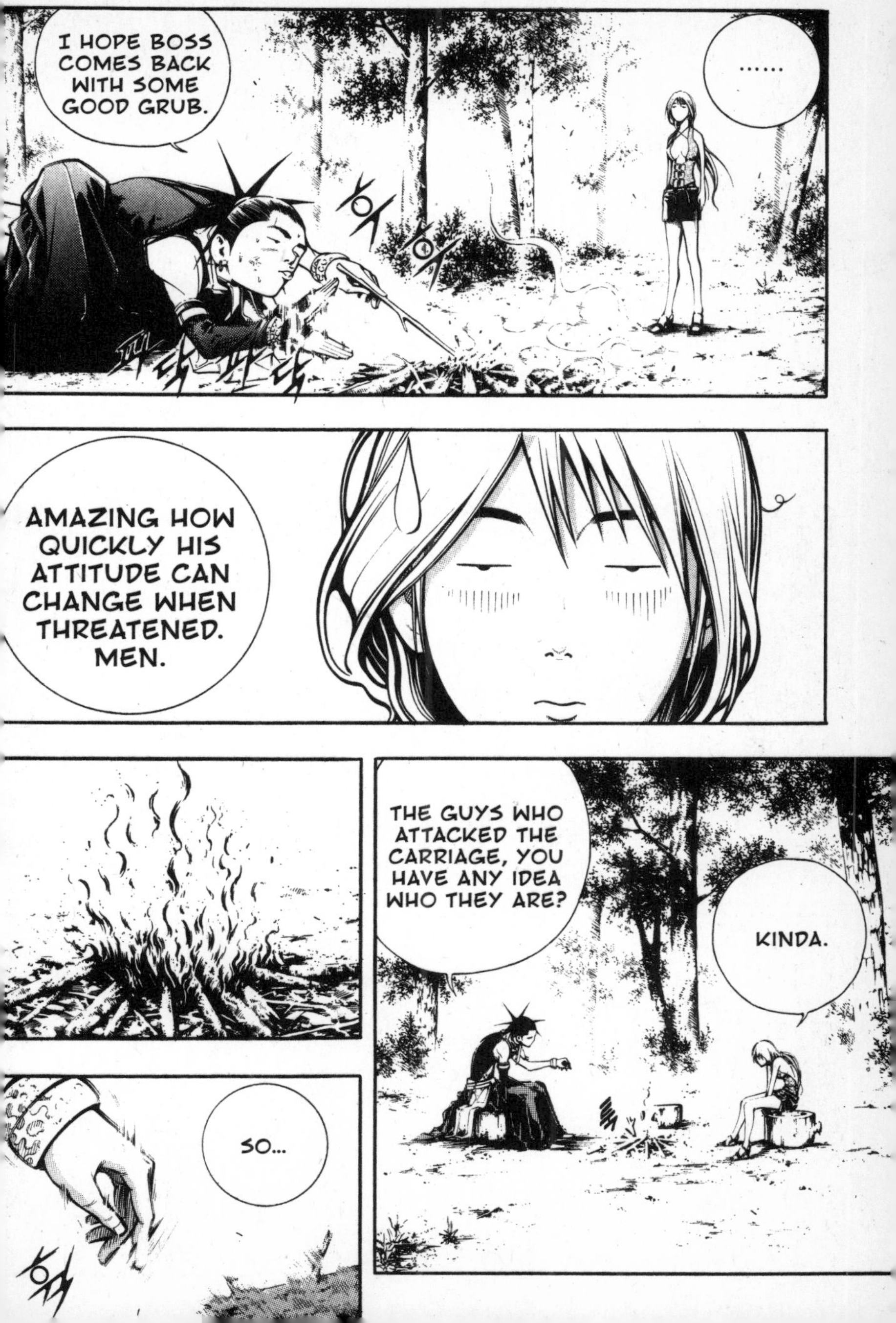
I HOPE BOSS COMES BACK WITH SOME GOOD GRUB.
......
AMAZING HOW QUICKLY HIS ATTITUDE CAN CHANGE WHEN THREATENED. MEN.
SO...
THE GUYS WHO ATTACKED THE CARRIAGE, YOU HAVE ANY IDEA WHO THEY ARE?
KINDA.

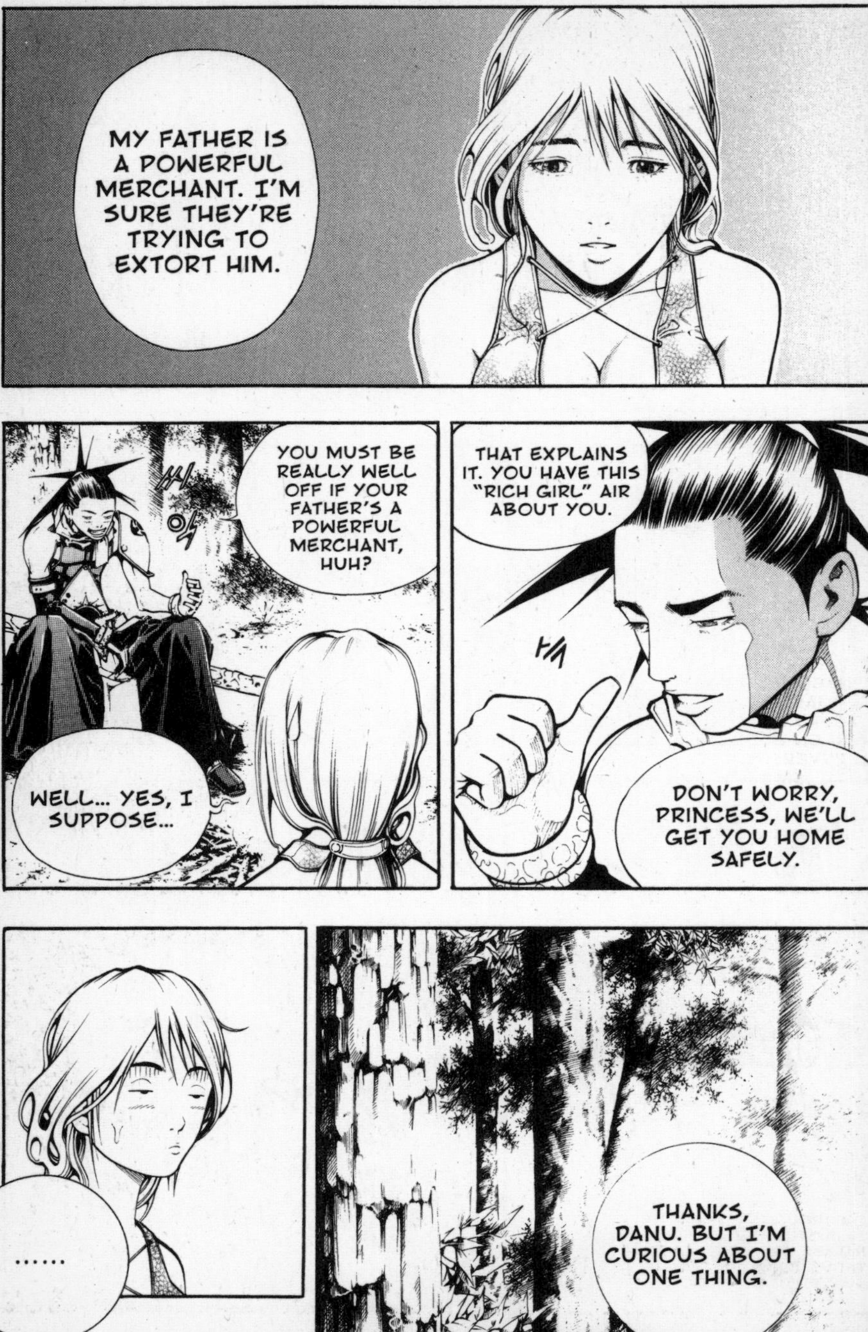
MY FATHER IS A POWERFUL MERCHANT. I'M SURE THEY'RE TRYING TO EXTORT HIM.
YOU MUST BE REALLY WELL OFF IF YOUR FATHER'S A POWERFUL MERCHANT, HUH?
WELL... YES, I SUPPOSE...
THAT EXPLAINS IT. YOU HAVE THIS "RICH GIRL" AIR ABOUT YOU.
DON'T WORRY, PRINCESS, WE'LL GET YOU HOME SAFELY.
......
THANKS, DANU. BUT I'M CURIOUS ABOUT ONE THING.

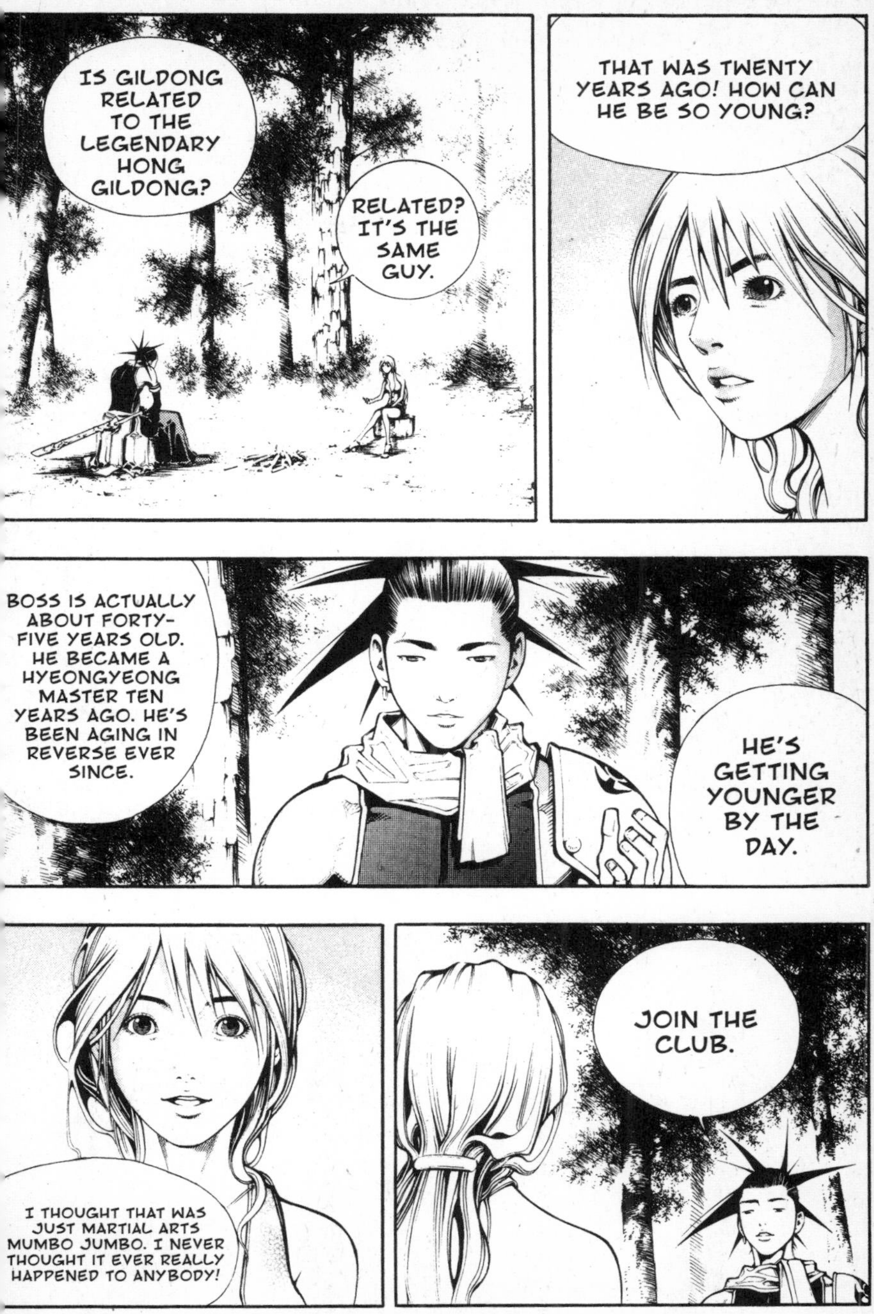
IS GILDONG RELATED TO THE LEGENDARY HONG GILDONG?
RELATED? IT'S THE SAME GUY.
THAT WAS TWENTY YEARS AGO! HOW CAN HE BE SO YOUNG?
BOSS IS ACTUALLY ABOUT FORTY-FIVE YEARS OLD. HE BECAME A HYEONGYEONG MASTER TEN YEARS AGO. HE'S BEEN AGING IN REVERSE EVER SINCE.
HE'S GETTING YOUNGER BY THE DAY.
I THOUGHT THAT WAS JUST MARTIAL ARTS MUMBO JUMBO. I NEVER THOUGHT IT EVER REALLY HAPPENED TO ANYBODY!
JOIN THE CLUB.

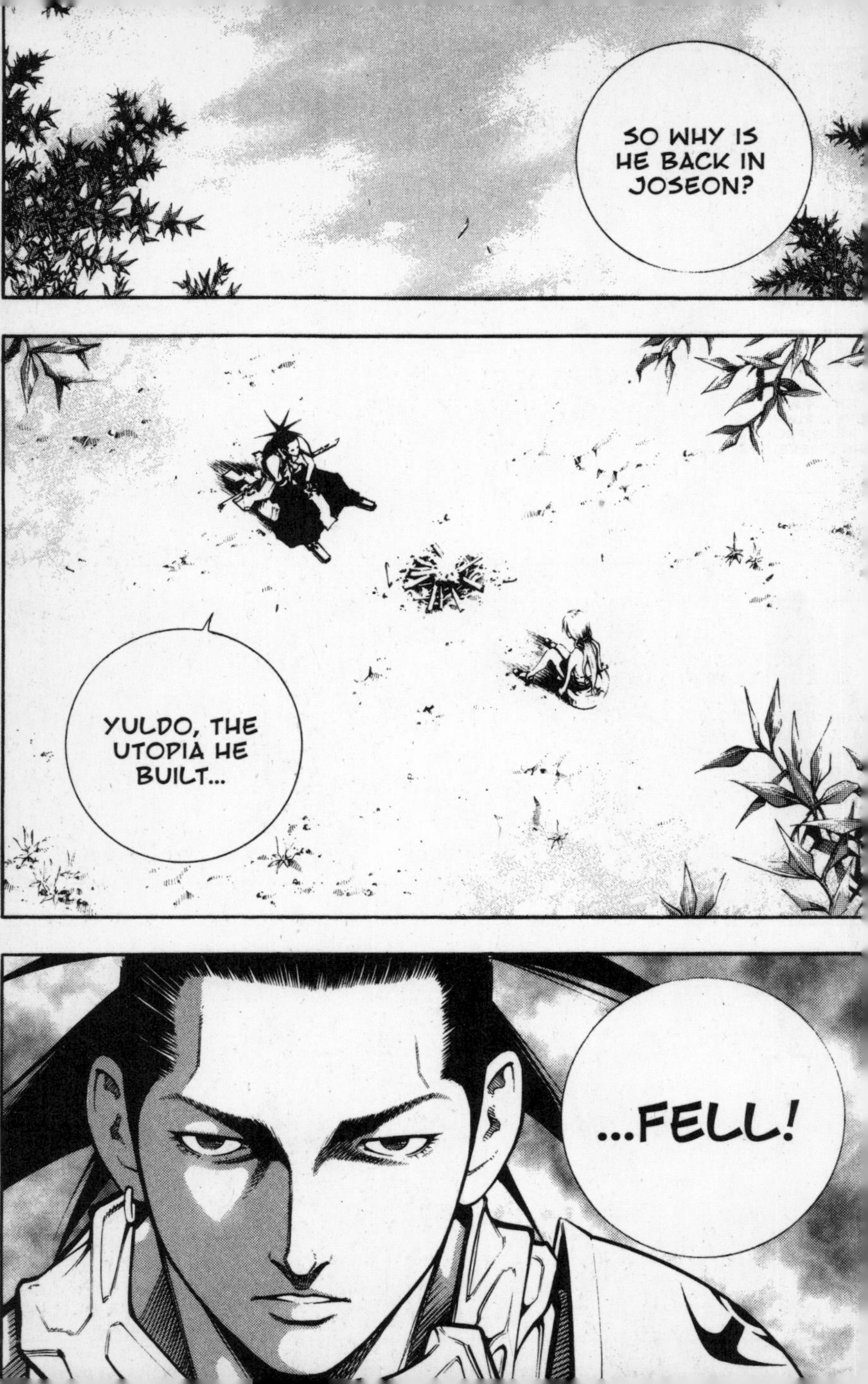
SO WHY IS HE BACK IN JOSEON?
YULDO, THE UTOPIA HE BUILT...
...FELL!

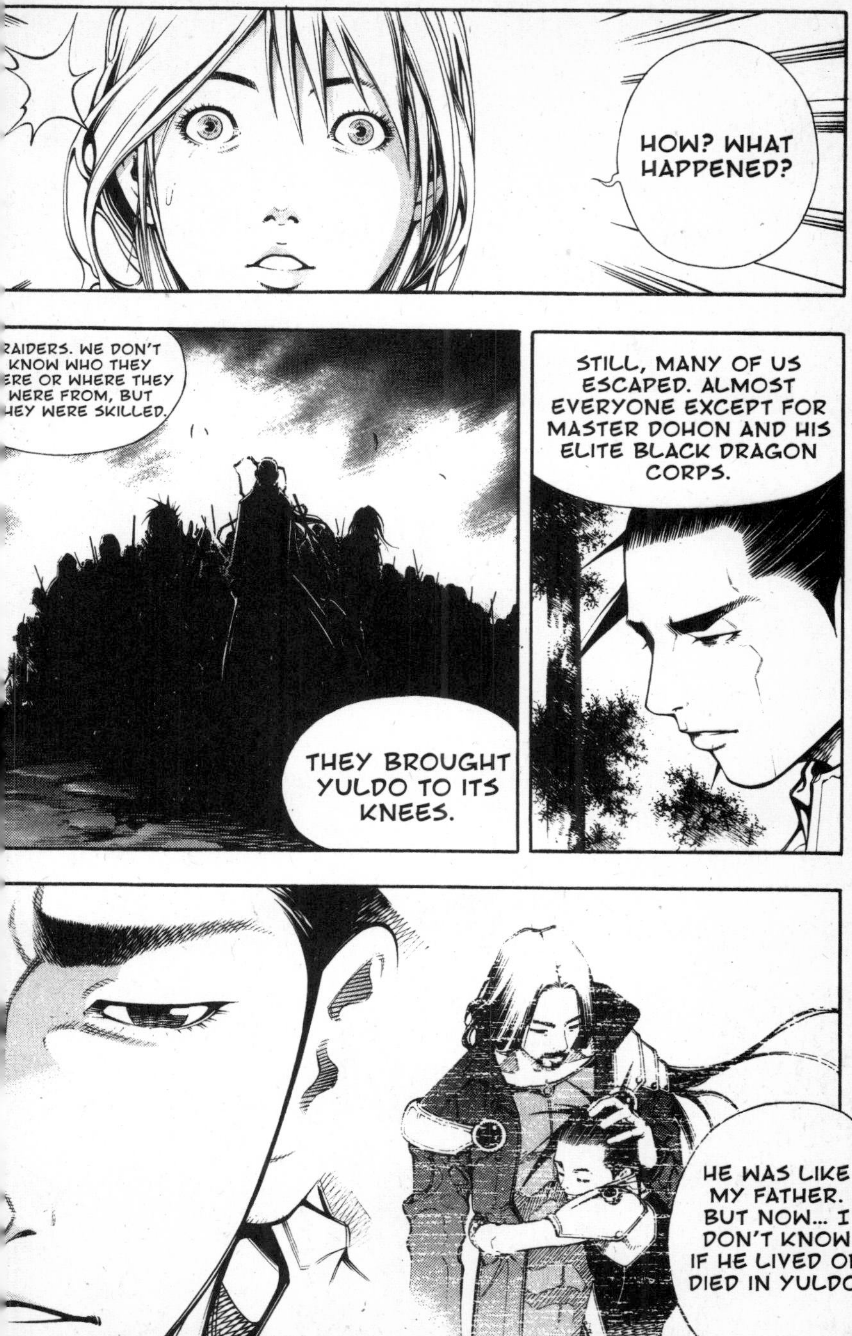
HOW? WHAT HAPPENED?
RAIDERS. WE DON'T KNOW WHO THEY ERE OR WHERE THEY WERE FROM, BUT HEY WERE SKILLED.
THEY BROUGHT YULDO TO ITS KNEES.
STILL, MANY OF US ESCAPED. ALMOST EVERYONE EXCEPT FOR MASTER DOHON AND HIS ELITE BLACK DRAGON CORPS.
HE WAS LIKE MY FATHER. BUT NOW... I DON'T KNOW IF HE LIVED OR DIED IN YULDO.

WE'RE BACK IN JOSEON FOR TWO REASONS.

THE FIRST REASON IS FINANCIAL. TO FUND THE REBUILDING OF YULDO.

THE SECOND IS TO FIND OUT WHO THOSE BASTARDS WERE, AND MAKE THEM PAY.

I'M SORRY, DANU. I THOUGHT YOU WERE A COUPLE OF SELFISH BOUNTY HUNTERS.

WHAT'S WITH THE HEAVY MOOD, GUYS? DANU?

DID YOU SAY OR DO SOMETHING YOU SHOULDN'T HAVE?

NO BOSS, JUST MAKING SMALL TALK.

WOW, BOSS, THIS IS A NICE PLUMP VARMINT!

HE PUT UP QUITE A FIGHT FOR BEING SO FAT.

IT'S IMPOLITE TO STARE, 'KNOW?

SORRY... I WASN'T... I MEAN.

WHAT-EVER.

DANU! HURRY IT UP! I'M HUNGRY HERE!

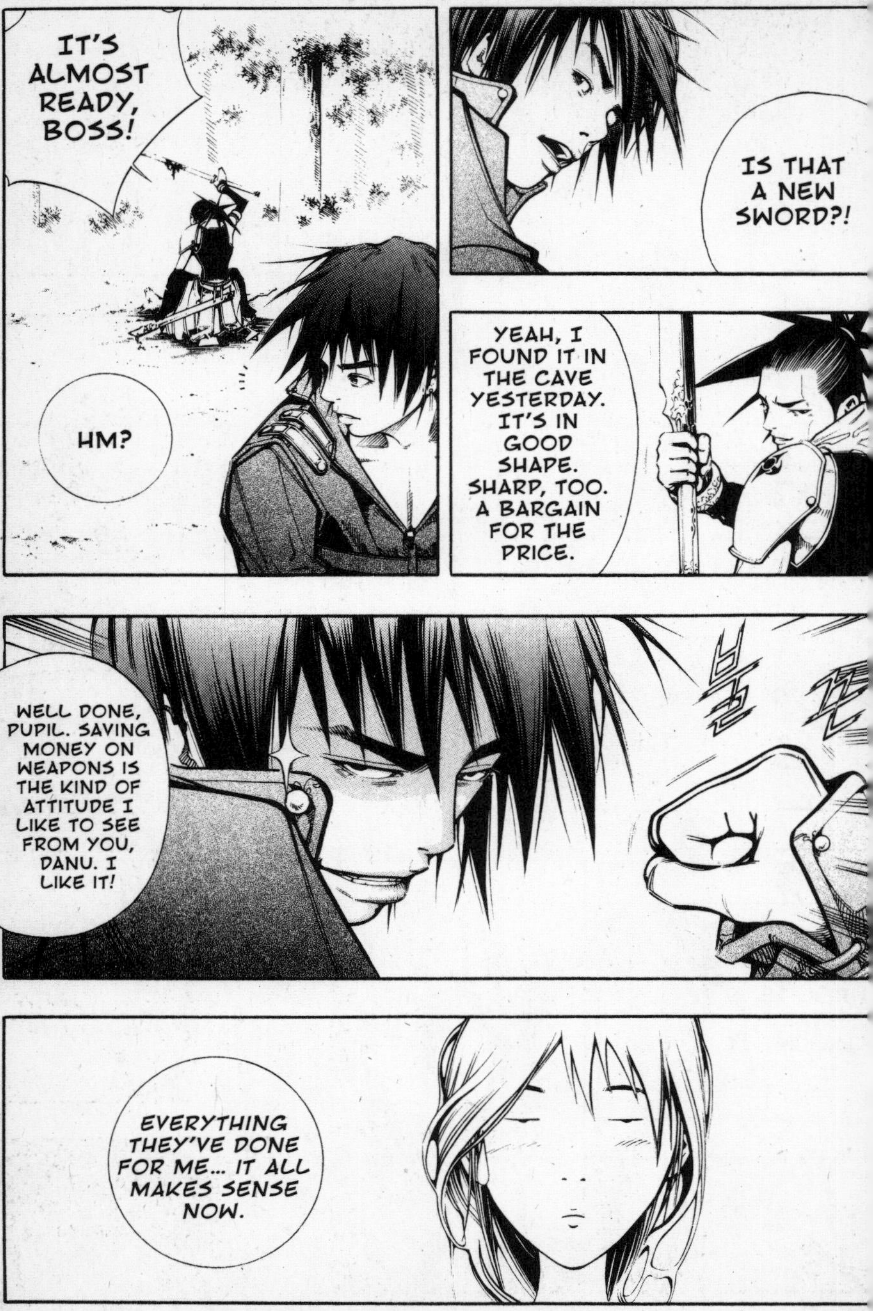
IT'S ALMOST READY, BOSS!
HM?
IS THAT A NEW SWORD?!
YEAH, I FOUND IT IN THE CAVE YESTERDAY. IT'S IN GOOD SHAPE. SHARP, TOO. A BARGAIN FOR THE PRICE.
WELL DONE, PUPIL. SAVING MONEY ON WEAPONS IS THE KIND OF ATTITUDE I LIKE TO SEE FROM YOU, DANU. I LIKE IT!
불끈
EVERYTHING THEY'VE DONE FOR ME... IT ALL MAKES SENSE NOW.

WHAT'S
THAT?

IT'S MY LAST LITTLE PIECE OF YULDO...

......

NOTHING YOU'D UNDERSTAND.

HOLD ON!

I'VE SEEN THIS BEFORE!

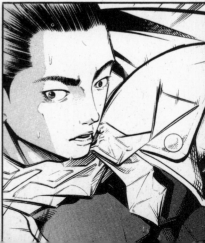

Chapter 5
The Last Piece of Yuldo

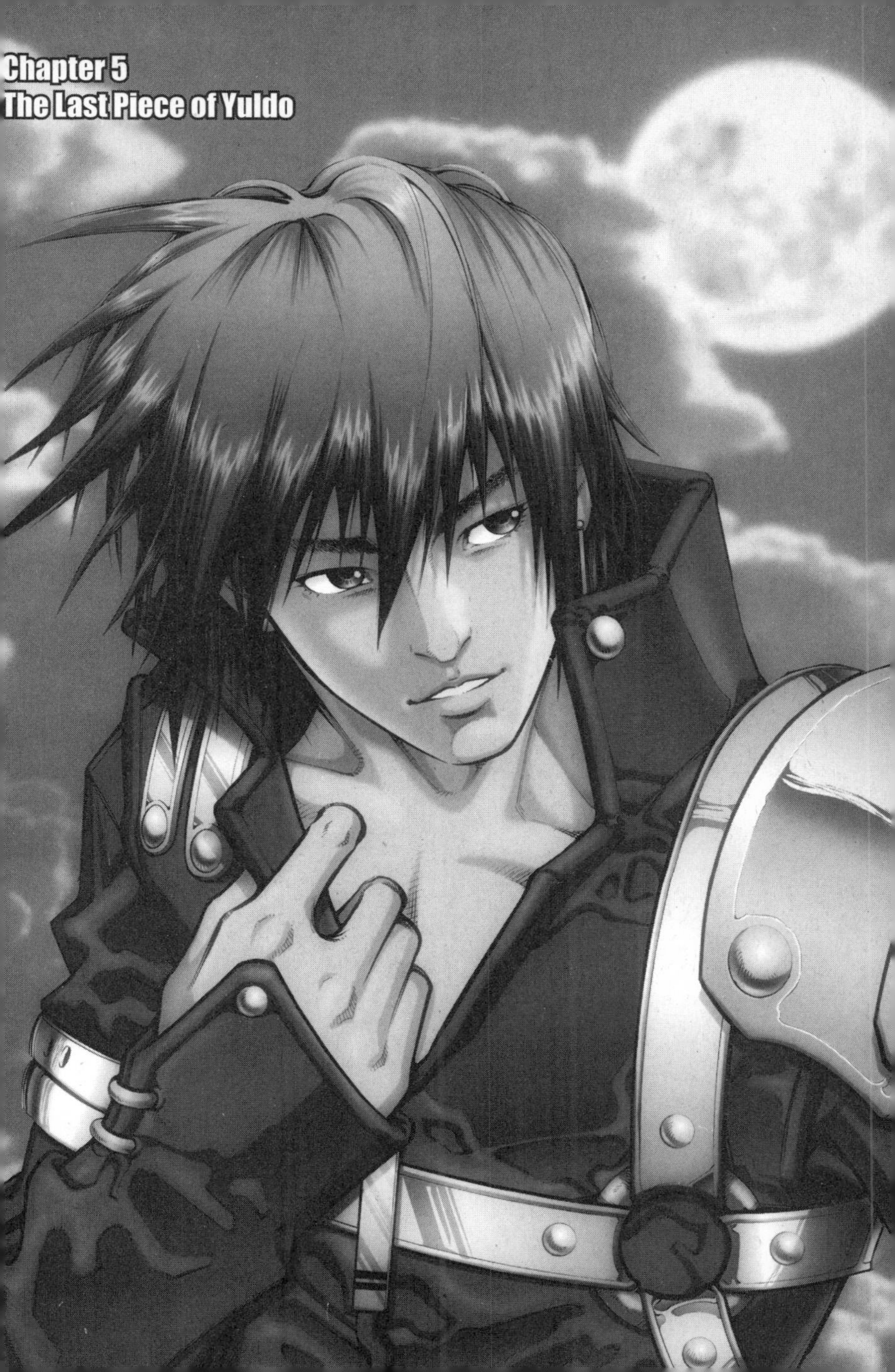

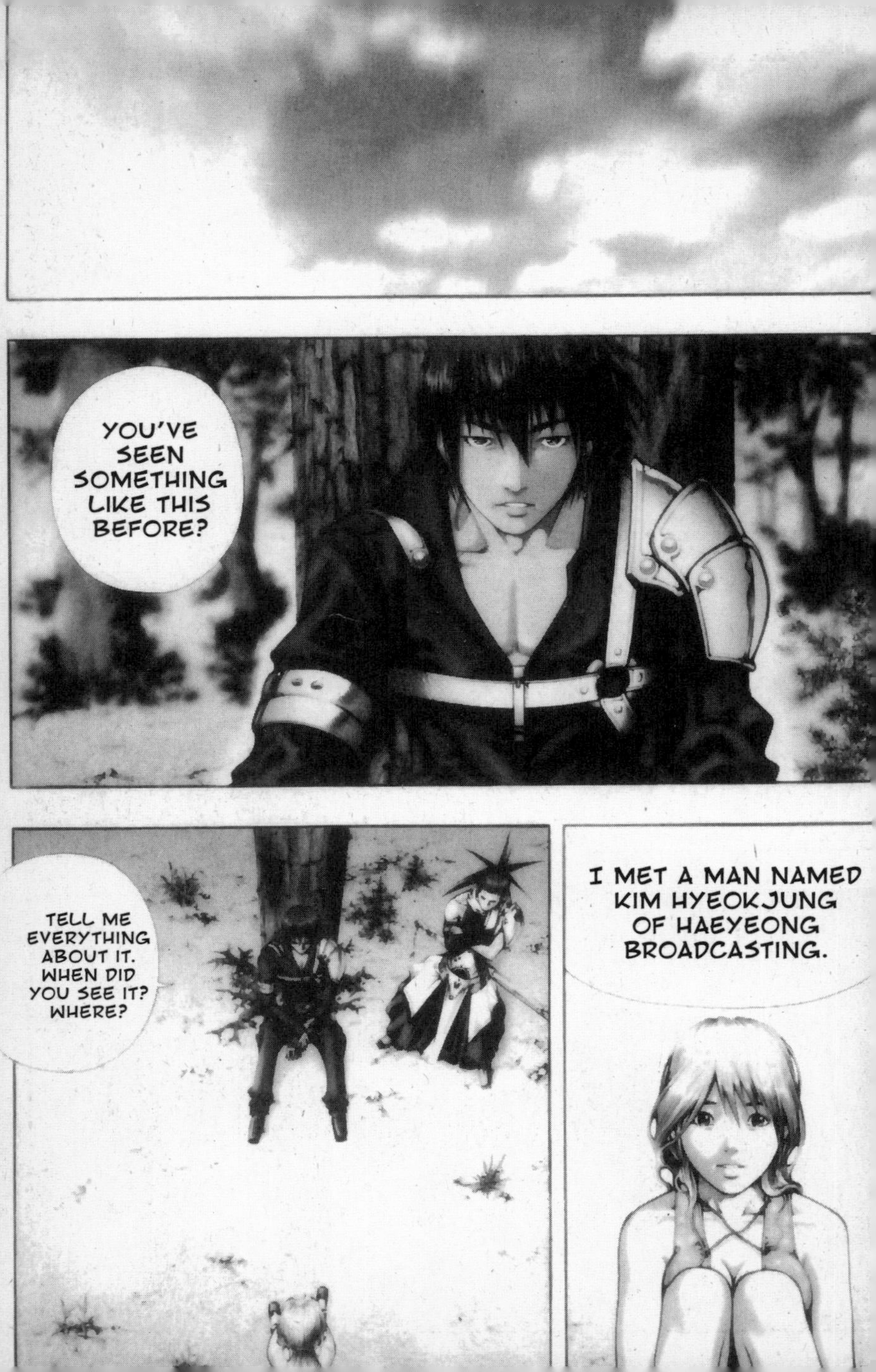
YOU'VE SEEN SOMETHING LIKE THIS BEFORE?
TELL ME EVERYTHING ABOUT IT. WHEN DID YOU SEE IT? WHERE?
I MET A MAN NAMED KIM HYEOKJUNG OF HAEYEONG BROADCASTING.

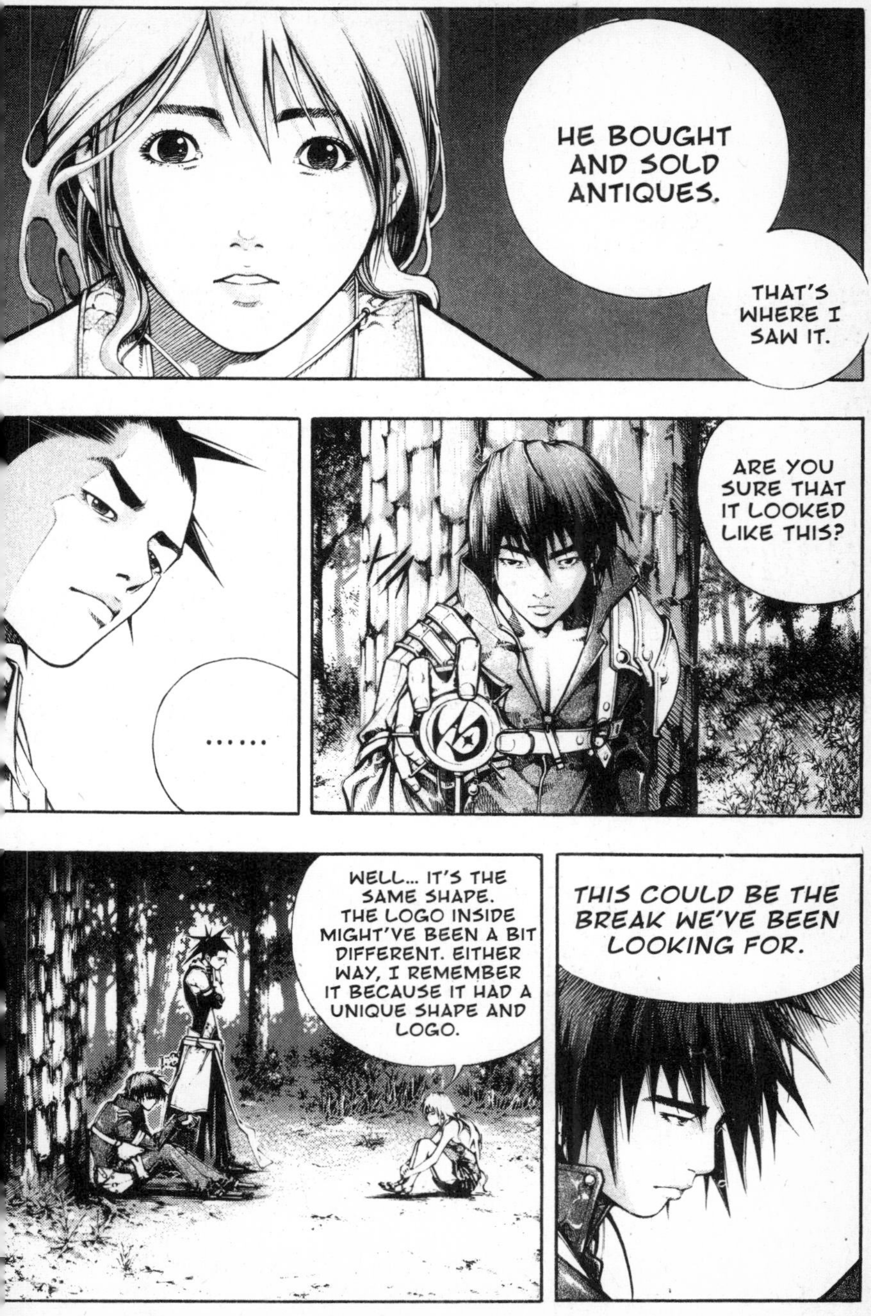
HE BOUGHT AND SOLD ANTIQUES.
THAT'S WHERE I SAW IT.
ARE YOU SURE THAT IT LOOKED LIKE THIS?
......
WELL... IT'S THE SAME SHAPE. THE LOGO INSIDE MIGHT'VE BEEN A BIT DIFFERENT. EITHER WAY, I REMEMBER IT BECAUSE IT HAD A UNIQUE SHAPE AND LOGO.
THIS COULD BE THE BREAK WE'VE BEEN LOOKING FOR.

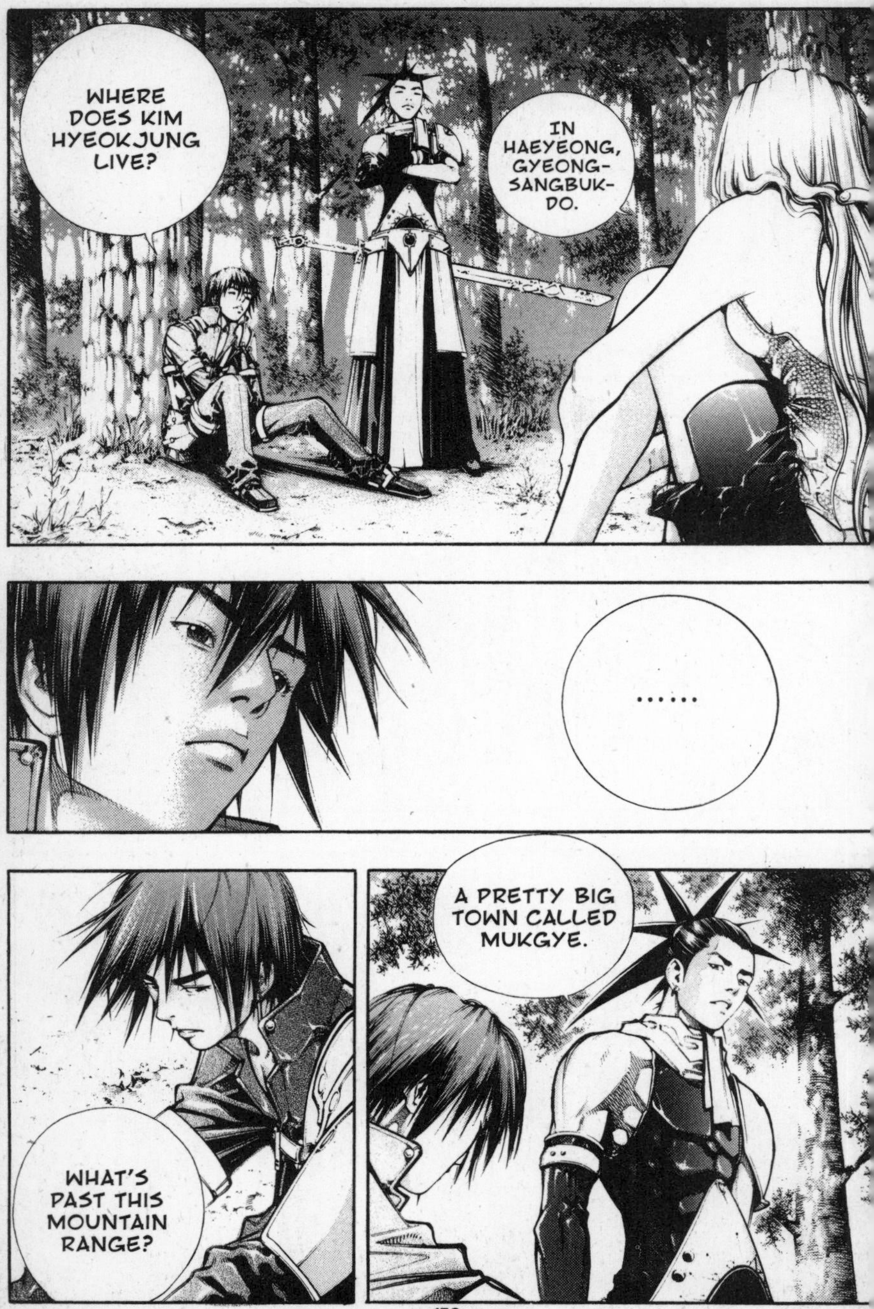
WHERE DOES KIM HYEOKJUNG LIVE?
IN HAEYEONG, GYEONG-SANGBUK-DO.
......
A PRETTY BIG TOWN CALLED MUKGYE.
WHAT'S PAST THIS MOUNTAIN RANGE?

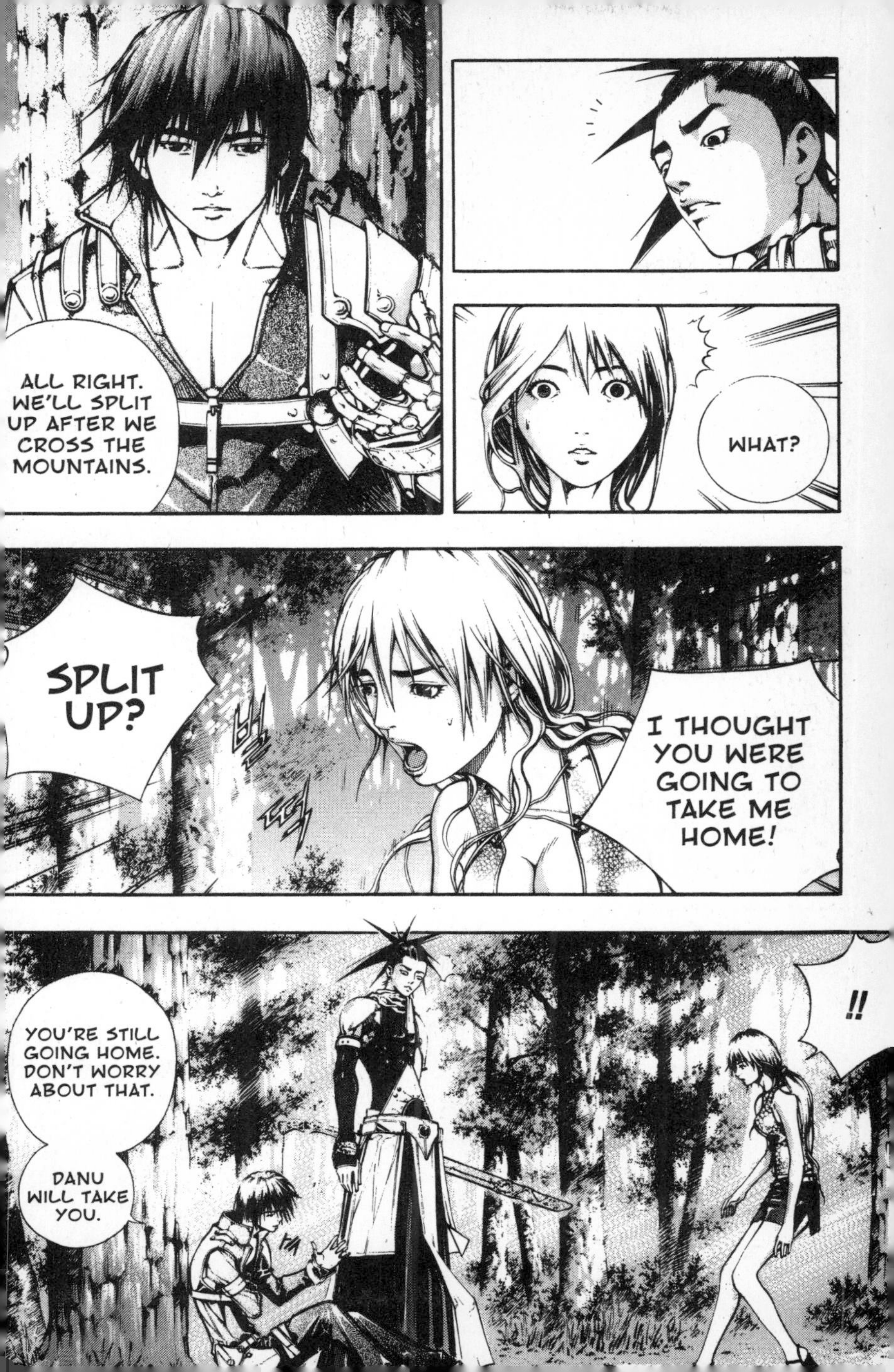
ALL RIGHT. WE'LL SPLIT UP AFTER WE CROSS THE MOUNTAINS.
WHAT?
SPLIT UP?
I THOUGHT YOU WERE GOING TO TAKE ME HOME!
!!
YOU'RE STILL GOING HOME. DON'T WORRY ABOUT THAT.
DANU WILL TAKE YOU.

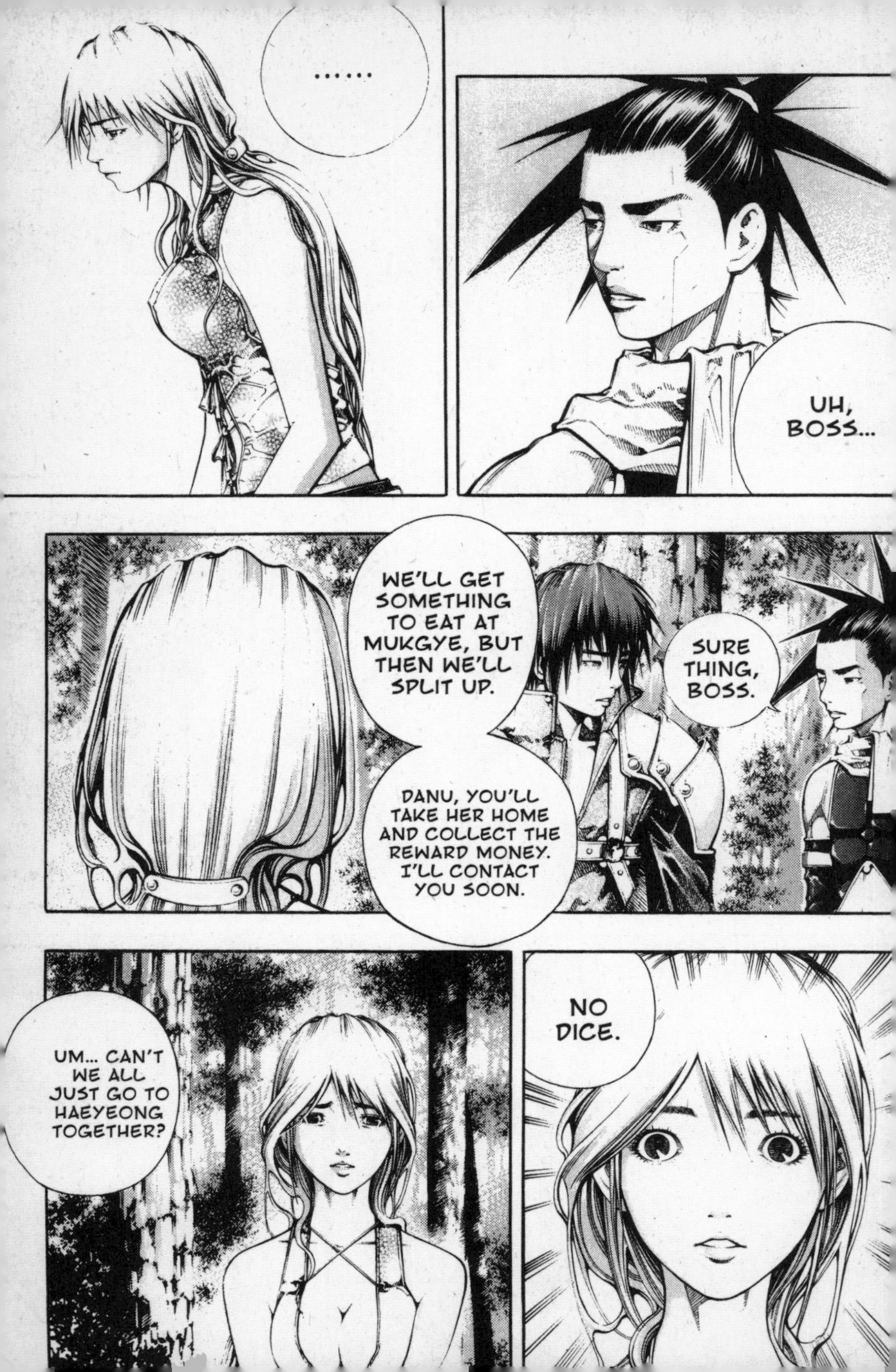
......
UH, BOSS...
WE'LL GET SOMETHING TO EAT AT MUKGYE, BUT THEN WE'LL SPLIT UP.
DANU, YOU'LL TAKE HER HOME AND COLLECT THE REWARD MONEY. I'LL CONTACT YOU SOON.
SURE THING, BOSS.
UM... CAN'T WE ALL JUST GO TO HAEYEONG TOGETHER?
NO DICE.

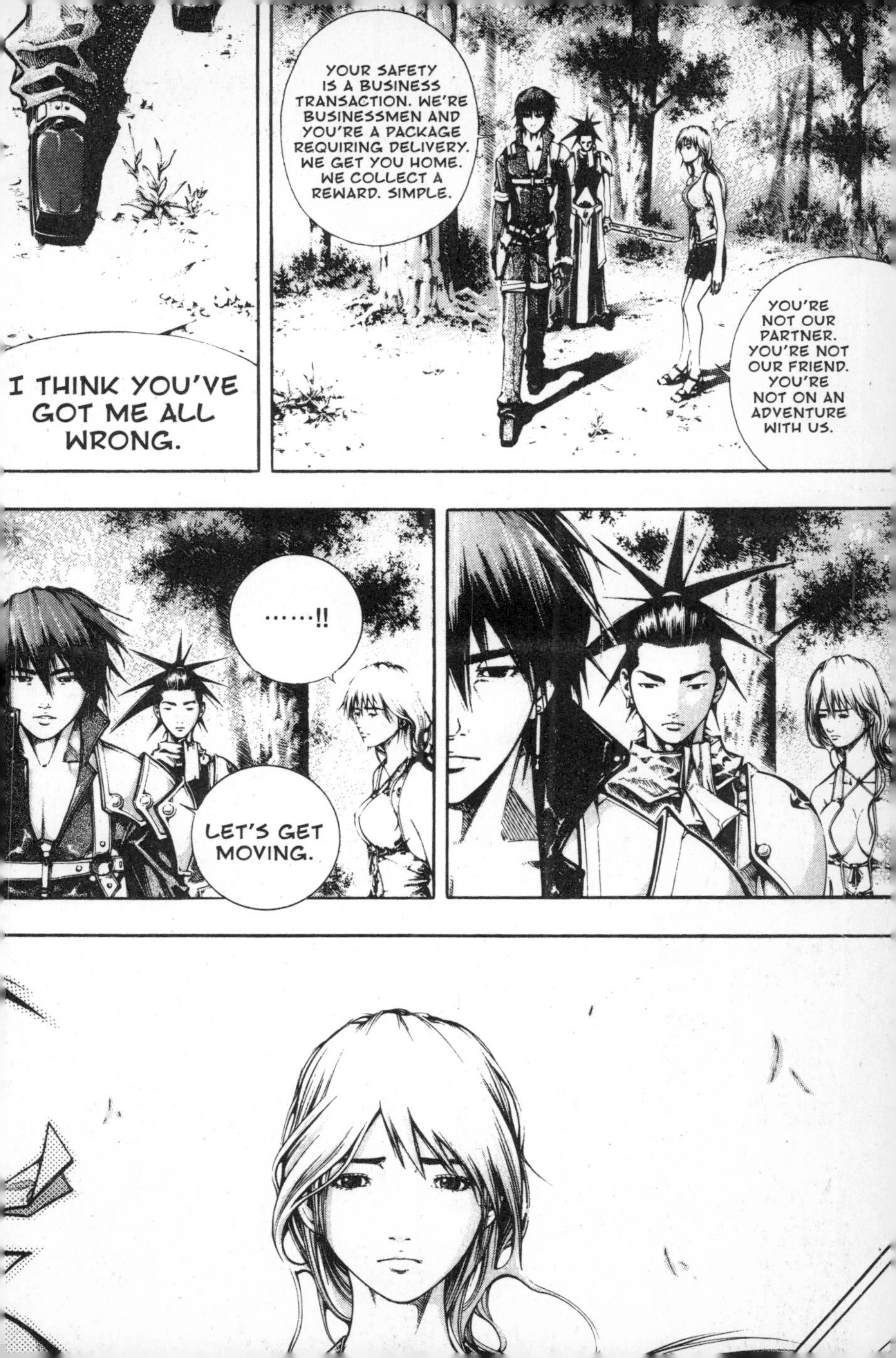
YOUR SAFETY IS A BUSINESS TRANSACTION. WE'RE BUSINESSMEN AND YOU'RE A PACKAGE REQUIRING DELIVERY. WE GET YOU HOME. WE COLLECT A REWARD. SIMPLE.
YOU'RE NOT OUR PARTNER. YOU'RE NOT OUR FRIEND. YOU'RE NOT ON AN ADVENTURE WITH US.
I THINK YOU'VE GOT ME ALL WRONG.
......!!
LET'S GET MOVING.

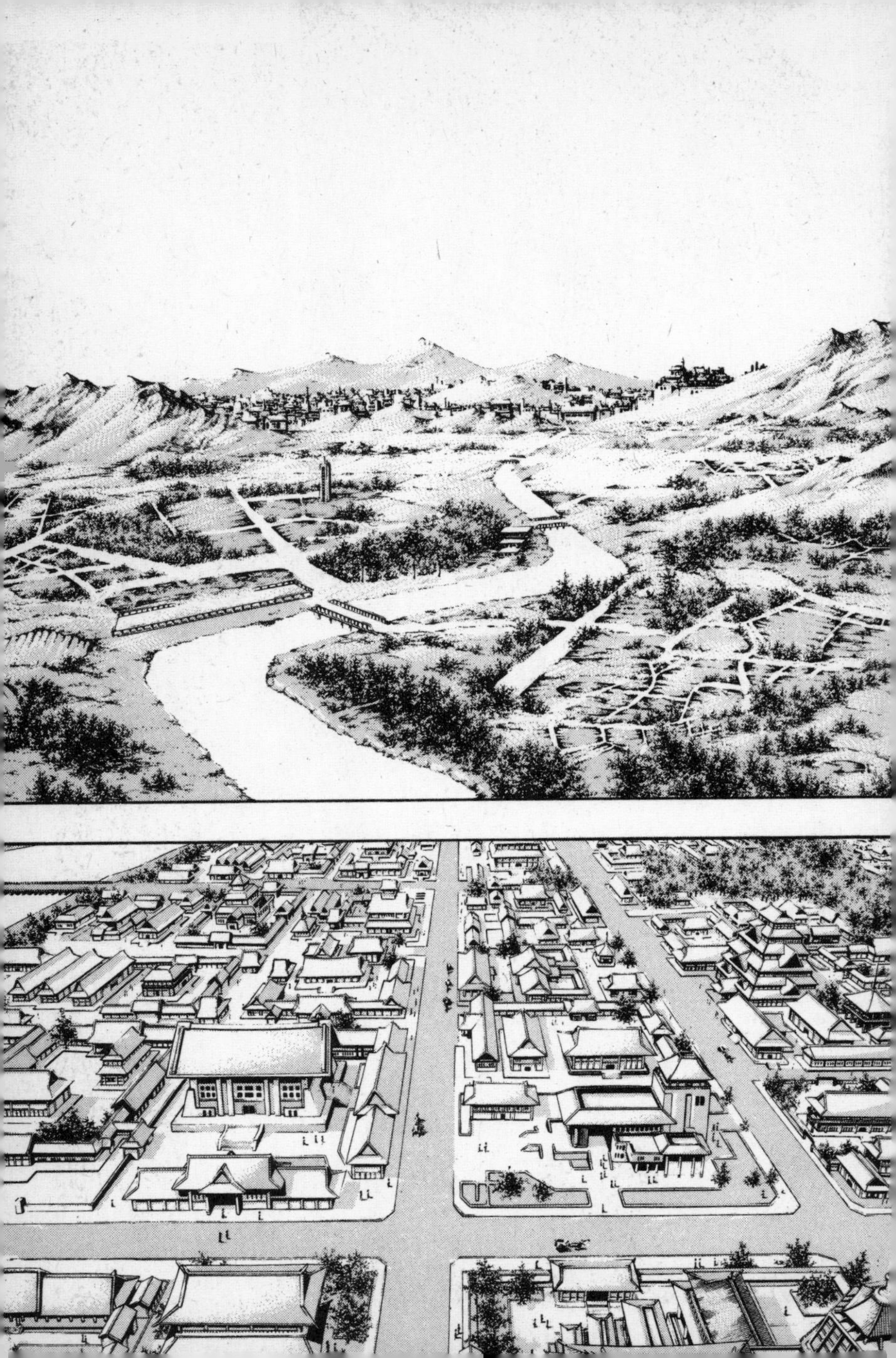

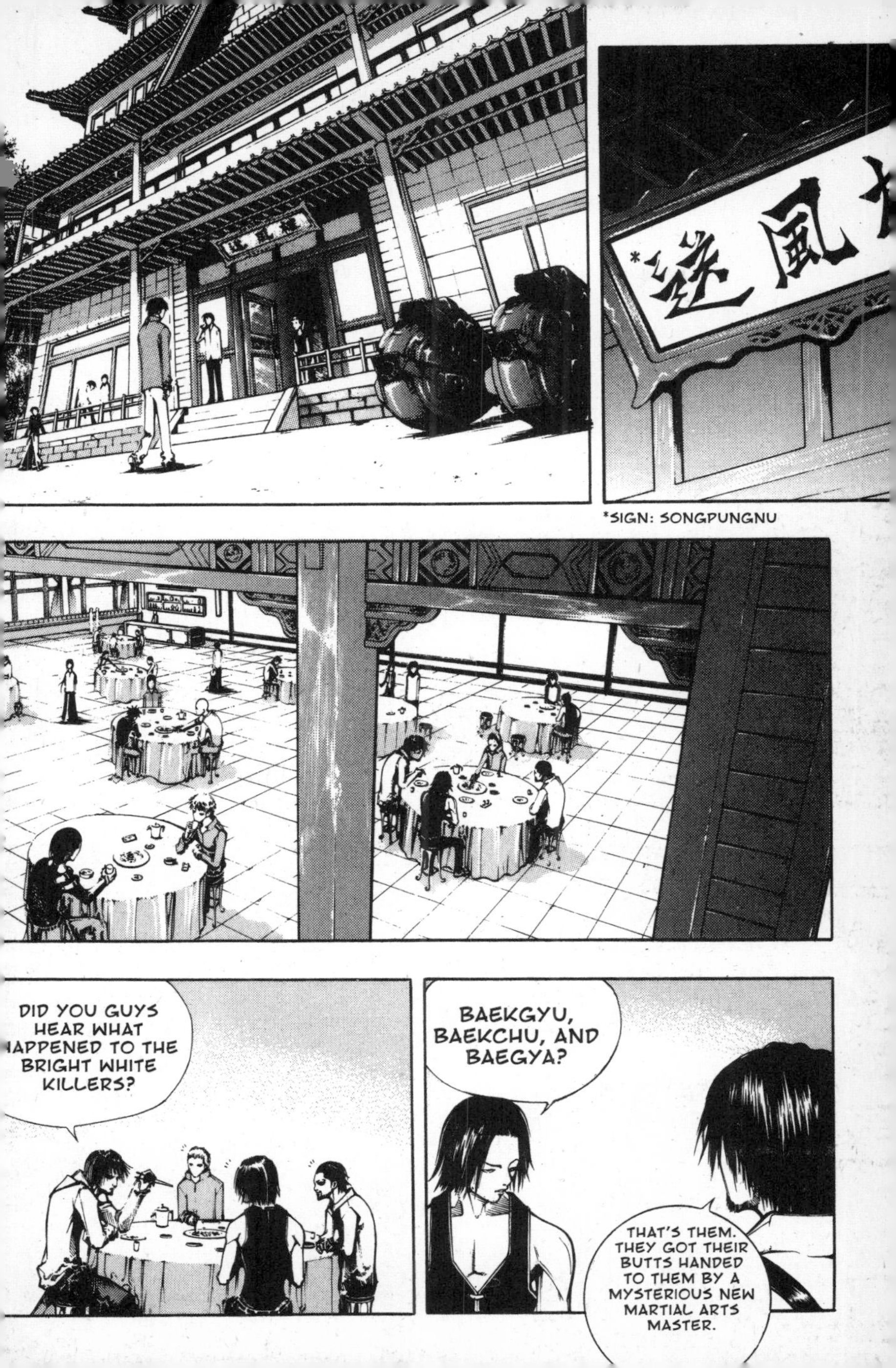
*SIGN: SONGPUNGNU
DID YOU GUYS HEAR WHAT HAPPENED TO THE BRIGHT WHITE KILLERS?
BAEKGYU, BAEKCHU, AND BAEGYA?
THAT'S THEM. THEY GOT THEIR BUTTS HANDED TO THEM BY A MYSTERIOUS NEW MARTIAL ARTS MASTER.

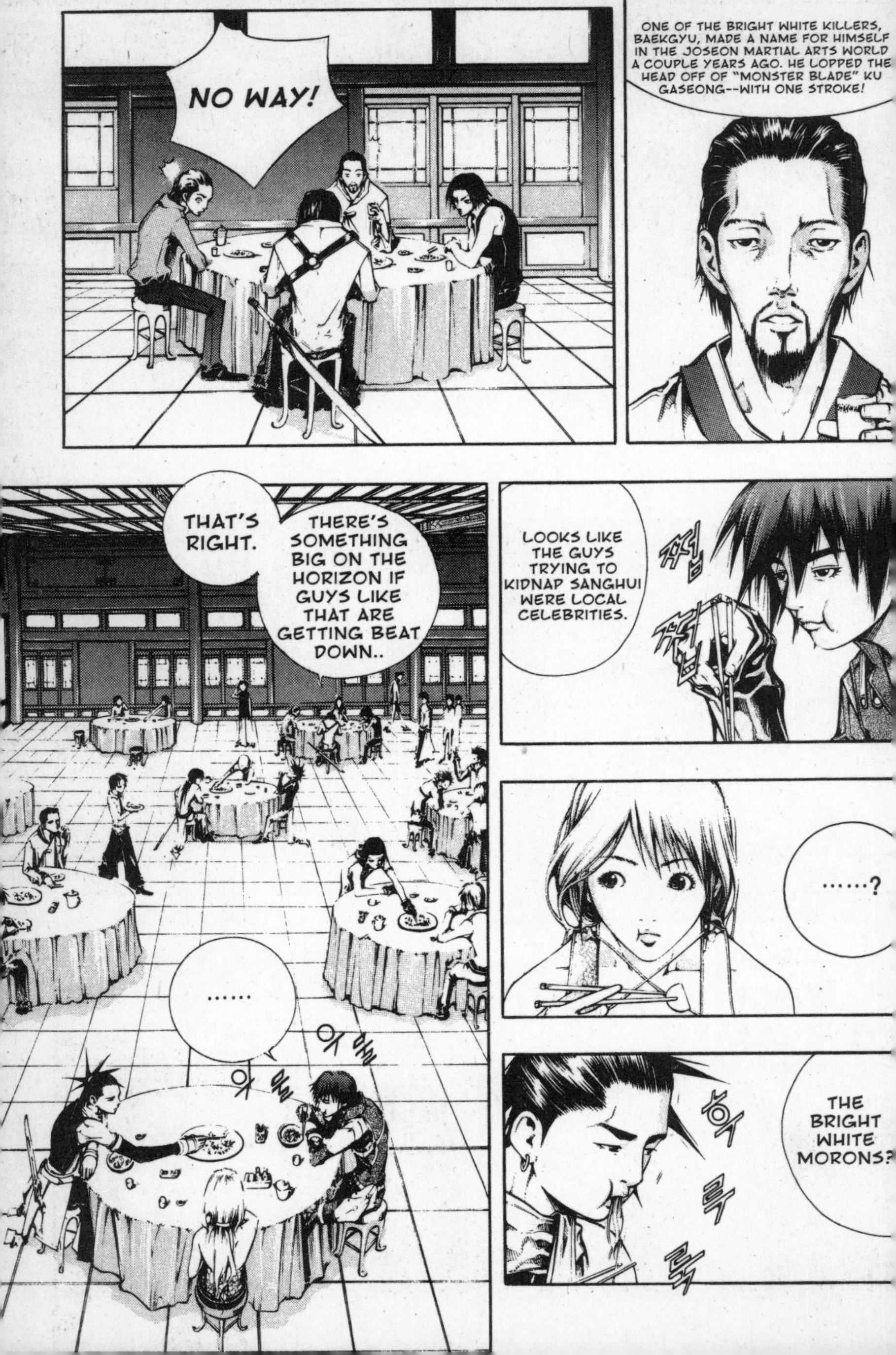
NO WAY!
ONE OF THE BRIGHT WHITE KILLERS, BAEKGYU, MADE A NAME FOR HIMSELF IN THE JOSEON MARTIAL ARTS WORLD A COUPLE YEARS AGO. HE LOPPED THE HEAD OFF OF "MONSTER BLADE" KU GASEONG--WITH ONE STROKE!
THAT'S RIGHT.
THERE'S SOMETHING BIG ON THE HORIZON IF GUYS LIKE THAT ARE GETTING BEAT DOWN..
......
LOOKS LIKE THE GUYS TRYING TO KIDNAP SANGHUI WERE LOCAL CELEBRITIES.
......?
THE BRIGHT WHITE MORONS?

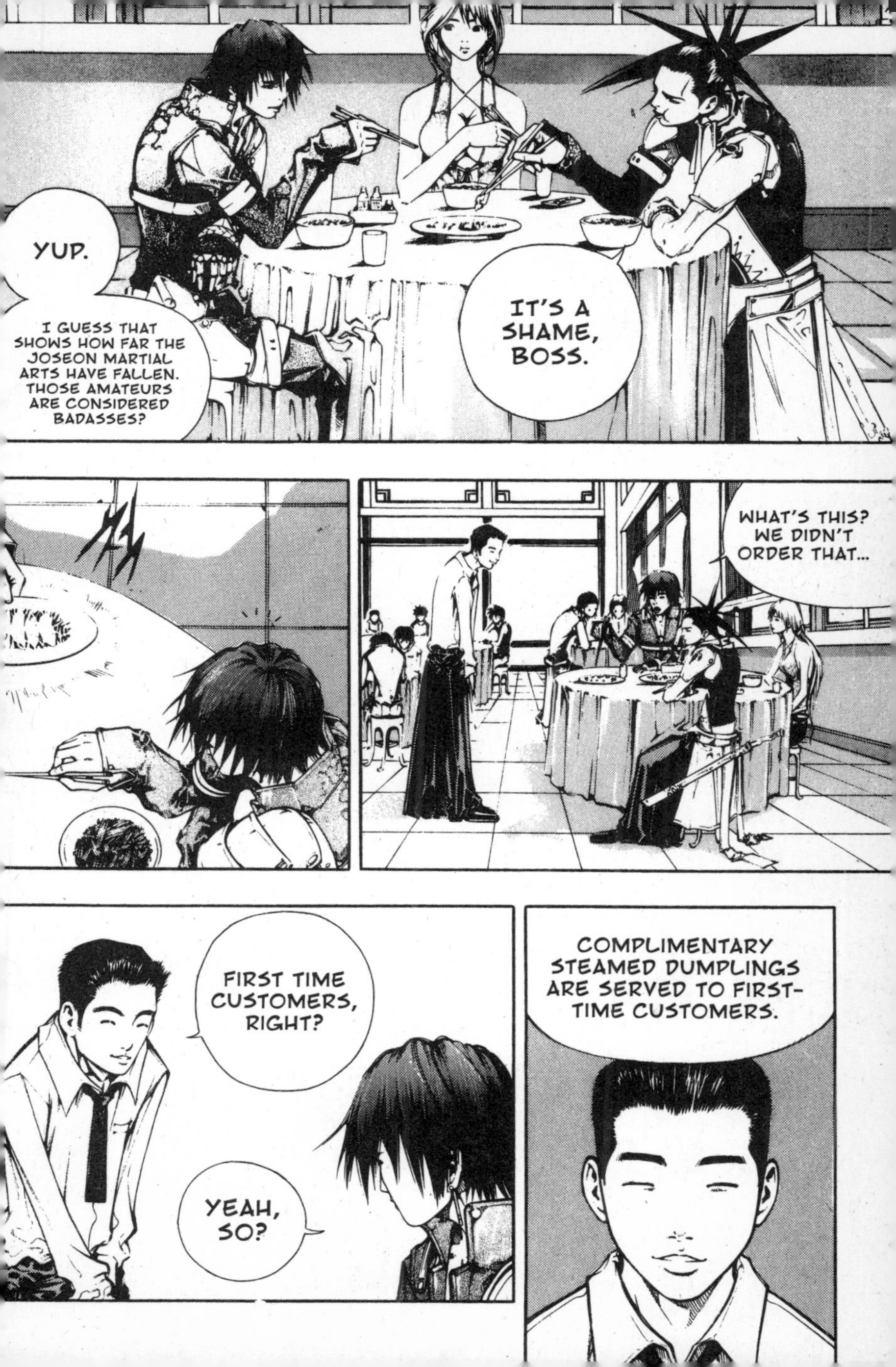
YUP.
I GUESS THAT SHOWS HOW FAR THE JOSEON MARTIAL ARTS HAVE FALLEN. THOSE AMATEURS ARE CONSIDERED BADASSES?
IT'S A SHAME, BOSS.
WHAT'S THIS? WE DIDN'T ORDER THAT...
FIRST TIME CUSTOMERS, RIGHT?
YEAH, SO?
COMPLIMENTARY STEAMED DUMPLINGS ARE SERVED TO FIRST-TIME CUSTOMERS.

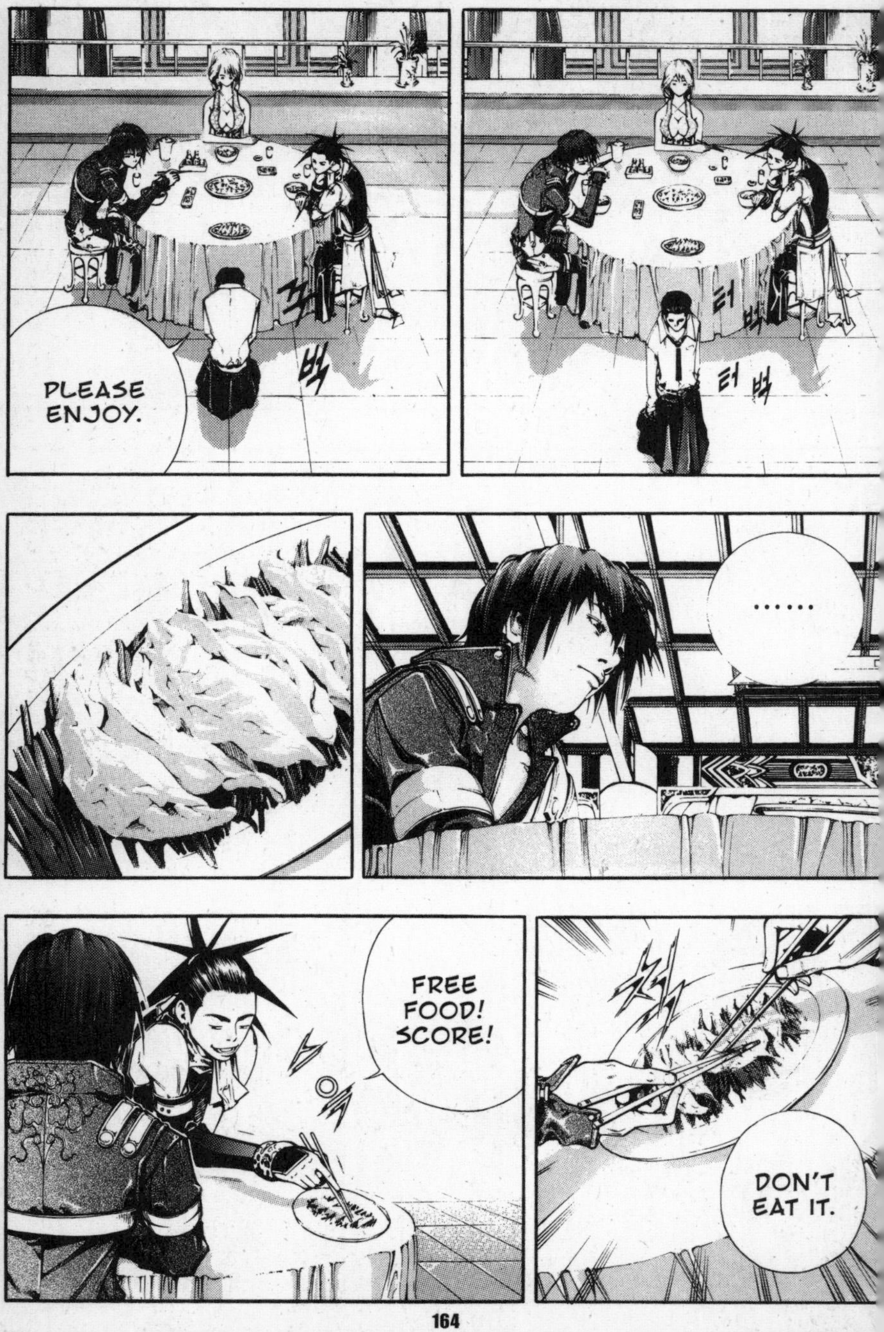
PLEASE ENJOY.
터벅
터벅
......
FREE FOOD! SCORE!
DON'T EAT IT.

SOMETHING FISHY IS GOING ON.

WAITER! HOLD UP.

YOU SHOULD KISS SOMEONE BEFORE YOU TRY TO SCREW THEM.

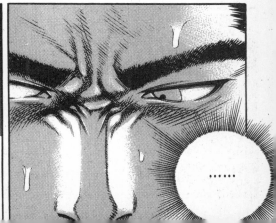

......

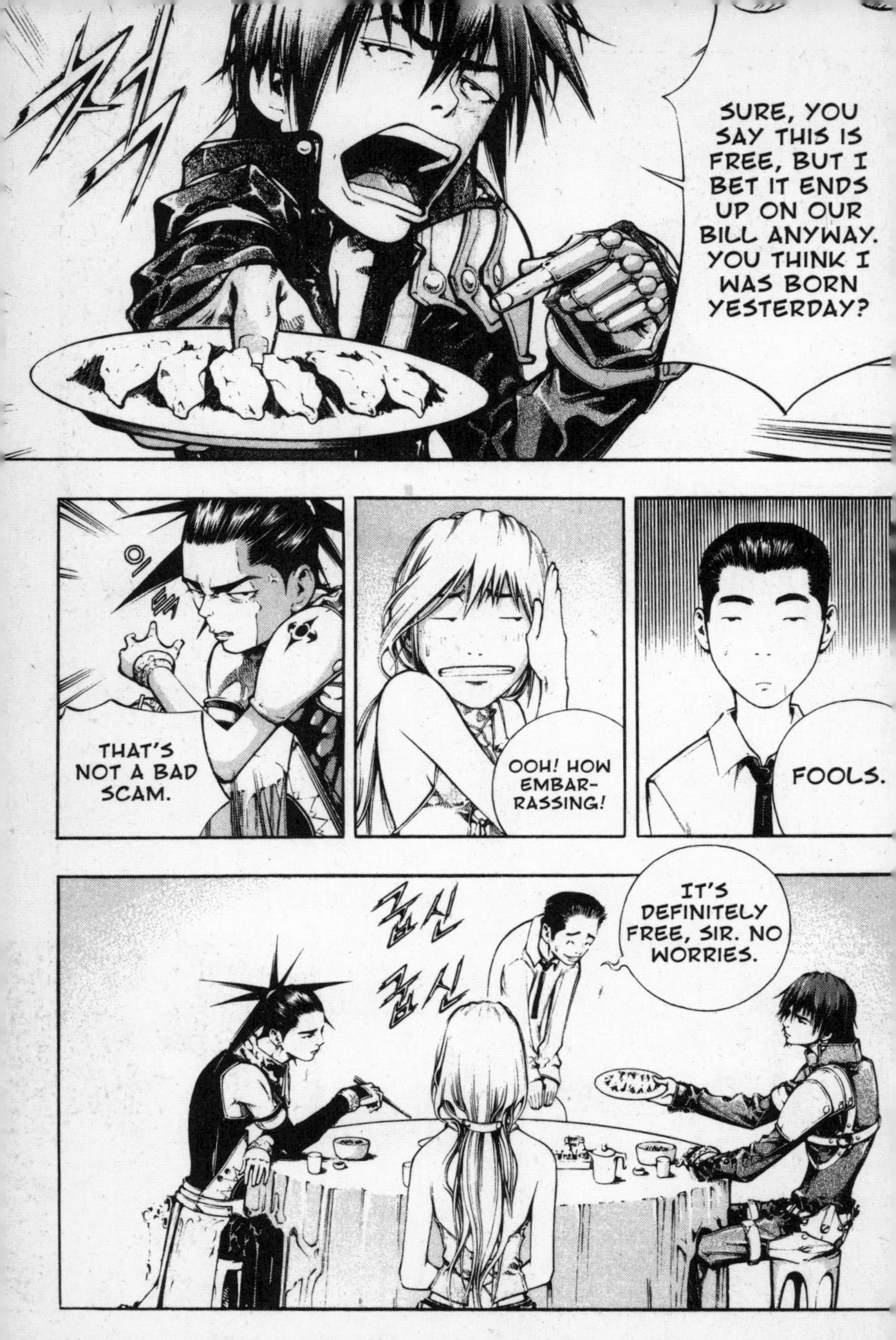
SURE, YOU SAY THIS IS FREE, BUT I BET IT ENDS UP ON OUR BILL ANYWAY. YOU THINK I WAS BORN YESTERDAY?
THAT'S NOT A BAD SCAM.
OOH! HOW EMBAR-RASSING!
FOOLS.
IT'S DEFINITELY FREE, SIR. NO WORRIES.

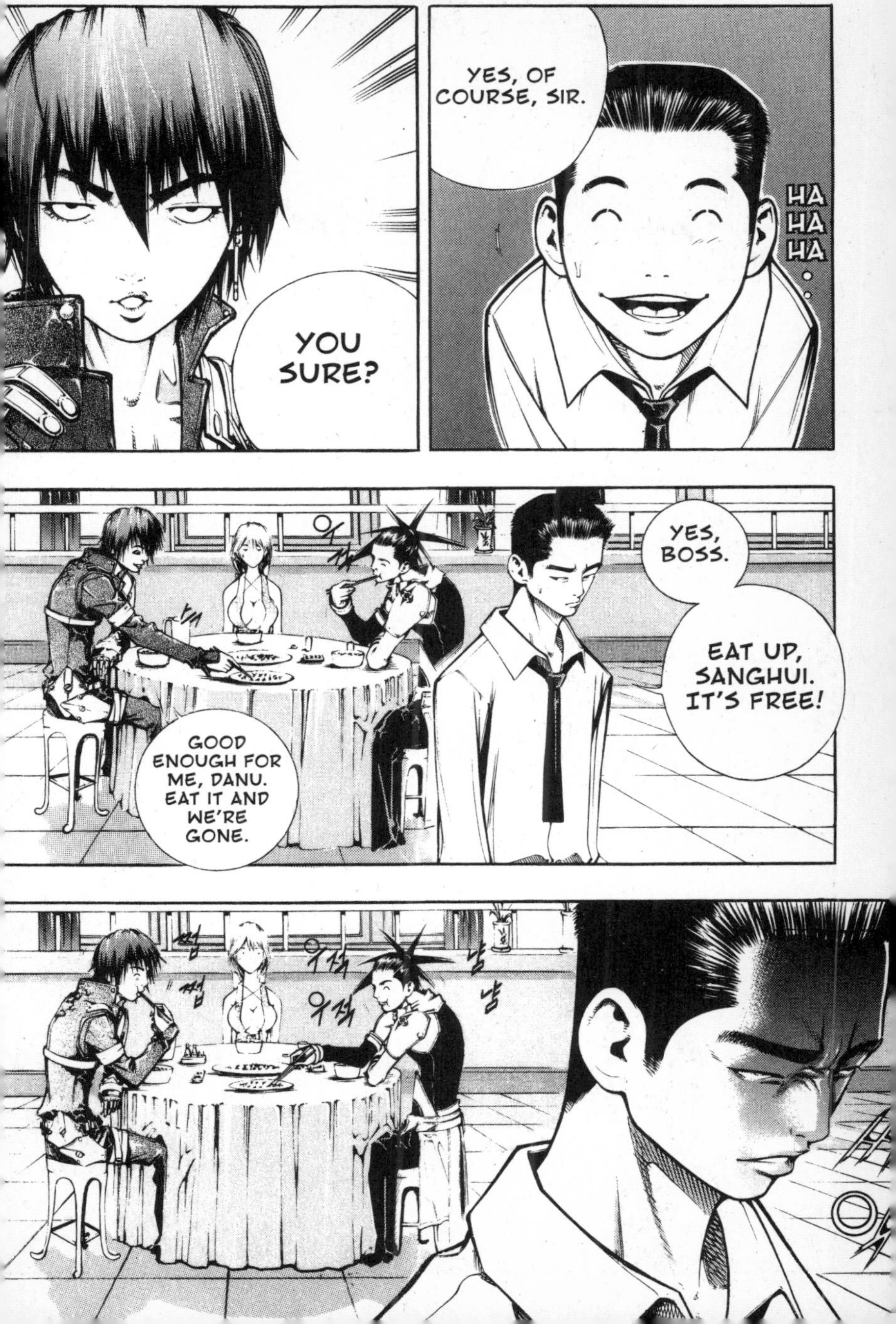

YOU SURE?
YES, OF COURSE, SIR.
HA HA HA..
YES, BOSS.
EAT UP, SANGHUI. IT'S FREE!
GOOD ENOUGH FOR ME, DANU. EAT IT AND WE'RE GONE.

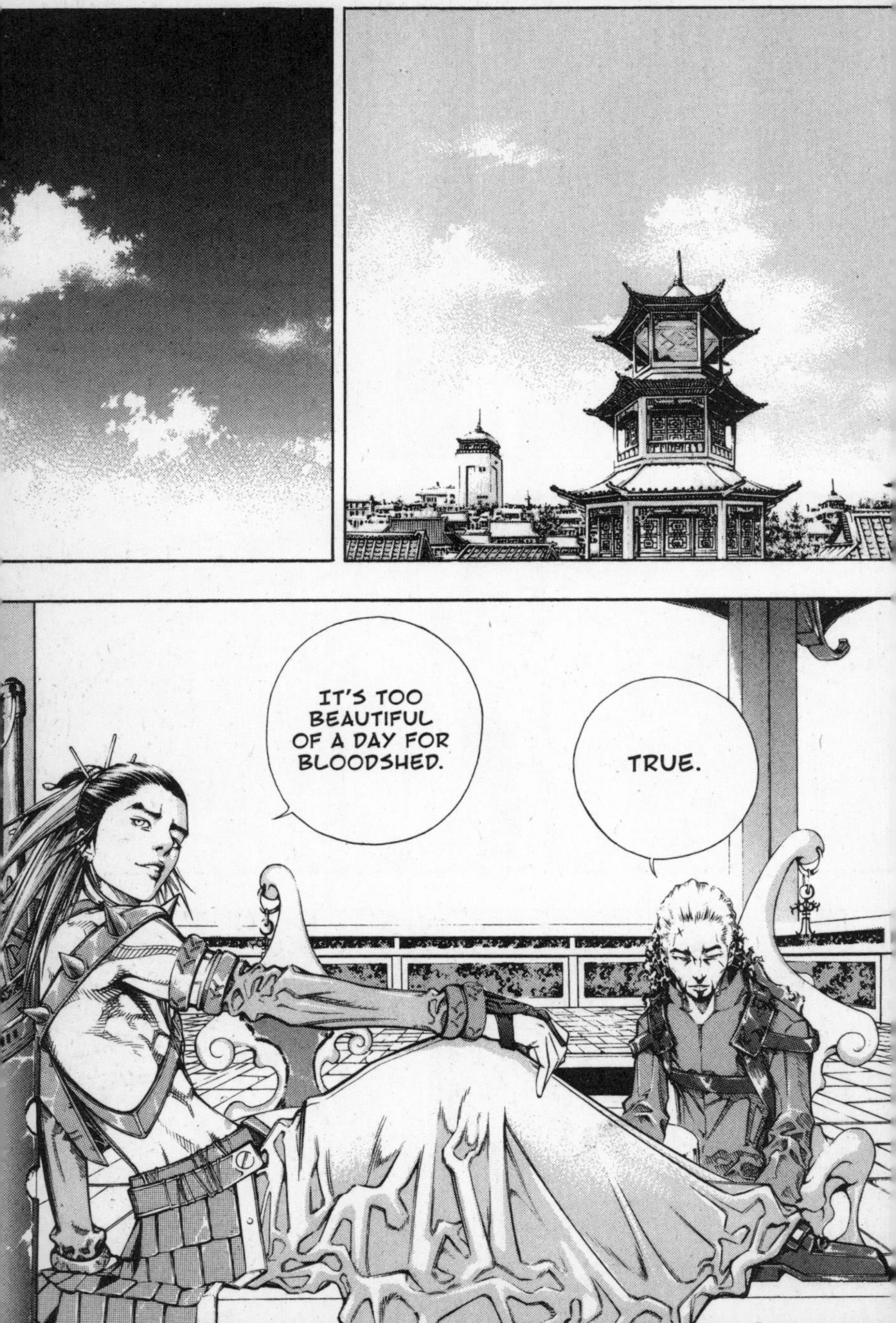
IT'S TOO BEAUTIFUL OF A DAY FOR BLOODSHED.
TRUE.

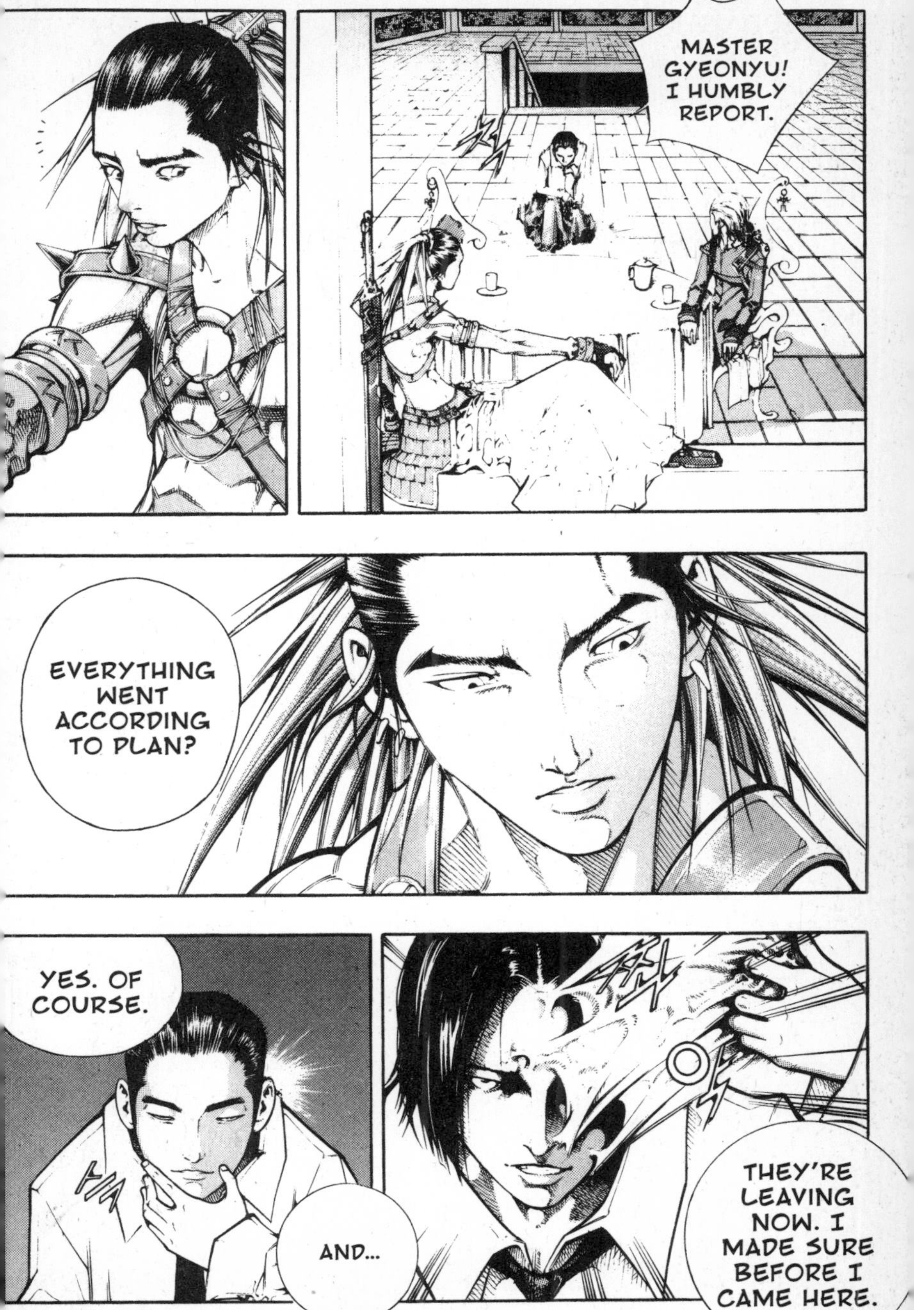
MASTER GYEONYU! I HUMBLY REPORT.
EVERYTHING WENT ACCORDING TO PLAN?
YES. OF COURSE.
AND...
THEY'RE LEAVING NOW. I MADE SURE BEFORE I CAME HERE.

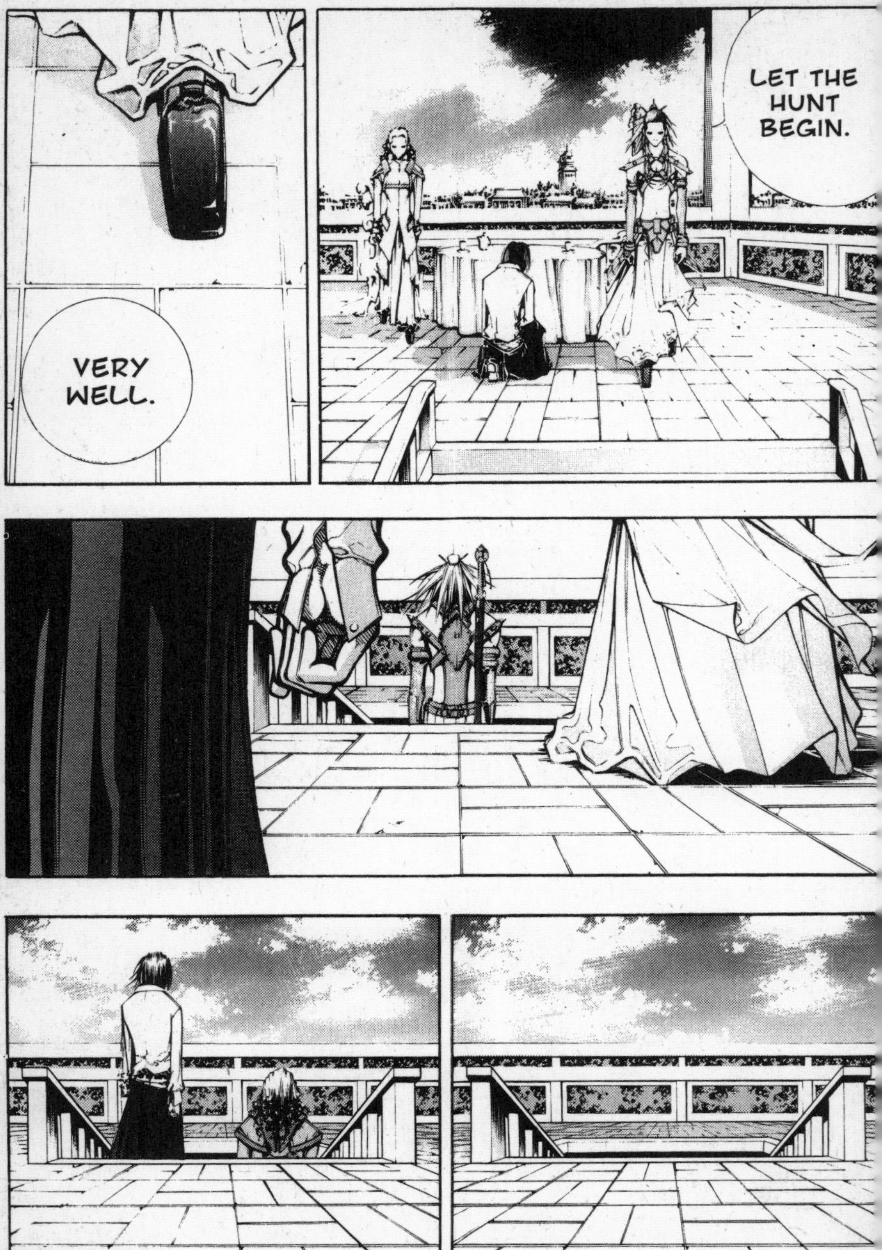
LET THE HUNT BEGIN.
VERY WELL.

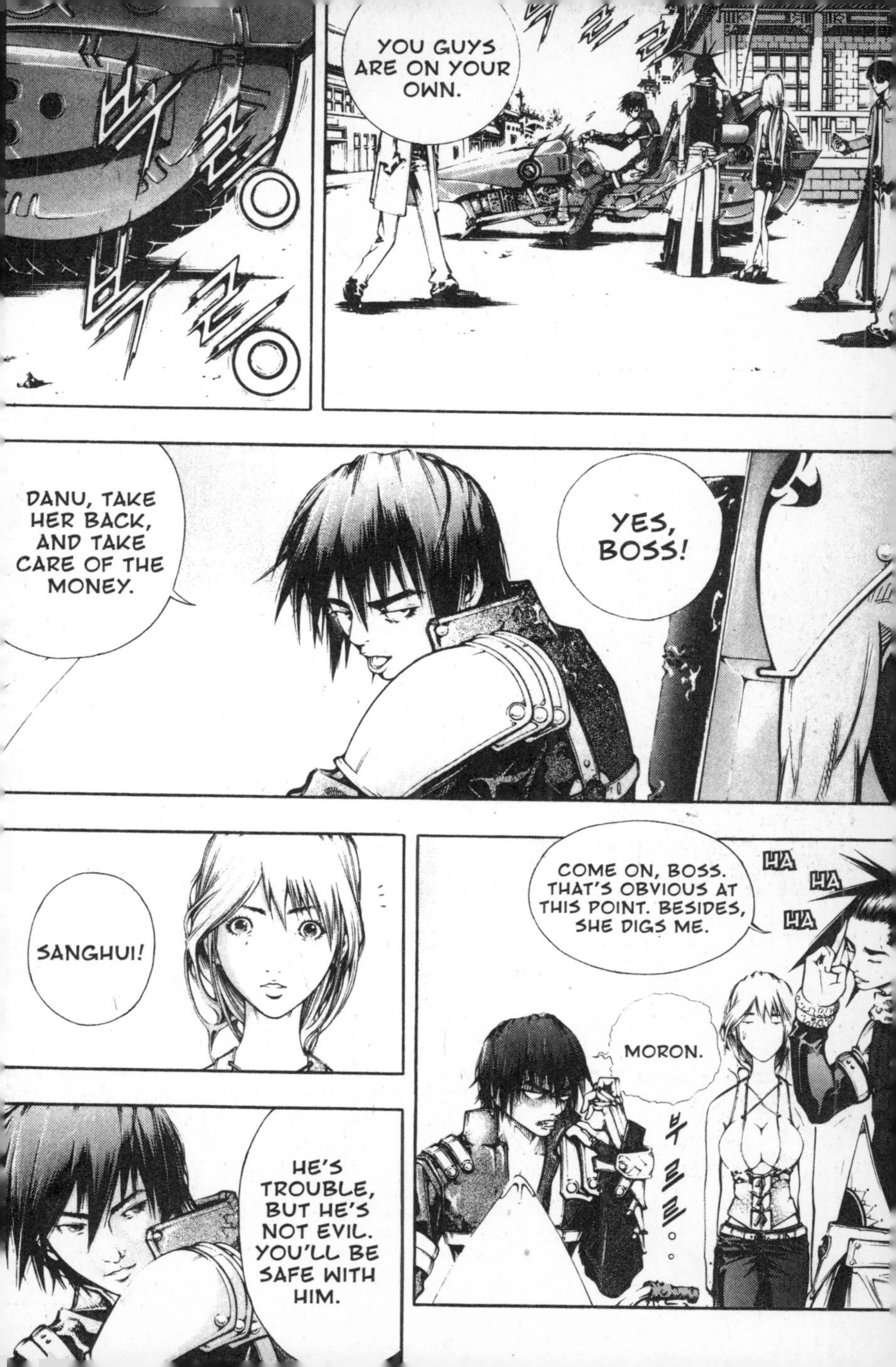
YOU GUYS ARE ON YOUR OWN.
DANU, TAKE HER BACK, AND TAKE CARE OF THE MONEY.
YES, BOSS!
SANGHUI!
HE'S TROUBLE, BUT HE'S NOT EVIL. YOU'LL BE SAFE WITH HIM.
COME ON, BOSS. THAT'S OBVIOUS AT THIS POINT. BESIDES, SHE DIGS ME.
HA HA HA
MORON.

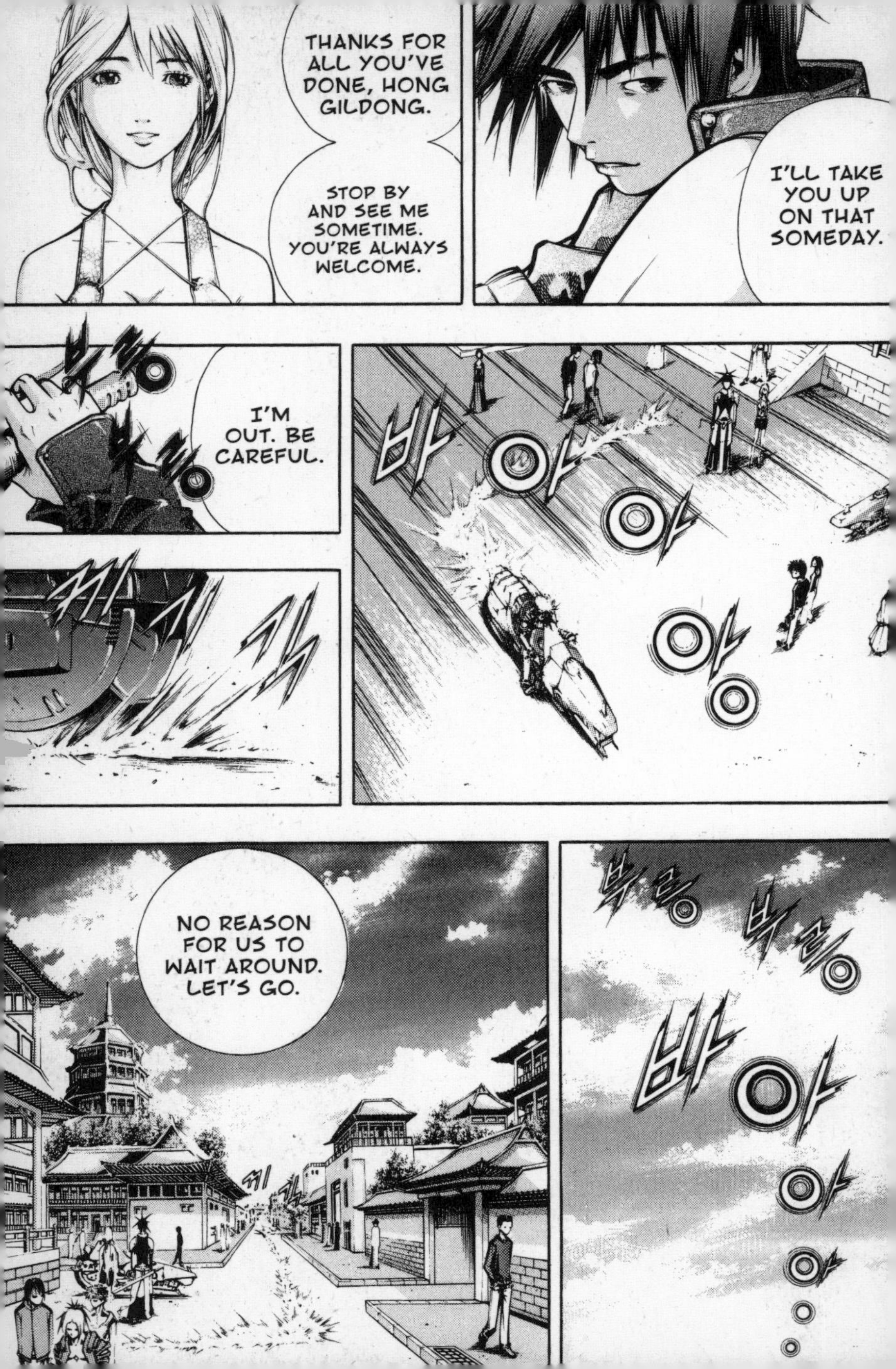

THANKS FOR ALL YOU'VE DONE, HONG GILDONG.
STOP BY AND SEE ME SOMETIME. YOU'RE ALWAYS WELCOME.
I'LL TAKE YOU UP ON THAT SOMEDAY.
I'M OUT. BE CAREFUL.
NO REASON FOR US TO WAIT AROUND. LET'S GO.

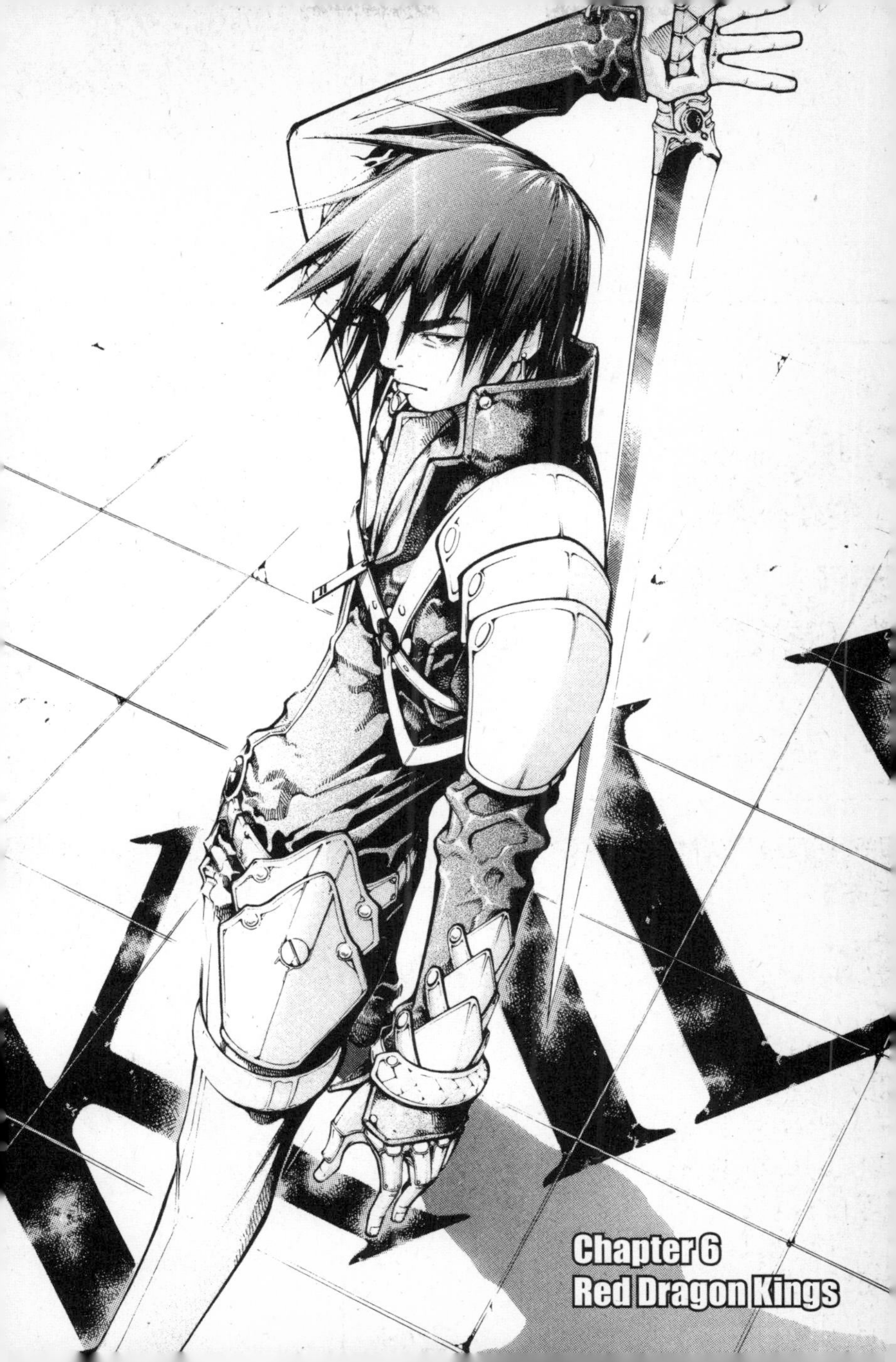

Chapter 6
Red Dragon Kings

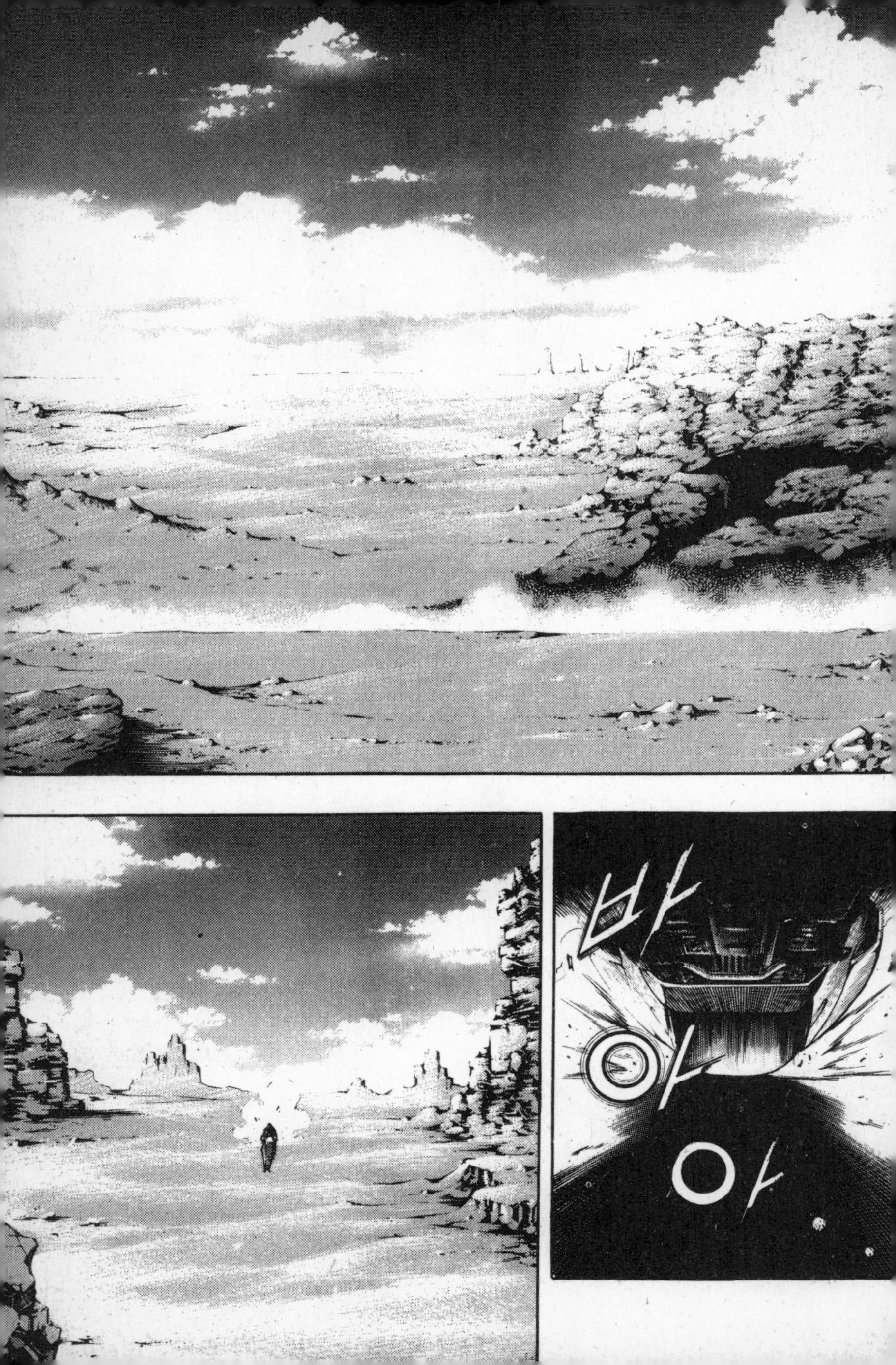
바아아

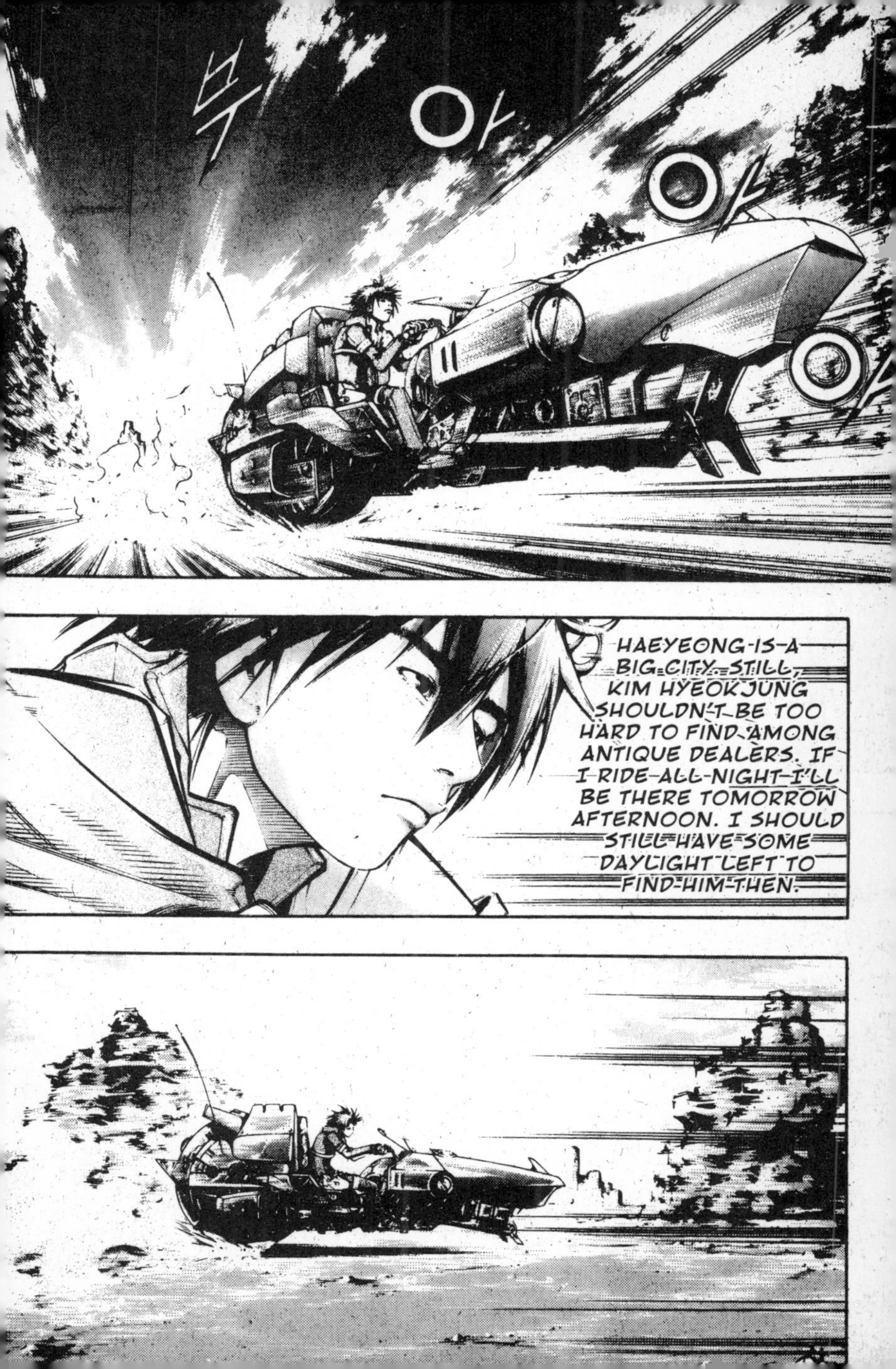
HAEYEONG IS A BIG CITY. STILL, KIM HYEOKJUNG SHOULDN'T BE TOO HARD TO FIND AMONG ANTIQUE DEALERS. IF I RIDE ALL NIGHT I'LL BE THERE TOMORROW AFTERNOON. I SHOULD STILL HAVE SOME DAYLIGHT LEFT TO FIND HIM THEN.

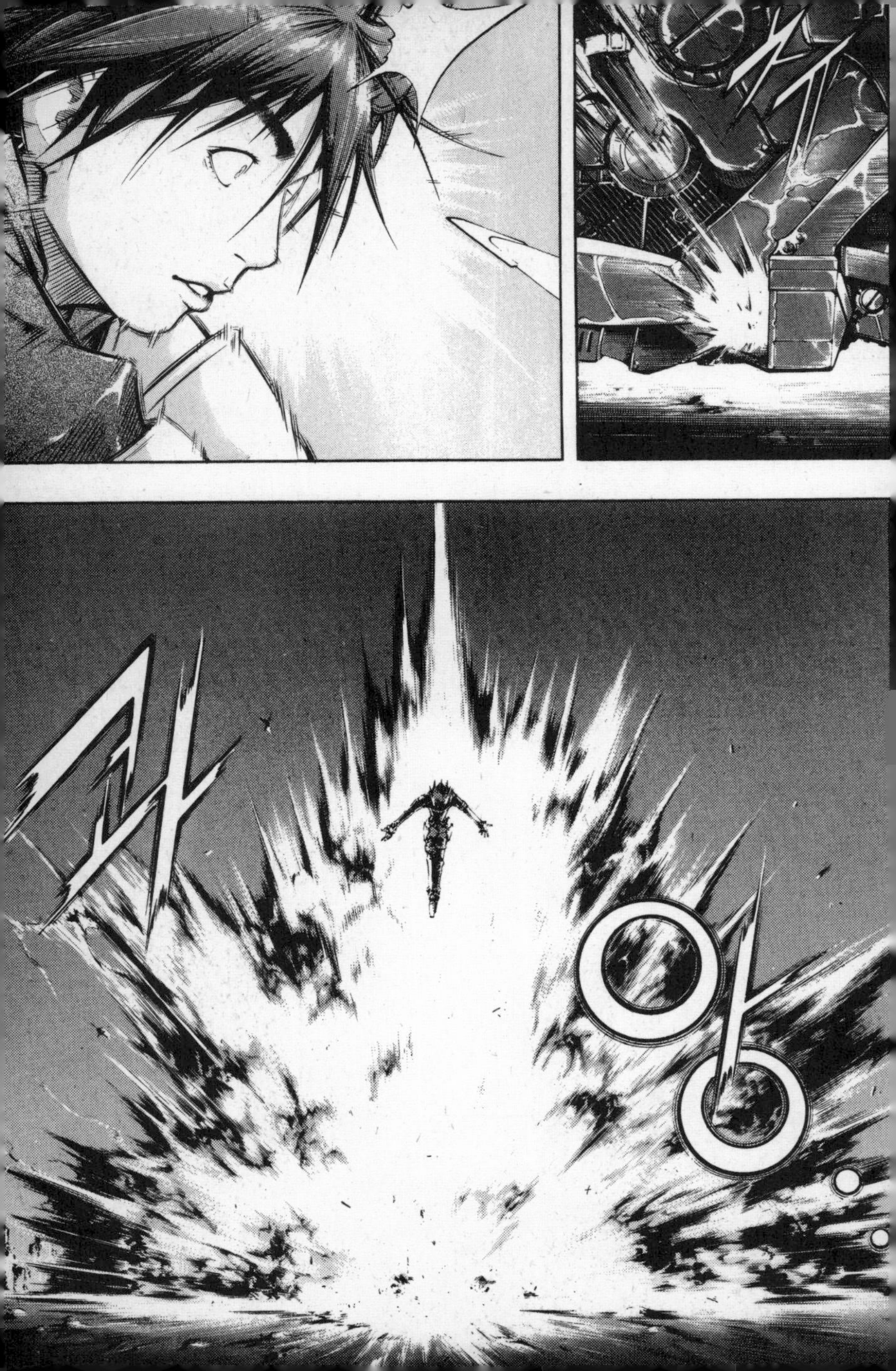

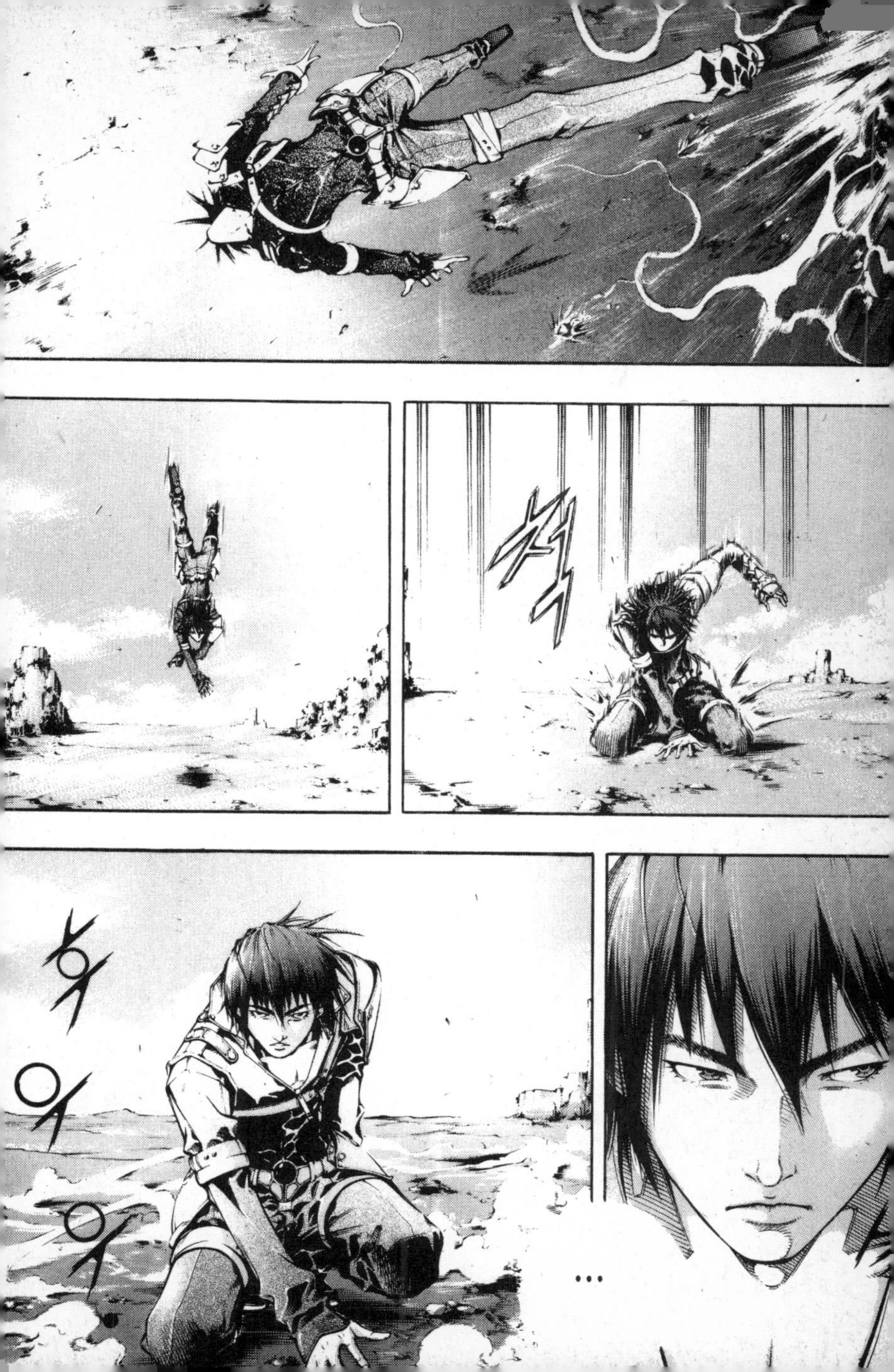
...

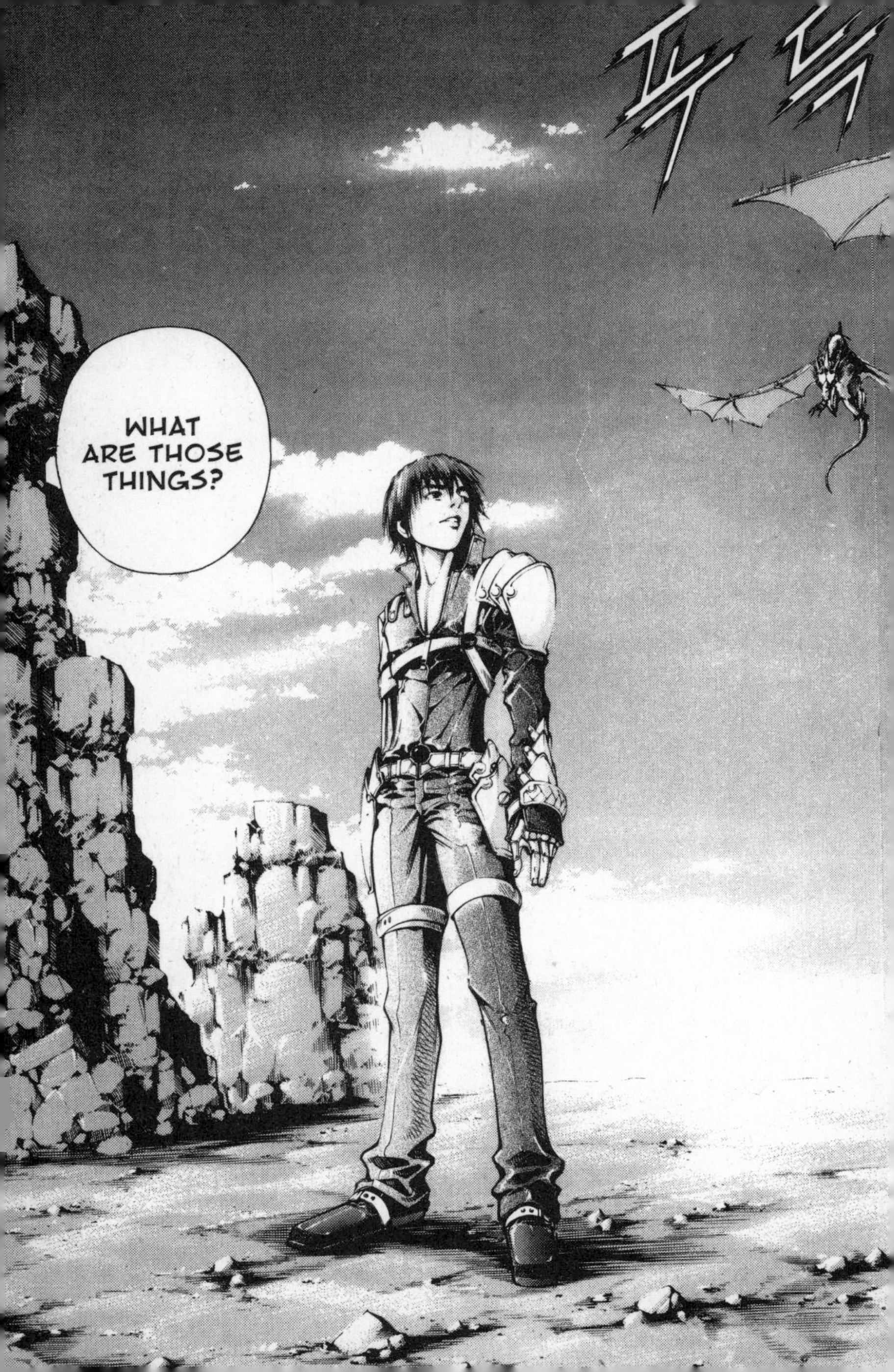
WHAT ARE THOSE THINGS?

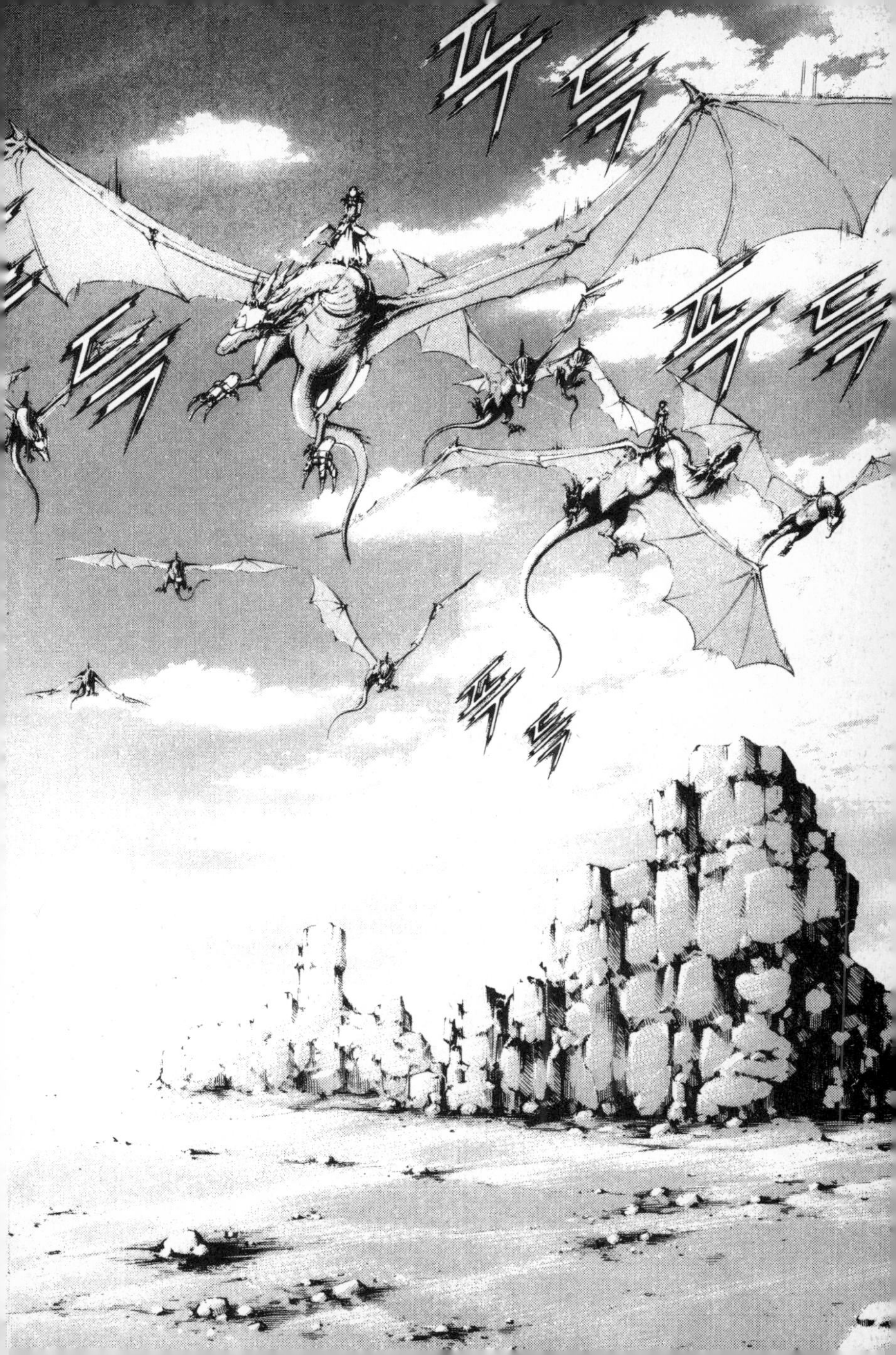
푸득
푸득
푸득

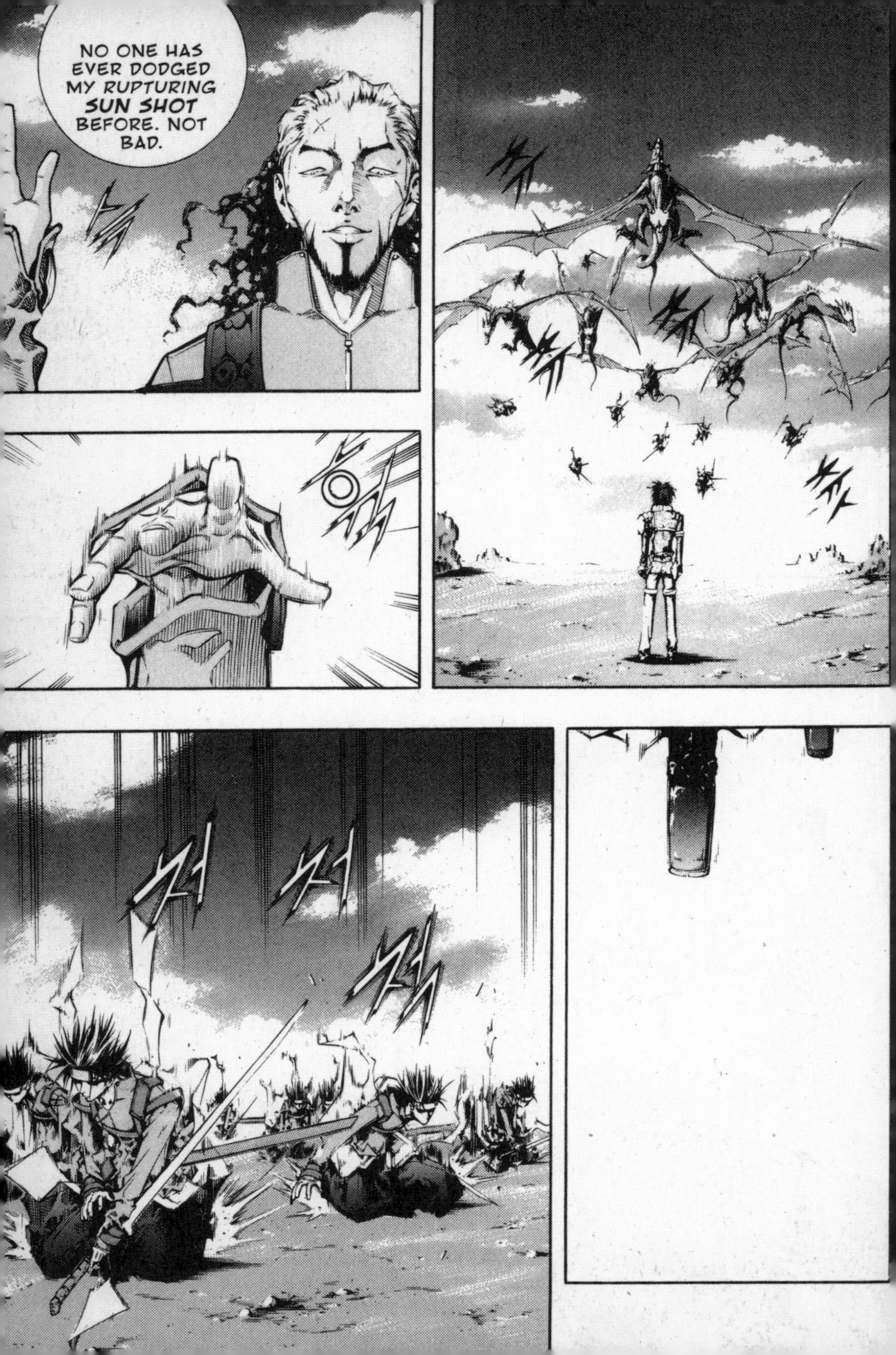
NO ONE HAS EVER DODGED MY RUPTURING SUN SHOT BEFORE. NOT BAD.

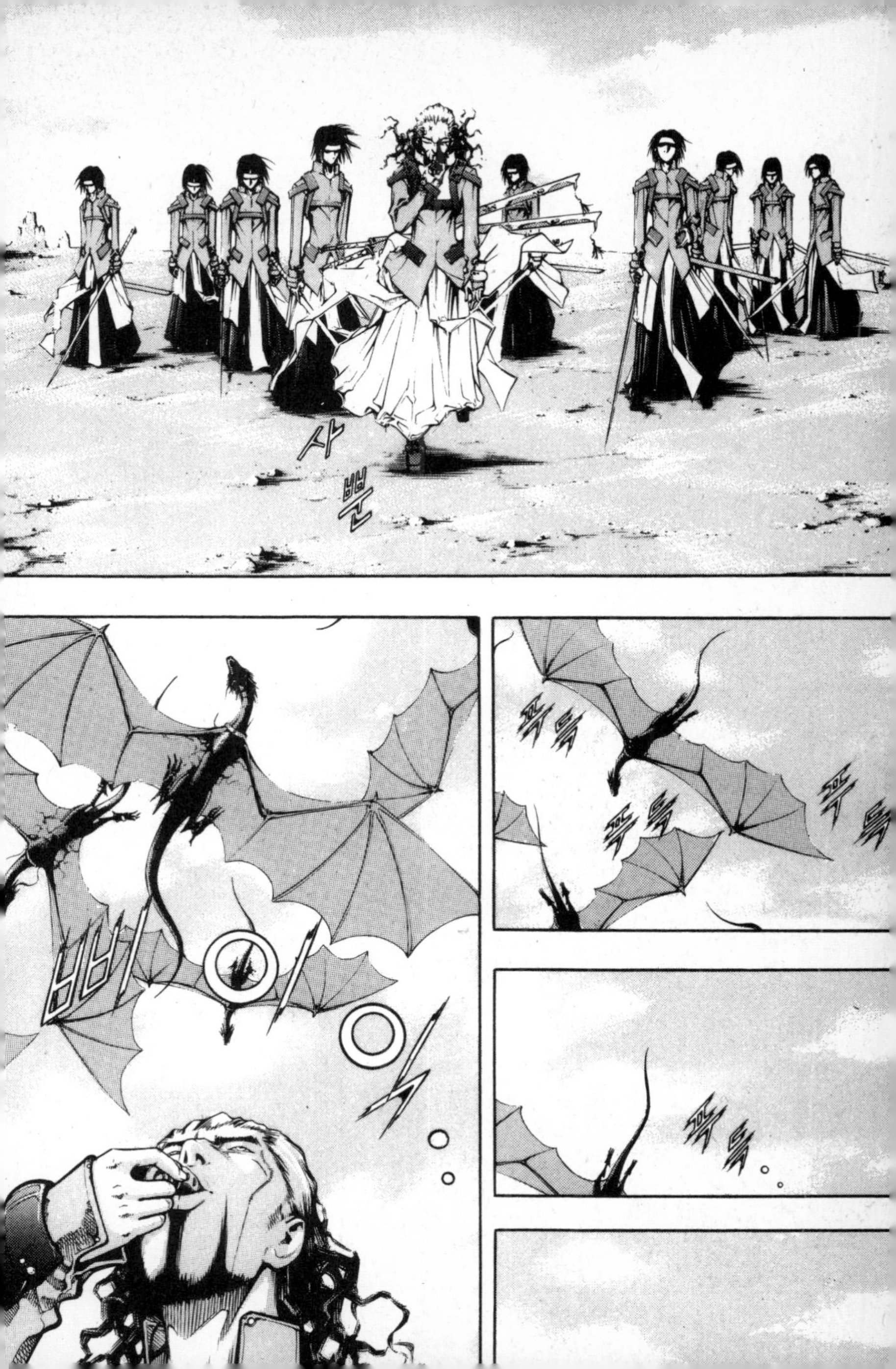
사뿐
삐이이~
푸득
푸득
푸득
푸득…

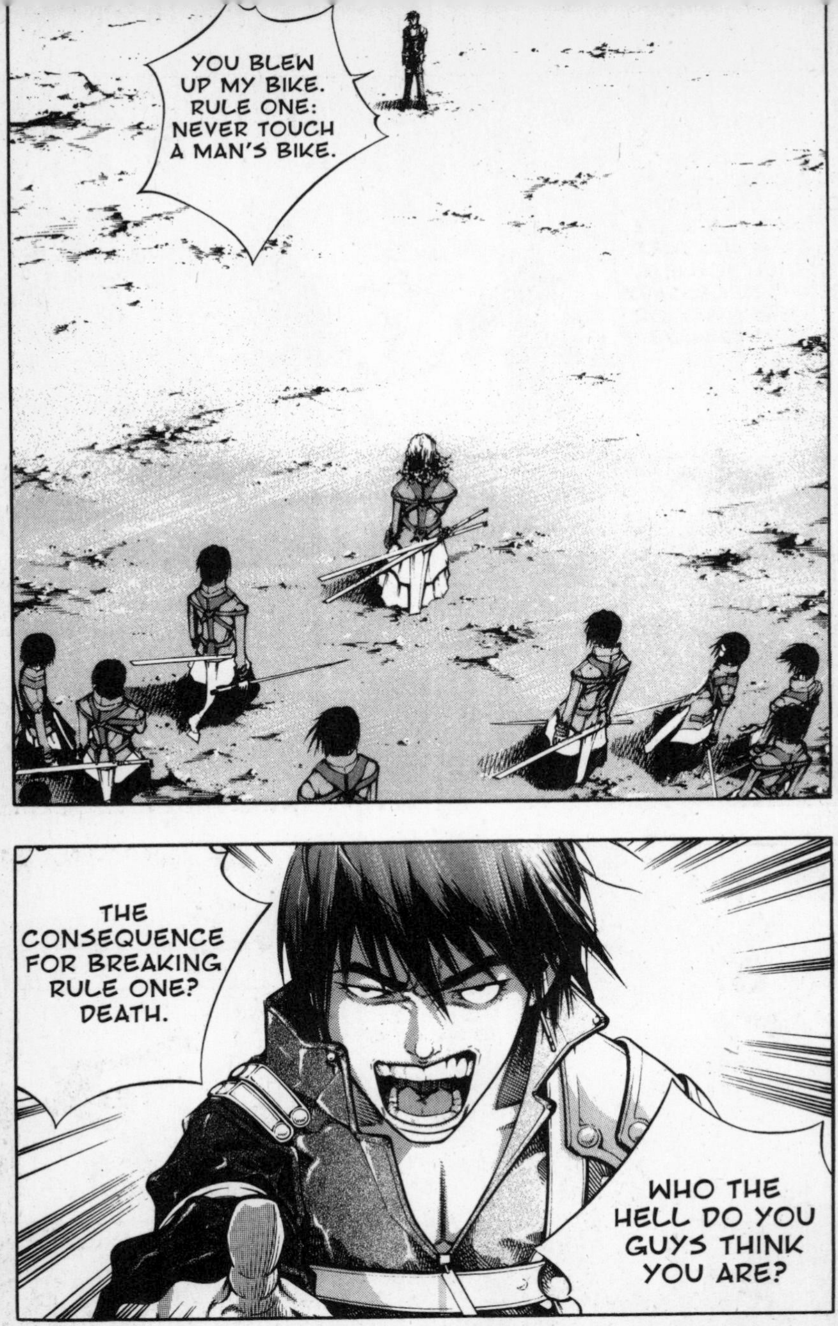
YOU BLEW UP MY BIKE. RULE ONE: NEVER TOUCH A MAN'S BIKE.
THE CONSEQUENCE FOR BREAKING RULE ONE? DEATH.
WHO THE HELL DO YOU GUYS THINK YOU ARE?

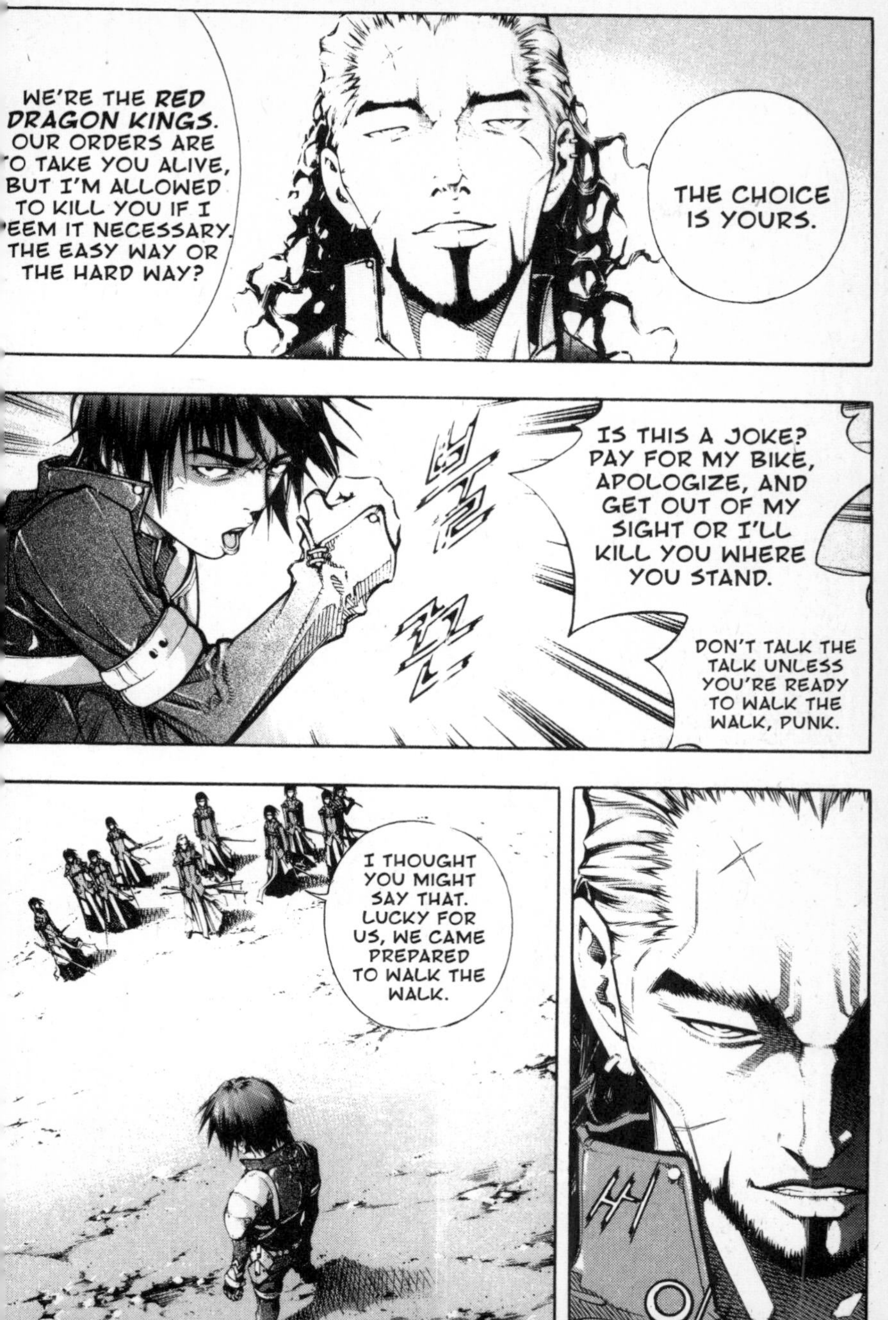

WE'RE THE RED DRAGON KINGS. OUR ORDERS ARE TO TAKE YOU ALIVE, BUT I'M ALLOWED TO KILL YOU IF I DEEM IT NECESSARY. THE EASY WAY OR THE HARD WAY?
THE CHOICE IS YOURS.
IS THIS A JOKE? PAY FOR MY BIKE, APOLOGIZE, AND GET OUT OF MY SIGHT OR I'LL KILL YOU WHERE YOU STAND.
DON'T TALK THE TALK UNLESS YOU'RE READY TO WALK THE WALK, PUNK.
I THOUGHT YOU MIGHT SAY THAT. LUCKY FOR US, WE CAME PREPARED TO WALK THE WALK.

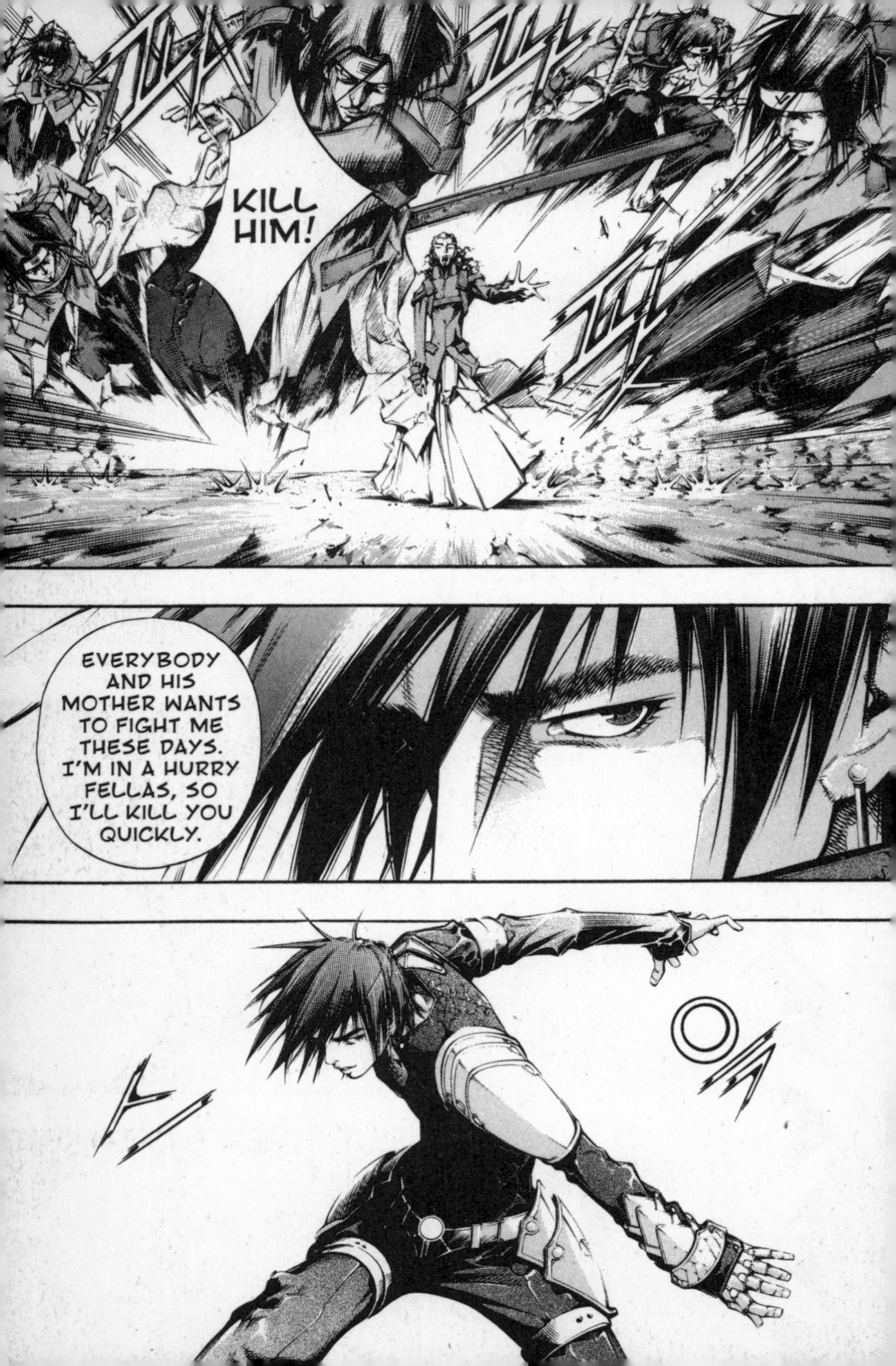
KILL HIM!
EVERYBODY AND HIS MOTHER WANTS TO FIGHT ME THESE DAYS. I'M IN A HURRY FELLAS, SO I'LL KILL YOU QUICKLY.

MY CHI!

I CAN'T CHANNEL MY CHI!

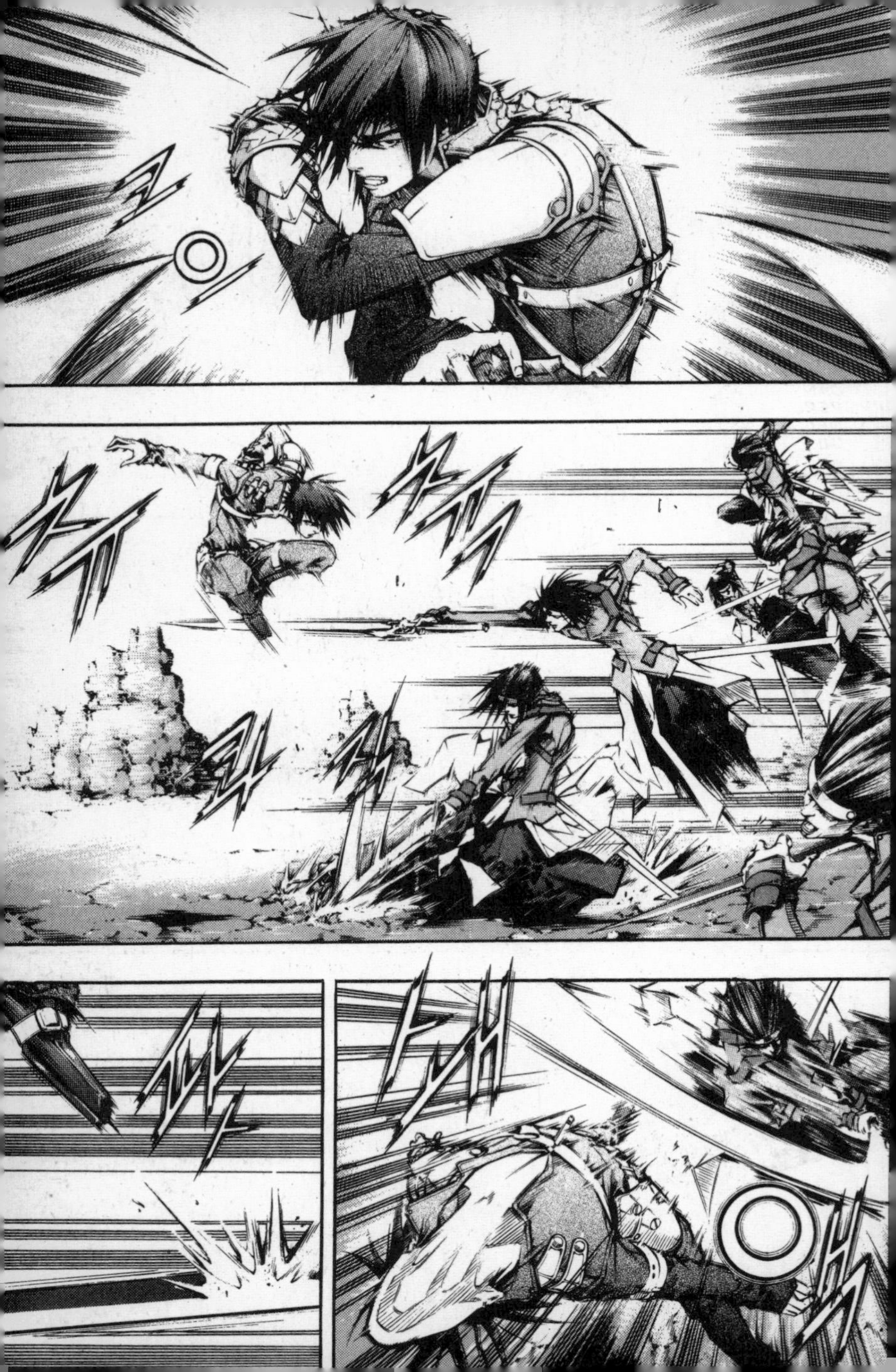

LET'S SEE HOW LONG HE LASTS WHEN HE CAN'T PROPERLY CHANNEL HIS CHI.

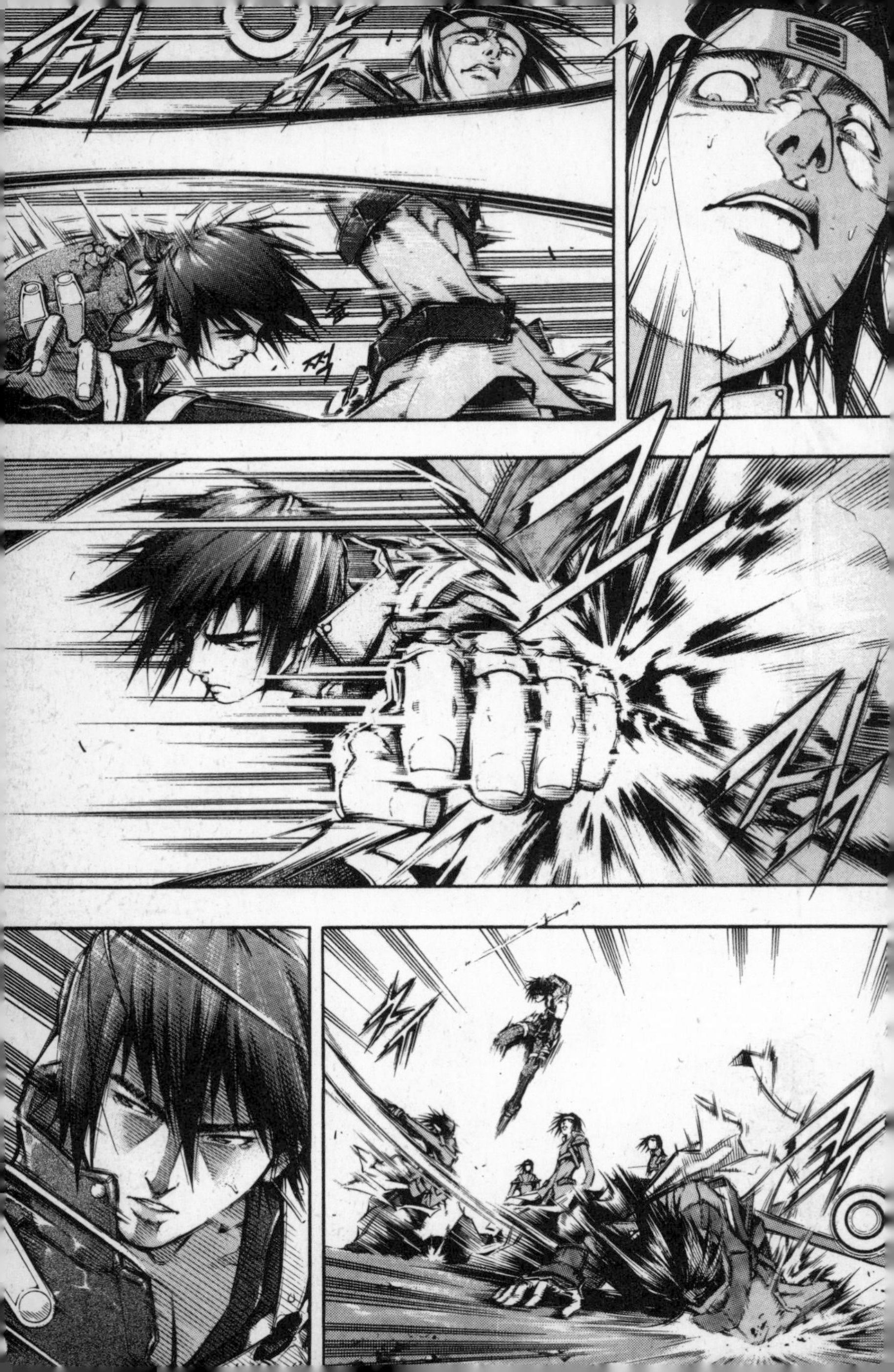

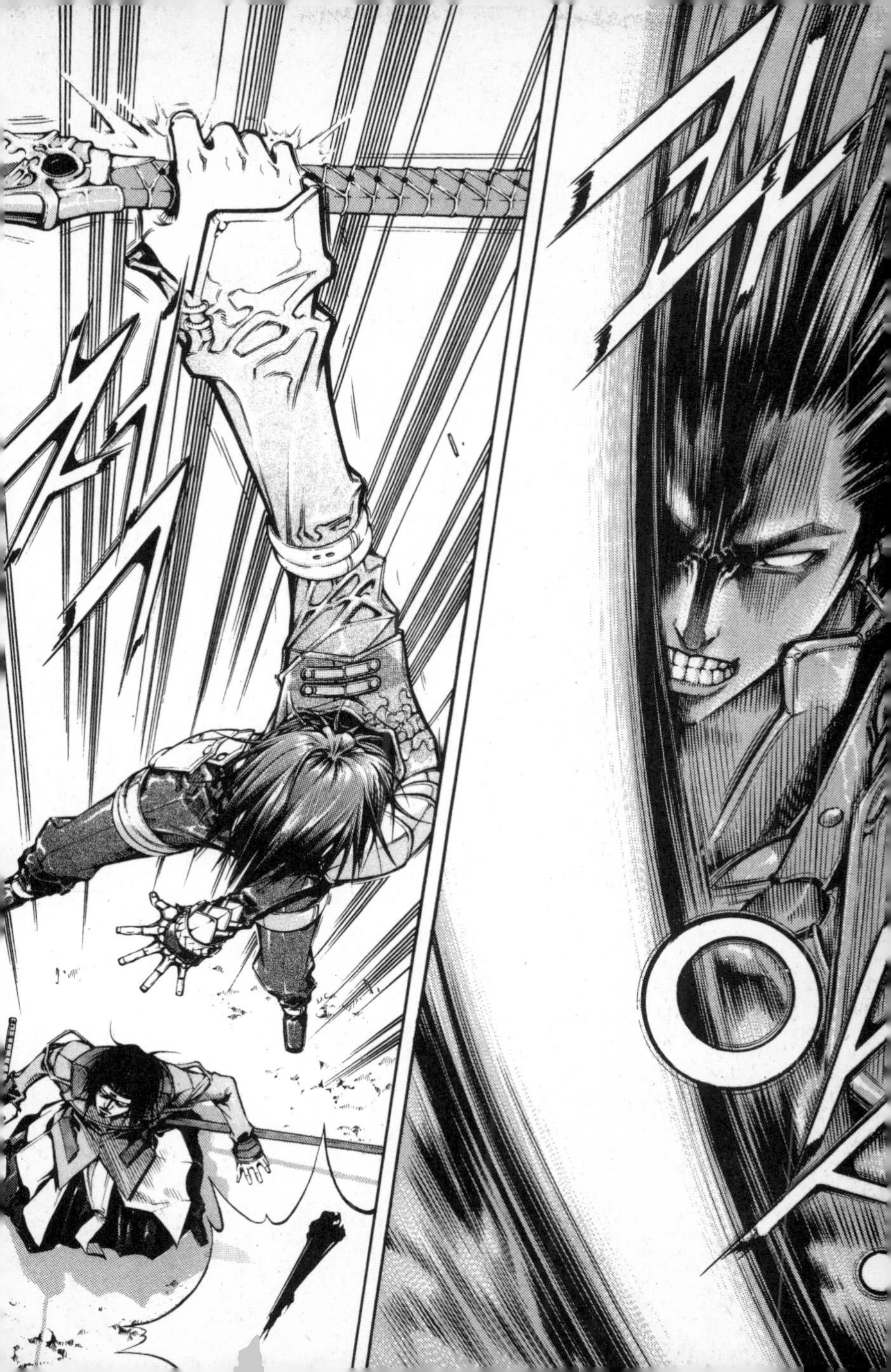

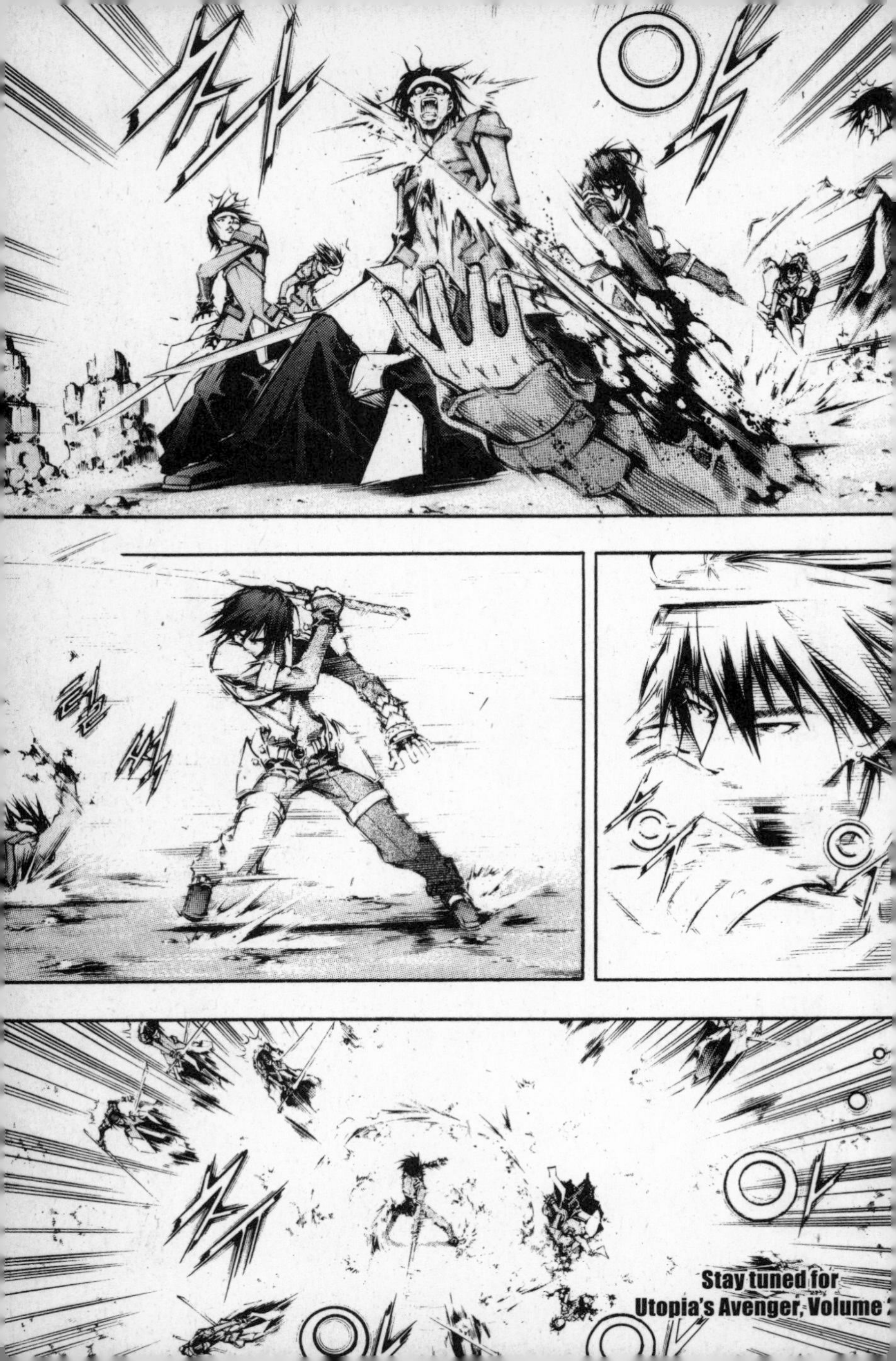
Stay tuned for
Utopia's Avenger, Volume 2

In the Next Exciting Volume of

WITH THEIR FORCES DIVIDED, GILDONG AND DANU
HAVE NO ONE BUT THEMSELVES TO DEPEND ON
WHEN THEY ARE EACH ATTACKED BY THOSE WHO
STAND IN THE WAY OF THE RESURRECTION OF
YULDO--THE LOST UTOPIA.

GILDONG HAS A TOUGH TIME OF IT WHEN...
IN THE MIDST OF BATTLE, HE REALIZES
THAT HE IS UNABLE TO CHANNEL HIS INNER "CHI."
A FACT THAT COMMANDER YAHWAN INTENDS TO
TAKE FULL ADVANTAGE OF.

MEANWHILE, DANU'S GOT HIS OWN HANDS FULL AS
HE VALIANTLY TRIES TO PROTECT SANGHUI FROM
THEIR ATTACKER. BUT GYEONYU'S NO PUSHOVER,
AND SMART-ALECKY DANU MAY FIND HIMSELF
WITHOUT A SNAPPY COME BACK...PERMANENTLY.

BE HERE FOR VOLUME 2!

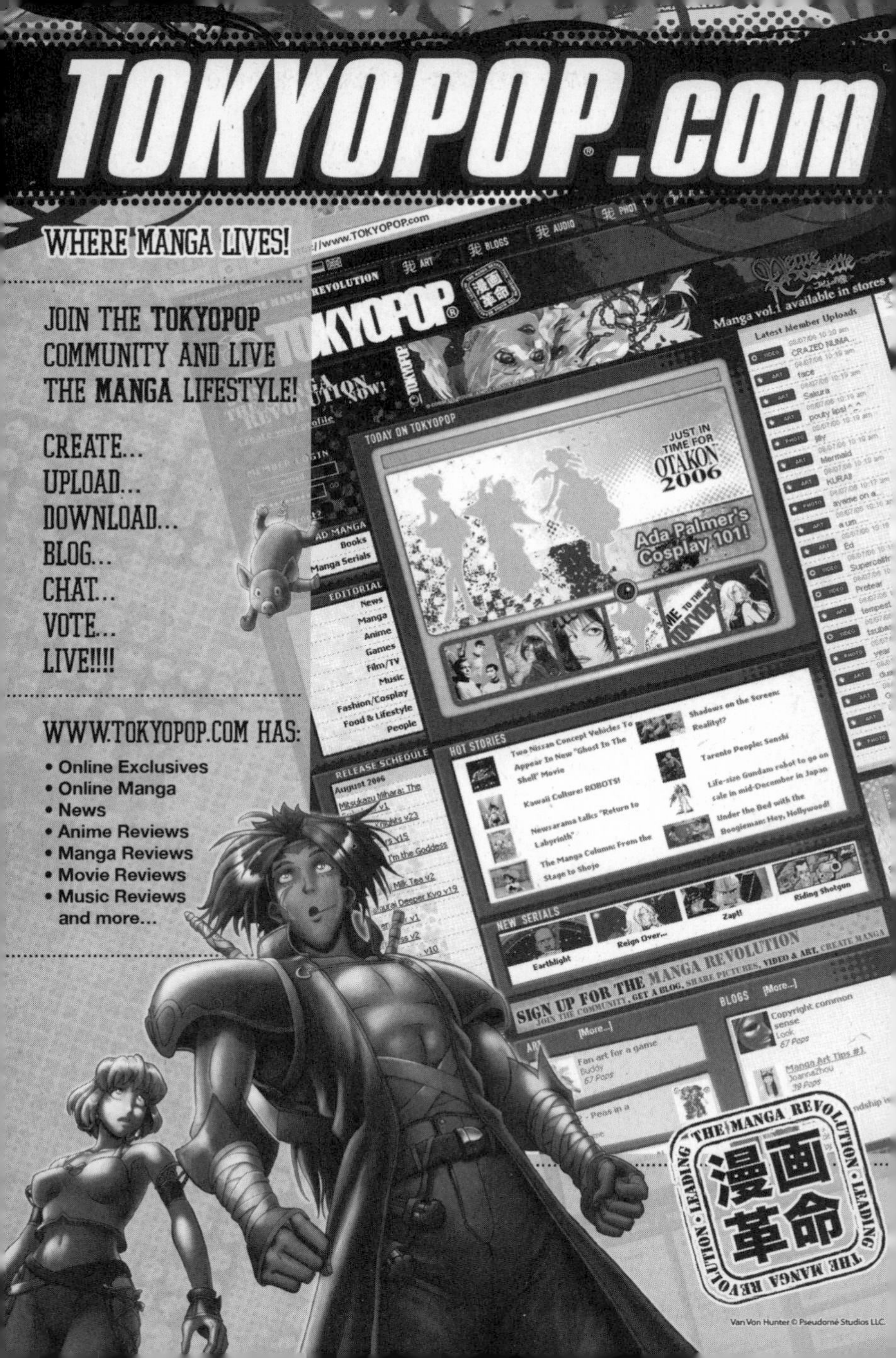
TOKYOPOP.com
WHERE MANGA LIVES!
JOIN THE TOKYOPOP COMMUNITY AND LIVE THE MANGA LIFESTYLE!
CREATE...
UPLOAD...
DOWNLOAD...
BLOG...
CHAT...
VOTE...
LIVE!!!!
WWW.TOKYOPOP.COM HAS:
• Online Exclusives
• Online Manga
• News
• Anime Reviews
• Manga Reviews
• Movie Reviews
• Music Reviews and more...
TODAY ON TOKYOPOP
JUST IN TIME FOR OTAKON 2006
Ada Palmer's Cosplay 101!
HOT STORIES
RELEASE SCHEDULE
NEW SERIALS
SIGN UP FOR THE MANGA REVOLUTION
THE MANGA REVOLUTION
漫画革命
LEADING THE MANGA REVOLUTION
Van Von Hunter © Pseudomé Studios LLC.

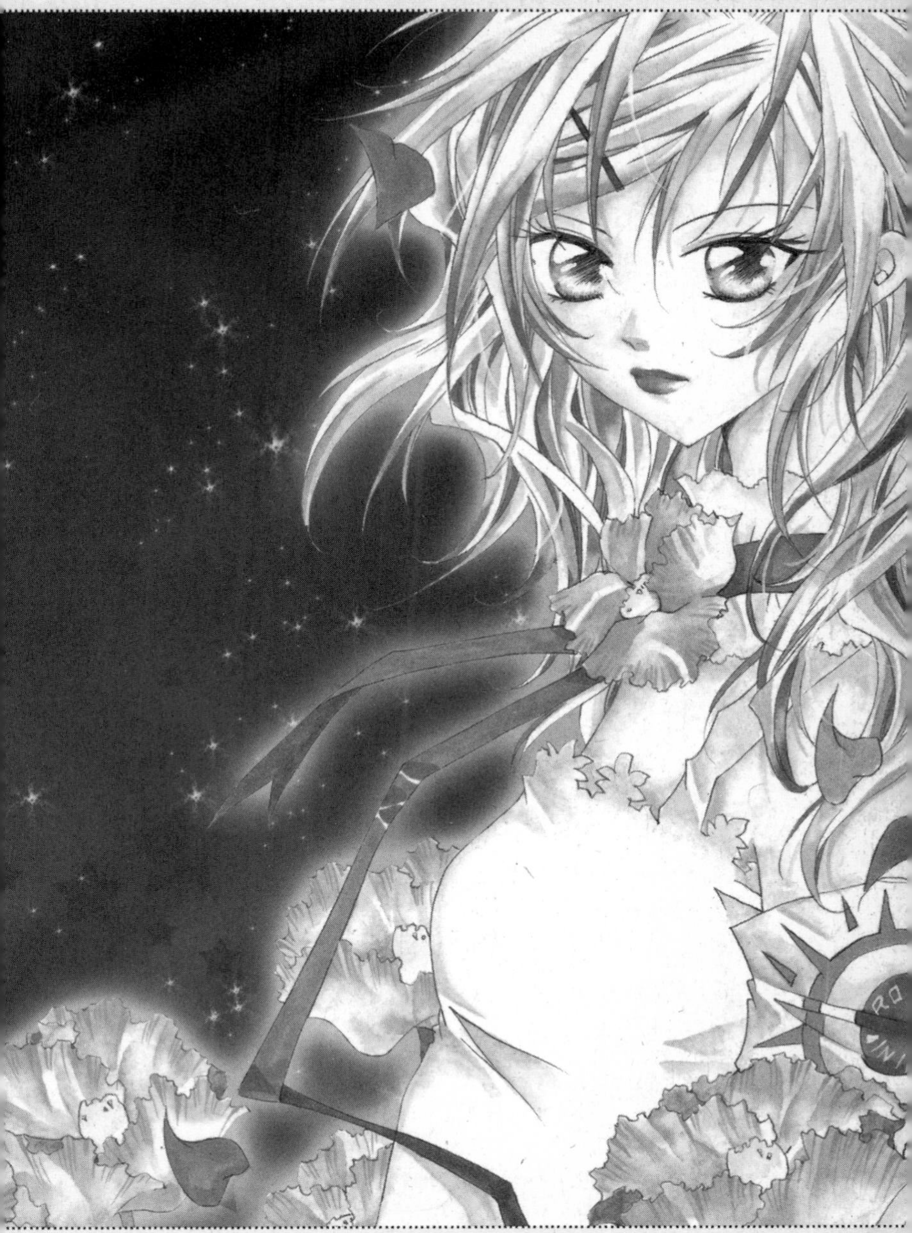